RITUAL

by

William Heffernan

A SIGNET BOOK

NEW AMERICAN LIBRARY

A DIVISION OF PENGUIN BOOKS USA INC.

NAL BOOKS ARE AVAILABLE AT QUANTITY DISCOUNTS
WHEN USED TO PROMOTE PRODUCTS OR SERVICES.
FOR INFORMATION PLEASE WRITE TO PREMIUM MARKETING DIVISION,
NEW AMERICAN LIBRARY, 1633 BROADWAY,
NEW YORK, NEW YORK 10019.

SIGNET TRADEMARK REG. U.S. PAT. OFF. AND FOREIGN COUNTRIES
REGISTERED TRADEMARK—MARCA REGISTRADA
HECHO EN DRESDEN, TN, U.S.A.

SIGNET, SIGNET CLASSIC, MENTOR, ONYX, PLUME, MERIDIAN
and NAL BOOKS are published by New American Library, a division of
Penguin Books USA Inc., 1633 Broadway, New York, New York 10019

First Signet Printing, February, 1990

3   4   5   6   7   8   9

PRINTED IN THE UNITED STATES OF AMERICA

For Larry Freundlich, a man who knows everything about books, and even more about friendship. Thanks, Lorenzo.

ACKNOWLEDGMENTS

I'd like to express my gratitude to Maureen Baron and Gloria Loomis, and especially to Stacie Blake, who types her fingers to the bone, and makes life wonderful.

Prologue

THE VOICE WAS soft and soothing, and it flowed out over the audience so gently it seemed to contradict its message, like a lullaby not yet set to music.

"I want you to envision something. Something that will challenge your concept of right and wrong, your basic understanding of what is good, and what is evil.

"Imagine yourselves standing in the jungles of Quintana Roo more than seven hundred years ago. You are there to witness a Toltec ritual that has been repeated for centuries, a ritual that has been described by some scholars as an act of human barbarism, and by others as one of great spiritual love. But now you are there, and a religious procession passes before you. An early morning mist rises from the jungle floor, then hangs, in a thick vapor that obscures the path along which the procession moves.

"There are three priests in the procession, each dressed in identical plumed robes, and the iridescent feathers of red and blue and green seem to shimmer in the morning light as they move along the path. Each priest wears a stone mask, suspended by a leather thong around his neck, a long green-bladed knife at his waist.

"Behind the priests a fourth man follows, dressed only in a loincloth, holding an intricately carved bronze ax high above his head. And behind him, two men

9

hold the end of a rope, tied to the wrists of a naked woman who walks proudly between them.

"All about them the jungle is silent, as the birds and monkeys lie hidden in the dark green foliage. Even the air seems suspended, hanging thick and heavy as it often does before a sudden storm.

"As the procession nears a large clearing, a stone pyramid comes into view. It rises a full two hundred feet until it dwarfs the surrounding jungle. At the base of the pyramid several hundred people have gathered, dressed in their finest robes, and as the priests approach, a soft chant flows from them, creating a beat as steady as that of a human heart.

"Slowly, majestically, the procession climbs the face of the pyramid until it reaches a flat area at its top, an area marked only by a triangular stone at its center. There the priests and the man with the ax take up the major positions of the compass, as the two men in charge of the woman lift her and hold her suspended above the triangular stone.

"Below, the chanting grows to a crescendo, then abruptly stops as the priests fit the stone masks to their faces and slowly withdraw the long obsidian knives at their waists.

"Now it is time. Now the sacrifice can be offered, a final act that bears no guilt, and offers only dignity and love."

*****

November 9, 6:30 P.M.

Rolk looked up briefly as Devlin entered his office, then returned to sorting the papers strewn across his desk. "I want you to pick up Lorenzo tonight," Rolk said. "Drag his ass in here and book him for his wife's murder. Take Moriarty and Peters with you."

"You're not going?" Devlin asked.

"No. Why should I?"

"You broke the case. I just thought you'd want to be there," Devlin said.

"I've got other plans," Rolk said. "I'm going to a lecture at the Metropolitan."

"Another lecture? What's this one about?"

Rolk looked up into Devlin's grinning face. "It's about Toltec ritual murder." He stared Devlin down. "That's right, another lecture on murder." Rolk leaned back in his chair. "What's the matter, you afraid you can't handle this porno star all by yourself?"

Devlin's grin widened. "I just thought maybe you'd spend the night with Superstud and I'd go to the lecture. Who knows, maybe I'd learn something."

Rolk fought off his own grin. "Just do as you're told. You'll learn something by doing that for a change."

"You think we've got enough on Lorenzo to make it stick?" Devlin asked.

Rolk leaned forward and placed his forearms on the desk, hunching his shoulders above them. "The guy's a big porno star with a prior for selling drugs. His wife was the daughter of a very nice, very rich family who gave her everything she ever wanted. Then she meets Lorenzo and she decides what she really wants is to get her brains screwed out and to stick needles in her arms. We don't *need* a lot to lock up this clown. We wouldn't even have caught this case if the victim's family hadn't been rich and prominent. The precinct detectives would have caught it, and they would have done the same thing we're doing—a week ago. Besides, Lorenzo'll get a good lawyer and the assistant DA won't give a damn whether he's guilty or not. All he'll care about is getting another conviction on his record, so he'll plea-bargain the charge. Lorenzo'll do five years in the slam, and then he'll be out dropping his drawers in front of the cameras again." Rolk looked down at his desk and began shuffling papers again. "Be realistic. Forget guilt and innocence and just clear the damned case. That's what the job is about."

*****

November 9, 9:35 P.M.

Cynthia Gault's cheek was pressed against the path, but she could feel neither the cold nor the roughness against her skin. She tried to move but nothing happened. Her legs and arms seemed to have disappeared; only her eyes told her where she was. She tried to speak, but only a gasp of air rushed past her lips.

Then her body was dragged across the path onto the grass, and through low evergreen branches that brushed against eyes she was no longer able to close. When the movement stopped, her body was turned, sending a kaleidoscopic rush of foliage across her line of vision. She was on her back.

Her eyes darted in every direction, searching for something that would tell her what had happened. Something must have fallen on her. Then she had been dragged to safety. But where was the person who had dragged her, and why couldn't she feel anything?

A figure loomed above her, and Cynthia gagged, fighting for speech. A briefcase was placed next to her head, and a plastic raincoat was withdrawn from it. Her eyes darted back to the figure that hovered above her, and she watched in disbelief as the plastic was slowly, almost majestically fitted over a dark topcoat.

The hands dipped into the briefcase again. Cynthia stared as a long green-bladed knife was slowly removed. It looked ancient, like something out of a movie or . . . Her mind froze momentarily. Or a museum. She gasped, fighting for words that would not come. The figure bent over her, the hands unbuttoning her coat, then the blouse beneath it. She watched, terrified, as the clothes were stripped from her body, folded, and placed neatly next to the briefcase.

She was naked now, but she couldn't feel the cold, and she watched with growing horror, as a stone mask replaced the figure's face. There was the faint sound of sharply drawn breath. The exhalation through the mask was a barely distinguishable hum. The figure straddled her, the mask bending toward her, the humming louder now, the eyes behind the mask soft and distant; even the stone mouth of the mask seemed to be curved into a smile that appeared gentle, almost tender. A gloved hand raised the knife in front of her face, then began to move slowly down. Tears ran along Cynthia's cheeks as she struggled to scream, to plead. Her mind raced with the words, but nothing escaped her lips.

"You are only prelude," a soft voice whispered.

The knife dropped lower, and Cynthia Gault watched it move in quick, slicing motions. A fountain of bright, red liquid surged suddenly, splattering the figure that crouched above her. It spurted again and again, and she watched it, trying to grasp what was happening. Then her vision began to fade, slowly at first, then in an accelerated rush, until there was nothing but a faint gurgling sound, and the distant hum of steady breathing.

*****

November 9, 7:45 P.M.

The limousines stretched up Fifth Avenue like a line of long, sleek predators, each awaiting its turn to disgorge another well-dressed couple before the wide stone staircase that led to the Metropolitan Museum. Occasionally taxis would cut ahead of the line to discharge equally well-dressed patrons, as the drivers, already thinking of their next fares, blatantly ignored the formality of the line.

At various levels of the well-lighted staircase, couples with tanned faces that spoke of privilege would stop to speak, some making plans for events still to come, others musing about the unusual lecture they were about to attend. Above them a long rectangular banner announced the coming exhibit that the lecture introduced: *The Smiling Gods of Human Sacrifice*.

*****

November 9, 7:30 P.M.

The two women faced each other defiantly as the middle-aged Catholic priest stared at each in turn, a look of nervous disbelief etched across his face.

"You are turning this exhibition into a show-business fiasco." Grace Mallory's lips were drawn into a tight, thin line, and despite her well-modulated voice, her eyes glistened with the fierceness of a mother protecting her child.

Kate Silverman's back stiffened under the rebuke. "I'm doing what works, Grace. What will bring people into this exhibit."

"And if our scholarship gets lost in the process, I suppose that's just an acceptable but regretable end result."

The priest continued to look at the women, confused by the soft tone of their voices, which contrasted with the fierce combativeness in their eyes.

"The scholarship means as much to me as it does to you, and you know that," Kate answered. "But scholarship exists in an environment of economic necessity, and if we don't get people into the museum, we're out of work."

Grace Mallory offered the younger woman a derisive smile. "And I suppose that's why you've conjured up this ludicrous lecture on Toltec ritualistic murder, and then turned it into a fund-raising event for Father LoPato's pathetic refugee program for the poor Mayans of Quintana Roo."

"That's right," Kate said, an edge coming into her voice for the first time. "That's what brings the important money people in. And it brings them in because it offers them two things they need. It allows them to expose themselves to something bizarre and horrific without touching the safety of their privileged lives. And it also allows them to open their wallets and help a group of downtrodden people. It soothes their sense of guilt. And it doesn't matter that they don't know the difference between a Mayan and a Ubangi. It works."

Grace Mallory began to object, but Kate raised a hand, stopping her. "And when *The New York Times* comes out tomorrow and reports that the Trumps and the Kissingers and the Rohatyns and the governor and God knows who else, were here, there will be lines out into the street when the exhibit opens. People like to ride the coattails of big money and power. They like to feel they have the same interests those people have. And that works too."

"Really, Grace, it is doing a great deal of good," Father LoPato said, interjecting himself for the first time, his voice weak and uncertain. "These people do need our help."

"Oh, stop it, Father," Grace snapped, her eyes boring into the priest's. "Nobody gives a damn about helping those people. If they did, the money you raised would be used to help them where they are now. How much good do you really think you're doing by plucking them out of a primitive environment they understand, and dropping them into tenements in Brooklyn and the Bronx? At least be honest about it. You and your superiors want them *here* to fill all those empty churches you're faced with. And now we're helping you do it so we can fill our empty museum."

"That is deeply cynical, Grace," Father LoPato said, anger coming to his own voice now.

Grace Mallory let out a cold, harsh laugh. "When it comes to cynicism, Father, I'm afraid I take a back seat to both of you."

"Perhaps you're right, Grace." Kate's voice was soft and even again. "We have a great exhibit, perhaps the finest work of scholarship ever put together on the Toltecs. It took you thirty years to reach this point, to even have the opportunity to gain the recognition you've deserved for so long. Now I'm a part of that opportunity, and I don't want to see it slip through our hands.

I don't want to wait another thirty years for *my* next opportunity. So if it takes a little showmanship to make this work for all of us, I'm willing to do it."

Grace Mallory stared at her young peer. "Then do it," she said coldly. "But don't expect me to applaud you."

*****

November 9, 8:30 P.M.

Kate Silverman stood before her audience, a plumed Toltec cape draped around her shoulders, the iridescent feathers shimmering under the stage lighting. In one hand she held a long obsidian knife; in the other, an intricately carved bronze ax.

"So you see, what we, in our society, would regard as an act of ritualistic murder, was, for the Toltecs, the ultimate act of love." She smiled. "I know it's difficult to accept the idea of ritualistic beheading as one of great love, but for the Toltecs it was exactly that. It was the greatest gift one could offer, and they were quite particular about whom it was bestowed upon."

Kate returned the knife and ax to a long case on the table beside her, then slipped the cape from her shoulders. "And for the Toltecs it was also an act of great joy, something that can be seen in their art, in the smiles on the faces of those involved in the sacrifice. They also considered it an act of transformation. When the priests donned the stone masks of the gods, they in fact became those gods, not unlike the concept of the Eucharist, the changing of bread and wine into the body and blood of Christ.

"And for those sacrificed, it was also a transformation, for in being sacrificed, they too became gods, and for that reason they went happily, even willingly, to their deaths.

"So here we have a stark contrast to our own religious beliefs. The Toltecs were happy killers, while for those who follow Judeo-Christian beliefs, the act of human sacrifice has always been a fearful one. We have only to recall the torment of Abraham, when asked by God to sacrifice his son Isaac, or the sorrowful image of Christ on the cross.

"Perhaps that is why the Toltecs were very particular about who was offered this great act of love. For the Toltecs, only the nobility were worthy, only the educated elite, the few among many." A small smile played across Kate Silverman's lips. "Looking out over this audience, I can't help but think that each of us here would be very high up on the Toltec list."

A spate of nervous laughter rippled through the audience, and Kate joined it before continuing. "Now," she began again, "I would like to turn to the other purpose for this gathering, the need to ease the suffering of the present-day Mayan people. To do that, please allow me to introduce a man who has worked among these people, both as a distinguished anthropologist and as a Catholic priest, Father Joseph LoPato."

*****

The cocktail party that followed the lecture seemed to swirl about her, placing her at its center, and Kate reveled in it. People came up to her—people who mattered a great deal in the museum world—and told her how much they had enjoyed the lecture and that they looked forward to the opening of the exhibit.

Across the room Kate could see Grace staring at her, her face a mask of perplexed irritation. It made Kate uncomfortable, but in a way, it pleased her as well. It had all worked, just as she had known it would. And Grace would have to admit it, at least to herself.

Kate took a glass of champagne from a passing waiter, then turned and found herself facing a man who seemed decidedly out of place among the other guests. He was middle-aged and rather rumpled, and for some reason she couldn't quite grasp, Kate found him extremely attractive.

"The name's Rolk," he said. "I just wanted to tell you how much I enjoyed the lecture."

Kate cocked her head to one side, trying to recall something the name and the face had provoked. "Why does that name sound so familiar?" she asked, then paused again, struggling to remember. Her face suddenly brightened. "You're a police officer," she said, instantly pleased with herself. "There was an article about you in the *Sunday Times Magazine* a few weeks ago." Rolk said nothing and Kate continued to pull the memory back. "They called you something . . . 'the scholar of death' or something silly like that. And they said you spend all your time studying murder. Is that why you're here?"

He nodded. "Something like that. But I got a lot more out of it than I expected."

"Thank you." She smiled up at him, flattered. "Is it true, what they said about you? That you're so single-minded that your job is all you ever think about?"

Rolk offered a faint smile, and Kate wondered if she had unwittingly offended him.

"Maybe we're alike in that way," he said. "You seem very devoted to what you do, and it's obvious you've spent a great deal of time studying it. Is that the major focus of your life? Your work, I mean?"

Kate felt herself blushing and she did not understand why. "Sometimes it seems that way," she said. She laughed, partly at herself and partly at what he had said. "But I'd hate to think that's all there is, just years of investigating ancient cultures and piecing together fragments of old funeral urns."

Rolk's smile was full and real this time. She was very beautiful, and he found he had to resist the impulse to tell her so.

"I know the feeling," he said, leaving it at that. "Well, again, thank you for a very enjoyable evening."

He turned, and as he moved away through the crowd, Kate watched him, wishing he had stayed longer.

One

STANISLAUS ROLK STOOD quietly, hands thrust deep in the pockets of his overcoat, his body bent slightly forward. He was on a small knoll that looked down on what was left of the woman's body. He remained motionless, his lined face impassive; only someone who knew him well might recognize the pain in his eyes. To anyone else he would simply appear tired, or, perhaps, even bored. Rolk kept his eyes on the woman for a long time. The contours of the body were now flaccid in death, but there was enough to tell him she had been relatively young; enough to tell him she had been physically attractive, the kind of woman men would have looked at more than once. Of course, she could have had a homely face, but he would have to wait to be sure. Wait until someone identified the body and gave them a photograph. Or until they found her head.

Below, the crime scene had been cordoned off in a large circle and portable arc lights cut through the early morning darkness, giving the area the bright glare of midday. The section of Central Park was isolated, a small clearing surrounded by a copse of trees, yet located no more than three hundred yards from Fifth Avenue and Eighty-first Street. The two uniformed officers who had discovered the body had responded to a 911 call about a woman's clothing found at the base of Cleopatra's Needle. The clothing had been folded, the smaller garments placed in a trail that led to the body. The woman's purse—or a purse

19

they assumed hers—had been left where the head should have been.

Rolk glanced at the two officers who were now standing at the inside edge of the circle, talking nervously to other officers assigned to keep reporters at bay. He had spoken with them when he had arrived an hour earlier and they were still green and sickly. But they were both young; in a few years the sight of human horror would no longer make them ill. And that, he told himself, was the unresolved sadness of the job they had all chosen.

Rolk's eyes moved back to the body and the tall, slender man who stood next to it jotting observations in a notebook. Paul Devlin was only thirty, a cop for nine years, and Rolk's partner in Homicide the last four. But Rolk knew the sight of this mutilated body would not disturb Devlin any more than it did him, and he wondered if that callousness, learned over time, was something to be envied or pitied.

As Paul Devlin closed his notebook and looked up at the knoll where Rolk stood watching him, a small smile played momentarily on his lips. Rolk was as rumpled as ever. His topcoat looked as though he had slept in it. His thick hair, streaked with gray, always seemed groomed with fingers instead of a comb. Rolk had a sharp, softly lined face. Not a cop's face, but the face of a bachelor uncle who appears for dinner every other Thanksgiving or Christmas, then fades from memory for the next year or two.

A hand touched Devlin's arm, and he turned to face a uniformed sergeant.

"The meat wagon just pulled into the park," the sergeant said. "The lieutenant said he wanted to know when it got here."

"I'll tell him," Devlin said. "Who's the assistant ME who caught this one?"

"Jerry Feldman. Doctor Death."

Devlin nodded. Feldman was probably the best pathologist in the medical examiner's office, but a man with such a morbid and cutting tongue that most cops avoided him.

"I can't wait to hear what he has to say about this one," Devlin said as he turned and started up the knoll toward Rolk.

"Me neither," the sergeant said to his back.

Devlin slipped the notebook in his pocket as he reached Rolk. At six-foot-two, he was three inches taller than the lieutenant, but his slender frame seemed to tower over Rolk's broader, more muscular body.

"The ME's just pulling in," Devlin said.

"Who?" Rolk asked, his eyes still fixed on the crime scene.

"Jerry Feldman."

Rolk nodded. "Any luck finding the head?"

"Nothing. Not in the immediate area anyway." Devlin glanced at his watch. "We should have sunrise in about half an hour, and they'll expand the search then." He gestured with his head toward the area behind Rolk. "The Emergency Service boys are checking in New Lake. It's shallow all the way across, so if it's there, they'll find it."

Rolk thrust his hands deeper in his coat pockets and started down the knoll. "Let's see what Jerry has to say."

The morgue wagon pulled up to the outer circle of the crime scene, causing an immediate rush of the press, whom uniformed officers fought to keep back. Television lights went on as Feldman emerged from the passenger seat, and camera crews jockeyed for position, drawing shouts of protest from members of the print media they tried to push out of their way.

Feldman turned and scowled, ignoring even those reporters and cameramen he knew. He was tall, vastly overweight, and red-faced, with black hair that had receded to the middle of his scalp. He had compensated for the baldness by allowing the hair on one side of his head to grow long, then combing it up and over the top, which only served to emphasize his lack of hair and make him look mildly ridiculous.

Feldman stopped at the barrier and slipped an over-sized lab coat over his tan polo, then stepped through and walked casually toward the body. He patted the lab coat as he reached Rolk and Devlin. "Cashmere," he said, of the coat beneath. "Hell to get blood out of."

Getting no response, he dropped his medical bag and stared down at the body. "Shit," he began.

Rolk removed one hand from his pocket and pointed at the body. "Tell me about her."

"She's dead," Feldman said. "I make it official."

"Thanks. What else?"

"Where's her head?"

"We're still looking."

Feldman adjusted his glasses, then knelt over the body. He slipped on a pair of rubber gloves and began probing the gaping wound at the base of the neck. "Nice cutting," he said. "Very neat. Something that took a bit of time." He looked up and gestured to a uniformed cop. "Help me turn her over," he ordered.

The cop hesitated, then noticed the angry glare in Feldman's eyes and complied.

"Jesus," Feldman said. He looked up at Rolk. "Have you seen this?"

"We haven't touched the body," Rolk said, stepping to Feldman's side.

Feldman pointed to the woman's back, where a long, gradually widening strip of skin had been removed, exposing raw muscle and areas of bone along the spinal column.

"Skinned," Feldman said. "And again, very skillfully."

Devlin had joined them. "Someone with medical training?" he suggested.

Feldman glared up at him. "You'd love that, wouldn't you?"

"Only if it turned out to be a pathologist," Devlin replied.

"That good he wasn't," Feldman said. "A butcher, even an experienced hunter could do this." He traced a finger along the spinal column, stopping at a deep wound five inches below the base of the neck. "Sharp, axlike instrument. Something like a tomahawk or hatchet. Probably the first blow struck. It severed the spinal column."

Rolk stared at the wound. "Was that the cause of death?"

"Can't tell, but I doubt it. I can tell you she was killed here, just from the amount of blood. The rest?" He shrugged. "You're going to have to wait until I finish the post."

"I'll need it fast, Jerry. Very fast," Rolk said.

Feldman nodded. "Yes, indeed. This'll make for ugly headlines. And that always makes the people upstairs nervous."

Rolk squatted next to him. "I want as little of this to get out as possible."

Feldman lowered his glasses and peered out over them again. "You've got more than a dozen reporters and cameramen standing a hundred yards away," he said. "'Every cameraman has a telephoto lens. They know our little friend here doesn't have a head anymore."

"But that's all I want them to know. Nothing about the skin being removed, or whether or not we've found the head, or any other details." Rolk glanced up at the uniformed cop who had helped turn the body. "That goes for you too," he warned.

"And how long do you think you can keep all that quiet?" Feldman asked, staring into Rolk's sad, tired eyes.

"I'm hoping at least forty-eight to seventy-two hours. We should have questioned everyone connected with the woman by then, and there's always the chance somebody might say something they shouldn't know."

Feldman snorted.

"That's right, Jerry. It's all bullshit, but I need the time. So just do it my way."

Feldman momentarily bristled at the remark, then

grunted agreement. "I'll do the post as soon as we get back to Club Med for the Dead," he said.

Rolk winced at Feldman's term for the morgue, then jerked his thumb toward Devlin. "I'll send Paul with you. I'll be there in a couple of hours, with somebody who can ID the body, I hope."

Feldman looked Rolk up and down, then gave a slight shake of his head. "You better go home and spruce up for the TV cameras," he snapped.

"I'd never look as good as you, Jerry," Rolk said. He patted his topcoat. "Just wool, not cashmere."

Rolk and Devlin climbed back up the knoll as the morgue attendants began loading the corpse into a rubber bag. Behind the high luxury apartment buildings that lined Fifth Avenue in the distance, daylight had just begun its faint early-morning glow, giving an austere beauty to the cold concrete boxes of the wealthy.

Rolk stared at the jutting line of buildings. "Christ, why couldn't this have happened someplace else?" He gestured toward the buildings with his chin. "Half those rich bastards will call their councilman today." He clamped his jaw shut, his eyes narrowing. "Well, at least there won't be anything in the *News* or the *Times* until tomorrow."

"Wait till the *Post* hits the streets this afternoon," Devlin said.

Rolk nodded. "Yeah, they'll love the headless-woman routine." He stuffed his hands back in his pockets and walked in a small circle, thinking. He withdrew one hand and placed it on Devlin's shoulder. "Make sure the lab boys sweep the area thoroughly. Leave somebody behind to stay on their tails. And you stay on Feldman's. He's good, but he's lazy, and he'll take his time getting everything together if we let him." Rolk stared into Devlin's eyes. "And don't let him bully you. I want everything. Cloth and tissue fragments from her fingernails; any indications of drugs or alcohol in her body; any fragments from the weapon left in the wounds, especially dealing with the material the weapon was made of, and approximately when and where it was made. And I want it all this morning, along with the routine checks he'll make about sexual assault, what she had for dinner, everything." Rolk paused, his eyes becoming distant. "The ID in the purse gave the woman's name as Cynthia Gault and a West Side address. She was wearing a wedding ring, so send two men there to see if we can locate a husband. Tell them to try to have him down at the morgue by ten. We need a positive on her as soon as possible."

"You got it," Devlin said.

Rolk glanced at his watch. "It's seven now. Stay on Jerry's ass, then pick me up at my house by nine-thirty. I'm going to take his advice and get cleaned up."

"You have an idea about this one, don't you?"

Rolk nodded. "But I need the information from the post before I'll know whether I'm right or not."

"You want to give me a hint?"

"Not until I'm sure. So climb on Feldman's ass, and stay there."

Stanislaus Rolk's apartment was located on West Eighty-seventh Street between Columbus and Amsterdam avenues, in a four-story brownstone he and his wife had purchased fifteen years earlier, two years after their daughter had been born. Rolk had just been made a lieutenant, and the rise in salary, along with the city's decision to provide urban-renewal loans for the renovation of run-down West Side buildings, had made their dream of a home in Manhattan possible.

They had renovated the building, doing most of the work themselves, creating two apartments on the upper floors to satisfy the conditions of the city loan, and converting the two lower floors into a duplex apartment with a rear garden and play yard for the child.

A few years later the Upper West Side was discovered. Other buildings were bought and renovated, and the cost of real estate and apartment rentals began to soar. It was at that same time that Rolk's wife and child disappeared. There had been a note, simple and unemotional. His wife had fallen in love with someone else. There had been no name, no destination, and all efforts to find them had failed. Now, fifteen years later, he still occupied the same apartment, filled with the same furniture, the same memories of what he had lost. And he still tried to understand why it had happened.

Rolk stepped through the front door of the lower level and into the stale, musty air of the hall. Have to remember to open windows, he told himself. Air the place out every day. Smells like a damn tomb in here.

He dropped his topcoat on a hall chair and climbed the stairs to his second-floor bedroom. Years ago he had stopped worrying about the excessive space he occupied alone. Once he had accepted the fact that his wife would not return, the idea of five rooms and a full basement for one man had seemed an extravagant use of living space. But the idea of moving to one of the smaller apartments, of selling off the extra furniture, required more energy or willpower than he possessed. So he remained in the house, just as he remained a lieutenant, never seeking to change either his place or position. Stagnation was what some people called it. But it was what he wanted; it suited him.

Inside the large, second-floor bathroom, Rolk stripped off his shirt and lathered his cheeks with shaving cream. The face stared back from the mirror, worn and weather-beaten. The eyes were tired. Tired of climbing out of bed in the middle of the night to go and stare at the torn and battered bodies that the city seemed to cough up with regularity.

But this morning's was worse than most, Rolk thought. He had seen bodies more severely mutilated, but there was something about this, something about the way the clothing had been folded and laid out to be found. The way the body had been positioned, almost as though it had been arranged for burial. Feet together, hands folded on the stomach. He shook away a shudder. What the hell was she doing walking through the park at night? An ordinary woman, perhaps a visitor to the museum. If she had been a hooker he might have found an explanation. But the wedding ring, the identification in the purse, the fact that nothing had been taken, all pointed in another direction. Maybe she had picked up a man in a bar, he told himself. Maybe she had been just another married woman on the make, one whose luck had run out in her choice of men. Maybe that's what had happened to his own wife. Maybe she too was dead now. He forced the thought away and stared at his image in the mirror, slightly disgusted with himself. It's the job, he thought. You've been doing it too long, and it's getting to you.

The razor was poised in his hand, but he waited, still staring at his face. You'll be fifty next year, he thought. Almost thirty years on the job. A couple of years and the pressure will begin for you to retire. Retire and do what? he wondered. And if they find out about the doctor's report, about that blip in your last EKG, it won't even be a question of pressure or time. He drew the razor across his cheek. But that was *his* doctor, not the department's. And police surgeons were notoriously lax. Rolk grimaced at his image in the mirror. If they weren't lax, dozens of psychotics now wearing badges would be working as security guards.

Rolk put on a clean shirt, wishing it were less wrinkled, a neutral tie that was miraculously free of spots, and a suit coat that seemed far less rumpled that its matching trousers. He started down the hall, then stopped by the door to the second bedroom. Opening it, he stepped inside. The room had changed over the years, slowly, and with concerted effort. It was no longer the room of a three-year-old child. The crib had been replaced by a single bed of painted white wood covered by a canopy. Stuffed animals still occupied prominent positions about the room, but now there were also books on the matching white dresser, and framed prints on the walls and other objects better suited to a young woman whose intellect was beginning to grow. Jenny. Little Jenny. She would be eighteen next year, and far from little anymore. If she were somehow to return, her room was ready and waiting for her.

He opened the door to the small closet. He had changed, and the clothing had changed as well. He had had to guess at the sizes, and the shopping had been difficult, but the colors were bright and alive and pleasing to look at. Running a hand over a blue print dress, he wondered if his daughter would like it. He wondered if he would ever know the answer.

His hand began to tremble then, and he pulled it back and closed the closet door. The room seemed smaller now with the larger furniture. It had seemed more spacious when it had held only a crib and a bassinet and a few toddler's toys. The wallpaper had been different then too, and he could still see his wife working with him, struggling with the paste and the water, her blond hair in disarray, intermittently laughing and cursing at their clumsy efforts.

They had been happy then, or at least he had thought so. But he had also thought she was happy on the last day he had seen her. Kathy had been seated at the small kitchen table, staring into her coffee. He had watched her from across the room, her blond hair partially obscuring her face, and he had thought how beautiful she was.

She had been quiet that morning, but she had always been a person who disliked conversation when she first awakened. Or had that only been in the later years? It was hard now to remember. Perhaps she had gradually grown more quiet, more introspective, and he had simply failed to notice.

Too busy with your work, he told himself now. Too busy to see what was happening in your own life.

Rolk's hands momentarily clenched.

"Be careful today." The last words he had heard her speak.

He had mumbled some incoherent response, then

reached down and run his hand along his daughter's head. She had been sitting on the floor, watching a children's program on the small kitchen television set. She had giggled at the program, not even realizing he had touched her.

A pain surged across his forehead, and he closed the door to Jenny's room and returned to his own. He sat down, waiting for the headache to ease. He would give it a few minutes, just a few, then he would go back to work, back to whatever other horror the day would hold.

Two

THE ROOM WAS dark, womblike. A soft, cold breeze filtered in from the partially open window, causing the curtains to sway slightly as though someone or something were standing behind them.

The figure lay fully clothed, eyes closed, features smooth and relaxed, breath coming in a rasping, barely distinguishable hum. Behind the eyes the vision of the sacrifice replayed itself again and again, each nuance studied in detail, each gesture judged against the requirements of the ritual.

It had been nearly perfect. Only the need to rush had marred the austere beauty of the ceremony. But the woman had tried to escape the indisputable need of the ritual, a vile attempt to disrupt the order that was so important to it all. She should have been punished for that, but there had not been time.

At least she had been blond. That had been the most important reason for choosing her. She had been prelude to the one who would come later, the one who would fulfill the final ritual. That one—the important one—told everyone her name was Kate Silverman. But that was not her true name. Her true name was known only to the keeper of the ritual, and to one other.

And that other could destroy the ritual out of ignorance, something that must not be allowed. Death must be offered to the one chosen as the ultimate act of love. It must be given beautifully and without pain so that the purity of the gift could be maintained. And the one to receive it must know that she would be welcomed with beauty and with love. She must know that death awaited her, not because she was evil, but because she was wonderful.

Three

PAUL DEVLIN STOOD before the barred garden-level door and rang the bell a second time. The morning had grown colder and his face was flushed from the wind that pushed its way along West Eighty-seventh Street. But the cold didn't matter: he barely felt it. The weariness of the long night had already set in, and that, combined with the knowledge of the work yet to be done, served to dull his senses.

Devlin ran his fingers through his wavy black hair as he waited for Rolk to answer the door. His thin, almost fragile face seemed strikingly vulnerable for a cop's, something that had served him well in allaying the fears of nervous suspects. Now his features seemed to have collapsed, and his dark eyes were streaked with red. He felt weary to the core. It was the morgue, he told himself. It always had the same effect. The sight, the smell, and, yes, even the feel of it.

The door opened and Rolk appeared, looking fresh and relaxed.

"You look like shit, Paul. Come in and have some coffee."

Devlin followed Rolk down a narrow hallway. "You'd look like shit too if you hadn't slept in two days. I just got the Lorenzo thing wrapped up when the call came in from Central Park."

Devlin took a cup of coffee and sipped it gratefully.

"How did Lorenzo take it? I never asked you."

"Just about like you said he would. First he squealed like a stuck pig, then blubbered a little about how much he loved his wife. Then, when he saw his bullshit wasn't going to float, he got serious, shut his mouth, and got on the phone to his lawyer." Devlin sipped the coffee again. "You were right—they'll plea-bargain it down. You could almost see it coming last night. And after watching his act, I don't care whether he did it or not. The clown deserves to do time, just for being the callous little prick he is."

Rolk nodded. "Just don't say that in public." He sipped his own coffee. "Did Jerry come up with anything?"

"He says he'll have most of it together by the time you get there. But he's not happy about being rushed."

"Jerry wouldn't be happy if I gave him until next month," Rolk said. "What about the woman's husband?"

"Peters and Moriarty found him at the Gaults' apartment. They said he's pretty busted up, but they'll have him down at the morgue as close to ten as possible."

Devlin wandered into the living room, the coffee still in his hand. He always marveled at the size of Rolk's apartment, the paintings that hung on every wall, the rows of bookcases that held volumes of every description. He turned back to face his partner.

"You know this house is the best damned thing you ever did," he began. "Christ, what it must be worth today. You don't even need your pension with the rentals from the apartments. I guess that's why you can tell the bosses to piss off when they get on your ass."

"I can tell them that because I'm good at my job and they know it." Rolk paused, taking in Devlin's knowing smile. "And if you like this house so much, maybe I'll leave it to you in my will." He paused again. "That is, if you don't screw up this case too badly."

"I'll take it," Devlin said. "My kid would love it. But I'll be damned if I know why you want a place this big all by yourself. You're never here, and cleaning it must be a pain in the ass."

Rolk's eyes became oddly shrouded, then cleared. "Just too lazy to move," he said.

Devlin set his cup down on a small desk, and noticed the papers carefully arranged there. He looked up at Rolk. "More work on finding your daughter?" he asked.

"Yeah. More."

"What are you trying this time?"

"College boards. She'll be eighteen next year, and I thought she might be applying to some schools. I'm going to ask them to run her name and her mother's maiden name."

Devlin nodded, but said nothing. The man was going to drive himself crazy with his constant search for a fifteen-year-old ghost.

"Well, I hope you come up with something this time," Devlin said.

"It's a shot," Rolk said. "No worse, no better than the others I've taken." He put his own cup down next to Devlin's. "We better get our tails down to Jerry's office. It's going to be a long day."

"Yeah," Devlin said. "Long and lousy."

Four

DEVLIN PULLED THE car into the wide ramp that led to the basement of the medical examiner's office on East Thirtieth Street. Climbing out, Rolk glanced across the street at the main entrance to Bellevue Hospital, a red-brick fortress that seemed more ominous than any hospital should. He wondered what the city had had in mind when it had placed the unloading area for the morgue in clear view of the psychiatric wing. "Therapy," he mumbled to himself as he turned and started down the ramp. "Or entertainment."

Rolk and Devlin moved down the blue-tiled hall. It was spotless, yet pervaded by the smell of rotting meat. At the end of the hall they entered the first of the large autopsy rooms. Feldman was at the far end, leaning over a microscope. In the center of the room the headless body lay on an autopsy table, as an older woman, known to her peers as "The Seamstress," sewed up the Y-shaped incision left by the postmortem.

"What have we got?" Rolk asked as he moved past the body.

Feldman's head snapped up from the microscope. "I'll tell you what we've got. We've got a young cop who's one enormous pain in the arse." He jabbed a finger in Devlin's direction.

Rolk slipped off his topcoat and dropped it on a metal chair. "A problem?" he asked, his face impassive.

"Don't play innocent, Rolk," Feldman ranted. "I know this pathetic excuse for a detective is only following your orders." He jabbed another finger at no one in particular. "This is science, not some goddamned butcher shop." He waved his hand, taking in the room, the building, the world, for all Rolk knew. "I've got thirty thousand bodies coming in here every year. Thirty thousand! That's one-third of all the god-damned people who croak in this city annually. And seven *thousand*, five *hundred* of those stiff-limbed motherfuckers have to be autopsied. Do you hear me, Rolk? Autopsied!"

Rolk shook his head. "It's an awesome task, Jerry. And nobody but you could do it."

Feldman's face reddened, his cheeks filled, and then with a rush of air he began to laugh. "You are an unmitigated bastard, Rolk. Unmitigated."

Rolk blinked his eyes and inclined his head to one side. "I'm not even going to ask you what that means, Jerry, because I'm afraid you'll tell me. So just let me know what we've got."

Feldman looked at Devlin and shrugged. "He's going into his dumb act now," he said. "Have you ever been in his house?"

"Just came from there," Devlin said.

"Then you know how the place is full of books," Feldman continued. "Not just books. Classics, art books, you-name-it."

"Tell me what we've got," Rolk interrupted.

"Come to my office," Feldman said. "I need to put my fat ass on something soft."

Rolk and Devlin followed him down another blue-tiled hall. Rolk held his topcoat in one hand, dragging it along the floor, picking up dust.

Feldman kicked open his office door and collapsed into the chair behind his desk. "You want coffee?" he asked as Rolk and Devlin took chairs. When they said they did, he activated an ancient intercom console and cooed into it, "Elvira, dear. Bring us three coffees, please." He released the button and stared across at Rolk. "Last week she told me getting coffee wasn't in her job description." He smiled as evilly as he could. "I threatened to autopsy her alive," he growled.

Elvira came with the coffee, her face a cold mask.

She left without saying a word. Feldman settled back in his chair, grinning, mounds of flesh overlapping the armrests.

"So?" Rolk asked.

"Not good," Feldman began. "The newspapers are going to go out of their minds." He leaned forward with effort, clasping his index finger with his other hand. "First, no drugs, no alcohol, no sexual assault. She had a salad and tea for dinner. And that's *all* the good news."

Rolk sat forward, imitating Feldman's intensity. "Don't draw it out, Jerry," he said.

Feldman nodded. "Death was due to a massive loss of blood, caused by the severing of every goddamned vein and artery in her neck. The wound in the back was administered first. It virtually severed the spinal column, making her an instant quadriplegic. He raised a cautioning finger. "It's highly probable, however, that our victim was conscious when her killer began to cut off her head." He waved one hand, warding off an anticipated question. "It is also probable, although I can't know for certain, that she felt nothing in the final minutes, since the spinal column was severed."

"What about the skinning?" Rolk asked. "Was it before or after the head was removed?"

"After," Feldman said. "The abrasions on the muscle show it was pulled down the length of the body, and away." He hesitated. "The final, and most unpleasant point," he began. "Our victim was two months pregnant."

Rolk closed his eyes. "Great. Now, if we find out she was a nun wearing civilian clothes, the case will have everything."

"Exactly," Feldman said.

"Any ideas about why the skin was removed from the back?" Devlin asked.

"Nothing you're going to like," Feldman said. "You want my opinion, I've got to say it involved some kind of ritual."

"Why?" Rolk challenged.

"The cutting was too precise. It's almost in the shape of a cape. Intentionally so."

Rolk fumbled in his shirt pocket for a cigarette, lit it, and blew a stream of smoke at the floor. He looked up at Feldman. "What about the murder weapon, Jerry?"

"I found some fragments in both wounds." He shrugged. "Cutting through bone always takes some toll. They're being analyzed now." He looked down at his watch. "Another half-hour maybe," he said.

Feldman's telephone rang and he picked it up. "Okay," he said, dropping the receiver back in its cradle. He looked back at Rolk. "Two of your men have the victim's husband upstairs. I don't think showing him the body on closed-circuit television is going to work in this case," he said. "He's going to have to look at scars and moles to get a positive."

Rolk nodded, then turned to Devlin. "You better bring him down here. Tell Moriarty and Peters to wait there. The fewer people around, the better."

When Devlin had left, Rolk stared at the floor for several minutes, then looked back up at Feldman. "Let's find some way to cover up the head . . . area," he said. "Let's make it as easy for this poor bastard as we can."

Feldman nodded, then slapped his palms down on his desk and pushed himself up. "This is the part of this job I really hate," he said. "It makes me feel like a goddamn undertaker."

Stephen Gault was a tall, well-built man in his thirties who, Rolk thought, under normal circumstances would be considered handsome. Now his face was ashen and his hands and lips trembled uncontrollably.

They led him into a small room where the victim's belongings had been stored. Feldman stood with his back to the door, divorcing himself as much as possible from the proceedings. Rolk and Devlin stood on either side of the trembling man before a long wooden table.

"Mr. Gault," Rolk began, his voice soft and distant, "the first thing we'd like you to do is look at some belongings. Then, if it's necessary, we'll ask you to identify the victim."

Gently Rolk began removing items from a large cardboard box—a purse, a ring, a wristwatch. He heard the sharp intake of breath, the words *"Oh My God"* repeated over and over. He removed the folded clothing, the shoes, a delicate designer scarf. He could feel Gault's trembling increase, heard the sobs mixed with gasps for air. He took the man's arm and moved him to a chair against the wall. "Please sit down, Mr. Gault," he whispered.

He stood over the man, giving him time, then pulled another chair from the wall, placed it in front of him, and sat. "Do you feel those things might have belonged to your wife?" he asked unnecessarily.

Gault drew a deep breath and nodded. "They're hers," he said, his voice no more than a croak.

Rolk waited again. He wanted the information quickly so he could act. But not at this man's expense.

"We're going to have to ask you to look at the body, Mr. Gault," he began. "Normally we'd do that over closed-circuit television. But in this case that's not possible."

Gault was silent for several moments, until the words finally registered. His head snapped up and he stared into Rolk's sad, weary face. "Why not?"

Rolk placed his hand on the man's arm and leaned toward him, choosing his words carefully. "The head of the victim was removed," he said softly. "And we haven't found it yet."

He watched the man's eyes widen, first in disbelief, then in horror. A gagging sound came from his throat, and Rolk reached out, taking his shoulders in his hands, steadying him. He waited for the horror to subside, then continued in a soft, hesitant voice. "Did your wife have any scars or other marks on her body that might help identify her?"

Gault was silent, breathing hard again, then seemed

to take some control of himself. "Appendix," he said, then fought for breath again. "And a birthmark. Red. On her upper thigh." He looked up at Rolk, his eyes pleading. "She thought it was ugly," he said. "It bothered her when she had to wear a bathing suit." His eyes continued to bore into Rolk's.

Rolk kept all expression from his face. He had seen the scar, and the birthmark, but that would not be enough. The law required more. "I'd like you to look at the body," he said.

They entered a large room with a long wall of tiered stainless-steel boxes. The door of each box contained a slot with an index card fitted into it. The cards were marked only with numbers.

Rolk and Devlin stood on either side of Gault to one side of the door; Feldman stood on the other. The pathologist opened the door and slid out a long tray. The body was naked, a white towel drapped over the lower portion of the neck.

A low moan began deep in Gault's throat, and his body sagged. Rolk and Devlin each took an arm, supporting him. Gault's eyes roamed the once familiar body—a body he had made love to, Rolk thought, had held and caressed. He knew it had been nothing like the pale gray, flaccid piece of waste he was looking at now.

"Is it her?" Devlin asked softly.

Gault's head bobbed up and down like some toy dog's in the rear window of a car. Suddenly his hands rushed to his mouth, and he began to retch.

Rolk circled his shoulders with one arm and turned him away from the body, as Feldman quickly slid the tray back. Gault bent double, and vomit spewed from his mouth. He gagged and retched, Rolk continuing to hold him, the vomit splattering both their shoes and the bottoms of their trousers.

When there was nothing left, Gault staggered forward and began to apologize. Rolk kept his arm around him and moved him away from the vomit-covered floor. "Let's go to the men's room and get you cleaned up," he said. "Then we'll have the men who brought you here take you home."

Feldman's office was empty when Rolk and Devlin returned, so they sat down to wait.

Devlin drummed his fingernails on the arm of the chair, as though deciding what to say next. He turned toward Rolk and noticed that his face seemed to sag with weariness, almost as though he had absorbed the pain of the man they had just sent home to grieve.

"How much time do you want us to spend on the husband?" Devlin asked.

"As a suspect?" Rolk asked, not needing an answer. "As much as you normally would." He looked across at Devlin. "But if he killed her," he said, "I want him sentenced to twenty years in Hollywood."

Devlin nodded agreement, then reached into his pocket and withdrew a photograph. "Moriarty picked this up at the apartment," he said. "It's the most recent photo her husband had."

Rolk took it and held it out before him. A distant wave of recognition moved through him, grew stronger, then began to fade. He studied the picture more closely, the laughing smile, the happiness and humor that leapt from the eyes. He heard Devlin's voice and looked up at him. "What?" he asked.

"I said her husband told Peters and Moriarty that she went to that lecture at the Metropolitan Museum. The same one you were at. She was big on museums and galleries." He paused a beat. "You might even have seen her there. Funny we didn't find the invitation among her things."

All the weariness seemed to vanish from Rolk's face and his eyes bored into Devlin's. "Did you check the pockets of her clothing, her purse?"

"While you were helping Gault in the men's room. Nothing." Devlin waited, studying the change in Rolk. "The husband didn't go because he says he doesn't like that sort of thing. She could have gone with a boyfriend and he might have kept the invitation. Maybe it's something we should look into."

Rolk held up the photograph again, studying the woman's face. Was that what she had done? He doubted it. She certainly didn't look the type. But you couldn't always tell. No, this was something far worse. He continued to stare at the face, thinking about the unborn child the woman had carried. He wondered if she knew. Certainly she suspected. Then he wondered if she had told her husband. He hadn't asked, and they hadn't volunteered the information. That would come later. In a few days, Rolk knew, the man's grief would ebb. Then anger would replace it and he would call and want to know what was being done, how such a thing could happen to his wife, how much suffering she had endured. Then he would learn about the child. Unless the newspapers told him first. Rolk knew it took a while for the survivors to think rationally again.

Feldman burst through the door. "Christ, what a bitch of a day," he growled. "They had a fire on the Lower East Side. I've got a half-dozen charred bodies coming in." He flopped into his chair, grunting.

Paul Devlin squeezed his eyes shut and groaned. The morgue would soon be pervaded by the smell of burnt flesh, and he wanted out of there before it happened. Rolk remained expressionless. He handed the photograph across the desk. "This is what Mrs. Gault looked like," he said.

Feldman stared at the photograph, his eyes softening with regret; then he handed it back. "Beautiful woman," he said, drawing himself up in his chair. "You better find this bastard fast." He shook his head as though fighting away an unpleasant thought. "And I think you better bring in the department shrink."

"Why?" Rolk asked, his voice eager now.

"Because I don't think this is a one-shot deal. I think you've got a crazy on your hands, and I think he's going to do it again."

"What makes you say that?" Devlin asked.

"The fact that it was a ritual."

"That's still only a theory," Devlin said.

"Less of a theory than before," Feldman said. He

stared at Devlin, then turned to Rolk. "A preliminary report came in on the fragments from the weapons. And it's not going to make you happy." He hesitated, as though trying to convince himself of the words he was about to speak. "Two different weapons," he began. "A hatchetlike weapon that did the damage to the spinal column, and a sharper-edged weapon that was used to remove the head." He let out a long breath. "According to the analysis, both of them are approximately seven hundred years old."

Five

ROLK'S OFFICE, AS head of the Borough Homicide Task Force, was located in the Thirteenth Precinct on East Twenty-first Street. Like the man himself, the office had a cluttered, ill-used look, with a paper-strewn aging wooden desk, three scarred institutional chairs, and a worn leather sofa, where Rolk often slept. There was a map of Manhattan on one wall that was marred by coffee stains, although no one could explain how they had gotten there, and there was a pervading smell of stale cigarette smoke. Rolk added to that smell now as he absently puffed on his fifteenth cigarette of the morning, his eyes studying Jerry Feldman's report one more time.

"You look like you found something in that report," Paul Devlin said from a chair opposite Rolk. "I'm reading the same thing and I'll be damned if I can find anything to be happy about."

Rolk glanced at Devlin, then at Charlie Moriarty and Bernie Peters, two other detectives he had assigned to the case. "It's the lecture," he said. "That's the thing that ties it all together. But let's go through the physical evidence before we get into that."

Rolk leaned back in his chair. The ash on his cigarette was an inch long now, and it fell, dusting the front of his tie. "Feldman puts the time of death between five and eight hours before the body was found. That would mean between eight P.M. and eleven P.M." Rolk ground out his cigarette, stared at his desk for a moment, then slowly lit another. "Given the fact

44

that the body was dragged from the path into the bushes, and that the clothes were neatly laid out at the base of the monument or dropped in a trail leading to the body, I can't see the murder happening when there were a lot of people around. That means the earliest would be nine to ten o'clock." Rolk drummed his fingers on the desk. "What have we got on the husband for that time period?"

Moriarty flipped open his notebook. He was a bulky man, whose clothing, though neater, fit almost as badly as Rolk's, and his smooth round face, which belied his forty-five years, made him seem almost boyish, as did his close-cropped blond hair. He cleared his throat and spoke in a voice unnaturally high for a man his size. "According to the doorman at his building, Gault got home around five-thirty, and left again a little after eight. He said he went to a party after leaving a note for his wife. She was supposed to meet him there after the lecture. The note was still in the apartment."

"Did the people who gave the party say when he got there?"

Peters leaned forward in his chair, making his small frame seem even thinner and narrower. There was a predatory look about him. His hair was dark and thin, and combed straight back, giving it a slick, oily look, and his eyes were closely set around a pointed nose. His voice had a rough, grating quality. "Approximately eight-thirty," Peters said. They couldn't be any more exact than that. The woman who gave the party said he started to look annoyed around ten, then later, a little nervous. He left around eleven-thirty."

"Did he call his wife while he was there?"

"Once." Peters said. "Left a message on their answering machine in case she missed his note. I listened to the tape. He sounded pissed as hell that she hadn't shown up at the party."

"So, unless he hired somebody, we can pretty much rule him out." Rolk pulled on his nose. "Christ, I can't see this as the work of a pro."

Devlin closed his notebook and returned it to his inside pocket. He had been making notes of Peters' and Moriarty's reports, but the information had provided little. A lot of mutilation murders, he knew, were homosexual crimes, and almost always involved mutilation of the genitals; in lesbian cases, often the breasts. No, this was just what Feldman had called it. The work of a maniac. He pushed the question away. "Charlie and Bernie are still checking out possible marital problems with the couple's neighbors and friends, and the possibility that either one of them had something going on the side. But it doesn't look promising," he said.

"And even if they both had something going, it might not mean a damned thing," Rolk said.

"So that leaves the lecture, and the fact that Mrs. Gault was on her way to do it when she was killed," Devlin said.

"Or she had already been there and was on her way home," Rolk offered. "Or was somehow lured outside. We'll have to check out all three possibilities."

"I still don't see how it fits, except to put her at the murder scene," Devlin said.

"You wouldn't unless you'd been there." Rolk ground out his cigarette and lit another. "The lecture was about ritualistic murders performed by the Toltecs, who were one of the tribes of the Mayan civilization." He paused, looking at each man in turn. "One of the ways they sacrificed their victims was to behead them and skin them. And they were doing this seven hundred years ago."

"Were there weapons at the lecture?" Moriarty asked.

Rolk nodded.

"Jesus," Devlin said. "Then you think somebody involved with that lecture decided to get in some practice?"

"Or somebody who heard it and got turned on by the idea," Rolk said.

"So that's our angle," Devlin said.

Rolk sat forward, dropping his forearms on the desk. "It may be the only angle. At least until this freak does it again."

"You think he will, don't you?" Peters said.

"Yeah. But I'm sure as hell not going to say that to anyone else, and I don't want any of you to either. I wish we could drop the whole damned thing right back into the hands of the PDU and forget it."

The other detectives knew exactly what Rolk meant. The Precinct Detective Units handled routine murders, and turned over only the sensational or high-publicity crimes to the Homicide task force Rolk headed. This one had qualified on all fronts right from the start.

"The age of the weapons," Devlin said. "That points to somebody at the museum, doesn't it?"

"It could," Rolk said. "But people in this city collect all kinds of crap." He rocked back in his chair. "Still, it's our only angle right now." He glanced at each of the men. "I want to find out how many people have access to that kind of museum piece. Could a museum guard get his hands on something? A janitor? Or would it have to be somebody higher up? And I want to know if there were any collectors at that lecture."

There was a light rap on the door; then a uniformed officer stuck his head in.

"Sorry to interrupt, Lieutenant, but the deputy commissioner for public information is on line two. Says he has to talk to you."

Rolk stared at the phone and grimaced. He had little use for the deputy, Martin O'Rourke. Like the other deputy commissioners, he was a political appointee of the mayor. But his office served one useful purpose. It dealt with the press, and could shield him and his men from a constant barrage of questions.

Devlin watched Rolk as he reluctantly picked up the phone, then listened to the terse, one-sided conversation.

"Hello, Martin.

"Yes, it's a beauty.

"No, we don't have much right now, except the positive ID, the ME's report, which I imagine you've seen, and the physical evidence we gathered at the scene.

"I'm sure every reporter in town *is* driving you crazy, but there isn't a helluva lot I can tell you right now to ease the pressure.

"Look, the *Post* can write anything they want, and if the husband refuses to bury the body until we find the head, Christ, what can we say except that we sympathize and are doing everything we can to find it?

"No, it looks like the killer took it with him." Rolk squeezed his eyes shut and began massaging them with his thumb and index finger.

"Well, the *Post* reporter's right about that. She was at that lecture at the Met, or on her way to it. I've got men there now, and I was about to head there myself.

"We're going to *have* to interview everyone who was there. There's no choice, unless somebody walks in and confesses.

"Look, Martin, I can't help it if those people don't like cops showing up at their door. I've got a woman who had her head lopped off either before or after she got to that lecture, and as you can see from the ME's report, it was probably done with a seven-hundred-year-old weapon. That makes the Met and the lecture a legitimate avenue of investigation. And I've got to pursue it.

"Right. No problem. I'll tell my men to ruffle as few feathers as possible.

"Of course I will, Martin. As soon as we have something solid, I'll let you know."

Rolk put down the phone and stared at it for a moment. "In a pig's ass, I will," he added to no one in particular.

Rolk pushed himself up from his desk and struggled into his topcoat.

"The museum?" Devlin asked.

"That's right. The deputy commissioner needs information. So we better get our tails in gear and find them some."

Devlin fought back a smile as they headed out the door. "Sounds like the brass are a little worried about this one," he said.

Rolk envisioned the days ahead, the murders he knew were coming. "So am I," he said. "And in a few days you will be too."

Six

KATE SILVERMAN SAT in the sterile modern office, patiently waiting for Alexsandra Ross to complete the telephone call that had interrupted their meeting. She struggled against listening to the irritating sound of Alexsandra's voice as she tried to intimidate the caller. Instead she allowed her eyes to glance around the cold, sophisticated room, the glass-and-chrome surfaces, the stark postmodern prints against even starker white walls, the garishly painted mobile suspended by almost invisible wires that dominated one corner. The overall effect, she decided, was as jarring in the Metropolitan Museum as the sound of Alexsandra's voice.

Readjusting herself on the uncomfortable contemporary sofa, Kate turned her attention to the full-length mirror affixed to the back of the office door. She looked herself over carefully. Everything seemed to be in place, as she had planned it. Smart. Professional. She grimaced at the thought, though it was an accurate description of herself. She knew she was attractive, and had even been called beautiful. Her soft blond hair and green eyes were appealing, and her bone structure was flawless. She studied her blue-gray suit. The well-tailored and expensive raw silk gave her the look she had struggled to achieve. The same could be said for the green silk blouse, with its turned-up collar, that offered little hint of the very good figure beneath.

Kate turned her attention to Alexsandra and found the comparison satisfying. The woman had a style about her too, a presence. She was pushing forty and was only moderately attractive, but her face was artfully made up, accenting just the right features. Her black hair was cut short and combed casually to one side so it fell forward, partially obscuring one of her large brown eyes. And her clothing seemed to say everything she wanted it to, clinging to her body, moving with each gesture, fluttering like the feathers of a preening avian.

Kate returned to her own image in the mirror. It was a far cry from the eighteen-year-old who had come to New York ten years earlier to study anthropology at Columbia University. But it was exactly the image she had wanted to create even then. A doctor of anthropology, working for the American Museum of Natural History, who looked as though she had just stepped out of the pages of *Vogue*. She smiled at herself for ever wanting it to be so, but she knew she wanted it just as much today.

Alexsandra slammed the phone down noisily, bringing Kate back. "Damned incompetent fool," she snapped. She leaned forward, her eyes and mouth accenting her annoyance. "There are some people in this world," she said, "who, if you tattooed your instructions on their ass, could still manage to screw everything up."

Alexsandra closed her eyes and sat back in her chair. "Where were we?"

"We were trying to decide which objects to photograph for the publicity posters and advertisements."

Alexsandra began drumming long polished nails against the surface of her desk. "You know," she began slowly, "I really can't understand why we at the Met ever agreed to a joint exhibit with the Natural History."

"It was a question of scholarship," Kate offered. "Together—in this one area, at least—we have the ability to put together one of the finest exhibits of Toltec art ever seen, something that neither of us could have done individually."

Alexsandra waved a dismissive hand, stopping Kate in mid-thought. "Scholarship is all well and good. And I'm not trying to denigrate your museum. We all know the Museum of Natural History here is one of the finest of its kind in the world. But when we talk exhibitions, my dear, we are talking showmanship, and that means drawing people in. Now, I'm not dismissing what you did last night. It was excellent and it was well-thought-out. But the money people came because it was held at the Met. To be perfectly frank, the Met draws and your museum simply doesn't. So, for the life of me, I can't see why we're doing this with equal billing. And I certainly don't see why the publicity end of things can't be left to me alone."

Kate smiled to herself. She realized Alexsandra was envious of last night's success, but she wanted to avoid any battles with the woman. "Dr. Mallory simply wants to have some—"

"I know," Alexsandra said, cutting her off again. "The old warhorse wants to keep a tight rein on the project. Christ, I understand she was even annoyed about last night."

In more ways than you know, Kate thought, and was about to say it when the telephone interrupted them again.

Alexsandra answered it with an angry, snapping voice, then almost immediately slammed it back down. "Christ," she said.

"What's wrong?"

"Now we have the police at the door," she said. "Something about a murder in the park last night. This is just more than I want to deal with this morning."

Kate turned as the door swung open to reveal the oddly attractive man she had met the previous evening, who now looked as though he had slept in his clothing.

Alexsandra stood behind her desk and appraised Rolk openly. "I'm Alexsandra Ross," she said.

"Lieutenant Rolk," he said, extending his identification.

Alexsandra looked from the card to Rolk, again appraising. "Stanislaus," she said, her lips curving slightly upward. "That's an unusual name."

"Not in Warsaw," Rolk said.

The woman arched her eyebrows. "Oh, were you born there?"

"No," Rolk said, returning the card to his pocket.

Alexsandra stared at him incredulously, then let out an exasperated breath and sat back in her chair. After a brief glance at Kate, he turned his attention back to Alexsandra.

"What can I do for you, Lieutenant?" Alexsandra asked.

Rolk stared at a nearby chair, then back at the woman, who waved an offering hand toward it. As he eased himself into the chair, his rumpled topcoat bunched up around him. "What you can do for me, Ms. Ross, is answer some questions. Then you can tell me who I can see to get some other questions answered."

Alexsandra lit a cigarette and exhaled the smoke in a long, irritated line. "I really don't have a great deal of time, Lieutenant. We're trying to put together the promotional work for a major exhibit."

The word "we" obviously referred to Kate, and Rolk looked toward her, smiled faintly, and nodded. Kate returned the greeting with a smile of her own, then watched as Rolk turned back to Alexsandra, all pleasantness gone from his eyes. "I guess your secretary didn't tell you there was a woman murdered just outside the museum."

"She didn't fail to tell me, Lieutenant," Alexsandra said, a slight edge to her voice.

Drumming his fingers against the arm of the chair, Rolk stared at the wall behind Alexsandra, where a large and, to him, totally incomprehensible painting hung. Slowly he eased himself up from the chair. "I certainly don't want to interrupt your office routine," he said. "I'll have one of my men bring you down to the Thirteenth Precinct, along with anyone else we need to talk to. We can handle the matter there."

Alexsandra shot forward in her chair. "That is *not* what I meant," she snapped.

Rolk stared down at her. "I don't care what you meant, Ms. Ross. I'm telling you what *I* mean."

The door opened, breaking the tension, and a second man entered.

"This is Detective Devlin," Rolk said, nodding toward the door.

Kate watched Alexsandra survey every inch of the handsome new arrival. Always appraising, she thought. And this time she liked what she saw.

Paul Devlin exchanged greetings with Alexsandra, then turned to Kate and nodded.

Kate smiled up at him. "Kate Silverman," she said. "It's nice to meet you, Detective."

Devlin continued to look at her, longer than necessary, Kate thought, until Rolk's words brought him back.

"What did you find out downstairs?"

From the air of tension in the room, Devlin guessed that one of the women—the one behind the desk, he thought—had ruffled Rolk's feathers and had discovered exactly what that could produce.

"A few of the guards thought they recognized the picture, but nothing positive. Our people are still trying with the rest of the staff."

"I hope you realize this is very disruptive. To *everyone* in the museum, staff and visitors alike."

Alexsandra had directed the remark to Rolk, and Devlin held his breath, waiting.

Rolk's face was like a large flat stone. "I'm sure Mrs. Gault would regret any inconvenience."

The woman's sharply defined eyebrows rose, questioning the name.

Rolk's face remained impassive, his voice soft. "Cynthia Gault. The woman who attended your lecture here last night, and who then had her head removed a few hundred yards from your back door." He turned to Kate. "Very much in the way you described the Toltec ritual, Dr. Silverman."

The two women stared at Rolk and then at each other. Kate's face paled. Alexsandra's expression moved quickly from shock to renewed anger.

"You can't be serious," Kate said, her voice carrying a slight tremor.

"Almost to the last detail," Rolk said. "As you know, I was there. I heard the lecture."

Alexsandra looked at the man more closely, finding what he was saying now especially hard to believe. "You . . . were there?"

"Yes. And I enjoyed Dr. Silverman's lecture very much. At least until about five o'clock this morning."

Alexsandra Ross broke the momentary silence that followed. "Very well, Lieutenant. Let's just get on with it as quickly as possible. Exactly what are you looking for?"

Rolk returned to his chair, and Devlin seated himself next to Kate.

"For starters, I need a list of everyone who attended last night's lecture."

"That's what I was afraid of," Alexsandra snapped. "You're going to make the museum sound like some sort of stalking ground to some very important people. And *that*, Lieutenant, is *not* going to do us a great deal of good."

"We'll be as discreet as possible," Rolk said, staring across the desk at her. "And we won't try to frighten anyone away."

Alexsandra closed her eyes, annoyed. "What else?"

"Our preliminary analysis shows the weapon used was old enough to qualify as a museum piece."

"How old?" The question came from Kate. Her face was still ashen, and a tremor remained in her voice.

Rolk hesitated, trying to decide how specific he wanted to be. He studied the young blond woman, who now seemed to have lost all the grace and confidence she had demonstrated during the lecture the previous night. "Seven hundred years, maybe older," he said at length. "Fragments have been sent off for a more accurate analysis."

"What type of material?" Kate caught a hardening of Rolk's eyes. "You'd have to know that to get *any* date. I've been involved in the process myself, on occasion."

Rolk nodded. "That has our pathologists a little confused. We have traces of bronze, and also another material that seems to be some kind of volcanic mineral, almost like glass. Very similar to the knife you showed the audience last night."

"Obsidian."

"What?"

"The material," Kate said. "The knife I used in the lecture was made of obsidian. It's a very hard glasslike material that's indeed volcanic. It was used by most of the Mayan tribes in South America and Mexico to make weapons and tools."

"Sharp enough to . . ." Rolk let the sentence die.

"More than sharp enough," Kate said. "It can be honed to a razor's edge. In fact the Mayans used obsidian for razors. It dulls quickly, but sharpened, it could certainly accomplish . . ." She hesitated. "What you described."

"What about cutting through bone?"

"Some of the swords the Mayans used had serrated edges. They could cut through some very resistant material."

"Where are the weapons you used in the lecture last night?" Rolk asked.

"They're downstairs in the workroom we're using here at the Met."

"I'd like to see them."

"Certainly."

"Are there other weapons as well?"

"Yes. Some are here, and there are others over at my museum, the Museum of Natural History."

"I'd like to see those as well."

"There are quite a number of them. Hundreds, perhaps."

Rolk stared at her a moment, surprised by the information. "Are there any private collectors who might have this type of weapon?"

Alexsandra interrupted, her voice dripping sarcasm. "Only a hundred or so serious collectors in the greater New York area alone."

"Alexsandra's right," Kate said, seeking to cool the moment.

"Any collectors who were here last night?"

"One that I know of," Kate said. "He's lent us material for our exhibit, in fact, but—"

"Who was that?" Rolk asked.

"Now, just a minute," Alexsandra said, leaning forward as though she was about to leap across her desk. "The last thing we need is an alienated collector who, because of his generosity, finds himself hounded by the police."

Rolk matched the woman's defiant stare. "Somehow I don't think I'm getting my message across to you. Because if I were, I don't think I'd be sitting here listening to all this. So let me try again. He hunched himself forward and raised one index finger. "First, we have a woman—a very nice, well-educated, middle-class woman—who was murdered in an exceptionally brutal way, a way that was a great deal worse than what you may or may not have heard about on the morning news, and one I'm not going to describe because I don't want to see your breakfast sitting on your desk." He put up a second finger. "Next, if she followed the plans she outlined to her husband, Cynthia Gault was killed last evening shortly after she left this museum, apparently with a weapon that could qualify as a museum artifact, several of which can be found right here." A third finger went up. "And finally—based on more years of experience than I care to remember—this is not the type of murder that happens only once. And if that's the case, what we may have is someone who's using your museum to audition corpses, and that means I'm going to talk to everyone here *I* feel it's necessary to talk to. And *anyone* who tries to interfere with that will find herself slapped with a charge of obstruction of justice. Now, Ms. Ross, have I made the picture a little clearer?"

Kate watched Alexsandra's face turn several shades of red, her fingers clench into tight white-knuckled fists, and her mouth harden into an angry line. Alexsandra was used to devouring people when challenged. But not this time, Kate thought. *This time, Alexsandra, you've met someone with much bigger teeth.*

Alexsandra stared at Rolk for several seconds, then ran her palms over her desk and sat back in her chair. "Very well, Lieutenant, tell me what you want."

The hint of a smile played on Rolk's lips. He knew a complaint would be telephoned to headquarters as soon as he walked out the door. He knew it with the same certainty that he knew O'Rourke would scream when the complaint was received. He also knew he didn't give a damn in either case.

"First, Ms. Ross, I'd like a list of everyone who attended the lecture yesterday. I'd also like a list of every person known to the museum who collects this type of weapon." He turned to Kate. "Your museum as well. And finally," he said to Alexsandra again, "I'd like to talk to the people at both museums who handle this kind of artifact. And I'd like to do that right now."

Alexsandra scratched notes on a pad, then stared at him coldly. "The lists will be ready by three if you'll send someone to pick them up." She glanced at Kate. "And I think Dr. Silverman can introduce you to the people here you're interested in." She hesitated a beat, then smiled without warmth. "Right now."

Kate led them to the basement of the Met, and through a labyrinth of corridors with closed-off work and storage areas. She stopped before a door marked only by a number, then turned to face them.

"Lieutenant, I have to know something before we meet the other people involved in the exhibit."

Rolk studied her closely. As he had observed the previous night, she was extremely beautiful; her clothing and manner spoke of someone who had learned all the moves needed to make her beauty and intelligence work for her. He had seen it during the lecture, and again today when he had entered Alexsandra Ross's office. But since she had learned about the murder, she had become frightened and unsure of herself. Perhaps even more than was warranted.

"I'm limited in what I can tell you, Dr. Silverman. What exactly did you want to know?"

Kate twisted her hands together, her eyes growing even more fearful. "You seemed to imply that my lecture last night might have played a part in this . . . this . . . That it might have inspired someone to act out the sacrifice ritual I described. Certainly you can't believe that."

So that was it, Rolk thought. She was afraid of being drawn into it, afraid of being accused of prompting a murder.

"Dr. Silverman, all I can tell you is that it's one possibility we're exploring."

"But, Lieutenant, the type of people who were here last night—certainly you must have noticed—they're simply not the kind of people who hear a lecture about ritualistic killing and then run out and try it."

"Dr. Silverman, I told you that was only one possibility. A security guard or maintenance person who's not quite all there could have heard your lecture and decided it sounded like a great idea. Or it could have been someone on the museum staff who did it for other reasons we're not aware of yet. But in any case, you certainly can't be blamed for it, and if I know New York, it'll probably help your exhibit more than it will hurt it. People will show up who wouldn't have come otherwise. New Yorkers, I'm afraid, love violence. They're fascinated by it because it frightens them, and because it's all around them. You let somebody shoot four punks on a subway, and they'll make him a national hero, without ever thinking that he might have killed some innocent slob who just happened to be on the train when he decided to start shooting. So don't worry about being connected with this. It may even help."

Kate's hands attacked each other again. "You just don't understand, Lieutenant. It's not what it will do to the exhibit. Oh, there'll be concern about that, certainly. But it will pass when the exhibit succeeds in spite of it."

Kate folded her arms across her breasts in an effort to keep her hands still. She looked at Paul Devlin. "I've already been accused of sensationalizing the promotion for this exhibit, and this . . . this could just confirm all those accusations in certain people's minds." Kate's mouth and eyes became suddenly angry. "Dammit, I've worked too hard on this, and I've worked even harder getting where I am. People are jealous here, and they look for excuses not to give you opportunities. I know how it works. A year from now someone will suggest me for a project, and someone else, who doesn't want me, will say, 'Oh, yes, she's very qualified, but she does have a tendency to get mixed up in messy situations. Not her fault, of course, but I really don't think we can afford the risk.' "

Kate unfolded her arms as she turned back to Rolk, and her hands were doing battle again. "Lieutenant, I just don't want to see my career go down the drain because of this. I know it sounds selfish, but dammit, it frightens me, the idea of losing everything I've worked for because of some madman."

Rolk stared at her for several moments. "What if it's not a madman, Dr. Silverman?"

Kate's eyes widened in disbelief. "What do you mean? That someone might have done this to intentionally harm me or the exhibit? That's insane."

The trace of a smile played across Rolk's lips, then faded. "Perhaps we're looking for someone who believes in your ritual, Dr. Silverman."

"That's even more insane."

"We see a lot of insane things every week," Devlin spoke up for the first time. "But right now, we really have to talk to these other people."

Kate felt suddenly numb, and she nodded woodenly. "Yes, of course," she said. "But I think it would be better if I went in first and told them what this is all about. Things will go much more smoothly for you if I do."

Rolk and Devlin stood just inside the door and watched as Kate approached her colleagues.

"What did you mean when you said we might be looking for someone who believed in her ritual?" Devlin asked.

Rolk continued to watch Kate, who was talking to an older woman who appeared to be in charge. As the woman listened, her face hardened. She was in her early fifties, as best as Rolk could gauge, and still reasonably attractive, despite severely cropped gray hair. Kate was speaking more rapidly now, and with each word the woman's body seemed to stiffen noticeably.

"I asked you what you meant about someone believing in the ritual," Devlin said again.

Rolk's eyes remained on the group before him. "The lecture last night," Rolk said absently. "It was tied into some refugee movement to help poor Mexican Indians who've been brought into the country."

"And you think—"

"You never know."

The older woman had turned her back on Kate now and was speaking to two men, one well into his sixties, the other younger, late twenties to early thirties. Rolk noticed that the muscles in the woman's jaw seemed to dance as she spoke.

At a nod from Kate, Rolk and Devlin approached the group. The younger man stared at them with amused interest. He was tall and slender, with long blond hair that covered his ears and collar, and a face so structurally perfect it would be considered beautiful on a woman.

"My goodness, officers," the younger man said. "This certainly livens up an otherwise dreary day."

"Be quiet, Malcolm." The older woman stepped around a table laden with artifacts and brushed past

Kate as though she didn't exist. "I'm Dr. Grace Mallory," she said. She inclined her head to the left. "That's Dr. George Wilcox, who's curator of Mayan art here at the Met, and this one grinning like a Chesire cat is one of my assistants, Dr. Malcolm Sousi. He and I are with the Museum of Natural History."

"This is terrible, terrible." The older man stepped forward. He had a neatly trimmed head of pure white hair that dominated a long thin face, and a curved, almost birdlike nose. He was short and slight and his hands trembled as he spoke. "Are you sure this poor woman was the victim of a Toltec ritual?"

"We're not sure of anything," Rolk said. "But there are some rather strong similarities to what Dr. Silverman described in her lecture last night."

Grace Mallory's jaw tightened. "The lecture was sensational claptrap. It should never have been given." The woman stopped herself, as though some other thought had rushed into her mind. "Were you there?" she asked.

"Yes, I was."

"Are you interested in Toltec rituals?"

"I'm interested in murder," Rolk said. "And I try to attend anything that deals with it."

"Sort of a busman's holiday." It was Sousi again. Grace Mallory shot him a withering glare.

"I'm sorry we're interrupting your work," Rolk began again. "But in homicide investigations we're always pressed for time."

Grace Mallory waved a dismissing hand. "That's perfectly all right, Lieutenant. I'm afraid we're all just a bit upset that still more sensationalism is being tied to our work. It is not what I intended," she said in a clipped, severe voice, then drew a deep breath, and continued, her voice softer and more businesslike. "Dr. Silverman tells us you feel the murder weapon may be an artifact from one of our museums. Can you tell me what you know about the era and the type of material?" She listened as Rolk explained the little they did know. "You're sure we're talking about a period approximately seven hundred years ago?" she asked.

"As far as we can tell. The fragments have been sent away for a more detailed analysis," Rolk said.

"Where?" Dr. Mallory asked.

"The Peabody Museum at Harvard. Our medical examiner has an arrangment with them."

"Couldn't go to a better place. They can run the whole gamut of tests. Carbon-fourteen dating, an electron-microscope scan, spectrophotometer, radio carbon, even the new neutron-activation analysis, if needed."

"Why are you so concerned about the date?" Rolk asked.

Grace Mallory smiled at the question. "Because of the apparent present of obsidian. That would almost guarantee the weapons were pre-Columbian."

"Why do you say that?" Devlin stepped closer to the table to get a better look at some of the objects there.

Dr. Mallory stuffed her hands in the pockets of her lab coat and drew herself up as if preparing to deliver a lecture. "All the Mayan tribes, whether Aztecs, Toltecs, whatever, were a brilliant and talented people. Yet they were highly primitive in certain areas. They built magnificent cities, reservoirs, pyramids—all incredible feats of engineering—but they had no knowledge of the wheel. Their tools and weapons were crude by the standards of European or Asian or African cultures of that period. The Mayans had no knowledge of iron, for example. Their tools and weapons were made of chert and obsidian. So if the weapons you're concerned with had come from another culture of the same period, you'd be dealing with ancient iron, not obsidian."

"Dr. Silverman said obsidian is sharp enough to . . ."

"Oh, Lord, yes." George Wilcox had stepped around the table and stood next to Grace Mallory. "A few years ago, when I was at the dig at Rio Azul—that's in northern Guatemala—some of the native workers we used there still shaved with obsidian."

"There are some examples here." The younger man, Malcolm Sousi, spoke up, and Rolk noticed his eyes still held amusement, almost as though he were viewing them all through a microscope.

Sousi held out a piece of green, glasslike material that could once have been the blade of a small sword or large knife. The edge appeared serrated. "This is an excellent piece," he offered.

Rolk ran a finger along the serrated edge. "Pretty dull," he observed.

Grace Mallory's laugh was full and throaty. "We don't keep them sharpened. There's no need, and if we did, I'm afraid we'd soon find ourselves without any pieces at all through sheer attrition."

Rolk turned to Kate, who had remained silent throughout the conversation. Like a small child, Rolk thought. One who had been caught doing something wrong, and was now hoping the floor would swallow her up. "The knife you used at the lecture last night. It seemed newer than these, and it looked as though it could have been sharp."

"It was a fake, Lieutenant." She watched Rolk's eyebrows rise at her words. "I used it because it looked more . . . dramatic." She spoke the final word with difficulty, then continued. "And also because if it was dropped or damaged in any way, its loss wouldn't have been of any consequence."

"There are quite a number of fakes around," Grace Mallory said. "The Indians make them and sell them to the tourists, sometimes claiming they're original. And sometimes it's hard to tell from the blade alone, since the obsidian used can be quite old. Usually we have to rely on the handle to get a true date."

"And the ax?" Rolk asked. "Was that a fake too?"

"No," Kate said. "It was original. I felt it was safe to use, since it was bronze and there was little chance of damage."

"Actually, Lieutenant," Grace Mallory said, "the knife was mine, a gift from one of the natives who worked for us on a dig several years ago. I kept it as a memento."

"Are there any other fakes around?" Rolk said the word "fake" with something that bordered on distaste. He glanced in turn at Silverman, Wilcox, and Sousi.

"I only buy authentic pieces," Sousi said through a grin. "Whenever I can afford to, that is."

Wilcox shook his head firmly. "I've never been fond of weaponry. I'm afraid my personal collection is quite limited in that area."

Kate simply shook her head. Going into hiding again, Rolk thought. He nodded. "You have quite a bit of the authentic stuff, I imagine," he said to Mallory. "Here at the Met and at your museum."

"Quite a bit," Dr. Mallory said. "I could find out exact figures, but it would take some time."

"Any of it sharpened?"

"I don't believe so."

"Would you know if any of it was missing?"

"We could certainly find out. That would take a *great deal* of time and effort, but we could do it, if necessary. And, of course, there would be no guarantee something hadn't been removed and returned later."

"What about private collectors? Have you ever seen any pieces that had been sharpened? Or any sharp fakes?"

Grace Mallory thought for a moment, then shook her head. "A collector wouldn't bother showing us a fake, and as far as an authentic piece . . ." She shook her head again. "It would simply be too destructive, and no collector would want to risk that."

Rolk studied the dull obsidian blade again. "I understand there was a collector here yesterday who loaned you some pieces. Who would that be?"

"Father Joseph LoPato," Grace Mallory said. "I imagine you saw him at the lecture last night, making his pitch for his refugee movement. He's assigned to St. Helena's Church on the West Side, and he does, in fact, have an extensive collection of ancient weapons."

"A priest collecting ancient weapons?" Devlin asked.

"Among other things," the older woman said. "He's an anthropologist by education, and a good one. And he was also a missionary in the Yucatán for a number of years, which is where he became involved in this ridiculous refugee movement." A note of anger had returned to Grace Mallory's voice.

Rolk looked at her briefly, then made a notation on his pad. "One more thing, Doctor. When pieces are removed from your collection—say, to bring them here, for example—how is that done?"

Grace Mallory shrugged. "Usually one of us will just stick them in a briefcase, if they're not too large."

"It's that easy to take things in and out of the museum?"

Grace Mallory smiled. "It's not supposed to be done that way, but I'm afraid most curators bend the rules if they want to have a piece examined by an outside authority or something like that." She inclined her head toward Sousi. "Malcolm brought over that obsidian blade you're holding this morning in *his* briefcase."

Rolk returned the blade to the table. "Would only curators be able to do that, or could anyone working in the museum?"

"Well, I suppose anyone could, but it would certainly be more difficult for anyone other than a curator or an assistant."

"Just one final thing," Rolk said, turning again to Kate. "I'd like to see the pieces you used in last night's lecture."

"Certainly," Kate said. "I put the weapons and the mask I used back in the box I brought them in. It's there on the table."

Rolk and Devlin both moved toward the long wooden box, not unlike an oversize briefcase. "Is this the same box you put them in after the lecture?"

"Yes."

"And then you brought it back down here?"

"No, one of the security guards did. I'm not certain exactly when. I stayed for the cocktail party we held after the lecture. But it was here this morning when I arrived."

Devlin raised the lid. The box was lined with green felt, but the weapons were not inside. Instead, there was a printed notice announcing the lecture, with Kate Silverman's name circled in black ink. Next to the name there was a large feather of iridescent blue.

Wilcox leaned over the box, his face suddenly pale. "It's a votive," he said, his voice little more than a croak.

"What do you mean, a votive?" Devlin asked.

Rolk looked up at him. "Dr. Silverman explained it at the lecture last night," he said. "It seems the Toltecs used to leave offerings for people they planned to sacrifice. So they could prepare themselves for the honor that awaited them." He turned to Kate. "That's right, isn't it?"

Kate nodded, her eyes still fixed on the case.

Rolk turned to Devlin. "Let's find that security guard," he said, then switched his attention to Mallory. "Then I'd like Dr. Silverman to take Detective Devlin to your museum to take a look at the collection there."

Grace Mallory stepped to Kate's side and slipped an arm around her. "Of course, Lieutenant. Anything. Anything at all."

Kate looked up sharply and stared into Rolk's eyes. "This is mad," she said, her voice firm, almost angry. "This is some insane joke."

Rolk studied her for several moments. "I hope so," he said softly. "But I think, Dr. Silverman, that right now you have a bit more to worry about than your career."

Seven

THE AMERICAN MUSEUM of Natural History occupied a ponderous slice of New York real estate. Stretching from Central Park West to Columbus Avenue, and West Seventy-seventh to West Eighty-first Streets, it was even more imposing than the Metropolitan Museum, if not in sheer size, then in the formidability of its architecture. The facade facing Seventy-seventh stood castlelike, seemingly impervious to the surrounding residential neighborhood. Its massive brownstone presence was given further rigidity by the turrets at its corners, suggesting a structure that could just as easily pass as a prison, or an armory, or an aging Gothic hospital for the insane. The newer addition facing Central Park was more traditional and less grim-looking.

It was the madhouse comparison that had always struck Paul Devlin, and he thought of it now as he was led into the rabbit warren of work and storage areas that comprised eighty percent of the building. He had come alone with Kate Silverman while Rolk took on the task of seeing the art-collecting priest. It had puzzled Devlin. Normally calls were made by two detectives as a matter of department policy. But then, Rolk had never worried about throwing policy out the window, and he probably didn't consider a beautiful anthropologist and a Catholic priest very dangerous quarry. Devlin glanced at the young woman and decided she certainly looked dangerous to him, although not in any way that would have worried Rolk.

They turned into a hall that ran along the south side

of the building. One side held glass-fronted cases, crammed with pre-Columbian artifacts.

Devlin stopped and allowed his eyes to follow the cases that extended several hundred yards ahead of him. "This is the collection?" he asked.

"Most of it," Kate said. "There are some smaller storage areas, and, of course, some objects are on display, and there are others in people's offices and laboratories for study."

Devlin pursed his lips and let out a soundless whistle. "Damn. I don't even want to know how many objects we're talking about."

She smiled at Devlin. "I'm glad you don't, because I'm not sure I could tell you without doing several hours of research."

Kate stared at the rows of cases and recalled how she, too, had been overwhelmed by the size of the collection when she had first come to the museum. But now she simply took it for granted, not unlike someone with a spectacular view outside his window who had learned not to notice it until something unusual called it to mind.

She led him up into an office housed in one of the turrets, its rounded walls paneled waist-high in heavy, polished mahogany.

"Some office," Devlin said, turning in a half-circle.

"It's Grace Mallory's," Kate said. "Several years ago it belonged to a lady named Margaret Mead."

"Should that give me some idea about the kind of weight Dr. Mallory has around here?" Devlin asked.

Kate shook her head. "I wish it did." Not only for Grace, but for myself as well, she thought. "No, I'm afraid museums, like universities, are very male-dominated. Margaret Mead, for example, was never made a full curator of ethnology here until 1964, even though she had been a world-renowned scholar for well over thirty years. She also taught at Columbia at the same time and was never promoted beyond the rank of adjunct professor." Kate paused a beat, then continued, almost as though talking to herself, "But it could be different for Dr. Mallory, especially if this Toltec exhibit goes as well as we think it will."

Devlin watched Kate absentmindedly perch on the edge of a desk, her thoughts still distant. She crossed her legs, which, Devlin noticed, could have belonged to a fashion model rather than an anthropologist.

The woman still seemed nervous, but she also appeared to have regained a great deal of her composure since her upset at finding that votive.

Devlin looked up and found Kate staring at him curiously. She had caught him looking at her legs. He tried to recover. "Why do you think this Toltec exhibit might make a difference?" he asked.

"Probably just wishful thinking. But then, maybe not." Kate seemed to be talking to herself.

"Why 'maybe not'?"

The question seemed to snap Kate back; her eyes blinked several times, and she looked at Devlin as though surprised to find him standing there. She drew herself up.

"Grace and I have been battling over the exhibit," she began. "I was put in charge of promotion, and she's objected to some of the things I've done. The lecture, for example. And the tie-in with the refugee movement. She feels I've been sensationalizing the promotions in order to raise public interest, and that the scholarship we've put into the show may suffer as a result." A shiver passed through her body. "I'm afraid your murder may have made that argument moot."

"But you still think you were right, don't you?"

"Yes." There was a look of determination in Kate's eyes that surprised Devlin. It was a sort of inner toughness he hadn't seen before.

"You see, Detective Devlin, we're living in the age of the blockbuster. Books, movies, everything. And museums haven't let that pass them by." Kate slid off the desk and walked slowly to one of the windows that looked down on Central Park. "To understand what I'm talking about, you have to know something about exhibitions," she said, her back to Devlin. "First, they're damned expensive. You have to bring work together from other museums, collectors, even governments. It all has to be professionally crated and shipped, and the insurance costs alone would shock you. Before it's all over, a major exhibit can cost an institution millions." Kate turned and began moving back toward Devlin. "Naturally the institution wants to earn that money back, and to do it they travel the show to other museums for a hefty fee. And if a show has a lot of glitz and celebrity, everyone wants it, and the money comes rolling in. If not . . ." She shrugged.

"But that doesn't happen to all shows," Devlin coaxed.

"Don't we wish it did." Kate leaned against the desk again. "You remember the King Tut show a couple of years ago?"

He nodded.

"Well, Tut had all the glitz and glamour anyone could want, and the Met hasn't stopped counting the money yet. Then, a few months after Tut opened, the Brooklyn Museum opened a show on Nubia that, from a scholarship standpoint, was head and shoulders above Tut. But no glitz, no glamour, and Brooklyn lost millions on it."

"What if a show has both?"

Kate shook her head, a little sadly Devlin thought.

"Then you have a dream come true, and the people who put it together become very important, very fast."

Devlin walked to a long table and picked up an intricately carved bronze ax. "You know, you just gave me an excellent motive for this murder," he said. "If it's eventually tied to your exhibit, people will be crawling over each other to get in."

Kate stared at him, a hint of anger in her eyes. "And if one of the curators is sacrificed, it will be even bigger, won't it?"

Devlin stood quietly, taking in the fear and anger that flashed across the woman's face. "We're going to see that that doesn't happen," he said finally.

*   *   *

Kate stood at the window staring down into the park, Devlin's final words replaying in her mind. "We're going to see that that doesn't happen," he had said, and then he'd left. She closed her eyes and exhaled heavily. Of course he had meant they would find the killer, not guard her against the killer. Still, he could at least have offered to see her safely home. She shook her head, annoyed with herself, annoyed with the fear the votive had produced. One ridiculous feather from the ceremonial cape she had worn during the lecture. It was a joke; it had to be. She closed her eyes again. But the dead woman in the park hadn't been a joke.

She shivered at the thought, and looked back down into the park. She forced the thought away. It was the detective, Devlin, she told herself. He didn't seem the protective type. Not like the other one. Rolk.

Stanislaus Rolk. She played the name over in her mind. An odd name and an even odder man. But somehow strangely attractive. She wondered how old he was. Easily into his late forties, but then, half of her friends dated older men. Kate shook her head again. You're being ridiculous now, she told herself. Some madman threatens to make you part of a ritual sacrifice, and you stand here wondering if a police lieutenant you only met last night is too old for you or not. God, it's all so insane; it has you terrified, and that's the last thing you can allow to happen. Concentrate on your work, on the career you've worked so hard to carve out for yourself. The career that could be going up in smoke while you stand here scaring yourself witless and fantasizing about men you don't even know.

Kate ran her hands through her hair and turned away from the window. And you have some work to attend to right now, she told herself as she started back toward Grace Mallory's desk. The bronze ax sat in one corner. She lifted a briefcase that had been left next to the desk and carefully placed the ax inside. It would have to go to the Met in the morning, and before then she would have to retrieve the documents on its provenance from the library. Might as well do it right now, she decided.

She drew the briefcase up under one arm, pressing it to her side and using her hip to take some of the weight. The briefcase was heavy and unwieldy with the ax inside. The killer had used an ax. The thought sent a shudder through her body, and she pushed it away as she moved quickly out of the office and toward the stairwell that led up to the library.

She entered the empty Gothic room, secreted away on the top floor of the museum. The old library had been replaced years ago by a more spacious and modern one in one of the museum's newer wings. Now this relic of the past was used to house documents and papers for ongoing exhibits and related research.

Kate placed the briefcase on a large worktable, then climbed the circular metal staircase that led to the mezzanine with its stacks of books and papers. The floor of the mezzanine was made up of thick glass squares that transmitted light from below. The effect was an eerie glow that seemed to rise up beneath one's feet and make the floor appear slightly ethereal and impermanent.

Methodically Kate went about selecting the documentation she needed, and carried it to a narrow table set against a wall. She thumbed through the papers, jotting notes as needed, her mind concentrating on the detail she knew Grace would require. The woman was demanding, and rightly so. Kate wished they could put aside the bitterness that had surfaced in recent weeks, could become closer somehow. There was so much to learn from the woman, if only she would consent to be a mentor.

A sound from below jarred her. It had sounded like the gentle swish of a door being quietly closed. Kate listened carefully, trying to detect some other sound of movement. She waited, and hearing nothing more, stared down at the documents again. Then it came again, this time only slightly more distinct. It was a low, rasping noise, almost like someone breathing with difficulty. She walked to the railing and looked down into the library's main floor, but the sound had stopped.

"Is someone there?" she called out. "Hello?"

The soft swishing sound came again, and she hurried to the staircase and made her way down. She passed the table that held the briefcase and moved quickly to the library door. It was closed; no one was there. She turned and looked behind her, searching out each corner, each shadow. No one, nothing. She started back toward the staircase, then abruptly stopped, her eyes riveted to the table that held the briefcase. Next to the briefcase there was a single sheet of paper, and atop it, at its center, a large iridescent red feather.

Kate approached the table, her entire body trembling. She stared down at the single white sheet. Above the feather, a message had been printed in capital letters: SOON YOU WILL BE WITH THE GODS. NOT BECAUSE YOU ARE EVIL. BUT BECAUSE YOU ARE WONDERFUL.

Eight

THE ROOM WAS largely in shadow, lit only by a single table lamp. The wallpaper, the carpet, and the heavy pieces of furniture were old and faded. It reminded Rolk of parlors he had seen in old-fashioned funeral homes, rooms intended to be comforting, but which were only dark and depressing.

The housekeeper at St. Helena's asked him to wait while she searched out Father LoPato. She had said "search out," as though the man were in hiding and she disapproved of whatever he did in private. Rolk smiled faintly at the idea. You've lived too long without a woman around, he thought. And it makes you wary when you see one in charge of a house.

Father Joseph LoPato entered the room abruptly, an oversize cassock flapping about his tall, slender body. He was a gaunt man in his early forties with prematurely white hair; his eyes, set deep, were surrounded by dark, discolored flesh. But it was the overall effect of the fact that struck Rolk. He thought it was the saddest face he had ever seen on another human being. Or was it sadness? Perhaps it was just a face filled with regret.

"The housekeeper tells me you're a police lieutenant," the priest began, taking a chair, ignoring any need for formal introductions. "What can I do to help you?"

"I'm investigating a murder," Rolk said.

"One of our parishioners?"

Rolk shook his head. "No. A young woman, killed last evening not far from the Metropolitan Museum."

"I'm sorry, but I haven't seen a newspaper all day. I've been working, and when I do, I tend to get preoccupied." The priest shifted in his chair. "But I don't understand. What connection does this death have with our parish?"

"No connection at all," Rolk said. "The connection is with you, Father. Indirectly, at least." He watched the priest lean forward, his expression curious. "The woman was killed in a particularly brutal way," Rolk continued. "Her head was severed, apparently while she was still alive—perhaps even conscious—and the weapons used seem to have been ancient Mayan."

"Dear God." The priest's face had suddenly gone pale; then he seemed to catch himself. "And of course you found I had loaned some ancient weapons to the museum."

Rolk stared at the man, his eyes cold and flat, offering nothing. "It's a bit more complex than that," he began. "We believe the woman was a guest at last night's lecture, which was also used to raise funds for the refugee movement you're sponsoring."

The priest nodded almost imperceptibly. "Tell me about the murder," he said.

"There's not much that I'm permitted to tell you. But I can assure you the killing bore a striking similarity to the ritual sacrifice described in Dr. Silverman's lecture."

"You can't possibly be certain of that."

Rolk continued to stare at the priest, noting that his hands had begun to tremble badly. "Yes I can, Father. I was at that lecture. And I was at the murder scene. So you see, I'm interested not only in your collection of weapons but also in any people you've brought here who might still believe in that ritual."

The priest looked at Rolk. His eyes blinked several times; then he offered a weary smile. "I see," he said. "Are you trying to tell me in a gentle way that I, and the unfortunate Indians I've tried to help, are suspects?"

"There's nothing gentle about it, Father. And I need answers. So let's just start with your collection of ancient weapons."

The smile faded, then returned, as if the priest had remembered he *should* smile. "The collection isn't limited to weapons, Lieutenant. I'm an anthropologist by education, and a Jesuit. We're the scholars of the clerical world, and our order allows us to devote much of our time to our individual academic disciplines." The priest leaned back in his chair, his eyes becoming distant. "I worked in Mexico—in the Yucatán—first as a student, and then exclusively, as a priest, for twelve years. During that time I collected quite an assortment of artifacts, some of them weapons, many more of them objects dealing with Toltec and Aztec religious ritual, especially those involving Quetzalcoatl. He was a Toltec god, or perhaps 'prophet' is a better word, who some think had ties to Christianity." Father LoPato abruptly rose from his chair. "But it might be better if I show you. I have something of a workshop downstairs, and there are some weapons there I'm sure you'd like to see."

Rolk followed the priest down a narrow, dust-covered staircase, noting the stoop to his shoulders, like that of a man who has spent a lifetime carrying heavy physical burdens. At the bottom of the stairs Father LoPato flicked a wall switch that flooded a large open area with fluorescent light.

Rolk stared at the transformed room. Glass-fronted cases covered one wall, and behind each panel of glass he could see a shelf crammed with artifacts. In the center of the room three tables were arranged to form a large U-shaped work area, each covered with objects and notebooks and photographs. He nodded to the priest and said, "I'm impressed."

The priest waved a long, slender hand, taking in the room. "You have before you the laboratory of the mad scientist, Father Joseph LoPato, Doctor of Anthropology." He smiled wearily again. "Almost twenty years of work, and it's only a scratch on the surface of the work ahead."

Rolk walked to the table, glanced at it quickly, then asked, "Then why are you here in New York?"

"I was ordered back to do parish work." He paused. "For the good of my health." The priest walked to the table and picked up a pottery fragment, weighing it in his hand. "I had been living in the jungles of Quintana Roo, not far from the ancient ruins at Chichén Itzá. Probably the most desolate part of the Yucatán." He smiled. "At least when you're there it certainly seems so. There was the isolation, as well as a bout with malaria. The isolation's gone, but the malaria still comes back from time to time." He shrugged. "Anyway, I'm here now, working from books and photographs instead of in the field, and performing the religious duties I was trained to do."

"Didn't you work as a priest in the Yucatán?" Rolk asked.

"Yes, to several small villages of Indians. But I'm afraid their religious beliefs were more Mayan than Christian. Oh, they knew of Christ, and I think some of them believed in him. But their strongest beliefs were well-mixed with the gods of their ancestors." Father LoPato returned the piece of pottery to the table. "I suppose that adds fuel to your theory. And it actually suited my intellectual interests rather nicely at the time, as well. I think my superiors were a bit put out at the idea of my spending more time studying the beliefs of the villagers than I did trying to change them." The priest drew himself up as though shaking off the past. "But that's not what I'm doing in our refugee movement, so let's not dwell on that. Let me show you what you came to see."

He walked to the center of the row of display cases and opened one. "You'll find all of the weapons in this case, except, of course, for the ones I've lent to the exhibit."

Rolk walked along the row of cases, his eyes roaming the contents of each. The priest watched him, his own eyes suddenly amused. "Of course you can look in the other cases as well, Lieutenant," he said.

Rolk nodded, his eyes still on the cases. "Thank you, Father," he said. "I'll do that."

At the weapons case Rolk removed a long blade of green obsidian, the dull edge still showing signs it had once been serrated.

"A sword," the priest explained. "Of course, the handle rotted away centuries ago."

"How old is it?" Rolk asked.

"Approximately twelfth-century. It was found near the ancient city of Tula, north of what is now Mexico City."

Rolk removed another blade, then another and another. From the rear of the case he removed a short, thick blade with a wooden handle still attached. He drew his thumb along the edge and flinched. Looking down at his thumb, he saw a thin line of blood. "This one's been sharpened," he said, looking at the priest.

"Yes, I'm sorry about that. I should have warned you. I'll get you a Band-Aid and some disinfectant."

Rolk held up a hand, stopping him. "It's okay. We can do that later." He looked down at the green blade of the knife. "I was told these artifacts are never sharpened, because it eventually destroys them."

"That's true," the priest said. "But this isn't an artifact. The Indians make these. Use them as well. But mostly they're sold to dealers who then sell them to unsuspecting tourists who fancy themselves collectors. They're forgeries. One of the villagers gave this to me after I explained that he was harming the history of his ancestors by making them for corrupt dealers. For a while I used it as a letter opener, but it's so incredibly sharp I was afraid to leave it on my desk upstairs. So I locked it away in the case."

"Any other forgeries around?" Rolk asked.

"No. That's the only one." He looked at Rolk levelly. "Forgeries aren't something an anthropologist keeps on hand. This was more of a personal memento. It marked one of my few successes in performing my priestly duties."

Rolk nodded. "Do you mind if I borrow this? Just for a few days. I'd like my men to get an idea of what this type of weapon looks like in its sharpened state."

The priest stared at Rolk, his eyes saying he understood far more than the detective was saying. "Of course, Lieutenant. Keep it as long as you like."

Rolk offered him what passed for a smile. "Tell me about Mayan weapons, Father. Tell me how they might, or might not, relate to this dead woman."

The priest's face became pale again. "You said her head was removed. Perhaps even while she was alive, even conscious. I asked you before, and I have to ask you again, was there any other . . . ?" He hesitated, as though the words he was about to speak frightened him. "Any other mutilation."

Rolk remained silent, trying to decide how much he wanted to say. "There was a very large section of skin removed from the back of the victim," he told him, finally.

"Oh, dear God." The priest leaned back against one of the tables.

"It fits in with something you know about?"

"Yes. I'm afraid it does."

Rolk waited, just staring into the priest's weary, almost battered face. "Tell me about it."

The priest's back remained against one of the tables, his hands tightly clenched to its edge. "It's complicated, but I'll try." He drew a deep breath; his lips seemed to tremble slightly. "First you have to understand Quetzalcoatl, who's represented in Mayan mythology as the plumed serpent.

"Legend has it that Quetzalcoatl came to the Toltecs from the sea and brought them their religion. He was said to be a tall man with a fair beard. Many scholars believe he was a Mediterranean seaman whose ship was lost at sea, and who was carried to the Yucatán by the tides." The priest looked at Rolk for the first time since he had begun speaking. His eyes now seemed frightened. "You must remember," he continued, "we are talking about a period not long after the death of Christ."

"You said some scholars believe that. What about others?" Rolk asked.

"Some believe he was Oriental. Others, myself among them, believe it was the apostle Thomas evangelizing in the New World." He smiled faintly. "There are solid reasons for that belief, but that would only obscure what I'm trying to tell you.

"In any event, Quetzalcoatl brought the Toltecs their religion, one that spoke of gentleness. Unfortunately that new religion was later corrupted by Toltec priests, who decided to include former practices of blood rituals. Then Quetzalcoatl left—again by sea—and promised to return in the holy year of Acatl. The Spanish conquistador Hernan Cortez arrived in that year, and Montezuma, king of the Aztecs—who had inherited the Toltec religion—believed Cortez *was* Quetzalcoatl and refused to resist his conquest."

The priest smiled at Rolk, a faint, sad smile. "I know I'm digressing, but I wanted you to understand that the religion began as a gentle one." He lowered his eyes. "But perhaps ancient peoples needed blood sacrifice. The Old Testament is certainly filled with sacrifices made to, and supposedly expected by, *our* God." The lips trembled slightly again. "In any event, blood became the mortar of the Toltec religion and the religions of the other Mayans and Aztecs as well. And the victim's head with the capelike skin was even worn by the priest as part of the ritual."

Rolk remained silent for several moments, then stared directly at the priest. "You said many of your parishioners in these Mayan villages still believed in their ancient religion. Was there ever any indication they were still practicing these blood rituals?"

The trembling intensified and the priest had difficulty forming his words. "There were rumors," he began, then hurried on. "But there always are in villages like these. You have to understand that these are a very simple, uneducated people who are prone to superstition. Someone is missing—usually because he fled the poverty around him—and suddenly there are stories being circulated that this person must have been sacrificed to the gods."

"But never any hard evidence that such a thing might have happened?"

The priest looked away. "Nothing I could ever substantiate."

Rolk rubbed the palms of his hands together in a slow circular motion. "You make me feel as though you're trying to protect these people," he said at length.

The priest looked at him sharply. "That *is* my job."

"No, Father. Not if it means protecting a killer." Rolk paused a beat. "How many people have you brought to this country under your refugee movement?" he asked.

"Perhaps a dozen families. Forty people or so."

"And how many are here in New York?"

"Two families. Both with small children."

"I'd like to meet them." Rolk's voice was flat and unemotional, carrying no threat.

"I'm afraid I can't do that, Lieutenant." The priest clasped his hands, almost as though preparing to offer a prayer. "These people are under the protection of the Church, and I've vowed to keep them safe. Immigration officers would arrest and deport them if they learned where they were staying."

"You don't seem to understand. We have someone running around who might be preparing to cut off a few more heads."

"You make it sound like a madman."

"Do I?" Rolk blinked several times, as though confused by the remark.

The priest shook his head, trying to clear his own thoughts. "Let me try to explain. If the person you're looking for is indeed a Mayan, then you're dealing with a Toltec priest." He walked quickly to one of the cabinets, removed a stone mask, and extended it toward Rolk. "You see, the priest didn't believe he actually performed the sacrifice. He would wear the mask of one of the gods, like this one of Quetzalcoatl. He would wear it on his face, or chest, or belt. And, while wearing it, he became that god, was transformed into him. So the god did the killing, and the priest did not even think he had done it. Because, you see, the sacrifice was an act of great love, not of punishment. And only a god could be capable of giving such love."

"And you think the Toltec priest might not even remember performing the sacrifice?"

Father LoPato nodded. "It's possible."

Rolk took the mask and held it in both hands, staring at it. "I'll still have to talk to your refugees," he said. "At least the ones here in New York."

"I'm not sure I can help you," the priest said.

Rolk's eyes rose slowly from the mask to the priest's face. "Yes, you can, Father," he said. "And I assure you, I *will* talk to them."

Father LoPato sat alone in his small study, the stone mask before him on the desk. He ran his hand over the surface, which was pitted with age. He had fled to his study once the lieutenant left, bringing the mask with him as a reminder of the horror that was happening again.

But it couldn't be. Even if everything the detective had said was true, it couldn't have followed him all the way from the Yucatán. He couldn't have brought it here. He crossed himself and lowered his head, but found he could not pray. He forced himself, trying to mouth words he had committed to memory so many years before. But the words became confused, intermingled with others that did not belong. It happened often now, almost every time he offered his personal prayers to God. The only time it didn't happen was during Mass, when he was offering prayers for others. But during Mass there were the doubts to cope with, doubts about his own beliefs.

The doubts had begun three years ago, in the Yucatán. He had been saying Mass and he had turned to offer a blessing to the congregation of the dilapidated village church. The faces had flooded toward him, filled with wonder and curiosity, some eager, some expectant, as if awaiting something profound. And then all the faces became one, a single, simple face with a knowing smile, like someone who had watched a magician and had discovered the secrets of his trickery.

And it had struck him then that perhaps it was trickery and nothing more. Perhaps all the teachings were only hollow words meant to give order to people's lives. Perhaps there was no single Being who cared and who ordered the existence of man. Perhaps it *was* only man's trite means of dealing with the reality of death. Or perhaps these simple Indians were correct and there were many gods who cared for man only as long as he appeased them and did not defy their will.

If one removed the concept of the single all-loving God, was that belief indeed so different from that which he had been taught to believe? And was there divine love, given the pain and suffering in the world? Given the misery? Given the senseless barbarism? The disease? The cruel accidents of fate?

The face had continued to smile at him, and he had stood frozen on the altar, fighting to shake free of the sudden doubt. But it had not dissipated. It had lingered and grown. Like a cancer that had affixed itself to his mind, it fed on the contradictions in the very beliefs to which he had devoted his life.

And the Indians had sensed that doubt, had watched it fester within him. The horror had begun then, fed, he knew, by the doubt he had allowed them to witness. But to follow him here? No, it just couldn't be possible. Even if the doubt had grown, it simply could not happen.

The priest's face was gray, the dark lines beneath his eyes deeper and more pronounced. He lowered his face slowly to the mask, and his chest heaved with deep, racking sobs. And as he remained there he recognized his torment for what it was. Despair, the final and deadliest of sins.

Nine

KATE SAT IN her office, anxiously glancing from her watch to the open door. She had telephoned the number Paul Devlin had given her as soon as she had returned to her office, only to reach a gruff man with a grating voice who had informed her Devlin was en route home. She had asked for Rolk and had been told he was out. Then she had explained the situation and been met with the slightly bored response that someone would be there as soon as possible.

Christ, she told herself now, the bloody fool hadn't even told her not to touch anything.

Kate swung around in her chair and began taking stock of her small, cramped office. The floor-to-ceiling bookcase was overflowing, and she had begun to stack books like small tables in convenient corners. There was a long, narrow workbench that ran the length of one wall, a single window at the room's center. The windowsill, too, was overflowing with the artifacts she was studying. A stone mask from the tenth century, an intricately carved gold necklace, a relief depicting Quetzalcoatl from the Pyramid of the Sun in Teotihuacán, fragments of a Mochica pot—all the trappings of a young anthropologist obsessed with her work. She smiled at the thought, at herself really, then allowed her eyes to roam the office again.

Cramped and crowded and well-suited to your rank and sex, she thought. Then again, Malcolm Sousi's office was also an oversize closet. But she knew very well that he would move to a larger one long before she did. Unless . . .

She pushed the irritating thought away. Concentrate on the fact that some maniac is sending you love votives. And not even the right kind. The thought flew into her head for the first time. This last votive, and the one before, had been nearly identical. And they were not supposed to be.

Did that mean they were dealing with someone who did not understand the ritual, someone who did not have the background and training to know? Or was it someone who did, who was merely trying to deflect attention from himself?

A comment Rolk had made came back to her. He had said they might be looking for someone who actually *believed* in the ritual. But even that did not necessarily imply someone who understood it completely. Even Mayans she had worked with had confused notions of what the original ritual included. Facts that had been handed down by word of mouth for centuries had simply gone astray. But Rolk's idea was mad. It could only point to one of the Mayans now being brought here by the refugee movement. And none of them were at the lecture. Except . . .

Juan Domingo *could* have been there. He had been working as their personal janitor on the exhibit, and the fact that he was a Mayan illegally in the country had been hidden from everyone but those working on the exhibit.

Juan's gentle, stoic face flashed across her mind, a face that lacked any malice, any ability to cause harm. But then, the priests never caused the harm. The gods did.

A shiver passed through her and she hugged herself, wondering if she should tell the police, if she *could* tell them, and risk bringing harm to Juan and his family. Only if they asked her, she told herself. Only in response to a direct question she could not avoid.

Could Juan have been confused about the votive? She could find out, could innocently ask him what he had been taught about the ritual as a child. As innocently as possible, anyway. Perhaps he misunderstood the meaning of the votives.

The votives. The latest one was in the library where she had found it, and suddenly she could not remember if she had locked the library door. She had fled the place so quickly, she could not be certain. If the police came and the feather was gone, they would think she had imagined it all, that she was just the "hysterical woman" so many men expected to find.

"But not this lady," she said aloud as she pushed herself up from her chair and headed for the door.

The library door was locked when Kate reached it, and she quickly produced a ring of keys and opened it. Across the room she could see the votive on the table where she had left it. She closed the door, turned, and leaned back against it.

At least you did *this* right, Kate told herself, then realized that museum regulations about locking all rooms that contained anything valuable were so ingrained in her she would have done it in her sleep. Well, then, she thought, at least you're well-trained.

As Kate started back down the hall, she noticed the door of a storage room standing ajar. She moved to it and stepped inside. The room was largely in shadow, the only light coming from the hall. It held an amalgamation of items from various departments, the floor dominated by large mounted animals that had been used in long-forgotten exhibits, the walls covered with mounted fish and fish skeletons. There was even a Mayan cape, identical to the one she had worn at the lecture, draped across the shoulders of a dummy, its back toward her, the high collar standing well above the dummy's head.

There was no one there. Someone had simply forgotten to lock the door. Someone not as well-trained as you, she thought, and turned to leave.

"Kate, I am here."

The voice came in a harsh whisper that seemed to swirl about the room, offering no hint of where it had originated.

Kate froze momentarily, then quickly crouched behind the stuffed body of a male lion, the odor of the preserving chemicals filling her nostrils, the coarse fur of the animal's mane brushing her cheek. Her eyes darted around the room; her arms and legs trembled as she fought to control them, fought even the sound of her own breathing, afraid even that might give her away. She reached down and removed one of her high-heeled shoes and held it before her like a hatchet poised to strike, then slipped off the other, so she could move more freely.

A rustle of movement came from her right, and she turned quickly, the toes of her left foot striking the base on which the lion was mounted. She fought back an urge to cry out as tears of pain filled her eyes. Slowly she began to back away, her body crouched low, her eyes darting from side to side. Her back struck something hard and she jumped forward, forcing back another scream. Slowly, fear rising in her throat, Kate turned her head. Behind her were the gaping jaws of an African crocodile, its huge daggerlike teeth gleaming in the light that filtered in from the hall.

Kate eased herself around the mounted reptile, lowering her body even closer to the floor, her eyes staring between the open jaws. Another sound came from her right, and she thought she saw movement near the mounted form of an ostrich. She stared at the giant bird, and, yes, the tail feathers appeared to move, to flutter lightly. Then the voice came again.

"The ritual, Kate. You must be sacrificed because you are perfect."

Kate turned and scrambled back away from the sound of the whispered words. Ahead of her the massive body of a Kodiak bear stood like a wall, mounted on its hind legs, arms stretched wide. It rose nearly fourteen feet, the top of its head only inches from the ceiling. Kate ducked behind the huge beast and stared out between its treelike legs. The muscles of her right hand suddenly cramped and she realized she was holding the shoe above her head in a vicelike grip. She loosened her hold on it.

A hand clutched her hair from the back, jerking her off her feet. As her back hit the floor, pain shot up her spine. The shoe fell from her hand and spun away, her eyes following it as she prayed it would not go too far.

"Here," the voice hissed.

Kate tried to twist away, but the unseen hand held her hair tightly. Now the breathing filled her ears, the soft, rasping sound of air drawn over teeth, followed by a faint hum as it fled over slightly parted lips.

Suddenly the hand released her and she spun away, then pushed herself back along the floor on her buttocks until she was stopped by the legs of the Kodiak bear. The figure loomed above her in the dim light, and she stared up in disbelief.

The figure seemed huge, the body encased in the bulky iridescent plumed robe, the face hidden behind a stone mask. Slowly a hand moved from the folds of the robe, and the light from the hall glinted off the shiny green blade of an obsidian knife.

"Soon," the voice hissed again.

Kate struggled slowly to her feet, her legs threatening to give way as they shook beneath her. She began to inch her way back around the mounted bear. The figure seemed to glide forward, then stopped. Kate turned and bolted, darting around the various animals she had used earlier for cover, stumbling once, righting herself, then racing out into the corridor.

Without hesitation she ran to the door of the library, fumbled for the keys in her pocket, then struggled to find the correct one, her eyes glancing repeatedly over her shoulder, expecting at any moment to see the plumed figure moving toward her.

The door opened and she pushed inside, slamming and locking it behind her. She stood there panting, her eyes staring at the solid wood door as though she could see through it, see the danger as it approached down the hall.

"A telephone," she whispered, then fought to remember if there was one in the old library. There's another door, she told herself. Off the mezzanine that leads to a catwalk, then up to an area under the eaves of the roof, the place where hundreds of elephants bones were stored. She shuddered at the thought, knowing she did not want to find herself trapped there.

The telephone. She turned, eyes searching the room. The handle of the door twisted behind her, was stopped by the lock, and she jumped back, a cry of alarm exploding from her throat.

"Dr. Silverman?" The voice filtered through the door, sounding confused. Then it came again, this time with a note of alarm.

"Who is it?" Kate asked, her body pressed against the door as though she might hold back whoever, *whatever*, was on the other side.

"It's Lieutenant Rolk."

Kate's body sagged slightly. "Oh, God," she whispered.

Her hands were trembling so, it took several seconds for her to work the lock. When she finally pulled the door away, Rolk stood there looking much as he had that afternoon, slightly rumpled, slightly gruff, but Kate thought he was the finest sight she had ever seen. She fell against him, her entire body shaking with both fear and relief.

Rolk put his arm around her for several moments, then straightened her up. "They told me at the office you received another votive." He stared into her eyes, studying her reaction. "It must have been some votive to frighten you this much. Where is it?"

Kate tried to speak, found she could not, and simply pointed toward the table where the votive had been left.

Rolk followed her gesture, then looked back at her. "Another feather?" he asked.

"And . . . a . . . note," Kate stammered, her voice choked. "But it's wrong," she suddenly blurted. "It's all wrong."

Rolk stared at her intently. "What do you mean?"

"It's . . . it's almost identical to the first one." Kate struggled with the words. "And it shouldn't be." She drew a deep breath. "The votives should increase in importance. It's . . . it's the way it was done."

Rolk's eyes clouded, then suddenly hardened as though he had finally grasped Kate's meaning.

"But it's not just that." Kate clutched at the sleeve of his topcoat. "I saw him . . . it. Someone dressed in a ceremonial robe and a stone mask. And the knife. The obsidian knife."

"Where?" Rolk demanded.

"Across the hall. In the large storage room just a few doors down." She pointed.

Rolk pushed her back gently. He withdrew a .38 from inside his coat, fumbled in his pocket for a moment, then began inserting bullets into the open cylinder.

"Your gun wasn't loaded?" Kate said, her voice and face astonished.

"I don't like them," Rolk said. "Sometimes I don't even carry one at all."

"But—"

Rolk pushed her well into the room. "Don't worry, I know how to use it. That's one regulation I've never been able to avoid. Now, you stay here," he said. "Lock the door behind me and don't open it for anyone *but* me. I'll say it's Stanislaus, so you'll know. And if anyone tries to open the door, scream like blazes."

Minutes passed—minutes that seemed like hours—and Kate paced in a small circle behind the locked door. The note had said she had been chosen because she was *wonderful*, and the figure in the robe had said she was *perfect*. A shiver passed through her body. Why me? None of it made sense to her. She was nothing more than a struggling young anthropologist. Certainly not prominent, and certainly not from an aristocratic background. Christ, she had waited tables to work her way through school. She had used scholarships and grants and loans. And suddenly I'm worthy of a Mayan sacrifice, she told herself, pressing her hands together, feeling the sweat between the palms.

She started at the knock on the door, then heard Rolk call out his name. When she opened it, there was a museum security guard standing behind the detective.

"Did you find anyone?" she asked.

Rolk shook his head. "The cape and the mask were on the floor. But that's all. No knife, no person." He hesitated a moment, still studying her. "And these," he added, raising one hand. Her shoes dangled from his fingers. "Yours?" he asked.

Kate nodded and took the shoes. Rolk continued to watch her. Somehow she seemed smaller, less imposing, without the shoes, seemed to have lost some of her bearing without the few inches of false height, he thought.

"How long before I came did you see this person?" Rolk asked.

Kate shook her head. "Five minutes. Ten, maybe."

Rolk's jaw tightened. "I went to your office first, looking for you. Then I came up here, thinking you might have stayed with the votive." He glowered at no one in particular. "Dammit. I wish I had gotten here a few minutes sooner."

Rolk turned abruptly to the security guard. "You lock this door and stand outside it. Nobody goes in until our forensic people get here," he ordered.

He took Kate's arm and led her down the hall. "This person you saw," he began. "Could you tell if it was a man or a woman? An approximate age? Hair or eye color? Anything?"

Kate lowered her eyes and shook her head. "The person seemed big, but then the cape is very bulky, and I was on the floor with it standing over me. And the mask covered the face." She shook her head again. "I just can't be sure."

"What about the hand holding the knife? Did it look like a man's or woman's hand? Young or old?"

"I don't even remember seeing the hand," Kate said. "Just the knife."

Rolk pursed his lips. He had heard it too many times before, the shock of what had happened making it impossible for a victim or a witness to identify someone he had seen clearly. "What about the shoes?" he asked. "Did you see the shoes this person was wearing?"

Kate shook her head again. "I'm sorry," she said in a weak voice.

"It's okay," Rolk said, guiding Kate toward the stairwell. "It happens this way more often than you'd think. Let's go back to your office. You might remember more later."

Outside Kate's office, Grace Mallory, Malcolm Sousi, and Father LoPato stood in a small group, facing Paul Devlin. When Devlin saw Kate and Rolk come down the stairs, he moved quickly toward them.

"I headed back as soon as I got the message," Devlin explained to Rolk, then turned to Kate. "I thought the votive was found in the library," he added.

Kate's eyes blinked as she returned Devlin's gaze, trying to understand what he was getting at. "It was," she said.

"Then why did you move it to your office? Didn't you realize it shouldn't be touched?"

"Hold it, Paul," Rolk said. "She didn't move it; it's still up there. I just put a guard on the door to keep everybody away from it."

Devlin stared at Rolk momentarily, then turned to Kate. "I'm sorry." He looked back at Rolk. "Then we've got two. Because I found another one on Dr. Silverman's desk when I got here about ten minutes ago."

Kate stood in her office feeling emotionally drained. Her face was pale, almost ashen, and her hands were trembling noticeably. She willed them to stop without success, and realized she was staring at the long green-bladed knife lying in the center of her desk, a piece of paper folded around its handle, traces of a crusty dried brown material smeared along its edge. She could not tear her eyes from it.

Rolk hovered over the knife, peering at it like an ornithologist studying a dead bird. "It hasn't been moved?" he asked.

Devlin came up next to him. "No. When I got here, I just assumed it was the votive. Essentially because of the stains on the blade. It looks like blood to me."

"I think it is," Rolk said. "But we'll find out for sure."

"The murder weapon?" Devlin suggested.

"It's a good bet. And it wasn't here when I came to look for Kate less than half an hour ago," Rolk added.

The paper rolled around the knife handle was held there by a rubber band. Taking a leather case from his jacket pocket, Rolk laid it on the desk, removing a small pocketknife and a pair of tweezers. Carefully he raised the elastic band and cut through it, then, using the tweezers, slid the paper from the handle and spread it open on Kate's desk. It held a single drawing and a hieroglyph.

"What the hell does this mean?" Rolk said, more to himself than to anyone else.

Grace Mallory, who, along with Sousi and Father LoPato, had been standing just inside the doorway, stepped to the desk, brushing Rolk aside. She stared at the hieroglyph and exhaled heavily.

"What does it mean?" Rolk repeated.

"I've seen a glyph like this before," Grace Mallory said. "As well as I can remember, it was at the Altar of Sacrifices in Guatemala." She pointed at the carefully drawn image of a woman dancing with a snake, next to a blocklike depiction of a deformed face staring at a hand holding a misshapen heart. "The woman dancing with the snake indicates something taking place in the underworld after death, a joining with the plumed serpent. The only place I've seen anything like it was on mortuary offerings placed inside someone's tomb."

"And this?" Rolk pointed to the blocklike hieroglyph.

"It's Mayan for 'He Let Blood,' " Grace explained.

"So this is some kind of threat," Devlin said.

"Not a threat," Grace said. "More of an offering for one who has died or will die."

"That sure as hell sounds like a threat to me," Devlin snapped.

Grace Mallory looked up at Kate, noting the fear that filled her eyes. "We can't be certain it was left for you," she said. "Your office is more out-of-the-way than most. Whoever left this may have considered it safer, more accessible."

"It would also make someone more noticeable if he—or *she*—was seen," Devlin said.

Grace's eyes met the younger detective's. She looked angry, and he wondered if it was because he had said something that might further unnerve Kate, or because he had implied the weapon might have been left by a woman.

"Could this knife be from the museum's collection?" Rolk asked.

Grace exhaled heavily again. "I doubt it. In fact it looks like the fake I lent to Kate for the lecture."

"Why?" Rolk asked.

"Well, the sharpening, of course. None of our artifacts—*none*—are sharpened. Then the handle. It's been well done, but it's new. I can't be certain, so many of the imitations look alike, but I think it is."

"And that could make it your murder weapon." It was Sousi, and Rolk noticed he was grinning again, enjoying the unexpected spectacle. If it *was* unexpected, Rolk added to himself.

"We'll be running tests, and we'll know soon enough," Rolk said.

"And that could also mean the killer has decided to stop." It was Grace Mallory this time, and she was looking at Kate reassuringly.

"Why do you say that?" Rolk asked.

"Because he's given up the weapon, of course."

Rolk nodded. "You could be right. Unless, of course, the killer has access to more weapons." In the silence that followed, Rolk thought of the weapon he had taken from Father LoPato earlier that day. He turned to the priest, who was still standing in the doorway. "I'm surprised to see you here, Father."

The priest smiled nervously. "I had some matters to discuss with Dr. Mallory."

"About?"

"The refugee movement."

Rolk turned to Grace. "That reminds me. When Dr. Silverman found the votive in the library, she was struck by the fact that the two votives were so similar." Rolk paused a beat, then continued. "That could mean our killer has been a little confused about the ritual. Could a Mayan—say, someone in the refugee movement—be confused like that?"

Grace Mallory didn't hesitate. "He could easily be confused, or perhaps 'misinformed' would be a better way to put it." She glanced at the priest—a hard look, Rolk thought—then turned back to Rolk. "Information about the ritual, and most other things concerning the ancient Mayans, have been handed down to the villagers by word of mouth. And as is so often the case, a lot gets lost or altered in the telling."

Rolk studied his shoes for a moment. "Do any of you—other than Father LoPato—know any of the Mayans involved in this refugee movement?"

Again Grace Mallory responded without hesitation. "Just one."

"Grace!" It was the priest, cutting her off.

Rolk pointed a finger at him. "Don't, Father. Not unless you fancy an obstruction-of-justice charge." He turned back to the older woman. "Go on."

"One of the Mayans—a man named Juan Domingo —has been working on the exhibit as sort of a personal janitor for us." She looked at the priest again, even harder this time. "And he could very well have been at the Metropolitan the night of the lecture. There was a lot of cleaning up to do. We had been unpacking crates all day."

Rolk looked across at the priest. "Is that what you wanted to talk to Dr. Mallory about? Juan Domingo?"

The priest closed his eyes. "Yes." He paused, as if waiting for something, then looked sharply at Rolk. "These people have suffered a great deal. What we are trying to do—"

"I'm not interested," Rolk snapped. "What I am interested in is finding a person who's already killed once and who appears to be getting ready to do it again." Rolk continued to look at the priest, but he could feel Kate's body stiffen next to him. "And you are not going to interfere with that again." Rolk turned abruptly to Devlin. "Get some uniforms to seal off this office until Forensic gets here. And then find this Juan Domingo. I'm going to take Dr. Silverman home, check out her apartment, and get a car to sit surveillance outside. When I get back to the office I'll want to talk to our little Mayan friend." He turned back to the priest. "And if you even *try* to stop that, Father, I'll lock your ass up."

Kate stood just inside the door as Rolk moved through her apartment. When he had finished, she poured each of them a drink and sat stiffly on a sofa, staring into her glass.

"This is turning into a nightmare," she said, her voice barely audible. Her eyes rose to his face. "If it's not one of the Mayans, it means it has to be someone inside the museum, or someone with access to it, doesn't it?" she asked.

"Or someone with a sick sense of humor," he said.

Hope flickered across her face, then faded. "Do you think that's possible?"

"Sure. But we can't gamble on that." He watched her features tighten again. "Look. This apartment building couldn't be more secure. No one enters the lobby without being checked, and you've got closed-circuit television on every elevator. Your door is solid, and the locks are excellent. Just don't open your door to anyone, and you'll be fine. I've already instructed the lobby that no one other than the police is to be allowed up to see you. And as I said, I'll be by each morning to take you to the museum until this is over."

"It could only be Malcolm Sousi," Kate said. She was staring at the curtains that covered the living-room window. Her face, he thought, seemed terribly fragile, delicate. "He's the only person I know who would play that kind of sick joke," Kate added.

She hadn't heard a word he had said, Rolk realized. She was simply grasping at the one hope he had held out.

"Especially if a woman was involved," Kate continued. "Malcolm hates women. Oh, he likes to palm himself off as some kind of playboy, or ladies' man, or whatever you call it, but he really doesn't like women at all, and he resents having to deal with them on a professional level."

Rolk took a chair opposite her and studied the conviction in her eyes. A beautiful woman, almost perfect, except for the small gap between her front teeth. And somehow that one flaw seemed to make her even more appealing. "If that's true, it must be hard for Sousi. I mean, he works for Dr. Mallory, doesn't he?"

Kate nodded. "And she treats him like a lackey most of the time, even though he's a quite competent scholar. And he hates her for it. But you can only tell that when she's not looking. Then you can see it in his eyes."

"How does not liking his boss carry over to a perverse joke against you?" Rolk asked.

Kate hesitated, then shook her head. "It doesn't, does it?" Her hands began to tremble and she put down her glass. "Oh, Christ. I'm just so damned scared it's making me think and act like an idiot." She looked up again, forcing a smile. "But he does hate women. Poor Malcolm. It was probably something his mother did to him, or didn't do for him." Kate let out a nervous laugh. "And now I'm accusing him of doing something terrible just to make myself feel better.

And I'm even accusing his poor mother of things. And all that coming from someone who never even knew her own mother." She shook her head again, dismissing her words.

"You were an orphan?" Rolk asked.

"Oh, not a real one, I guess." She took a cigarette from a box on the coffee table and lit it. The flame trembled in her hand, and she took a deep drag on the cigarette, then held it out and stared at it. "I gave these up months ago, and at the first little scare, I'm back to them." She dismissed the self-reproach and looked back at Rolk. "Actually, my mother was killed in an accident when I was very young, and my father never recovered from it. I was taken in and raised by my mother's sister and her husband. They gave me everything I ever needed. They even gave me their name."

"What was your name originally?"

"Warren." Kate laughed again, more easily this time. "From a WASP to a Jew in one stroke of the court's pen. It's caused a lot of confusion in my life, most of it quite amusing."

"How would you like to be named Stanislaus Rolk?"

They smiled at each other, and the tension seemed to slip from Kate's face.

"See?" Rolk said. "Life goes on, and we can still laugh if we try."

Her eyes clouded again. "Yes, it goes on. For some of us." She closed her eyes. "I keep thinking about that poor woman in the park. I have been ever since I saw that knife on my desk." She took a deep drag on her cigarette, and Rolk noticed her hand was trembling again. "God, I've handled knives like that for almost a dozen years, and I've never really thought about how they were used, not emotionally anyway." Her jaw tightened. "The things people do to each other, have done for centuries. How can a species like that survive?"

"At least we don't eat each other anymore."

"I guess that could be considered progress."

Rolk decided the note of sarcasm in Kate's voice

came from a sense of personal strength rather than any bitterness about the situation in which she found herself. He was really attracted to the woman, something he hadn't felt for any woman in a long time, and he knew it was something he would have to keep well under control.

Kate looked across at him suddenly and smiled, almost as though she had just decided it was time to laugh at herself.

"I wouldn't make a very good homicide detective, would I?" she asked.

Rolk shook his head. "Afraid not."

"How do you do it? Day after day, I mean?"

"I have a theory about homicide cops," Rolk said. "I think they have little closets in their heads where they store away all the things they can't deal with. And then, if they're lucky, they retire and die of old age before the door starts to push open and all the old horrors start creeping out."

The telephone rang before Kate could respond, and she answered it, then extended it toward Rolk. "It's for you," she said. "Detective Devlin."

Kate watched Rolk as he took the call, and she realized how attractive she found the man. His strength and competence. There was also something strangely threatening, something she found both disturbing and exciting. Suddenly she began wondering what he'd be like as a lover, whether the gentleness she had seen in his eyes would come through then as well. She pushed the thought away, telling herself that the man was there to protect her, not satisfy any erotic fantasies she might conjure up.

Rolk ended the call and returned to his chair and his drink.

"Are you married, Lieutenant?" Kate suddenly asked, surprising herself as much as Rolk.

"I was," Rolk said, hesitating for a moment. "My wife left me fifteen years ago. She took our three-year-old daughter with her."

"Where are they now?"

Rolk shrugged. "I don't know. I've been trying to find them—my daughter at least—since they left. I got a court-directed divorce from my wife a few years after she disappeared." He studied Kate's eyes for a moment. "Not a very good reputation for a man you expect to find a killer, is it?"

"But you'll find him. I know you will."

Rolk nodded. "That's right, I will. And I won't let anything happen to you in the meantime."

Kate crushed out her cigarette. "I'm sorry I'm acting the way I am. I don't usually frighten so easily."

Rolk nodded, certain she was telling the truth. "I'm afraid I have to go now. Devlin located Juan Domingo, and he's waiting at my office."

Rolk started for the door, with Kate behind him. When he turned, he saw she was trembling again.

"I'm sorry," she said. "The idea of being alone just hit me. I'll be all right."

Rolk put his arms around her and drew her to him. She pressed her head against his shoulder and he could feel her body become more relaxed. "You'll be safe here. I promise you. And I'll come for you in the morning."

"I know," Kate said, her voice almost hoarse. "And thank you. Thank you for caring about me."

Ten

JUAN DOMINGO SAT in Rolk's office looking small and poor and fearful—just like so many others who had sat there before, Rolk thought as he slid behind his desk and prepared to intimidate the living hell out of the man. He had seen Domingo's wife and two small children seated in the waiting area when he had arrived, and he had felt a pang of guilt at exposing them to what must seem like a scene from an old Nazi war film, with hard-looking men moving in and out, weapons hanging from their bodies.

But the guilt ended there. Now, seated across from this small, frightened man, Rolk felt only the need to batter him into an admission of guilt or innocence.

"Does he speak English?" Rolk asked Devlin, who stood menacingly behind the chair in which the small man sat.

"Not a word. Mayan or Spanish is all he can manage. When I picked him up he kept saying *'immigración'* over and over. The poor bastard thinks he's being deported."

"That's the least of his fucking worries," Rolk said, keeping his words harsh in case the man was only feigning a lack of English. "Is your Spanish good enough to handle a translation?"

"I doubt it," Devlin said.

"Then get Lopez in here. I want to get every word this sonofabitch says."

Mickey Lopez was what New York cops refered to as a "spade" Puerto Rican, and in fact his Negroid features had won him the nickname "Spade" among the detectives who worked with him. But all derisiveness ended there, and every detective was quick to acknowledge that Lopez was one of the best investigators in the unit, and certainly *the* best at playing "good guy" in the traditional interrogation game of "good cop, bad cop."

When Lopez had seated himself next to Domingo, Rolk jabbed a finger at the small frightened man. "Tell this little prick that he's in deep shit, and I'm his only prayer for a shovel," he snapped, keeping his tone of voice like his eyes—hard and cruel.

Rolk watched as Lopez began a long, elaborate translation. He was a large, soft, gentle-looking man, with the most sympathetic eyes Rolk had ever seen, and a perennial smile that seemed to illuminate a room when he entered it. But beneath it was a man as hard as Rolk had ever known, and he still winced at the memory of seeing Lopez beat the crap out of a suspect who had made the mistake of spitting in his face.

Domingo, by contrast, only looked frightened. Dwarfed by the chair he sat in, the Indian appeared even smaller and more frail than he was. As Lopez spoke, Domingo's dark eyes seemed to grow larger, until they dominated his classically Mayan features—a wide, full mouth and long curved nose that led into a narrow forehead.

Lopez turned back to Rolk. "I told him this was a murder investigation, but all he wants to know is whether or not we're gonna turn him over to Immigration." Lopez shrugged. "Whatta you want me to tell him?"

Rolk stared at Domingo. "You tell him I don't believe this shit about him not understanding English. You tell him, I find out he does, I'm gonna call Immigration and they're gonna bust his ass right back to that fucking jungle he came from."

"I speek leetle," Domingo said. His lips were trembling, and he seemed to have difficulty forming his next words. "You send *me* back. No send *mi esposa, mis hijas.*"

"Wife and daughters," Lopez translated.

Rolk glared at the man. "You tell him I don't make deals, but if he tells me about the murder, and the ritual, I'll think about it. And you tell him to answer me in English as much as he can."

Lopez translated and Domingo began babbling rapidly in Spanish, then seemed to catch himself and turned to Rolk. "*Es muy malo,* is very bad," he said. "But I no know about—only hear about from priest."

"Father LoPato?" Rolk asked.

Domingo nodded. "He tell me be careful, because *la policía* look for me."

"Ask him about the ritual sacrifice," Rolk told Lopez. "Ask him if he believes in it."

Rolk glanced up at Devlin while Lopez spoke to Domingo. "What kind of place does he live in?" he asked.

"A shithole in the South Bronx. But clean. The kids seemed well-cared-for too."

"You toss the place?"

"Yeah. Nothing there. I didn't have a warrent for the search, but since he's an illegal, I didn't think we had to worry about it."

"We don't," Rolk said. "And we could have invented enough probable cause if we did."

Domingo was speaking rapid Spanish, and when he stopped abruptly, Rolk turned his attention to Lopez.

"He says he doesn't believe in ritual sacrifice, but that other people in his village did. He said the ritual is still performed there. It's a place called Chatulak, by the way, and it's where the priest had his mission."

"Ask him if any of the villagers who believed in the ritual have come here as part of this refugee movement."

"I did," Lopez said. "He says no. Says they won't leave the village, because the jungle is the only place the gods can live. Says all their holy places are there."

"Did the priest know about the sacrifices in the

village?" Rolk directed the question at Lopez, but Domingo answered.

"*Sí*. He tell them is *muy malo,* very bad. But they no leesten, they no hear."

"Ask him if they left votives for their victims. Gifts, offerings."

Lopez translated.

"I no know," Domingo said. "Me *católico*."

"Bullshit!" Rolk thundered. He jabbed a finger toward Domingo's face. "You lie to me, I'll send your wife and daughters back with you."

Domingo trembled as Lopez translated, unnecessarily, Rolk thought.

The small man began to gesture with his hands as if trying to use them to find the English words he needed. Finally he turned to Lopez and spoke in rapid Spanish.

"He said they left jewelry, special clothing, things like that."

"Was there an order to it, something that had to be left at certain times?"

Domingo listened intently to Lopez, then turned to Rolk, his face a mass of confusion and fear.

"Never mind," Rolk snapped. "He obviously doesn't understand what I'm talking about. I'm not sure I do either." Rolk drummed his fingers on his desk, then leaned forward, hunched like a bear studying a morsel of meat. "I want to know the names and addresses of the other Mayans who are refugees connected with the priest," he said flatly.

The trembling began in Domingo's chin, then seemed to move down his body—shoulders, hands, legs—until it engulfed him in one uncontrollable spasm. Rolk continued to stare at him, unmoved.

"Priest say is sin. Beeg sin," the small man finally managed.

Rolk's eyes remained riveted to the man's face, his fingers still beating a tattoo on the desk.

The trembling intesified, and finally Domingo nodded.

"*Sí,*" he finally said. "*Por mi esposa y mis hijas.*"

*   *   *

"I don't see why you let him go," Devlin said after Domingo and Lopez were gone. "Immigration would have kept him on ice for us as long as we wanted. He skips now, somebody's gonna want our livers for lunch."

"I put a tight tail on him," Rolk said, dismissing Devlin's legitimate concern. "He's not exactly going to show up at Kennedy with his American Express card, is he? Besides, I want to see where he goes and who he talks to. And I want to see if he tries to get rid of anything."

"What about this Roberto Caliento he told us about?"

"He lives and works in Brooklyn," Rolk said. "I don't see him waltzing into the Met with Donald Trump and Henry Kissinger. But he could have been working with someone who did. Both of them could have."

"Like with who?" Devlin asked.

"Like the priest, maybe. Or any of the anthropologists, for that matter."

"Even Silverman?"

"You mean if she's faking this votive stuff."

"The thought crossed my mind."

"Mine too," Rolk said. He shrugged. "What else have we got going right now?"

"Inspector Dunne and your favorite deputy commissioner have been calling all afternoon. They sound hot to get hold of you."

"They'll still be hot tomorrow," Rolk said. He glanced at his watch. It was seven-forty-five. Let's give ourselves twelve hours. I've got the department shrink due in here at eight." Rolk shook his head; it brought a smile to Devlin's lips. He knew how much Rolk detested psychiatrists, how he considered them useless in police work.

Rolk fumbled with a folder on his desk, and Devlin saw it was the same one he had seen at his home earlier. His continued search for his daughter.

"You gonna work on that tonight?" he asked.

"Just for a little while. I've got a friend, a captain down in Princeton, where the Educational Testing Service is. I thought I'd give him a call and ask him to grease some skids for me."

"You want some help?"

Rolk shook his head. "No. You and Lopez are going to see this Caliento. Just in case."

Rolk walked along West Eighty-Seventh Street, his slow, lumbering gait giving him the look of a man mentally and physically exhausted. There was a package tucked under his arm. It held a woman's beige cashmere sweater he had purchased from a street vendor. Probably hot, he thought now, as he had then, not really caring. He had got it in a medium size, assuming his daughter would now be about the same size his wife had been. At least he hoped so. He paused briefly in front of his own house; he stared at the door, his forehead wrinkled with indecision; then he moved on, heading west.

The neighborhood was still a strange mix, though a far cry from what it had been when he had moved there fifteen years ago. There were elegant brownstones and apartment buildings, well-cared-for by their owners, intermingled with others that had simply been patched together quickly for the high rents they could bring. The old neighborhood stores and workingman's bars were largely gone now, replaced by small chic shops and trendy restaurants. In some ways the neighborhood had lost some of its charm, replacing it with prestige and upscale real estate, and he wondered where the poor Irish and Poles and Italians who had once lived there had gone. But some things had not changed. There was still a whorehouse only a block away, and enough street crime to keep the local precinct busy. But that was New York, and he doubted it would ever change. In many ways he hoped it wouldn't.

At Amsterdam Avenue he waited for the light, his eyes fixed on a tall black loitering a few doors down on the opposite side of the street. When Rolk was halfway across the street, a red BMW pulled to the curb next to the black man. The driver leaned across the passenger seat, stared up at the man, and tapped his nose with one finger. The man was halfway to the car when Rolk's words stopped him.

"You sell that yuppie one gram of coke and your ugly self is busted."

The hustler turned, stared at the shield in Rolk's extended hand, then smiled and raised both hands in surrender. "I ain't sellin' nothin', brother."

Rolk walked up to the man and smiled. "I'm going to tell you this once, so listen. I live in this neighborhood, and if I ever see your ugly, grinning face within five blocks of it again, you're gonna wish your mother hadn't lost the address of that abortion clinic she was headed for when you were born. You understand me?"

"You got it, my man. I am gone."

"Then do it," Rolk snapped.

As the dealer hurried around the corner, Rolk walked to the driver's side of the car, placed one hand on the top, and leaned down so his face was only inches from the driver, a well-dressed Ivy League type with a vested suit and horn-rimmed glasses. "Show me some ID," he said.

"Look, officer, I was just asking for directions to—"

"Show it to me here or at the precinct, I don't give a damn," Rolk said.

The man took a driver's license from his wallet and handed it to Rolk, who jotted the name and addressed in his notebook before returning it. "Now, you listen carefully. I don't really care what you buy to stick in your nose. But I *know* you're not gonna do it in this neighborhood, because the next time I see your cute little red car, the first thing I'm gonna do is find out where you work. Then I'm going to send two detectives there to bring you in for questioning in a drug case. Now, I don't know if your boss will like that or not, but I'll bet you a new attaché case that you won't be on the next promotion list."

The young man stared straight ahead, face red, mouth tight with anger. Rolk stared down at him. "I think you ought to toddle on home now," he said. "And when you get there, mix yourself a good strong Perrier. In fact, make it a double."

Rolk stepped back and watched as the car pulled from the curb and headed down the street. He shook his head, wondering at the stupidity of otherwise bright people. A street hustler like that would sell him cocaine laced with Drano and never bat an eye. He returned to the sidewalk and continued down the street, turning in at the gate of a nondescript brownstone.

The door to the garden floor, under the front stairs, was opened moments after Rolk rang the bell. He nodded to a large, elegantly dressed black man. "Good evening, Richard."

"Good evening, Lieutenant," the man said as he stepped aside. "Miss Rose is in the kitchen."

"Thanks," Rolk said as he moved down a long, dimly lit hall.

Rose Delacroix was a petite woman of about forty-five with red hair that was obviously professionally colored and hard, street-smart eyes above a smiling generous mouth.

"Rolk," she said as he rumbled into the kitchen. "It's been months, probably right around the last time you had that godforsaken suit pressed. "Sit down and I'll pour you a drink."

As Rolk took a chair at a round kitchen table, Rose poured out a liberal measure of Jack Daniel's, Rolk's favorite. "So what brings you to my door? You're sure as hell not here to show off your fancy new wardrobe."

Rolk leaned back and stared at her along the length of his nose. "Don't be fresh, Rose, or I'll have the public morals squad pay you an unscheduled visit."

Rose grinned at him. She had known Rolk for more than ten years now, ever since her husband had been murdered and she had taken over his bookmaking business. Rolk had never questioned the way she made her living, and they had become friends of a sort, more than friends on a few occasions. Still, there was something about the man that unnerved her. And it wasn't just that he was a cop. There was an intensity about him, almost a fanaticism about the way he pursued things. Like murder. Always reading books about it, attending lectures. And then talking about what he had learned. Then there was his daughter. Who the hell looked for somebody for fifteen years. Still, he had never shaken her down, never forced her into a compromising situation. And that was unusual for a cop.

"So what brings you here?" she asked again.

"Did you see the six-o'clock news tonight? The murder near the Met?"

Rose nodded. "Sounded awful. Are you handling it?"

"Yeah, I'm handling it." He took a long sip of Jack Daniel's. "Look, be careful if you go out. Take Richard with you. I don't think this is a one-shot deal."

"Sure," Rose said, staring at him intently. "You look like hell, Rolk. Have you been sick?"

"Just sick of the job. I'm starting to hate the things it makes me think about."

"You always did." Rose poured another measure into his glass. They had talked about it before, in quiet moments lying next to each other in bed. He had explained how cops tried to lock away the horrors they dealt with, and how sometimes the locks failed to hold. He had said it was why so many cops ended up killing themselves. Or, sometimes, other people.

"You ever think about retiring?" she asked. "You've gotta have almost thirty years in by now."

"Only once or twice a day," Rolk said. "But what would I do with myself?"

"You could find your daughter. If you worked at it, you probably could, you know."

Rolk shook his head, thinking of his futile conversation with his friend in Princeton. "I've about given up hope that I'll find her. Maybe someday she'll find me."

"Maybe," Rose said. "Maybe she will."

"So, what have you been doing with yourself," Rolk said, his voice gruff and forceful. "You look like you've put on a few pounds."

"You never learn, do you, Rolk?"

"Learn what?"

"That there are four things you never discuss with a woman."

"Oh? And what are those?"

Rose tilted her head to one side, then raised a hand and began ticking off the items. "Her age, her weight, the true color of her hair, and how many lovers she's had."

"I'll try to remember," Rolk said.

"No you won't. But I told you, anyway."

Rolk's lips pressed against each other in his vague imitation of a smile. "You're a tough bird, Rose. Maybe that's why you make me feel good."

"You want to talk about this case?"

"You don't want to hear the details. Nobody in their right mind would want to hear them." He downed half the liquor in his glass. "But it is bugging the hell out of me. It's almost as though there's something in the back of my mind, something I can't quite get hold of." He lapsed into momentary silence, as if trying to force the thought out. He shook his head, then looked across the table at Rose.

"I've got plenty of suspects, but one who particularly gets under my skin."

"So?"

"The guy's a goddamned priest."

Rose freshened Rolk's glass. "Don't count him out because of that." She leaned forward, both arms on the table. "A couple of years back, Maggie had this regular. A real sexual athlete who always wanted two or three girls at a time." She laughed softly. "She just thought he was some randy businessman whose wife had reinvented the chastity belt. Then one Sunday she's at Mass, and who's delivering the sermon but old blood and guts himself. A monsignor, he was.

"Oh, he was always very discreet, always showed up in civilian clothes. But he was always there, once a week, regular as clockwork."

Rolk grimaced. "A horny priest is a long step from one collecting human heads," he said.

"You afraid of what your bosses might say if you started investigating a priest?"

Rolk let out a rumbling laugh. "You know what they call the Archdiocese of New York? My bosses and all the politicians?"

"I know. The Powerhouse."

"And they damn well mean it." Rolk laughed again. "I've got a deputy commissioner who'd have a coronary right in my office if I even hinted at that." Rolk's smile faded. "But that's not the reason, Rose. It's like I told you. There's this something in the back of my head that I just can't get hold of. It's almost like I can't remember it. And I know that if I could, I'd know what direction to take."

Rose reached out and squeezed his hand. "It'll come, Rolk. It always does, doesn't it?"

"Yeah. It does." He stared across the table.

Roberto Caliento was short and broad and difficult, and unlike Domingo, very little Devlin and Lopez said seemed to unnerve him.

The Brooklyn apartment in which he lived was shabby and run-down, but obvious care had been taken to make it as clean and livable as possible. Caliento was alone when they arrived, explaining that his wife and child were out visiting friends, whom he had refused to identify, and Devlin suspected he had received a call warning him that the police might be on their way.

Lopez started out gently, trying to befriend the small hard-faced man. But that quickly ended with Caliento's terse, indifferent replies to each question Lopez posed. In the end Lopez was growling at him, threatening him with Immigration, demanding to know how long he had been involved in Toltec religious rituals.

Caliento had shrugged ignorance, answering only in Spanish and insisting the ritual was something foreign to his village, something practiced much deeper in the jungles by people he had never met, people he had only heard rumors about.

When they were leaving, Caliento smiled at them, and Devlin had to grab Lopez by the arm to keep him from throttling the little man.

"That little prick knows something," Lopez snarled as they drove away. "But he thinks we can't touch him because of that fucking priest."

"We're just giving him a little rope," Devlin said.

"We oughta turn his ass in to Immigration," Lopez snapped. "Let him sit in one of their filthy cells for a few days, then see if he wants to talk."

"That's not the way Rolk wants to play it." Devlin looked over at him and grinned.

"Shit," Lopez snapped. "So we just have somebody sit on his ass, right?"

"That's right," Devlin said. "At least for now."

Eleven

Dr. NATHAN GREENSPAN was a short, pudgy man, bald except for wisps of hair that fluffed out above his ears, with a plump round face that looked as though it had listened to too many woes over far too many years.

Seated next to Paul Devlin in Rolk's cluttered office, Greenspan seemed weary beyond what would be normal for eight o'clock in the morning. Rolk had just arrived, and had apologized for keeping the doctor waiting, but Greenspan dismissed the apology with a wave of his hand, as if serving as a police psychiatrist had left him with no greater expectations.

After listening to Rolk and Devlin, Greenspan leaned back in his chair and squeezed his eyes shut. Shaking his head slowly, he reopened them and stared at Rolk.

"If," he began, "—and it's a big 'if' right now, our killer hasn't deliberately tried to make this look like the work of a religious fanatic or a madman, then I'm afraid Dr. Feldman may be right. This is something that could happen again and again and again."

"When?" Rolk asked.

Greenspan offered a faint false smile and shrugged his shoulders. "If I could tell you that, I'd apply for your job." He rubbed his hands together, looking at them as if they belonged to someone else. "Almost everything we thought we knew about serial killers has been systematically contradicted by cases we've faced over the past ten years or so."

"That's not awfully helpful," Rolk said, his dislike of psychiatrists coming through.

114

"Well, what we do know is that the modus operandi usually remains identical, as does the weapon." Greenspan began fussing with a pipe, carefully stuffing tobacco into the bowl, then lighting it with a wooden kitchen match. "There *was* a theory," he began again through a cloud of blue smoke, "that claimed the period between killings became progressively shorter, almost as though the killer was in a growing frenzy, moving toward a crescendo, so to speak. But there have been cases where the killings stopped for months, even years, before they started again. For a time we thought territoriality was involved, only to later find ourselves faced with killers who moved across the country, killing as they traveled." He blinked several times, as if bothered by his own billowing clouds of smoke. "I *can* tell you that serial murderers of this kind are almost exclusively male. Women, when involved in multiple killings, invariably do it for profit. With men it's usually a matter of insane furies, mad possessions, or wild longings."

"What about religion?" Devlin asked.

"That could fit all three categories, actually." Greenspan noticed the smirk forming on Devlin's lips and raised a hand. "I don't mean that as a put-down of religion," he explained. "It's just a comment about what can happen when someone's thinking process goes over the edge."

"Exactly what kind of illness are we talking about in this case?" Rolk asked, poking through a pile of unanswered phone messages from reporters and department officials.

"If ritual is involved, we're probably dealing with a psychopath, someone who lives in a world we can't even begin to understand, and who gets enormous feelings of pleasure and power from the things he does to other people. This type of person could even believe he's some kind of godlike creature, or someone sent by God to pass judgment on the rest of us."

"Could a priest, or minister, or rabbi have that kind

of illness?" Rolk asked, and shoved the phone slips in his wastebasket.

"Sure, but it's unlikely. Usually, when they start to go over the edge there are so many people watching them it gets caught in the early stages." Greenspan sucked on his pipe again. "But then, look at that bearded bastard in Iran. He's a classic psychopath if ever I saw one."

Rolk ignored the political observation. "So you think I'm dealing with a psychopath?"

"That's my best guess if ritual is involved."

Rolk rocked back in his chair. "If there's another one—another killing, I mean—I'd like you to come to the murder scene. Is that possible?"

Greenspan's brow wrinkled with distaste. "One of the reasons I became a shrink," he said, "was that I loathe the sight of blood." He shook his head. "But if it would help."

"It might," Rolk said.

Greenspan nodded in surrender. "At least try to find the body at a reasonable hour."

"We'll do our best," Rolk said.

When Greenspan had left, Rolk sat toying with a pencil, using it to bat a paper clip back and forth along the top of his cluttered desk. "So what do you think?" he finally said, turning his attention to Devlin.

"I don't know. What he said about women committing murders for profit sort of grabbed me. It made me think about this exhibit and how publicity could make it a big success. But then, according to the doc, this murder really points toward a psychopathic male. And this murder sure as hell looks like the work of a head case."

Rolk winced at the unintended pun and narrowed his eyes at Devlin, who shrugged an apology. "I didn't mean to start sounding like Jerry Feldman," Devlin said.

"So you think the museums and the exhibit are the key." Rolk stated the question as fact.

"I don't see how we can think anything but." Devlin

ran a hand through his hair and leaned forward in his chair. "We have a murder committed in close proximity to both of the museums. Those museums at present are putting together an exhibit on Toltec art. The murder weapon, even if it's a fake, could qualify—at least from the standpoint of its physical material—as a knife or sword similar to those that will be shown in that exhibit." Devlin's voice got louder as he ticked off the points. "And the method used in killing Mrs. Gault closely resembles a Toltec religious ritual that at least six people connected to the exhibit are familiar with, including two—the priest and Domingo—who were personally exposed to it in the recent past."

Rolk put down his pencil, sparing the paper clip another batting. "And what does that tell you?"

"It tells me we're in a lot of trouble," Devlin said. "We've got to direct our investigation into two of the city's most prestigious museums *and* the Catholic Church, which is going to make the bosses downtown bounce off the walls."

Rolk pulled on his nose and repressed a smile. "That part of it can't be helped. What would you do next?"

"We better start checking out those six people with a microscope, and, if possible, begin some kind of loose surveillance on at least five of them."

"Why only five?"

"The older guy working on the exhibit—the one from the Met, Wilcox—I don't think he'd have the physical strength to commit the crime," Devlin offered.

"What if he had help?"

Devlin nodded. "All six of them. Seven if you want to include this other Mayan, Caliento."

Rolk hunched forward, picked up the paper clip, and tossed it in the ashtray. "I'll put Peters on Dr. Mallory, Moriarty on Sousi, you on the priest, Lopez on Wilcox, and I'll take Silverman. We'll leave the same teams on Domingo and Caliento. It's going to mean some night work for all of us, and the overtime won't make our leaders happy. But at least they won't bitch about that until we break the case."

Devlin grinned at him. "How come you get the only good-looking female suspect in the lot?"

Rolk stared at him for a moment, then tilted his head to one side as though considering the mock objection. "We'll switch suspects off and on later. I get her now because I'm the only one who can be trusted with her."

Inspector James Dunne sat in the rear of the unmarked police car, as far away from Deputy Commissioner Martin O'Rourke as he could get. Unlike Dunne, who was lean and hard, with sharp, angular features, O'Rourke was broad and overweight, and his slouching body required more than half the seat to satisfy his need for sprawling comfort.

"I don't know why the hell we have to take the time to go to Rolk's office," O'Rourke said, his pouchy, liquor-reddened face filling with a self-important petulance. "We should have just told him to get his ass down to headquarters."

"He wouldn't have come," Dunne said, staring out at the sluggish late-morning traffic. "Oh, he would have agreed to come, but then he would have sent word that something had come up on the case and he would have disappeared for the rest of the day. I've seen him do it before."

"The Polack bastard," O'Rourke snapped. "Who does he think he is?"

He knows who he is, that's just the trouble, Dunne thought. "It's the way he's always been," Dunne said. "Just a goddamned pain in the ass who likes to throw the rulebook out the window. Unfortunately, he's damned good at what he does."

"Nobody's *that* good," O'Rourke snapped back.

"His men think so. And they cover his ass four ways from Sunday whenever he needs it," Dunne said. "And the press acts like he's some goddamned supersleuth." Dunne turned to look at the deputy commissioner, wishing the man had had more time in the job so he could understand the delicacy of departmental infighting, that he wasn't just another political appointment putting in some time until a better offer came along. "If we push him too hard, he'll resist, and we'll be forced to either give in or replace him. And if we replace him, we'll get questions from the press that we don't need on this case."

"So what does that mean? We let him do things *his* way?" O'Rourke shook his head. "Not if the mayor gets all lathered up, we don't."

"Of course not," Dunne said. "But we *handle* him instead of pushing him. Believe me, it's the only way. I've known that sonofabitch since we were in the academy together. And pushing him won't work."

"Well, he damned well better understand that he's going to run this case the way City Hall wants it run. I need somebody I can deflect the heat to, and that's Rolk. I'm not going to take shit from the mayor because some Polack lieutenant wants to do things his own way."

"He'll do it our way," Dunne said. "Just let me handle him. I'll stay on his tail, and we'll keep the heat to a minimum." Dunne looked at O'Rourke and smiled. "Who knows, maybe he'll close this one out before the heat really starts. Then we'll all be off the hook."

"He'd better," O'Rourke said. "I don't want any more complaints from either the Metropolitan Museum *or* the archdiocese. *Especially* the fucking archdiocese. This is already the kind of murder that makes people crazy. Now this dumb sonofabitch has to start stirring up people who are going to make City Hall crazy. What the hell's the matter with this guy? Why can't he see that everybody gets burned when people like this aren't handled right?"

Dunne stared out the window again. And why do I have to have some pissy-assed politician who needs his hand held every time he thinks the mayor's about to scream, just so he can keep from wetting his pants? Dunne squeezed his eyes shut. And why was Rolk running the case? Because you fucked up, that's why.

You didn't move the lousy sonofabitch to some desk job the last time things were quiet. God, how he despised the man, Dunne thought. He was nothing but an arrogant ball-breaker who had to do everything his own way. He'd always been like that, right back to the time he started using the name Stanislaus, just to show he didn't have to be part of the Irish or Italian mafias who ran the department. Just to show he didn't have to kiss anybody's ass, even though the whole department was run on the basis of bend-over-and-pucker.

Dunne opened his eyes and watched people moving along the sidewalk. He drew a deep breath. Well, this time he's going to learn, dammit. And when it's all over—this time, he goes, no matter what. And if he fucks up, he goes even faster.

Rolk and Devlin were still plotting strategy when the door to Rolk's office swung open without the courtesy of a knock. Inspector James Dunne entered first, followed by the deputy commissioner, Martin O'Rourke, two top dogs in the department's Irish mafia, Rolk reminded himself.

"Well, I see we've got a beauty on our hands," Dunne said as he and O'Rourke took the two remaining chairs in the office. Devlin rose to leave, but Rolk motioned him back to his seat. Dunne was second-in-command to the chief of detectives, more politician than cop, in Rolk's view, and he always liked to have at least one witness whenever he spoke to the man. Now, with O'Rourke there—a *pure* politician—it was even wiser.

"It qualifies as one of our least-delightful cases," Rolk said.

O'Rourke leaned forward in his chair. "We're getting a lot of press on this, and it's going to get worse." He tried to stare Rolk down and failed. It seemed to make him both nervous and angry. "And we're also getting complaints about some of the methods you're using," he said in a harder voice.

"From whom?" Rolk asked, not really caring about the answer.

"The Metropolitan Museum for one. The archdiocese, for another." O'Rourke tried his stare again; failed again.

"Look, Stan." It was Dunne, interrupting before things got out of hand. "You can't play hardball with people at the Met or the archdiocese. These fancy museum types haven't the slightest idea what's involved in a murder investigation. And the archdiocese couldn't give a damn, not when you're fucking around with something as important to them as their refugee fund-raising. They've got empty churches, and they want to fill them up. It's business to them."

"You telling me I don't investigate a bunch of Mayans, when I've got Mayan ritual murder on my hands?" Rolk had kept his voice soft, but the threat was already in the words.

"You don't know that," O'Rourke snapped.

"Close enough to say it." Rolk paused a beat. "To you, if not to the press."

"Jesus Christ—" O'Rourke began, only to be cut off by Dunne.

"No one is telling you to back off on any suspects, Stan." Dunne was smiling; with some difficulty, Rolk thought. "Just don't go threatening to lock up some priest because he's trying to protect a couple of spic families." Dunne raised his hands in a gesture of surrender. "Look, if one of these greaseballs did it, lock 'em up. Just take it easy on the boys in the turned-around collars. That's all we're asking. And the same with these museum clowns."

Rolk leaned forward, a small smile forming, then disappearing from his lips. "The only hard suspects I have right now include three people who work at the Museum of Natural History, one who works at the Met, two Mayans, who are part of this refugee movement, *and* the priest."

"For Chrissake. Are you trying to tell me a priest could have done this?"

O'Rourke's outburst was stopped again by Dunne's raised hand. "Look, Stan, nobody's going to tell you who's a suspect and who isn't. But a priest?"

Quietly, slowly, Rolk rattled off the circumstances surrounding the priest's involvement, his work in the field, and with the museums, his work as a missionary in the Yucatán, where other ritual killings had supposedly taken place, his possession of the type of weapons used in the murder, and the possibility he had suffered a nervous breakdown while in Mexico, and had been brought back to New York to recover.

When he had finished, the other men sat quietly, and he decided to add the coup de grace. "Now, I can ease up on any of these people, but if I pick the wrong one, we're going to have some more bodies dropped in our laps—we may have them even if I don't—and that's going to raise a lot more heat than any pissed-off lady at the Met or any monsignor up at St. Pat's."

O'Rourke was visibly fuming now, and Dunne rushed ahead, hoping to silence him. "Stan, you're absolutely right." O'Rourke had turned to glare at him, but Dunne ignored it and continued. "You know, and I know, that *nobody* knows more about murder and homicide investigations than you do. Christ, you study it all the time; you even write papers on it." He paused, offering an insincere smile. "Hell, what is it the press calls you? The scholar of murder?" He offered the last more for O'Rourke's benefit than to mollify Rolk. "But just do us one favor, huh? Try not to alienate *every* important bastard you come across."

"I've got a lousy personality," Rolk said.

Dunne laughed without warmth. "That's right, Stan, you do. But try to give us a little help on this one." He stood to leave, touching O'Rourke's shoulder to urge him up and out the door. "Just try to keep a lower profile on this." He walked O'Rourke to the door, then turned back, keeping his eyes harder than his voice. "And keep us posted, Stan. Any good news you can give us will keep the press *and* City Hall off Marty's ass."

Rolk nodded and watched the pair leave, turning back to Devlin when the door had closed behind them. "It's a miracle we ever nail anybody," he said. "Especially with the goddamn assholes we've got running this department."

Devlin was laughing. He had enjoyed Rolk's performance. "Someday I hope I can break chops the way you do," he said.

"Wouldn't it be nice if nobody had to?" Rolk said. He leaned back in the chair. "Okay, what's your next move with the priest?"

"I want to skip the priest this morning."

Rolk's eyebrows rose.

"He's not going anywhere," Devlin said. "I telephoned the rectory before you came in, and the housekeeper said he was saying all the Masses this morning, and hearing confessions this afternoon. Seems like the pastor is sick, and he has to cover for him."

"So?"

"So I thought I'd like to check out this votive thing. With either Mallory or Wilcox. I told you yesterday, I have a hard time buying this leave-a-gift-before-I-kill-you crap and I'd just like to get a better handle on it."

"You think Silverman is faking it?" Rolk asked.

"I don't know," Devlin said. "But my gut tells me something's wrong with it."

"Then you ought to follow your gut," Rolk shrugged. "So do it. Just don't lose sight of that damned priest."

Twelve

"I'VE SPENT THIS time with you because I'm extremely concerned about your ability to protect Dr. Silverman." Grace Mallory stared across her desk, taking in Paul Devlin as though he were a specimen under a microscope.

She had spent the past half-hour explaining the intricacies of Mayan sacrifice, the random manner in which noble victims were selected.

"It hasn't helped you very much, has it?" she asked.

"If anything, it's made it worse," Devlin said. "Even if we know we have to protect Dr. Silverman, it doesn't mean that we'll stop the next killing by doing it. The next victim could be anyone. And while we're protecting Dr. Silverman, we have to spread ourselves even thinner than we already are."

"But you *will* protect her?" There was an urgency in Grace Mallory's voice.

"Yes, of course we will." Devlin stared across the desk. "But we can't surround her twenty-four hours a day. We just don't have the manpower. Not if we expect to catch this . . ." He let the curse he was preparing die in his throat.

"My, my, don't we sound angry."

Devlin turned to the sound of the new voice, and saw Malcolm Sousi saunter into the room, a smirk already fixed on his delicately handsome face.

"Where have you been, Malcolm?" There was an edge to Grace Mallory's words, and Devlin noticed that it produced a flash of anger in Sousi's eyes that he quickly masked.

124

"At the Met," he said. "Working, working, working."

"Was George Wilcox with you?" Grace's voice was openly suspicious and Devlin wondered if Sousi was the type who wandered away from work from time to time.

"No, old George left early," Sousi said. "Thinks he has a touch of the flu or something." He turned to Devlin. "And why are you here? Have we had another murder?"

"I had some questions about the obsidian knife—the sharp one—that was found in Dr. Silverman's office," Devlin said.

"Ah, so you think our dear little Kate is the killer," Sousi said.

"Don't be an ass, Malcolm," Grace Mallory snapped.

"No, but we are trying to find out who might have been in Dr. Silverman's office," Devlin said. "Were you, by any chance?"

"Never got within a hundred yards of it," Sousi said. He was grinning again. "But I'm grateful I finally made the list of suspects. I was beginning to feel left out of all this excitement."

Devlin studied him closely, wondering at the man's ability to be so completely unlikable. "We won't leave you out, Malcolm," Devlin said. "I may even move you up a bit on the list."

Sousi's grin disappeared, and Devlin decided to leave him in that state of uncertainty. He stood to leave. "Thank you again," he said to Grace Mallory. "If I have any more questions, I'll call you."

"Of course, Detective."

"Do you need me for anything, Grace?" Sousi asked.

"No, Malcolm," she said. "I've seen quite enough of you, thank you."

Sousi's eyes hardened, and he turned abruptly. "Then I'll walk out with you, Detective. Perhaps you can get me to confess on our way down in the elevator." The grin was back on his face again.

When the door closed behind the two men, Grace Mallory slumped back in her chair and exhaled deeply.

Idiot, she told herself. The man's an absolute idiot, like most of the men you've known in your life. She sat up again and opened the middle drawer of her desk. And it will be men who will be protecting Kate.

She stared into the drawer, at the private journal she kept there. She turned to the last entry and reread what she had written earlier about Kate. Such soft skin, she thought. Such soft, beautiful skin. She wet her lips, the taste of her own lipstick filling her mouth. She closed the journal abruptly. Stop it, she told herself. Just stop thinking about her.

Thirteen

"**S**O WHAT DO you do? For a living I mean?" There was a slight nasal inflection to the woman's voice that seemed to match the false shade of blond hair and the heavy makeup she wore about her eyes.

Sousi liked the lascivious touch her smile gave her wide mouth, as if she were offering something they hadn't yet spoken about, but would. But of course, it was already seven o'clock, and the women still occupying stools in this West Side bar had already decided the evening would be one for prowling.

"I'm a plastic surgeon," Sousi said. "Put a knife in my hand and I can make any woman a goddess."

"Yeah, and I'm a brain surgeon, so let's have a consultation." The woman returned to her drink, momentarily dismissing him.

Sousi slid a business card in front of her. It said only: Dr. Malcolm Sousi, followed by his home address and telephone number. "Oh, ye of little faith," he whispered.

The woman picked up the card, eyed it, and then Sousi, with renewed interest. "My name's Nicole. Nicky, for short." She turned to face him again, and the smile had returned. "So, you running any specials this week? A two-for-one tuck, maybe?"

"We're running a special on the bosom this week. We'll make it larger or smaller, lift it or lower it. Whatever the customer wants."

Nicky glanced down at herself playfully, then back up at Sousi. "And what if we like it just the way it is?"

"Then we'll offer it tender, loving, personal care."

Nicky let out a slightly harsh laugh that Sousi thought fit her perfectly. "That's just what every girl needs. A lot of tender, loving care." She toyed with her drink. "So tell me, why aren't you home with the wife and kiddies?"

"Don't have any of those. I'm a young, *struggling* plastic surgeon, just out of residency. I can't afford any extra baggage right now."

Nicky eyed him suspiciously, then tossed her hair to one side as though it didn't really matter anyway. "Just sticking to nurses right now, huh?"

"I hate nurses. Can't stand women in uniform. They all remind me of the nuns I had in school as a kid." He grinned at her, then tossed his own long blond hair for effect. He leaned closer. "I like women with large mouths and large tits," he said softly.

Nicky stiffened slightly. "Don't push it too hard, doc. Some people don't like the heavy breathing to start for at least five minutes." The line of her mouth was straight now and her eyes had lost their playfulness.

"Just carrying the conversation to its logical conclusion," he said. He was leaning on the bar, openly appraising her, confident he could have whatever he wanted.

Nicky stared at him in disbelief. "You're some piece of work, you know that? Just because somebody jokes with you, you think right away she's a piece of meat. You better wise up, fella."

Sousi's eyes became flat. He waved a hand, taking in the room. "We *are* at a meat auction, *aren't* we?" There was subdued anger in his voice that made the woman move slightly back on her stool.

She stared at him for several seconds, then her own eyes hardened. "You are a *creep*." She spoke the final word more loudly and with exaggerated emphasis, causing several people at the bar to turn.

Sousi's face reddened and his eyes brimmed with anger. "Do try to control yourself," he said, his voice soft and sneering.

Nicky offered him a smile that wasn't a smile. "I'm

just letting the other women here know exactly *what* you are. That way they won't have to put up with your crap either."

Sousi forced his voice to remain soft. "A sort of slut's Morse code?" he offered.

"Get away from me, you creep!" Nicky emphasized each word, peaking it clearly and loudly.

The bartender moved in quickly, positioning himself opposite Sousi. "What's going on here?"

Sousi glared at him, then at the woman, as he reached in his pocket, withdrew a handful of folded bills, and dropped a five on the bar. His face broke into a smile again. "Nothing," he said. He turned back to the bartender. "But you really shouldn't let hookers work in your bar." He let the words drop, then turned abruptly and walked toward the door, making it half-way there before the woman could recover and let loose a cry of rage.

As Sousi pushed his way through the door, Charlie Moriarty slipped a notebook from his pocket and scribbled quickly: *Put a knife in my hand and I can make any woman a goddess*. Rolk'll like that one. He heaved his bulk from the barstool and moved quickly toward the door. And a real slick guy with the ladies, he told himself. Like the man said, somebody who couldn't get laid in a two-bit whorehouse with a roll of quarters in his hand.

Moriarty pushed through the door just in time to see Sousi climb into a cab. He spun on one foot and sprinted, as quickly as his bulk would allow, to the unmarked car he had parked illegally a few doors from the bar.

Once behind the wheel, Moriarty swung the car into traffic. Up ahead he could see the cab two blocks further along the avenue. He pressed the accelerator down. "Too far," he said aloud, swerving to cut into a faster lane. A traffic light ahead turned red, and he jammed his foot down, making it across to a blare of horns. A bus cut in front of him, forcing him to hit his brakes, and he slammed his hand against the steering wheel and cursed.

In the cab, Sousi sat stone-faced, oblivious of Moriarty's pursuit. His features were dark and his hands were clenched. "Filthy bitch," he said in a voice audible only to himself. "Dirty little slut." Then his face softened. "But you put her in her place." His thoughts flashed to Grace Mallory and he immediately wished he could do the same with her. And someday he would. Someday he'd be in control and she'd be the one underfoot. And sweet little Kate Silverman as well. Then the department's female aristocracy would come crashing down and they'd get a taste of just what they'd been handing out. He watched an attractive young woman walking along the sidewalk. All of them. So superior. So much in control. What he had told that slut in the bar had been true too. About those nuns he had had to deal with as a boy. All so perfect in their starched little habits. Acting like they'd never done anything reprehensible in their entire lives, like the thought of causing anyone harm had never crossed their minds. And all the while pretending they were the only ones with any intelligence, and their students were nothing more than feeble little idiots who couldn't grasp the simplest thought. Even people who now had doctorates and were changing the way people thought, molding the way people *would* think for generations.

Sousi glanced at his watch, then ahead at the crush of traffic. "I'm in a hurry," he said to the driver. "Try another street."

The driver shrugged helplessly. "I'll cut over and try Central Park West, but I can't guarantee it'll be any better."

Sousi looked out the window. "Try it," he said. "I've got a warm lady waiting for me, and it's a cold night."

"Lucky you," the driver said. "All I've got is another six fucking hours in this cab."

Rolk sat on the edge of the bed in his daughter's

room, staring straight ahead at the small flowers that patterned the wallpaper. A book lay in his lap, open to a page of photographs depicting various Mayan ruins. It had been his wife's book, one she had used when studying for her master's degree in art history.

He had thought of the book when Father Lopato was relating the legend of Quetzalcoatl. The plumed serpent. He had heard the term before, and then he had remembered his wife, Kathy, had told him about it, about the legend and the sacrifices. It had lain dormant in his mind all those years, and then it had surfaced with the priest's words.

Kathy. He hadn't even spoken her name in years. Now so much came back, things she must have told him. It was as though he had already known everything the priest had said, as though he might even know things the priest had not mentioned. But what were they?

He lay back on the bed and closed his eyes. It's age, he told himself. It creeps in and grabs you by the throat and cuts oxygen to the brain. And you don't even know it's happening.

His hand shot up to his eyes, the pain cutting across his forehead. Some days the pain felt as if it would kill him.

He rubbed his thumb and forefinger against his eyes, trying to press the pain away. Sleep, he told himself as he lay back. Sleep the pain away. He struggled to ignore the pain, willing it to leave him, concentrating against it. Gradually his breathing became slow and regular; the book slipped from his lap and fell soundlessly to the carpeted floor.

Fourteen

PAUL DEVLIN CROSSED the small lawn and approached his front door, thinking, as he did at least once each month, that the mortgage payment would be due next week and that it would be a tight squeeze to get it in on time. He stopped to let his eyes roam the exterior of his home. He and his wife, Mary, had bought the slightly dilapidated house six years ago, and had laid plans to turn it into a neighborhood showplace. Then, a year later, and only a month after their daughter had been born, Mary had been killed in a car accident, and all plans for the house, and most other things in his life, had been forgotten.

It was then that his sister, Beth, had moved in with him—Beth, the older sister who had tormented him in his youth, who had never found anything he did quite up to her expectations, but now willingly cared for him and his daughter as if it were the most ordinary thing to do.

Closing the front door, he removed his revolver and placed it on a high shelf in the hall closet, then made his way to the kitchen, where he could hear his sister and daughter jabbering to each other.

The birth of his child and the subsequent death of his wife had produced an unexpected change in Beth. From a hard-driven career woman she had suddenly come forth with maternal instincts he never would have imagined. And somewhat to his surprise, he found the change had made him love her as he never had before.

Beth had given up her full-time job as a research

supervisor at a drug firm, determined to give his daughter her full attention until the child was in school all day. And it had worked. His daughter, Philippa—named for his father—was as bright and contented as any child he had ever known.

As he stepped into the kitchen, Philippa let out a cry of delight, wiggled from her chair, and ran into his arms, where she began a breathless recitation of the events of her day. He listened attentively, expressing approval or amazement, whichever seemed appropriate, while casting an occasional amused glance at his sister, who appeared to radiate pleasure with each sentence the child uttered.

Beth was dressed in jeans and a loose-fitting pullover, and her hair was pulled back in a ponytail with loose wisps falling about her ears. She wore no makeup, and beneath the smile she directed at the child, she looked tired and slightly harried. Devlin stared at her and tried to fight off the comparison with Kate Silverman that leapt to his mind. It was unfair and foolish, but he couldn't help it, even though he knew that five years earlier the comparison might easily have been in Beth's favor.

"See," Beth said, coming up to him and kissing his cheek, but speaking to the child. "I told you Daddy would be home for dinner tonight." Beth turned her attention to Paul. "She was upset when she thought you weren't coming."

"So was I," Devlin said. "But I found out the priest I'm tailing had evening confessions, so I thought I'd slip home, at least for an hour."

"A priest!" Beth grimaced, then squeezed his arm. "I keep hearing about the case on the news. It sounds grim. I suppose this means we won't be seeing a lot of you for a while."

"Afraid so. Everybody is all lathered up, and we already have more suspects than we can handle."

"Any good ones?" Beth's soft brown eyes offered a hint of hope.

"The best one's the priest, if you can buy that. Then

a couple of Mexicans. All the others are museum types, mainly because they had access to the type of weapon used."

"What about the usual criminal types? Your ordinary park rapist, mugger? Or the woman's husband?"

"You've spent too much time watching soap operas," he teased her, knowing she actually spent her spare time reading science journals. "You're beginning to think all husbands are evil philanderers who regularly negotiate with hit men to do in their wives."

"What's a hit man?" Philippa asked.

Devlin grinned at the child. "A baseball player," he said. "The one who hits the ball." His smile broadened. Next week the child would repeat the phrase, as she did everything else, and someone—her grandfather, no doubt—would ask where the hell she ever picked up an expression like that.

"What's for dinner?"

"Pot roast," Beth said as she placed a soup tureen on the kitchen table. "I thought I'd start making things that would be easy for leftovers so you could heat up something when you get home. *If* you get home," she added.

"Don't be a pessimist," he said.

"It's hard not to be."

"I know." He ladled a portion of pot roast onto his plate, and found his thoughts going back to the case, to Father LoPato, and the absurdity that the man might turn out to be a killer. But Rolk seemed hot on the idea, and he had a proven instinct that was hard to dismiss. Still . . . He pushed the thought away. He had another forty-five minutes before he would have to head back. And he was damned if he was going to spend it worrying about this case. Not when he could spend it with his daughter, whom he might not be seeing a lot of over the next few days.

The figure stood very still, waiting, ignoring the Fifth Avenue traffic, which was still heavy.

She'll be coming soon. You can feel it. She was still

*in her office when you telephoned. What time is it?
Look at your watch. Eight o'clock. The lady is working
late tonight. She was so annoyed when she answered
the phone and you didn't speak. Such an authoritative,
domineering person. One of the elite. One of the ones
who should be offered up for sacrifice. The briefcase.
Look and make sure everything is ready. Oh, yes. All
there. Everything that you need.*

*Look out from behind the hedge now and see if she's
coming. Not yet. Slow tonight. She doesn't know the
honor that awaits her. A much better place then the first
time. So much more like the place for which it was
intended. And so important if the ritual is to be upheld.*

*Look again. Oh, yes, there she is, just crossing
Seventy-ninth Street. Now you must step out and meet
her.*

The woman stopped abruptly as the figure dressed
in dark clothing suddenly appeared before her.

"Dear God, you scared the wits out of me." Alexsandra Ross pulled her arms about herself, her thin
leather briefcase clutched to her breast.

"I'm sorry. I've been waiting to talk to you. It's
really very important, or I wouldn't ask."

Alexsandra's face became incredulous. "What?
You've been waiting here? On Fifth Avenue?"

"I know you don't like to be disturbed when you're
working, so I thought I'd just wait here for you to
leave."

"But how did you know I was still working?"
Alexsandra pulled at the sleeve of her coat to reveal
her watch. "It's eight o'clock. How . . . ?" Her expression changed, her eyes growing harsh. "The telephone call," she said. "Why in heaven's name didn't
you say who it was?"

"You seemed annoyed by the interruption, so I
thought it best to just wait."

"Oh, *really*." Alexsandra let out a long irritated
breath.

"It's truly very important. Please. If we could just

step into this small playground and sit on a bench for a few minutes."

Alexsandra exhaled another exasperated breath. "All right, but let's make it quick, *please*." She turned and started down the narrow path that led to the children's playground just inside the park south of Seventy-ninth Street.

She's walking so quickly, almost marching. Hurry, hurry. Get the briefcase open and get the ax. Quickly now, but not too quickly. Be accurate. You must hit the spine exactly.

"Alexsandra?" the voice called softly.

She's slowed; she beginning to turn. Now. Now.

Fifteen

DEVLIN WAS ALREADY at the playground when Rolk arrived. It was a few minutes before midnight, and the traffic along Fifth Avenue was still heavy enough to allow minor tie-ups as drivers paused to stare at the arc lights that now illuminated the play area.

Rolk pushed his way through the reporters gathered outside the playground's tall iron fence, simply shaking his head at the shouted questions that poured from several dozen mouths. He moved immediately to Devlin's side, but his eyes remained fixed on the covered body that lay atop a triangular stone structure used as a children's climbing area.

"Was the body found on top of that thing?" He stared at Devlin. "Just like it is now?"

Devlin nodded. "It hit me the same way when I got here. The damned thing looks like a miniature pyramid."

"Is the head missing?"

"Just like the first one," Devlin said. "A clean cut with something that was very sharp. And the skin along the back is gone too."

"Jesus," Rolk said, staring at his shoes. He motioned with his head toward the waiting reporters. "They're going to kill us."

"Worse than you expect," Devlin said; his words caused Rolk's eyes to rise and meet his. "The woman, at least according to the identification we found in the purse, was Alexsandra Ross, that PR lady from the Met."

Rolk closed his eyes and drew several deep breaths.

137

When he opened them again Jerry Feldman was standing next to them, his white lab coat already in place, his medical bag dangling from one hand.

"Same as before?" Feldman asked.

"Paul says it's identical," Rolk said.

"That's what the boys at the morgue thought, so they called me at home." All the normal gruffness was gone from Feldman's voice. "Christ. Two in two days," he said. "I thought there'd at least be some time between them. There usually is."

"Maybe we stirred him up by getting too close," Devlin said.

Rolk studied Devlin's face. This thing is starting to scare him, he thought. Christ, it should. It scared the hell out of me, right from the start.

"Did you call Greenspan and ask him to come down here?"

"About an hour ago," Devlin said.

"Good, I'll wait for him. But right now I want you to find someone at the Met who can get us a look at personnel records tonight. I want to know everything I can about this woman as fast as possible." Devlin turned to go, and Rolk grabbed his arm. "And get Peters over to her apartment—check her ID and find out where it is. We need somebody who can identify her as quick as we can get them dressed and down to the morgue."

"Unless she had a husband or a steady boyfriend, that might be hard. Especially since—"

"I know," Rolk interrupted. "We may have to settle for someone who worked with her today. Somebody who can remember the clothes and jewelry she was wearing. I sure as hell can't, can you?"

Devlin shook his head, realizing he had paid far more attention to Kate Silverman. "Not very good for trained observers," he said.

"We were paying more attention to her mouth than what she looked like," Rolk said. "She was that kind of woman." He paused as if trying to recall something. "Check with all our men. I want a detailed report on the suspects they were assigned to follow. I want to know where they were last night. Every minute of it."

Devlin stared at his shoes. "We have a problem there," he said.

"We do?" Rolk was facing him squarely.

"I lost the priest a little before eight o'clock."

"How the hell did you do that?"

Devlin's jaw tightened. He had never felt more disgusted with himself. "He was scheduled to hear confessions until nine. So I thought I'd take advantage of it and go home and have dinner with my kid." He paused, his face reddening. "Apparently confessions were slow, so he left early."

"Where'd he go?" Rolk's voice was flat, unemotional.

"I don't know. I spoke to another priest there, but all he could tell me was that he went out a little before eight."

Rolk stared at him in silence for several moments. "Go take care of the other things I just told you about," he said at length.

Devlin nodded. "I'm sorry," he said.

"You should be," Rolk said.

Feldman was kneeling over the now-exposed body as Rolk made his way up the small stone pyramid. There was a flat area at the top, and the body had been placed there, just as the other victim had, as though arranged for burial.

"You see anything different this time?" Rolk asked.

Feldman glanced up at him. "No such luck. I'm just going through the motions. Even the way the skin was taken from the back. The angle of cuts, everything. I can tell you right now, you're dealing with the same killer." He shook his head. "What the hell was she doing in this playground after dark? Who the hell would she come in here with?"

"Why do you say that?" Rolk asked.

"Because she's been dead a good three or four hours. And there would've been too much goddamned traffic on Fifth Avenue then for somebody to force her in here without being noticed."

"So you think she knew the person," Rolk said.
"Don't you?"

Rolk nodded. "I just wanted to hear somebody else say it."

Greenspan stood next to Rolk as Moriarty detailed Sousi's barroom exchange with the woman, and his subsequent disappearance in traffic shortly thereafter.

"But he didn't go home, Lieutenant," Moriarty said, his normally pink face even pinker now. "At least I was able to check up on that."

Rolk nodded, then patted the bulky detective's shoulder. "Don't worry about it, Charlie. It happens."

Rolk turned to the psychiatrist. "That ring any bells for you? Anything that Charlie said?"

"Too vague. I can't diagnose a psychopath based on one comment in a bar. That good I'm not."

Rolk watched the psychiatrist stuff tobacco in his pipe, and wondered if the smoke was going to do him more harm than good. The man had spent time looking at the body and the area around it, and now seemed a little green about the gills. Rolk wished he could avoid the details for Greenspan's sake, but knew he could not.

"Sorry to have to subject you to this," he began, "but I wanted you to see exactly what we're dealing with. I'm convinced these killings involve some form of Toltec ritual that would fit in with this whole Toltec exhibit at the museum."

"I agree," Greenspan said.

"There's something you don't know," Rolk said. "One of the people at the museum received what we think are several threats from the killer."

Greenspan listened as Rolk told of the various votives left for Kate Silverman. He rubbed his chin thoughtfully. "This could be a classic example of the catch-me-before-I-kill-again syndrome, which also often fits in with an increased frequency of murders. Our killer may be asking someone to stop him in general, or specifically, before he kills Dr. Silverman. But in any case, there's one thing that's sure."

"And that is?"

"That you have to protect that woman, because if you don't, she's going to end up very dead." Greenspan glanced toward the body of Alexsandra Ross, then closed his eyes. "And I certainly don't want to have to look at another one like that," he added.

Two security guards and a drowsy personnel director lounged at the opposite end of the large office as Rolk and Devlin pored over Alexsandra Ross's file for the fourth time. A private telephone line had been made available to them, and an earlier call from Bernie Peters, who had been questioning tenants at her apartment building, had informed them that no close friends were available to identify Alexsandra Ross's body.

"This is one single-minded woman," Devlin said. "Not even a vacation in the past two years."

"Some people are dedicated," Rolk said. "Not like some civil servants."

Devlin studied his dour-faced partner, trying to determine if he was still being rebuked for his earlier failure. He decided he wasn't. "When was the last time *you* took any time off?" he asked.

"I can't," Rolk snapped. "People keep killing each other." He withdrew a cigarette from a pack on the desk and lit it. "Dammit. This woman has worked here for ten years. She's lived in her apartment for twelve. And she hasn't got one close friend in either place. According to her neighbors, lots of male visitors, but no steady boyfriends."

Devlin jabbed a finger at a personnel form that indicated both of the woman's parents were deceased. "No help there," he said. "And her secretary left town for a long weekend. That leaves us with exactly no one to identify her personal effects."

"*Almost* no one," Rolk said.

"Who?"

"Kate Silverman."

"Kate Silverman?" Devlin asked.

"That's right. She was in her office today, and I'm sure she at least noticed her clothes. Get hold of her and get her down to the morgue as fast as you can." Rolk stared up at his partner. "It's bad enough we can't find her head. If we can't even produce her name, the press and the politicians are going to hang us out to dry."

The telephone on the desk rang and Rolk picked it up. "Yeah, it's me. What have you got?" He listened, his face expressionless. "Tell him I want him in my office at nine o'clock this morning." He waited again, then stiffened in his chair. "Then bring him down to the morgue in half an hour. I'll question him there." He replaced the receiver roughly in its cradle.

"Who's that?" Devlin asked.

"Our man up at the rectory. Father LoPato was out last night from eight until after eleven-thirty."

"Did he say where he was?"

"A religious film series at St. Gregory's School auditorium."

"That's only a ten-minute cab ride from here."

"That's right," Rolk said. "And it's also someplace that was probably crawling with nuns and priests."

"Why are you bringing him to the morgue?" Devlin asked.

"Because he refused to be available at nine. Says he's scheduled to say Mass then."

"Seems awful dedicated for a man who couldn't hang around for the end of confessions," Devlin said. He hesitated. "The archdiocese is going to scream again, you know."

"That bother you?" Rolk asked.

"As far as I'm concerned, you couldn't *be* too rough on this guy."

"Or anybody else," Rolk said. "Not if our killer is on a victim-a-day binge."

Devlin nodded. "I'll call Silverman right now."

*   *   *

Kate sat at a long table, with Alexsandra Ross's personal effects spread out before her. Her face was drawn and tense, a fact accented by the absence of makeup, and her hands were tightly balled in her lap.

"You're sure?" Paul Devlin asked.

"No doubt at all." She spoke without looking up. "I admired the necklace and commented on it. She said it was very old, her grandmother's. I doubt there could be two like it."

"We'll be checking her fingerprints too," Devlin said, trying to keep his voice soft. "But normally it's not much help with women. Few of them seem to have prints on file."

"Do you know if Ms. Ross had any scars, moles, birthmarks? Anything like that?" Rolk asked, looking down at the objects on the table.

Kate stared at him, confused. "I never saw her undressed. And we never discussed anything like that. My only contact with her was through the exhibit."

Rolk shuffled his feet. "I was hoping you might have belonged to the same health club or something."

"Did she ever talk about any personal friends? Anyone she was especially close to?" Devlin asked.

"Never."

"I know this is difficult for you," Rolk said. "It's just that we want to be as sure as we possibly can."

Kate nodded. "That's just it. It's not difficult. It's just . . ." She let the sentence die, then began again. "I didn't know Alexsandra very well, and what I did know, I didn't particularly like." She shook her head slightly and shuddered. "Now I'm here identifying her as a murder victim, and I can't really feel a great deal, except that I don't want to be here." She looked up sharply. "I *am* sorry she's dead. I don't mean that I'm not. I just don't feel anything . . ." She paused, trying to find the right words. "Except fear." She shook her head again. "That sounds terrible, but it's true."

"It's a natural reaction to murder, especially if you knew the person. And this place doesn't help," Devlin said. "Everyone who comes here just wants to get out as quickly as they can. Even cops."

Kate twisted nervously in her chair. "Will I have to . . . look at her?"

"No. That won't be necessary," Rolk said. He watched Kate close her eyes and exhale heavily. "In fact we really won't need you for anything else."

Kate felt her muscles suddenly relax and she realized for the first time how tightly she had been holding herself. She stared again at the articles spread across the table; the now empty cardboard box beyond them. Her eyes moved about the sparsely furnished room they were seated in, and she noticed the rows of identical cardboard boxes neatly stacked along one wall, and realized that each of them contained the belongings of yet another person who had died unexpectedly. *God, you've spent most of your adult life dealing with the belongings of long-dead civilizations, of people, many of whom died just as horribly. But you didn't know them, you hadn't spoken to them the day before. And you never before had to consider the possibility that the same thing could happen to you.*

"Dr. Silverman?"

Kate turned to the sound of Rolk's voice and found him staring at her. "I'm sorry. It's this place, I think. I was trying to understand why it's affecting me this way." She smiled weakly. "I've been on digs where we've excavated tomb after tomb."

"It's different here," Rolk said.

Kate nodded. "Yes, it is."

She rose to leave, then stopped. "There's something I suppose I should tell you," she began. "Not about this. It's just that I have to go to Mexico City for a few days to oversee the packing and shipment of some objects we're getting from their National Anthropological Museum."

Rolk stepped forward. "How close is that to Chichén Itzá?" he asked.

"Not close at all, really. But by plane it's only a short flight. Why?"

"Could you go there for a day or two, if I asked you? The department would cover your additional expenses."

"Of course I could. In fact I'd love to. It's one of the finest archaeological sites in the Yucatán. But again, why?"

Rolk waved a hand, partially dismissing the idea. "Just something in the back of my mind. I'm not really sure it will be necessary. When are you leaving?"

"Tomorrow. I'll be in Mexico City for two days, then I'll be back."

"I'll let you know later if I decide it's necessary." He pressed his lips together, offering his imitation smile. The woman seemed confused. So did Devlin. "I'll call for a car and have someone drive you to the museum. I'd do it myself, but unfortunately there's someone else here we still have to see."

"That's perfectly all right," Kate said. "If there's anything else I can do, please let me know."

Rolk took her hand and held it. "There is one thing."

"Yes?"

"Do you think Dr. Mallory could spare you long enough later this morning to give me a complete tour of your museum?"

"I'm sure she'd be willing to," Kate said. "But you should realize that that could take most of the day. Especially if you mean the storage areas as well as the collections on display."

"You can skip the collections on display," Rolk said. "But I'd like to become very familiar with all the work and storage areas."

"Of course," Kate said. "I'll speak to Dr. Mallory first thing." She hesitated. "I won't mind having a policeman follow me around today." There was a faint tremor in her voice.

Sixteen

THE PRIEST HAD been left alone for two hours in a first-floor conference room. The detective who had brought him had remained outside, per orders issued by Rolk: "Leave him alone. Let him sweat. Let him get angry."

When Rolk and Devlin entered the room it was almost three A.M., but Father LoPato was neither sweating nor angry. He simply looked tired, and very relieved the detectives had finally made an appearance.

"Sorry to keep you waiting," Rolk began, taking a seat opposite the priest.

He nodded at Rolk and then at Devlin, who had remained standing by the door. "I guess I should have agreed to nine o'clock at your office," he said. "But the pastor is ill, and the other curate can't really handle all the Masses himself."

"The offer to let it wait until nine was a courtesy, Father. I really couldn't afford to let it go beyond then." Rolk fell silent, waiting for the priest to respond. When nothing came, he continued. "I'd like to know what you did last night."

The priest's brow furrowed and he seemed about to challenge the question, but after a pause he simply sat back in his chair.

"I finished some work I had been doing. Then, as I told the other detective, I went out to a film at St. Gregory's School. They're having a religious film festival—the type of film Hollywood doesn't seem to make anymore."

"Didn't you have dinner?" Rolk asked, suddenly realizing that he himself had not.

"I stopped at a small restaurant on Amsterdam, not far from the museum."

"What was the name of it?"

"I don't recall. It was a small diner type of place. I just sat at the counter." He offered a weak smile. "Food has never been one of the great passions in my life." He pulled open his suit coat revealing his lank frame. "As you can see."

"What film did you see, Father?"

"It was a documentary on Mother Theresa. She's the nun who—"

"I know who she is, Father," Rolk interrupted. "What time did it end?"

"Around eleven, or shortly before. I really didn't pay a great deal of attention to the time."

"Did you see anyone there you knew?"

"No, I'm afraid not."

"Weren't there other priests, nuns?"

"Oh, yes. But I've been back in this country such a short time, I really haven't met a great many other religious." The weak smile returned. "I'm afraid my work takes up most of my time, and other than that, I'm not a terribly sociable person."

"Did you take a cab back to the rectory? I assume you went right back." Rolk's voice was toneless, a flat, even, boring line.

"Actually I walked. Wandered, really, just enjoying the night. I got back somewhere around midnight."

"And you saw no one you knew all evening," Rolk spoke the question as fact.

"No, I didn't." The priest paused as if hesitant to say more. "Lieutenant, why are you asking these questions? I asked your detective, and he said you'd explain."

"There was another murder tonight—last night—near the Met."

"Oh, God."

From the doorway Devlin concentrated on the priest's

face. It seemed to shatter, to collapse from within, as though the last vestige of his faith was being ripped from him.

"Was it the same as the . . . the other?" The priest stuttered, struggling with the words.

"I'm afraid it was, Father." Rolk paused, drawing it out, wanting the maximum effect from what would follow. "A woman. Someone I believe you knew. She worked at the Met. Her name was Alexsandra Ross."

Father LoPato lowered his head. "God have mercy on her," he said, slightly above a whisper. He looked up at Rolk. "We met several times. The last time, the day I brought the objects to the museum. She wanted to list my name in the catalog, and couldn't quite seem to understand why I didn't want it there."

"Why didn't you?" Devlin asked.

The priest tried to smile, but failed. "We're taught to avoid temptations of pride. A good work without recognition is considered a greater good."

"Did you argue with her?" Rolk asked.

"No, of course not. She was very pleasant, even though she didn't understand. She was simply trying to extend a courtesy, and she found it difficult to understand why I didn't want it. But we certainly didn't argue about it."

The room fell silent for several minutes. Rolk used it to make meaningless notes. The priest, after a time, began to understand.

"Are you asking me these questions because you think some of the people I'm trying to help might be involved in this? And that I might be involved with them?" the priest finally asked.

"We're requestioning everyone we spoke to about the first murder," Rolk said. "For the time being, it's that simple."

The room fell silent again. Rolk stood and walked back to the door where Devlin was standing, then turned back to the priest. "Father," he began slowly, his voice drawing the word out, "when we spoke yesterday, you said the Mayans you worked with in the

Yucatán often mixed their old religious beliefs with their Christianity. You also asked some rather specific questions about the possible mutilation of our first victim." He paused as if gathering his thoughts, although actually concentrating on the priest's eyes and mouth, the first places any discomfort would show itself.

"When you were in the Yucatán, Father, did you experience something similar to what we're having here? Is that why you knew what might have been done to the body?"

The priest's hand shot to his forehead, the fingers trembling. "I would have known just from my studies," he said. There was a long pause. "But, yes. Something did happen there." He looked up at Rolk and Devlin, his eyes hollow, his features seeming to collapse even more. "The blood rituals began again— several people, mostly young women, disappeared." The eyes became imploring. "And it was partially my fault, you see. Because of my intellectual curiosity, I had asked questions about the past as they understood it, and later I feared I had unintentionally encouraged them. You see, I didn't lead them away from it. I didn't lead them toward Christ. I was fascinated, so completely fascinated. It was like reliving the past that I had studied for so long. And I didn't see where it was leading, didn't allow myself to see."

"How many people disappeared?" Devlin asked.

"I don't know, don't remember." He took a handkerchief from his pocket and began mopping his brow. "Later I suffered a breakdown, and much of it is still so vague."

"Did they ever arrest anyone?" Rolk asked.

"Not that I know of. But then, I left rather quickly. The order felt it was best for me, and as soon as I could travel, they sent me here."

"Do you know who was responsible, Father? Who actually performed the ceremonies—the blood rituals?"

The priest shook his head violently. "No. No. They were all so innocent, so childlike. The people of the village lived as though they were in a different century." He stared at Rolk, his eyes imploring. "Even the ones who did these things, did them without a sense of doing wrong. They wore the masks I told you about—and thus they became the gods—and because of that, they didn't feel *they* were performing the actual sacrifices." He lowered his face into his hands. "Oh, dear god, it can't be happening here too. It just can't."

"What was the name of the village, Father?" Devlin asked.

The priest looked up at them, his face confused. He shook his head as though trying to clear it. "Chetulak. It's about fifteen miles into the jungle, toward the coast, from Chichén Itzá."

"How many people from that village have you brought to New York, Father?" Rolk's eyes bore into the priest.

"Just the two families I told you about." His face clouded. "The only other people I knew from there were Dr. Mallory and Dr. Sousi."

"Sousi and Mallory?" Rolk asked.

The priest nodded slowly; his eyes seemed confused. "Why, yes, of course. I thought you knew that. It was where I first met them. Grace and Malcolm were working on a dig near there just about a year ago." He stared at each detective in turn. "I'm sorry. I thought you knew."

"Your one good solid suspect suddenly turned into three." Devlin shook his head as he spoke to Rolk.

"Better than none," Rolk said. "At least we've got people to investigate. And given what Kate Silverman told you, we may even have a motive."

Devlin took a chair in Rolk's office and leaned forward, resting his forearms on Rolk's desk. "I still find it hard to believe that someone would go on a killing spree to promote a show at a museum."

"A sane person wouldn't. But a sane person wouldn't kill people this way either." Rolk ran a hand across his face, feeling the nearly full day's growth of beard. "I'm not even sure the priest isn't right."

"About what?"

"About the possibility our killer may not even realize what he's doing." Rolk paused, then corrected himself. "What he, *or* she is doing. Christ, we could be dealing with someone who *believes* in this ritual."

"We're not sure how similar this thing in Mexico was," Devlin said. "The killings there—if there were any—may not be similar at all. And if they were, it could be coincidence."

"I don't believe in coincidences. And based on the priest's reaction, I'll bet you a suit they're damned similar." Rolk shrugged. "Anyway, you can find out with a phone call. And then we'll know whether it's worth my while to ship off to the Yucatán."

"You really might go?"

Rolk nodded. "That's right. And that means you'll be in charge for a couple of days."

Devlin sat back, stunned. "I'm not sure if you just decided to do me a big favor or screw my ass to the wall," he said.

"Probably a little of both," Rolk said. "Of course, if you solve the case while I'm away, I might be working for you when I get back."

Devlin stared at the floor, shook his head, then looked back at Rolk. "What are you going to look for on this museum tour?"

"Places where people could hide something?" Rolk said.

"Like what?"

"Like missing heads."

Rolk's telephone broke into the conversation, and he picked it up, issued a tersc thanks, and turned back to Devlin. "Inspector Dunne's on the other linc," he said. "I guess the complaint department at the archdiocese opens early these days."

Seventeen

GRACE MALLORY SAT hunched over her desk, a magnifying glass held before one eye, revealing the details of the mask set out before her.

It was a ceramic effigy of the merchant god, Ek Chuah, the narrow face marked by a long bulbous nose, fangs protruding from the corners of the mouth, and colored eye patches.

"This is an extraordinary piece," she said, her attention still concentrated on the mask. "I want this prominently displayed among the other Late Postclassic pieces."

Malcolm Sousi, who had been standing behind her, leaned over Grace's shoulder to get a better look at the mask, noting, as he did, the dandruff that littered her tangled mass of gray hair. His nose wrinkled involuntarily, and he wished the woman would make herself a bit less disgusting.

"Our problem," Sousi said, "is that we have so many outstanding pieces. One seems to overwhelm the next." He brushed back a spray of long blond hair that had fallen across his forehead, then stood erect, jamming his hands into the pockets of his white lab coat, unconsciously imitating Grace.

"That's why placement is so crucial, Malcolm." She lowered the glass and pivoted in her swivel desk chair. "It's what causes so many exhibits to seem less than they are."

Her eyes bored into Malcolm's handsome face. You, Malcolm, would have made a splendid Mayan yourself, she thought. With that long fine nose and narrow forehead, the way your lower lip turns slightly down. I can almost see you dressed in ceremonial regalia, preparing to take part in some ritual.

"Well, at least our problem is not having too few good pieces," he said. "It should have a staggering effect on the academic community." He paused, pursing his lips in thought. "And our connection with a murder investigation won't hurt us. The public's attraction to the macabre certainly should produce crowds."

Grace Mallory's brow wrinkled and her lips became a tight line. "Not exactly the sort of public I want to bring in," she said. "Those poor women. I almost choked on my breakfast when I heard Alexsandra's name on the morning news."

Sousi nodded. "Yes. I felt the same." He turned and walked a few steps away from the desk, his slender, athletic body seeming to glide along the carpet. "Although I must admit, I doubt I shall miss Alexsandra terribly. She was such an imperious bitch."

"That's a terrible thing to say, Malcolm." A small smile crept to her lips. "But it is an accurate description. She always reminded me of a—"

The sound of a fist striking wood caused them both to turn and take in the figure of Stanislaus Rolk framed in the doorway.

"I hope I'm not interrupting," he said.

"Not at all, Lieutenant," Grace said, beckoning him forward. "I was just discussing the morning's work with Malcolm."

"Ah, Lieutenant," Sousi said. "And we *are* delighted to see you. You are breaking up a morning that has been absolutely dreary with work."

Rolk studied the younger man, noting the well-developed shoulders, the large, powerful hands. "I thought I'd find everyone a bit subdued this morning," Rolk said. "Unless, of course, you haven't heard the news reports."

"You mean about poor Alexsandra?" Malcolm said.

"Oh, we've heard. I suspect it will have most of the women here in a state of near-terror." He inclined his head toward Grace. "Present company excepted, of course."

"Oh, do shut up, Malcolm," Grace said. "I'm sorry, Lieutenant. Malcolm has a tendency to run off at the mouth, given the slightest provocation. What can we do for you?"

Rolk walked around the room, studying its layout. "Actually, I'm here to get your okay on something, and to ask a few more questions."

"My okay?"

"Yes, it concerns Ms. Silverman," Rolk began.

"*Dr.* Silverman," Grace corrected.

Rolk nodded, as though the distinction meant nothing to him. "I understand Dr. Silverman is going to Mexico City to supervise a shipment coming here."

"Yes. But I don't see why that should involve the police, unless you feel she shouldn't go?"

"Not at all," Rolk said. "In fact I'd like her to make a small side trip. Actually, meet me in Chichén Itzá and help look into something."

"Chichén Itzá?" Confusion spread across Grace's face. "I don't understand."

Rolk shifted in his chair, rearranging the folds of his wrinkled suit coat. "It seems there were some killings down there. Ritual killings. Not unlike the ones we're having here. I believe you and Dr. Sousi were there at the time. Perhaps you recall it."

"Chichén Itzá—" Malcolm began, only to be immediately silenced by a sharp look from Grace.

"Yes, I recall," Grace said. "Of course, we were fairly far back in the rain forest, and what we heard of it we got from the natives working for us." She offered a slight shrug. "Frankly, we didn't pay a great deal of attention to it. The natives there tend to be quite superstitious. We were always hearing stories about strange or mystical things the gods were doing. I'm afraid we ignored most of it."

"Even reports of young women being killed?"

Grace leaned forward and smiled. "Young women often disappear in the Yucatán, Lieutenant. More often than not, they've simply packed their few belongings in a bundle and headed for a larger city. The natives, meanwhile, attribute the disappearances to the gods."

Rolk rubbed his chin. "Yes, young women show up like that in this city every day." His eyes suddenly hardened. "But in this case we confirmed a number of killings with the police down there. Seems it really did happen. Right around the time you and Dr. Sousi and Father LoPato were all there."

The room fell silent. Rolk looked toward Sousi. "You seemed about to say something before. Do you remember something about it?"

Sousi paused, pursing his lips again. "No, not at all. It's just as Grace said. We didn't put much credence in the rumors. To be honest, we were interested in what happened hundreds of years earlier, not modern-day superstition. Or at least what we thought was superstition."

Rolk nodded. "That's understandable." He looked back at Grace. "You did meet Father LoPato down there, didn't you?"

"Yes, we did. He was ill at the time. Malaria, I think. Some days, I'm afraid, he couldn't remember conversations we had the day before."

"Is that common with malaria?"

"Sometimes. The fevers can run fairly high, and hallucinations aren't uncommon. I had a bout with it myself once," Grace explained. "The mosquitoes that pass it on overrun that bloody jungle."

"Did you ever experience any loss of memory?" Rolk asked.

"Not that I recall." Grace laughed at the absurdity of the answer. "But that really doesn't say very much, does it?"

Rolk pressed his lips together as he too tried to

smile. "So there's really nothing you can tell me about what happened there."

"I'm afraid not," Grace said. She turned a stern eye toward Malcolm, who simply shook his head.

"Well, perhaps I'll find something," Rolk said.

"When will you be going?" Grace asked.

"I'm not sure," Rolk lied. "It will depend on scheduling. I take it you don't object to Dr. Silverman helping us?"

Grace sat back in her chair, her mood more pensive. "Actually, it would probably be a good idea to keep her away from here for as long as possible, given what happened the other day. At least we'd be removing her from any danger, and there would be the possibility you'd catch this person in the meantime."

"I had thought of that," Rolk said.

"So had I," Grace added. "It's one of the reasons I asked her to make the trip to Mexico City."

"For lack of a better name, we call this the Bug Room." Kate reached for the handle of the heavy metal door and pulled it slowly back.

The smell hit Rolk immediately, causing him to wince. It was the cloying odor of putrefied flesh, masked by a heavy deodorant. "Jesus," he said, taking a step back. "I know that smell. I've had to go into too many rooms where people have been dead a long time." He glanced at her. "I'm almost afraid to ask why I'm smelling it here."

Kate stepped past him, beckoned him inside, then closed the heavy door behind them as she switched on an overhead light. "We have to be very careful about keeping the door closed. If the occupants escaped, they'd wreak havoc on the museum."

"The occupants?" Rolk stared at her, waiting for more.

Kate smiled at him. "Sounds a bit like a horror movie, doesn't it?" She turned and walked to one of two long metal cases, placing her hand on it. "It's a rather primitive system, but to date no one has found a more effective one." She stuffed one hand into her lab coat and patted the top of the container with the other. "If we have an animal carcass, or a part of one, that we want to reduce to the hide and skeleton, we place it in one of these containers. Inside each are several hundred thousand carpet beetles, and in a matter of days they can eat everything edible on a fairly good-size animal."

She motioned Rolk forward and opened the container. Inside was the leg of a once large animal—or what was left of it—covered with the writhing bodies of thousands of small beetles, their mouths emitting a chorus of clicking sounds as they worked furiously on the remaining flesh.

"Christ!" Rolk stepped back, his eyes narrowing. "I feel like I just looked into an unprotected grave."

Kate studied Rolk, noting his discomfort, the obvious effort he had to make to see it through. Odd for a man in his line of work, she thought. Not at all what she would have expected. And such a lonely, sad man. Rolk's eyes were still fixed on the container, and she was able to study his features unobserved. He was an attractive man, and so comforting to be with. She pushed the image away. He was committed to finding another woman, a woman *and* a child. Just concentrate on your work, she told herself. It's the one constant you can depend on.

"What are these larger containers?" Rolk asked.

His question brought Kate out of her reverie, and she looked toward where he was pointing.

"Storage," she said. "Carcasses waiting their turn with the bugs."

Rolk winced and stepped forward, raising the lid of one. Inside, wrapped in canvaslike cloth, were the bodies, and parts of bodies, of various animals, packed in a liquid solution. Each piece of canvas bore a stenciled number. "The numbers?" he asked.

"It allows those using the room to locate their specimen without unwrapping others. It's just a time-saving mechanism."

"So if I had a specimen waiting its turn, I wouldn't necessarily know what other specimens were in here," Rolk said.

"That's right. There'd be no reason to." She smiled at him. "Most of the people working here are pressed for time, as far as their own studies are concerned. They really don't pay much attention to what their peers are doing. I doubt that the people in Entomology, for example, have even the slightest idea what those in Herpetology are up to." She smiled again. "And they probably couldn't care less. It's the nature of the scientific mind, I'm afraid. We tend to have tunnel vision about our own academic disciplines."

Rolk understood, and liked the woman's realistic explanations. She was highly intelligent, but not overly impressed by the fact. She seemed to accept it as something that was part of her, like her physical beauty, but something she could not take complete responsibility for, and therefore, little credit.

His wife flashed to mind. She too had been highly intelligent. But she had been consumed by the fact, just as she had been consumed by his own lack of a higher education. He had always thought it a major factor in her decision to leave.

"Are there other storage containers like this, in other parts of the museum?" he asked.

"Just in the dissecting room."

"Could you show me?"

Kate led him through another labyrinth of corridors, each more confusing than the last, and Rolk wondered how long it took a new employee just to find his way in and out of the building.

Already they had covered vast stretches of the museum—from under the eaves of the roof where the massive bones of elephants were stored, and into the basement, where the huge boilers that heated the museum competed for space with more than a dozen full skeletons of whales. They had entered rooms containing countless skins of great cats—cheetahs, jaguars, tigers—in such quantity, Kate had assured him, that a sizable portion of the population of New York might easily be clothed in fur, many with skins more than a hundred years old.

One storage area was called "the alcoholics" by the museum staff—areas where more than a million specimens were preserved in alcohol, allowing scientists, if the need arose, to determine if toxins or diseases plaguing animals today might also have been present fifty or a hundred years earlier.

At nearly every turn Rolk had found himself faced with mounted heads or entire bodies of animals, often in such unexpected places, he had to restrain himself from jumping back.

The place was overwhelming, a scientific enterprise so vast that its annual expenses exceeded thirty million dollars—expenses bolstered and supported by a hundred million dollars each in endowment and investments.

And now, he thought as Kate led him into yet another corridor, a scientific enterprise with a series of murders hanging over it like an all-enveloping shroud.

Kate stopped before another large metal door and pulled it open. "This is it," she said, leading Rolk inside.

Across the room, under the glare of fluorescent lights, lay the partially dissected body of a large ape, its lifeless form overflowing a stainless-steel autopsy table.

Rolk stared at Kate, disbelief in his eyes. "You do autopsies here?" he asked.

"Yes. We found it the only practical way to guarantee the quality of specimens." She watched Rolk raise a questioning eyebrow, so continued. "Most of the specimens we get now come from zoos. In the past, if someone wanted to study the brain of an ape, he would request *only* the brain when a suitable animal died." Her hands were back in her lab coat now, as she assumed the lecturing pose Rolk had seen Grace Mallory use before. Everyone seems to imitate that woman, Rolk decided, wondering if he too would find himself doing it before the investigation ended.

"But, unfortunately, it didn't work out well," Kate continued. "The veterinarians at the zoos would simply smash the animal's skull to get at the brain rather than properly dissect it, and we'd end up with a severely damaged specimen. "So," she added, gesturing around the room, "we decided to do it ourselves."

"And when you're through, off the animal goes to the Bug Room?"

Kate nodded. "In most cases, yes."

Rolk crossed the room to where several large containers lined one wall. Like those in the Bug Room, they were filled with canvas-wrapped animal cadavers. Slowly he closed the lid and allowed his eyes to roam the room.

Kate watched him from the door. "I know what you're thinking," she said.

Rolk turned to face her. "And what's that?"

"The heads of those women could be hidden here without a great deal of difficulty."

"Or disposed of in your Bug Room," Rolk said.

"Good lord. I hadn't thought of that."

"Not just that," Rolk said. "I was thinking you could hide just about anything in this museum. A weapon, for example. And it probably would never be found."

"Oh, it would be found," Kate said. "It might take ten years, but eventually somebody would find it."

Kate's office was off a workroom filled with Mayan artifacts. Seated across from her, Rolk reviewed notes he had made on the four-and-a-half-hour tour they had just completed.

"Did it help at all?" Kate asked.

"It added to the confusion," Rolk said. "But confusion always precedes resolution."

She let out a small laugh. "You're a strange man. You're more like a history professor than a policeman."

"I've been described as a lot of things, but never as a professor."

Kate tilted her head to one side. "Not even when it comes to murder?" She smiled.

Rolk lowered his notes, giving her his full attention now. "Maybe," he said. "I'm like some of the people who work here. I too tend to have tunnel vision about my particular discipline. But not because I love it."

"Is that why you walk around with an unloaded gun?"

He shook his head slowly. "I learned a long time ago that a gun impedes a person's ability to think. You have it, and you know you have it, and when somebody opposes you, you tend to rely on it rather than think your way through the situation."

Kate studied his eyes, noting how wise and weary they seemed. "I thought the police had regulations about guns. I thought you had to carry them all the time. Loaded, I mean."

"They have a lot of regulations," Rolk said. "A whole book of them. Unfortunately, the book isn't much good for anything but a paperweight. Besides, I hate guns. I've rarely seen them put to any good use."

Kate looked at him more intently than she had yet allowed herself. "You're a strange man, Rolk. As strange as your name."

Rolk smiled, genuinely this time. "It wasn't always my name," he said.

Kate raised her eyebrows, urging him to say more.

"Stanislaus Rolk." He laughed as he said it. "When I was getting ready to join the department, almost

thirty years ago, my name was Stanley Rolkacheweicz."
He made a face, as if the name now sounded peculiar
on his own tongue. "In those days, if you hoped to get
ahead in the department, you were much better off
having an Irish or Italian name, or a name that had *no*
apparent ethnic connection. So I changed my name to
Rolk. Then, after a time, I realized what donkeys all
the cops who put credence in that really were. But it
seemed like too much trouble to change the name
back. So I simply started to use Stanislaus. It drove
some of them nuts, but there wasn't a damned thing
they could do about it, except try to talk me out of
it."

"And, of course, they couldn't." Kate laughed.

"If they hadn't tried, I probably would have forgotten about it within a few months. But they wouldn't
stop, so Stanislaus Rolk became a fixture in the Detective Division."

"You sound a little like Dr. Mallory," Kate said.
"There's a great deal of prejudice in museums, as
well, although here one is much better off being a
male and a WASP. But she's taken some daring ap-
proaches to things—intellectual gambles—and they've
worked." Kate toyed with a pencil on her desk. "If
this exhibit is a success—and it should be—even the
old boys' network that controls things around here
will have a difficult time putting any barriers in her
way."

"You sound like you really care about her," Rolk
said. "Despite your disagreements."

"I respect her."

"How do you feel about helping me? In Mexico.
There's always the chance it will turn something up
that will hurt rather than help her."

Kate's eyes became momentarily clouded, as though
she had never considered that possibility. "I'm not
sure," she said. Her mind drifted. When Rolk had
suggested the trip earlier that morning, she had felt an
initial ambivalence. But the man's eyes had bored into

her as though he had suspected she might not agree. Now she wondered if she had agreed because she had not wanted him to think she was backing away from him. "Do you think that will happen?" she asked.

"You can never tell," Rolk said. "Will you still go?"

Kate looked at him and tried, unsuccessfully, to smile. "Yes. But I'm sure you won't find anything that will harm Grace," she said, wondering if she truly thought that.

"I'm glad you'll be going," Rolk said, taking her hand.

Kate smiled, without difficulty this time. "So am I."

Eighteen

GRACE MALLORY PACED her office, from the curved turret window to the desk, then back to the window. It was all getting beyond her, this intrusion of police into her work, into her staff. Now Kate would be gone even longer than she had planned, helping them in Chichén Itzá. And there was nothing she could do about it, nothing that would seem reasonable. Chichén Itzá. She remembered the killings there, the blood rituals that had begun almost a year ago. She had remembered them as soon as they told her about the death of the first woman in the park. But it was a coincidence. It had to be.

She hadn't mentioned it to Rolk—had even denied knowledge of it—because she wanted to protect the exhibit from more sensationalism. Even Malcolm hadn't told Rolk anything, and she was certain his reasons had been the same as hers. She clenched her fists. Already there had been too much talk about the publicity the murders would generate, and the probable public attention they would bring to the exhibit. It was insane talk. All it could do was tarnish the intellectual purity of all her work, turn the beauty of the Toltecs and their rituals into a grotesque sideshow. No, she could never allow that to happen. She could not allow it.

She raised a hand to the back of her head. The tension was building; she could feel it there and in her shoulders. She needed some release, some relief from it all. She was working much too hard, struggling to make the show everything it could be, must be.

She shook her head. There had been days she couldn't even remember if she had begun a given task the day before or had only thought she had. It was a block, brought on by overwork. And now there would be more work, more pressure, which would continue until the show opened.

And Malcolm was no help at all, gushing over this investigation, enjoying every minute of it. She had treated him like a son, helped him, nurtured him. She had corrected the errors he had made early on in his dissertation, the wild, undisciplined assumptions he had made about Toltec ritual. Things he had obviously picked up from the natives they had worked with, never realizing how imprecise, how impure their views of the religion were. Such beauty, such precision when viewed properly, within its historical context. God, how she would have loved to live in that era. Just to see the great works of art and architecture as they were created. To see the ritual of the Ball Court enacted live, rather than through hieroglyphic reliefs. She smiled at herself. The dream of every archaeologist, every anthropologist. The dream of every *human being:* to live the past, and to know the future.

She returned to her desk and stared down at the mask of Ek Chuah. There was another mask she had worked with in the past few days. But which one was it? She could not recall. Damn the overwork. Damn the show itself. No, not the show. Never the show.

"Grace?"

She looked up at the sound of Kate's voice. Pushing all other thoughts away, she smiled and beckoned her into the office. "Are you finished with our police friends?" she asked.

"I think so. I hope so. At least for today." Kate slipped into a chair opposite Grace's desk. "I'm exhausted," she said. "It's been a long time since I tried to cover the whole museum in one day. Thank God he didn't want a tour of the public exhibits as well."

"And now, when you finish in Mexico City, you'll be off to Chichén Itzá," Grace said.

Kate studied the older woman, trying to detect any irritation she might be harboring, but her face was expressionless. "I know this is all going to interfere with our work, and I'm sorry. I just didn't see any way to refuse."

"Did you want to refuse?" Grace asked, her voice flat and noncommittal.

"Very much," Kate said, not wanting to lie, but feeling she must. "I don't know what possible good I can do there. I belong here, working on the show with you and Malcolm."

Grace walked around the desk and gently stroked Kate's cheek, allowing her hand to linger on the woman's soft skin. "You look so tired, dear," Grace said, her hand still touching Kate's face, then moving slowly to her shoulder. "That ridiculous incident with the knife has put you under pressure. Perhaps you should just go home and rest. You won't be much good here if you're exhausted."

Kate pressed her cheek against the hand on her shoulder. "You're being too kind to me, Grace. You should be furious about the lack of real work I've done the past few days."

"She only gets furious with me." Malcolm's voice hit the room like harsh laughter and it seemed to match the grin on his face.

Grace's eyes darted toward him, and she quickly withdrew her hand from Kate's shoulder. "It's usually justified, Malcolm," she said, turning abruptly and walking back around her desk.

"Ah, see, Kate? You get tender caresses, and I get harsh words." Malcolm watched Grace's eyes flash momentary anger, but he prattled on, ignoring her. "Now you're off to Chichén Itzá to help solve the great murder mystery." He grinned again.

"Malcolm, please. I'm really far too tired for your humor," Kate said. "If I could have figured out how, I would have volunteered you for the job."

"Ah, Chichén Itzá," Malcolm sighed. "How I do love the Yucatán, the jungles of Quintana Roo." His eyes found Kate again. "But of course you were there last year, weren't you? I almost forgot that brief visit you paid us when we were on the dig. Do you recall all the talk then about the blood rituals beginning again?"

"No," Kate said. "That must have been after I left."

"Was it?" Malcolm said, glancing away. "Perhaps it was. Grace said it was all nonsense anyway, and I'm sure that's true. Odd the police should find it so fascinating. But then, they don't seem to be the brightest group, do they?"

"I wouldn't underestimate them," Kate said. "Especially this lieutenant."

"Oh, really," Malcolm said. "I would have thought you would have been more impressed with Detective Devlin." Out of the corner of his eye Malcolm caught another sharp look from Grace.

"Why do you say that?" Kate asked.

"Well, he's rather good-looking, isn't he?"

"I thought we were discussing intellectual capacities," Kate said.

"So we were." He turned to Grace. "I just popped in to collect the mask." He extended one long slender finger toward the mask of Ek Chuah atop Grace's desk, then walked forward and picked it up.

"Remember what I said about placement, Malcolm. I don't want it lost among lesser pieces." Grace's voice was cold, almost harsh.

"I shall remember." Malcolm started for the door, then threw a quick look at Kate. "And enjoy your trip. Who knows, maybe you'll actually solve the crime."

As the door closed behind him, the wry grin disappeared from Malcolm's face, replaced by one of dark anger, something close to hatred. Then the smile returned and his pace quickened. He moved down the hall, turning abruptly into his small office, swinging the door shut behind him. Ever since Kate had arrived, his position with Grace had steadily deteriorated. He wondered what she saw in her. Oh, she was bright enough, but certainly not exceptional. But then, he knew what Grace saw in her. Old Grace had always had an eye for a pretty woman. And little Kate certainly qualified on that score.

He snorted laughter. He certainly found her attractive. And he had backed off from any attempt to get close to her once Grace let it be known she did not approve. Funny, wasn't it, how all the victims of these murders had been women. He laughed softly again. But then, that was as it should be.

He picked up the mask of Ek Chuah and held it in front of his face.

"I wonder if you'd approve, old boy," he asked aloud. "No, you were the merchant god. This is more up Quetzalcoatl's alley, isn't it? The great plumed serpent. The morning and the evening star. The great discoverer of maize. The god for whom blood shall flow so the universe can be preserved."

Malcolm put down the mask and leaned back in his chair. His features became dark again. She shouldn't be helping the police, he thought. It's not her affair at all.

Kate sat wearily behind her desk, withdrew a notepad, and began listing things she would have to do before her flight left for Mexico. She closed her eyes momentarily, wishing she could put everything off until morning. The flight would not depart until early afternoon, and she tried to convince herself there would be adequate time tomorrow to put everything in order. But there would not be. The morning would be filled with last-minute instructions from Grace, about how certain objects should be crated, specific documentation and provenance that should accompany others, even suggestions as to how individual scholars at the Mexico City museum should be handled, which among them should be given special deference. She smiled weakly at the idea of how international museum politics became an important part of even the most routine job.

No, leaving things until morning simply would not work. She studied the notepad again, then began reviewing the items of clothing she would need, adding those things the unexpected side trip to Chichén Itzá would require.

Though she was not being entirely honest when she had told Grace she would have preferred to refuse Rolk's request, she had to admit her feelings about the trip were mixed. The idea of delving further into the horror that surrounded them was unnerving, even frightening. Still, there was also an underlying sense of adventure about it, a certain voyeuristic thrill of being close to something so far from her own experience that she felt an almost intellectual need to understand it. She sat back in her chair. And there was Rolk, but that was something she did *not* want to think about.

She leaned forward and checked the list again, then picked up her briefcase and made sure her airline tickets were tucked safely inside, and the notes on documentation she would have to take with her. The material that would allow her to get some work done in the evenings. Something that would also keep her away from a detective she found far too attractive, she added to herself.

Kate smiled at her own primness, then pushed herself away from the desk, taking a file of notes with her, and walked out of the office with far more energy than she felt.

Using her own keys, she opened the door to the pre-Colombian laboratory and switched on the lights, flooding the room with a harsh fluorescent glow that seemed to suddenly intensify the various objects that lay scattered about the oversize worktables.

The room was a labyrinth of bookcases, filled with scholarly papers offering detailed analyses of various pre-Columbian antiquities, not only those housed within the museum itself but also major pieces held in institutions throughout the world.

Kate went directly to the card catalog and began jotting down the location of files she would have to review, then on into the stacks, moving slowly from one file to the next, taking carefully detailed notes that would allow her work to be done quickly and professionally in Mexico.

More than an hour passed without notice as Kate concentrated on the files, even digressing occasionally when a particularly interesting fact or observation caught her fancy. She was completely lost in thought, as she often found herself when working, even to the point of not hearing the greetings or comments of peers, who could come and go without notice.

Closing the final file, Kate hesitated a moment, thinking about what she had read, then absentmindedly slid the folder back into its proper place in the stacks. She glanced at her watch, suddenly surprised at the passage of time, yet satisfied the work had been finished, knowing it would make the morning far less hectic.

The sound of movement on the opposite side of the stacks startled her, and she wondered if she had been so lost in her work she had failed to notice the presence of someone else. She remained still and listened, but the movement appeared to have stopped. Now your imagination is working overtime as well, she told herself as she turned and started down the narrow aisle between bookcases. Then it came again, fainter this time, more like a rustle of clothing or the sound given off by a lightbulb about to fail, an almost indistinguishable hum. She stopped to listen, then glanced at her watch again. It would have to be someone else from the department, also working late, or someone from Maintenance. She realized she was breathing more rapidly, and it made her feel foolish.

"Grace, is that you?" she called out. "Malcolm?"

There was no response and she shook her head, annoyed with herself, then started back down the aisle. The sound came again, directly opposite now, coming from the next aisle. She stopped again and tried to look between the folders. Nothing. Only the sound.

A tremor passed through her body and she felt her

bladder constrict with fear. She looked down at her hands, the fingers trembling, the palms moist with perspiration. She glanced furtively down the aisle and thought of running to the door. No, not that door. There was another at the rear of the laboratory, one that led into a small unused office, then out into a rear hallway.

Slowly, making as little noise as possible, Kate carefully removed her shoes and began moving back along the aisle toward the rear of the lab. The sound seemed to grow fainter as she moved away, her stocking feet sliding silently on the polished tile floor. She glanced over her shoulder, the movement altering her balance, causing her arm to brush against the folders to her right, jarring them enough to send several clattering to the floor.

Kate gasped at the sound, then forced herself into a dead run, rounding the corner at the end of the aisle and racing for the rear door.

The door swung back, slamming against a wall, the force propelling it back again behind Kate. She stumbled blindly across the small dark office, her hip striking the edge of a desk as she struggled to reach the glass-paneled door that led to the rear hallway. Pain shot through her hip, numbing her leg, but she ignored it, forcing herself forward, clawing for the handle of the second door until she finally pulled it free.

Out in the rear hall, the sudden light was blinding, and she paused, fighting to catch her breath. Pain shot through her hip again and she slumped back against the wall. The sound of movement came from the small office behind her and she jumped away from the wall, the pain forgotten now as panic again seized her.

To her right the hall led back to the central corridor and the safety of her office and others. But that route would also take her past the main entrance to the laboratory she had just fled. She hesitated for only a second, then turned left and hurried down the narrow hall, heading for the door that led to the skin-storage room where she had taken Rolk earlier that afternoon.

Working her keys with a sureness that belied her trembling hands, Kate pulled the door open and stepped inside. Immediately she was assaulted by the heavy odor of the chemicals used to protect the thousands of cat skins that hung from racks throughout the room.

Choosing not to turn on the lights, Kate felt her way from rack to rack, her hand brushing against the furs until she reached the room's center. There she moved down a narrow aisle between hanging rows of skins, her breath held in check, her stomach constricted in fear, listening for the slightest sound. Her mind demanded to know why she had put herself in this place with no other exit, no way of escape.

The sound of the door opening made her stiffen, and she could feel the perspiration burst from her body. As quietly as she could, Kate slipped in among the skins hanging along the row at her back, the heavy smell of the preservatives assaulting her nostrils. She recalled the warnings given to all museum staff, that long exposure to those chemicals could be a serious medical hazard. If only I live so long, she told herself, fighting to control the trembling that racked her body.

The overhead lights flashed on, flooding the room with surreal light, making Kate gasp and jump back involuntarily.

"Dr. Silverman?" The voice was broken and rasping with age. "Dr. Silverman?"

Kate recognized it at once: the lank, aging, almost cadaverous museum guard she knew only as Melvin.

The voice came again, and she stepped out from between the skins, her voice croaking out the word, "Yes."

Rounding the aisle, she found Melvin standing in the narrow doorway, his hand still on the light switch, his eyes staring at her incredulously. "Is everything okay?" he asked.

Tremors shook Kate's body again, and she told him what had happened, watching his eyes narrow, then widen again, feeling more foolish as each word tumbled from her mouth.

Melvin blinked rapidly, as though trying to grasp what he was being told. "I heard somebody running along the hall," he said. "And when I came around the corner, I saw you coming in here."

"Were you in the lab, the anthropology lab?"

Melvin shook his head. "No, ma'am." His eyes hardened. "But I'll go there now and check for you. You can be sure of that."

Kate reached out and laid one hand on his arm. "If you don't find anyone, please don't tell anybody about this." She drew a deep breath. "I feel so damned foolish. It's these killings, and having the police here every day. I think it's just getting to my nerves."

Melvin laid one hand atop hers. "It ain't foolish. You oughta be careful." He hesitated, then added, "And scared." He smiled a yellow—toothed smile. "And don't you worry. I ain't gonna talk to nobody about this unless I find somebody."

Kate thanked him, then followed him along the narrow rear hall, leaving him when he entered the small office that led back to the lab and continuing on toward the main corridor, her legs still shaky beneath her, her contradicting mind telling her with growing certainty that she had acted like some idiotic schoolgirl.

Rounding the corner into the main corridor, Kate nearly stumbled headlong into Grace Mallory.

The older woman's eyes widened in surprise, then narrowed abruptly. "Why are you still here?" She shook her head. "I thought I told you to go home and rest."

Kate fought to control her voice, not wanting to show any of the fear she had just endured. "I had to get some materials together for Mexico," she said. "Really, I'm fine, Grace."

Grace shook her head again. "You have to learn that some work can be left for the next day." She softened the words with a small smile.

"I've never seen my mentor do that herself," Kate said, returning the smile.

Grace huffed, feigning displeasure. "It's probably

just as well," she said. "Father LoPato stopped by a little while ago. He wanted to know if you could take some photographs for him while you're at the museum in Mexico City. I sent him down to your office. You see, I didn't really believe you'd listen to me about going home to rest. Did you see him?"

"No," Kate said, her legs weakening again. "I was in the lab. Do you think he went there?"

"Why should he? I sent him to your office."

Movement further down the hall caught Kate's eye, and she looked past Grace and saw the tall, gaunt figure of the priest coming toward her.

"Here he comes now," Kate said.

As she spoke, the door to the anthropology lab opened and Melvin emerged. He stared down the hall at Kate and shook his head as inconspicuously as possible. No one had been there.

Kate drew a deep breath and began to follow Grace toward the priest. It was all just foolishness, she told herself, vowing not to mention it to anyone.

Nineteen

THE BAR WAS located on Columbus Avenue and West Eighty-fifth Street, two blocks south of Rolk's home. It was an aging neighborhood establishment, one of the few that had survived the gentrification of Manhattan's West Side, eschewing the now popular glass-enclosed patios and hanging ferns, keeping instead its dark, grimy walls covered with signed photos of long-forgotten baseball players and boxers.

It was only eleven P.M. as Rolk slid onto a stool just inside the front door, and the bar was still crowded with the regulars who filled it each night, older men and women who lived in the nearby tenements that had not yet fallen victim to the neighborhood's endless upgrading.

An overweight, homely young woman approached him from behind the bar, croaking out a greeting in a broad Bronx-Irish accent. "Hey, Lieutenant. Ain't seen you in a while. Whadaya drinkin'?"

"Jack Daniel's, Patty. Neat."

He watched the young woman slosh a more-than-ample amount of liquor into a glass and slide it toward him as she snatched up the five-dollar bill he had laid on the bar. It was a long-standing policy, cash on the bar before anything was poured, and Rolk suspected it was due to the inability of the bartenders—all relatives of the owner—to handle the arithmetic necessary to keep a running tab.

Patty leaned against the bar, propped up by fleshy pink forearms. "So whatcha been workin' on, Lieutenant? You doin' that headless-woman thing?"

"Afraid so, Patty."

"Jeez, ain't he a crazy bastard, whoever he is? Cuttin' people's heads off. We oughta catch that weirdo an' hang 'im up by his you-know-what." The young woman raised her chin and stared at the oversized briefcase Rolk had placed on an empty stool next to him. "Whatcha got in there? Evidence of the murders?"

"Just stuff I have to read, Patty."

"Gawd, you gotta read a lot, don'tcha? You could fit halfa the Bronx in that thing."

Rolk put a protective hand on the briefcase; the other hand rose to his forehead, fingers massaging lightly.

"You got another one of those headaches?" Patty asked.

"Just starting," Rolk said.

The young woman leaned closer, lowering her voice. "I got some aspirin out back. I ain't supposed to, but I can get you some if you want."

"It's all right," Rolk said, tapping his glass with one finger. "This will take care of it."

A loud, rasping voice from the other end of the bar called Patty's name. Her head snapped toward the sound. "Keep your pants on, I'll be there in a minute." She rolled her eyes at Rolk. "Jeez, these guys," she said. "Their glasses get empty an' they start to get palpitations."

Rolk watched the young woman move awkwardly down the length of the bar, and felt relieved to be alone. He had come to the bar at least once a week for years now, never staying for more than two drinks, but always returning. He couldn't really explain why. The place wasn't either appealing or particularly comfortable.

Perhaps just to have a drink. He kept no liquor at home, afraid he might sit and drink whatever was there after a bad night. It was something he had decided when his daughter was born. He had known too many cops who had turned to liquor to escape the horrors of a bad case, and he had been determined that his daughter would not be forced to live with a drunk.

His daughter. Few days passed that he didn't think of her. His wife, the memory of her, had receded into bitter, vague thoughts that only occasionally assaulted him. But thoughts of his daughter were always there—wondering what she was like now, what kind of young woman she had grown into. Wondering too if she ever asked about him, and if she did, what she was told.

A visual image of the murdered women filled his mind. Thank God they were older. Over the years he had been forced to handle cases involving young girls, some the same age as his daughter. Those cases had tortured him, filled him with fear and rage. Just knowing he could not protect her, tell her how to best protect herself.

Push it away. Thinking about it accomplishes nothing, solves nothing. He rubbed his fingers against his forehead again. The headache would be bad tonight. It would blind him with pain until he could lose himself in sleep. Unconsciousness was the only thing that helped, a sleep that always came without dreams. Waking in the morning with the pain gone, he would recall nothing of the unconscious hours of sleep that had preceded it. Like awakening from death.

Rolk was looking toward the rear of the bar when the man slid onto the stool next to him, but he sensed the movement and turned to look into the smiling face of Tim Matthews.

"Shit," Rolk said, staring into the round, boyish face with a wavy lock of red hair dangling across its forehead.

"I usually get a better greeting," Matthews said. The man's grin carried to his blue eyes. He was sitting hunched on the stool, and his protruding belly hung well over his belt, far too much so, Rolk thought, for a guy in his early thirties.

Matthews was a reporter for one of the city's tabloids, a man Rolk actually liked and trusted, but someone he definitely didn't want to see tonight.

"You just happened to stop in here for a drink, I suppose," Rolk said, his voice a half-growl.

"Actually I remembered it was a place where you stopped occasionally, so since you won't answer your phone calls, I thought I'd give it a try. Before I rang your doorbell, that is."

"I shoot reporters who ring my doorbell," Rolk snapped.

"I know. But it takes you so long to load your gun they always have time to run."

Rolk's penchant for leaving his weapon unloaded was known even to the press, and had once been mentioned in a story—something that had drawn a stern warning from the police commissioner himself.

"It's loaded today. So don't do anything to irritate me."

"Tell me about these murders," Matthews said.

"You're irritating me."

"Come on, Rolk, this is too big to sit on. You know as well as I do it'll just cause a lot of wild-ass speculation if somebody doesn't open up."

"That's a shitty excuse for shabby journalism." Rolk lifted his drink and sipped it, watching Matthews' reaction in the mirror behind the bar. The man's face seemed to groan.

"At least tell me about the heads. Tell me if they've been found yet."

"No heads." Rolk stared at him in the mirror, his face stern. "But don't quote me, not even on that. Understood?"

Matthews raised his hands in surrender, then motioned to the bartender, indicating he would have what Rolk was drinking, along with another for the lieutenant.

"You gonna ply me with liquor now?" Rolk asked.

"If I thought it would work, I would. But you Polacks can hold too much." Matthews sipped his drink, then glanced at Rolk's briefcase. It was large and old-fashioned, the type that opened at the top like a great yawning mouth.

"I don't suppose you'd let me look through your briefcase," Matthews said. "Although anything I found there probably would have mold on it. Where'd you resurrect *that* thing from?"

Rolk ignored both remarks. His head was throbbing again and he sipped his drink, hoping it would dull the pain.

"Look," Matthews began again. "If I tell you what I'm hearing, would you at least confirm or deny it?"

"Probably not. But you can try me."

"Great. Then you find out what I'm hearing, and you give me nothing in return."

"It's my job to find things out."

"Mine too."

"Not from me it isn't."

"You're a pain in the ass, Rolk. You always have been and you always will be."

"It's a cross I'll have to bear."

Matthews laughed, then raised his middle finger to Rolk's image in the mirror. Rolk ignored that too.

"All right," Matthews said, a touch of surrender in his voice. "I hear—and I'm not going to tell you where I got this from either—that there seems to be some kind of ritual involved." Matthews stopped, waiting for some reply. When none came, he sipped his drink again. "The other thing we know is that it's all tied to an exhibit being prepared at the Met."

Rolk remained silent, content with swirling the liquor in his glass.

"No comment on either one?" Matthews asked. "Off the record, naturally."

"Sounds like Hollywood to me."

Rolk looked at the mirror again, his expression blank. "Look, Tim, there are four or five guys in the media I trust enough to talk to, and you're one of them. But not this time. This time, if you get it, you get it yourself. And as far as I'm concerned, I hope we've got this creep locked up three days before you do."

He held Matthews' eyes in the mirror. "And if that doesn't tell you how worried I am about this, you're dumber than I think you are."

"And if I use this stuff I've heard?"

"Don't." Rolk continued to hold his eyes. "All you'll do is give some other sick bastard out there some ideas he hadn't thought of yet."

"Then give me something, for Chrissake."

Rolk stared down into his drink. He wasn't surprised about the rumors; they were bound to come, either from cops at the scene who had heard too much, or from morgue attendants, who always seemed to hear everything, no matter how carefully everyone tried to keep the lid on. But if something was going to be printed, it would be better if it was something *he* decided to plant.

Rolk stared into the mirror again. "All right, I'll give you something, but only if you use one of your ridiculous 'well-placed-source' labels or some equivalent bullshit."

"How about a source close to the commissioner?" Matthews grinned as he said the words, well aware of Rolk's lack of friends among the top brass.

"I haven't even talked to the man in more than six months."

"That's close enough for me."

Rolk smiled, even though he didn't want to. "Use 'someone high up in the investigation.' "

Matthews raised his eyebrows. "You want that, you've got it. So give."

Rolk sat quietly for a moment, allowing the right words to form in his mind. He tapped his fingers against the bar. "What we're dealing with," he began, "is a psychopath who has a deep hatred of women—but a person who believes that he has a mission to fulfill. This person believes he or she has a *right* to do these things—may even have been 'chosen' to do them, and that the power guiding these acts will never allow him or her to be caught. But it's this warped thinking that has already led the killer to make several very serious mistakes. And it's those mistakes that are bringing us very close to an arrest." Rolk waited as Matthews scribbled the final words. "That do it for you, hotshot?"

The reporter stared at him, a crooked smile on his lips. "You're goading him?" Matthews tapped his pen against his open notebook. "I don't remember which case it was, but you did that several years back, and you ended up making the killer come after you instead of going for another victim. Is that what you're trying now, Rolk?"

"You're talking Hollywood again." Rolk stared at him with hard eyes. "You stick with what I gave you—and only what I gave you—and you'll get more later. If not, you'll get zip, just like everybody else."

Matthews nodded slowly, then shrugged. "I can play ball that way. But it doesn't mean I won't *look* for anything else. Just so you know."

"You look where you want. Just remember to be careful when you do it. You're dealing with a sick mother here, and there's no way of knowing what nerve you're going to touch if you go poking around the wrong place. Touch a bad one, and you just might wake up some morning and find you own head missing."

"Or yours," Matthews said. "Especially after this gets printed."

"It's what I get paid for," Rolk said. "Not you."

Rolk raised his glass and downed the rest of his drink, then climbed down from the stool, and, briefcase in hand, pushed through the heavy front door. Outside, the air was cold and biting. Snow had been predicted but none had come. He drew a deep breath, then started north, the briefcase a deadweight in his right hand. It held reports of other detectives, and photos of the murder scenes. And an old art-history book his wife had left behind, a book he was perusing, trying to remember things long forgotten. It also held the long, serrated, green-bladed knife he had taken from the priest. They had found two sharp obsidian knives, the first murder weapon and this one. But they still hadn't found the one that had killed Alexsandra Ross. Somewhere there was another knife, and it too was sharp. And there was also a seven-hundred-year-old ax that had been used on both women, and, if Rolk was right, would undoubtedly be used again.

Unless you find him fast. Find him and stop him.

There it was again, he thought as he turned into his street. When he thought about the killer, it was always *him* in his mind, even though he kept telling his men to keep themselves open to it being a woman. And why not? Why not Grace Mallory or Kate Silverman? It was certainly just as possible as Malcolm Sousi or Father LoPato. Or even the Mayan refugees, or someone they hadn't even found yet. No. By now another suspect would have surfaced. Someone with the opportunity, with access to the weapons. So far the only person eliminated was George Wilcox. As co-curator of the Toltec show, Wilcox had had the same opportunities as the others. But he had been away the evening of the first murder, attending a lecture in Philadelphia.

The priest. Rolk kept coming back to the priest, and that was the worst of all possible solutions, the one that would be the most difficult for anyone to accept. Rolk turned into his gate and moved wearily to the front door. Or maybe it wouldn't be, he thought. Maybe priests went just as mad as truck drivers, or schoolteachers, or even cops.

He closed the door behind him and made his way down the narrow hall to the large sitting room. He dropped his coat on a chair, the briefcase on a table next to it. All he wanted now was to sleep till morning, when the damned headache would be gone.

The cry for blood goes on. The need for sacrifice continues. But the proper victim must be found or the gods will not be pleased. You were too worried at first about finding offerings with blond hair, only because the final offering will be blond. But it only matters that they be of a certain class, a certain worthiness. Like Alexsandra. Someone who will not offend the ritual.

*Oh, your heart is beating so fast. Just pounding in
your chest. You have to rest. You have to be patient.
And you must be careful. If the gods are to be satisfied,
the ritual must be completed. But it will be. Who would
suspect you as the substitute of the great god Quetzalcoatl?
Who would think you capable of such a thing?*

*No. They might look. They might even question. But
in the end, who would believe them? And you can lead
them in any direction you want now. A finger pointing
subtly in another direction. And they'll never find the
weapons, or the heads. Not for years and years and
years.*

*It's a gift of the gods. Something you've waited for
for so many years. Years of waiting to repay the injus-
tice. Years of unwilling denial. Years of waiting to
prove you did not deserve what was taken from you. A
chance to prove . . . To prove what?*

*Your mind is so confused now. What is it you can't
remember? The reason for the killings. The need. It's
there. It has to be. But you can't remember what it is.
Rest. Relax. Breathe deeply now. It will come back to
you, it always comes back to you. Except when you're
that other person. That fool whose body you live in
each day.*

*But there has to be a reason. Everything has a rea-
son; it's something you've known all your life. There
are always facts that have to be proved, beliefs that
have to be upheld. There has to be an order to things,
and people who would destroy that order must be destroyed themselves. They are the criminals, the ones
who take from others, who take things that others have
a right to have. Yes, that's it. That's what you have to
prove. That you had a right, and that it was taken from
you unfairly. But they won't admit that. They'll even
steal your beliefs from you, say you aren't entitled to
them.*

*But they can't. Not if the sacrifices continue. Where
is the knife, where is it? There. There it is, close to you.
So green and so beautiful and so sharp. And the mask*

next to it. The simple piece of stone that elevates you beyond what you are.

But not now. Not today. There must be a period of rest, a period of waiting for the right person. It will confuse them if you wait. All the players must be in place when the next sacrifice is made. It has to be that way. Any other way would be a mistake. And mistakes cannot be made. Not now. Not ever again.

Twenty

A MANILA ENVELOPE with a Princeton, New Jersey, postmark was waiting on Rolk's desk when he arrived at his office. He slid into his chair and took it in his hands, holding it for several minutes, unwilling to open it, unwilling to face yet one more of many disappointments. Finally he tore it open and withdrew a thin sheaf of papers. The first was a note from his friend in the Princeton Police Department, and he read it quickly, then pushed it aside and stared intently at the documents beneath.

A Jennifer Morgan had taken the Scholastic Aptitude Test. Jennifer was his daughter's name. Morgan, his wife's maiden name. He scanned the personal-information sheet. It listed a Los Angeles address and a date of birth that was the same month but a different day from his daughter's. Pain gripped his stomach, then eased. It could easily be a typographical error, he told himself. Or something his wife had devised to keep him from locating Jenny.

He sat back in his chair, the papers dropping to his lap, and wondered if he had ever told his wife how the National Crime Computer worked—how accurate dates of birth were so essential to it in locating someone sought by the police. The radicals of the sixties had managed to hide so successfully because they discovered that simply by pretending false birthdates—and through those, new social-security cards and passports—they would fool the crime computer.

Still, Morgan was such a common name, as was Jennifer. He looked quickly through the pages. There was no photograph, of course. Federal regulations prohibited it as a means of thwarting racial discrimination. But he would contact the LAPD, would ask them to investigate quietly.

He raised the papers again, his hands trembling slightly. If it turned out to be nothing, it would only be one more false lead, one more to add to the list of many over the last fifteen years. But maybe, just maybe . . .

Inspector James Dunne pushed his way into Rolk's office like a fast-moving thundercloud, his face only lightly masked against the rage that filled his eyes. There was a folded newspaper in his hand. As he stopped in front of Rolk's desk he opened it to the offending page.

"Have you seen this?" he barked. His eyes widened as Rolk nodded. "Well, I don't like it, and I want it stopped before it gets worse. You have any idea who's behind this shit?"

"Could be anybody," Rolk said, his face blank.

"Dammit, it says right here it's somebody high up in the investigation." Dunne gripped the paper so tightly it began to crumple in his hand.

"You know how newspapers use those labels. As far as I'm concerned, it could mean some clerk on one of the upper floors at headquarters. Why don't you call Matthews and ask him?" Rolk suggested.

"I did," Dunne snapped. "The fat prick claimed he couldn't tell me." Dunne stared down at Rolk. "You think it was that shrink? I never trusted those fucking bastards."

"I doubt it," Rolk said. "He doesn't seem the type."

"Well, goddammit, find out. The commissioner called me at home at seven this morning, and that was because the mayor had just called him." Dunne began pacing in front of Rolk's desk. "They don't like people saying we've got a lunatic on the loose. And they don't like reading that we're close to nailing the killer, when they fucking well know we're not."

Rolk leaned back in his chair, his face calm, his

voice soothing. "Jim, it's no secret we've got a lunatic on our hands. People already know that. The newspapers have had a field day! Christ, somebody's running around collecting heads." He raised a hand, stopping Dunne's objection. "And the story just might help us. It might force the killer to lose his cool and make a mistake. Or it just might shake him up enough to lie low for a while. And either way, that's good for us."

Dunne placed both hands on Rolk's desk and leaned forward, a grim smile spread across his face. "Well, I've got something that's not good for us. There's a monsignor from the archdiocese sitting in your outer office. He was waiting for me when I got to work this morning. And guess who I'm turning him over to?"

"Be happy to see him," Rolk said. "And I'll send him away smiling. I promise."

"You damn well better, because he sure as hell isn't smiling now." Dunne spun on his heel and started for the door.

"Don't you want to stay and listen?" Rolk asked.

Dunne turned, the unfriendly smile back on his lips. "No, Stan, I don't. It's your pile of shit, and if you don't clean it up, you're the one who's gonna take the fall. I don't intend to be within a mile of this."

Rolk leaned forward as Dunne left the office. The smile on his lips gradually grew wider. "That's what I like," he said to himself. "A true leader of men."

Seconds later, Paul Devlin entered the office in response to Rolk's summons.

"You still have that voice-activated tape recorder?" Rolk asked.

"Yeah, it's in my desk."

"Well, set it up, stick it in your pocket, and then bring that priest in here."

Monsignor John Arpie was short and bald and plump, with a red face that would normally note a happy man, but as he introduced himself to Rolk, he appeared anything but happy.

Seated in a chair opposite Rolk, with Devlin next to him, Arpie explained that he worked in the public-relations office at the archdiocese, and, as such, had come to "express the rather strong concerns of the archbishop."

"I'm sorry to hear the archbishop is concerned," Rolk said. "I'd certainly like to help in any way I can."

"What concerns us is you," Arpie said. "And the harassing tactics you seem to be using against Father LoPato and some rather unfortunate people who have sought the help of the church."

"I really don't feel anyone has been harassed," Rolk said. "We're simply conducting a murder investigation, and talking to people when and where we find it necessary."

"Really?" Arpie said, leaning back in his chair. "You don't feel it's harassment to bring a priest to the morgue at three in the morning, or to threaten poor unfortunates like Juan Domingo and Roberto Caliento with deportation if they don't reveal the names of other unfortunates?"

Rolk leaned back in his chair, mimicking the priest. His voice remained soft, almost gentle. "Father LoPato was brought there only after he refused to come to my office at *nine* in the morning. As far as Domingo and Caliento are concerned, they *are* illegal aliens, they *are* suspects in two murders, and I was *forced* to question them about other illegal aliens, who might also be suspects, because Father LoPato *refused* to give me that information." Rolk leaned forward and smiled. "As far as threats about deportation, I probably violated my sworn duty by *not* turning them over to Immigration." The priest began to speak, but Rolk raised a hand, stopping him. "However, if you can suggest some alternative, I'm perfectly willing to listen."

Monsignor Arpie smiled for the first time. It was a friendly smile, with only a hint of falseness, a small note of satisfaction that he might be about to get his way. "First of all, Lieutenant, let me assure you that I've spoken with these people, and I'm convinced, in my own mind, that none of them could have been involved. Juan Domingo and Roberto Caliento are simple men who are so overwhelmed by their present surroundings, and so easily frightened, that it would be virtually impossible for them to commit such acts. Certainly not here in New York. Father LoPato . . ." Here Arpie raised his hands and let them fall back in his lap in a gesture of exasperation. "I'm afraid he, like so many of our clergy today, is an idealist who either cannot or will not grasp the Church's need for a favorable public image."

Rolk straightened in his chair, a quizzical look on his face. "You make it sound as though the archdiocese isn't thrilled with the refugee movement."

The monsignor opened his palms, stared at them, then pressed them together again. "That would not be a completely inaccurate assumption."

Rolk smiled at the choice of words. They were the indirect, meaningless words of a politician or bureaucrat, the type of person who could walk across a chocolate cake and not leave footprints.

Arpie's voice grew harder, more serious. "We find there are two types of clergy involved in the refugee movement: idealists who feel they can change the world by bringing a handful of uneducated peasants to a place that truly overwhelms them, and those who see their congregations rapidly diminishing and see this as a quick fix to that problem. What each fails to recognize is that, not only are the subjects of their interest badly served, but they also put an enormous strain on institutions that were never designed to serve them."

"Such as?" Rolk asked.

"Such as charitable organizations within the Church." Arpie hesitated, then smiled again. "It's not that we would not *like* to help. We simply aren't equipped for it, and because of that we feel certain members of the clergy should temper their idealism, and find other, more traditional ways of replenishing the size of their congregations."

Rolk steepled his fingers in front of his face and stared through them. "Then if Father LoPato has been such a thorn in your side, why haven't you just shipped him off somewhere else?"

Arpie tilted his head to one side. "It was discussed. But now, with your investigation, it might appear we were trying to shield him from an investigation. And that is not true. Nor do we want the impression to get about that we strongly oppose his movement."

Rolk nodded, more to himself than to Arpie. "I still don't see what you want from us."

"Two things, Lieutenant. And they are both purely cosmetic. First, if either of these Mayan men becomes tied to these crimes, either as suspects, or witnesses, or whatever, that no mention be made to the press of their connection to Father LoPato's refugee efforts. This would only tie them—and unfairly so—to the archdiocese."

"And second?" Rolk asked, intrigued now.

Arpie pursed his lips, then shook his head slowly, sadly. "If Father LoPato turns out to be even *indirectly* involved with the person who committed these crimes, we would appreciate being informed of that fact before the press learns of it. This would allow us to take"—he waved his hands in a small circle—"independent action that would separate the archdiocese from any scandal."

Rolk stared at the plump, red-faced monsignor for several moments. "As long as my superiors don't object, I don't *think* that should prove to be a problem."

"Then I think we agree on the matter, and I wouldn't anticipate any further difficulties," Arpie said.

He stood, preparing to leave.

"Tell me, Monsignor," Rolk said, halting him. "Did you ever hear anything about a breakdown Father LoPato might have suffered while working in the Yucatán?"

Arpie's face tightened noticeably. "I couldn't say that I had," he said, falling back on bureaucratic language. "But then, medical records, even for the clergy, are kept confidential. We would continue to keep them that way."

As soon as the monsignor left, Devlin removed the small voice-activated tape recorder from his breast pocket and dropped the mini-cassette on Rolk's desk. "I'm not sure if that's going to do us any good or not," he said, nodding toward the cassette.

Rolk picked it up and dropped it in a desk drawer. "We may have to go back to him for something one of these days. And I'm sure he wouldn't want the things he said here to fall into the wrong hands."

Devlin shook his head and smiled at Rolk's deviousness. "You think maybe they're a little concerned these Mayans and their priest might be involved in all this?"

"Could be," Rolk said. "You just never know."

Juan Domingo and Roberto Caliento were more than a little awed by Father LoPato's office in St. Helena's rectory. They had known the priest when he had worked in their battered, dusty village of Chetulak, but the church had been battered as well, and there had been no special office, no soft chairs, or desk, or pictures of saints on the walls. Seated behind his desk now, even the priest seemed different. He seemed to have the power of men they had only heard about— men who sat in the great buildings of Mexico City and decided how life would be for others.

This was not to say that in the village the priest had not been a man of importance. Everyone knew that priests spoke directly to God. So people understood that he was a man who must be listened to, a man who could judge you in God's name, who could send you to everlasting suffering or everlasting happiness when the time came to leave this life. And so he was greatly respected.

He had also brought them to this strange new country, a place where everyone—even the poorest of people—had the great miracles they had only heard about and seen from a distance, and envied. The bathrooms and the running water; the houses with light that came from small glass balls; the stores filled with food and clothing and furniture. And the automobiles and the television sets. And the children who seemed to have everything a child could ever want. And now the priest was warning them that all that might be lost.

Father LoPato sat behind his desk studying the effect of his words on the two men. Domingo, as always, just seemed small and frightened. Caliento, also small, but broader, with a hard, inscrutable face, seemed frightened now too, but only in his dark eyes.

LoPato loved these men, as he had loved all the people of the village, as he had loved their history and their heritage from the moment he had seen his first picture of the great cities of the past. But now he was failing them, just as he had failed the people of Chetulak. They had listened to him, had done as he asked. And now everything he had struggled to achieve was being threatened. And perhaps, he thought, there was no way to survive that threat. Still, he knew he must try.

"We are in danger," the priest said softly. "And the danger comes from the police. I must move you to new places, to new jobs, to avoid that danger. Do you understand what I am saying?"

Caliento sat stonelike, then turned his gaze on Domingo. His eyes were harder now, but the fear still hid beneath the stare.

"It is his fault," Caliento said of Domingo. "He spoke to the police. He told them about me and my family. I do not know what else he might have told them."

They spoke in Mayan, and the soft, musical quality of the language made the words seem more gentle than they were.

Domingo stared at the floor, ashamed. "These men, they gave me no choice. They said my wife and children would be sent away." He looked up at the priest, his eyes pleading. "They are powerful men," he said. "And I am a man with no power. I only have the strength that you give me, Father." He stumbled over the final word, then caught hold of himself. "But I told them nothing else, only what was necessary to save my family. I swear this to you."

The priest leaned forward, his eyes soft with understanding. "I believe you, Juan, and I know Roberto will believe you as well." He shifted his gaze to Caliento, and stared until Roberto lowered his eyes and nodded. "But just as you have in the past," he said, looking at each man in turn, "you must do exactly as I tell you. And one of you must make a trip for me."

Twenty-one

THE SMALL TWIN-ENGINE plane banked over the ruins of the ancient city, then turned and dropped abruptly to the cracked, weed-ridden strip of runway that had been laid out between wide rows of planted corn.

"This is it?" Rolk asked as the plane raced past patches of wild vegetation that seemed to grow from the battered concrete.

"We're lucky today," Kate said. "The last time I was here we circled for twenty minutes, waiting for a herd of goats to move off the runway."

"They were probably eating the weeds," Rolk said. He turned to Kate and again admired the thin sundress that revealed a beautiful figure and soft, creamy skin. When they met at the airport in Mérida, he noticed the change in her appearance. The contrast to her usual well-tailored business suits was both surprising and pleasing.

The plane pulled up to a small wooden building, little more than a shack. An elderly man stood in the doorway, while two others sat on a narrow bench along one wall.

"The terminal?" Rolk asked.

"Afraid so."

"Not exactly La Guardia, is it?"

"Later you'll be thankful it isn't." She smiled as Rolk raised his eyebrows, questioning her. "The ruins haven't been overwhelmed by tourism," she explained. "No graffiti on the walls. No empty Coke cans on the floors of the temple."

The pilot began unloading luggage, and Kate and

Rolk joined the dozen other passengers who were sorting out their bags. The three old men joined the passengers to hand out makeshift claim tickets for luggage to be delivered to nearby hotels. Kate negotiated quickly with one of the men, told him to take their bags to the Mayaland Lodge on the outskirts of the ruins, and watched as Rolk gave him the small number of *pesos* they had agreed upon.

"Will the bags ever get there?" Rolk asked as they moved away from the airstrip.

"Oh, yes," Kate said. "Sometime before dinner they'll arrive. Probably just before."

"But it's only two o'clock," Rolk said.

"It's also Mexico."

Since they could walk through the ruins to reach the hotel, Kate offered an impromptu tour of the ancient city, and Rolk was drawn along in the wake of her enthusiasm.

They went first to the Cenote Sagrado, or Sacred Well, which sat in the middle of dense jungle foliage at the end of a three-hundred-yard *saché*, or sacred road. Like a gaping wound in the heart of the rain forest, the well, Kate explained, was one-hundred-eighty feet in diameter and dropped seventy-two feet to the still surface of green-tinted water. The Mayans believed the well to be bottomless, but it actually went down another sixty-seven feet.

Standing at the edge of the sheer rock wall, Kate waved one hand, taking it all in. "This was one of the primary places of sacrifice," she said. "Even before the Toltecs overran the old city and raised the newer, major one. At first, it was believed that it was a place where virgins were sacrificed to the gods. But in 1968 an underwater archaeological dig was completed and the skeletons they found showed that most of the victims were children under twelve, of both sexes, and mature women who were either sick or deformed.

Kate turned to Rolk, her eyes still distant. "The ones who were sacrificed would be adorned with jewels and gold and copper, and then thrown into the well." She pointed down at the walls, sheer and smooth. "There was nothing they could hold on to, even if they could rid themselves of their ornaments, and so they drowned." She stared into the green water. "The spectacle must have been overwhelming, with hundreds, perhaps thousands, of believers standing around the edge of the well, dressed in ritual robes, chanting prayers to the god for whom the sacrifice was intended."

"Hmm, I imagine it was quite a sight," Rolk said. He raised one hand, pointing at the water, "for everyone except the person down there."

Kate turned back to him. "Yes," she said, then seemed to come back to herself. "Of course, if they somehow managed to stay alive until the next morning, a rope was lowered and they were brought up to spend the rest of their lives as living gods themselves."

"Knowing how to tread water would have been a definite plus," Rolk said.

Kate laughed. "Or being favored by the gods."

She led him back along the *saché* and into a broad expanse of manicured lawns. There, rising from its center, was the massive grayish bulk of El Castillo, the great sacrificial pyramid known as the Castle.

"This was the main edifice of the new city of Chichén Itzá," she explained. "The Spanish conquistadors renamed it the Castle because they used it as a fortress. Originally it was the great temple of Kukulcan, or Quetzalcoatl, as he's more commonly known." She pointed up. "These four massive staircases, each facing a point on the compass, have 91 steps each, which adds up to a total of 364–365 when the top platform is counted—or the number of days in the year. There are also fifty-two panels on the sides, corresponding to the number of years in the Mayan calendric cycle, and eighteen terraces on each side, representing the eighteen-month religious year."

"Was this used for sacrifices too?" Rolk asked.

Kate looked away, staring up at the wide steps. "I'm afraid almost everything you'll see here was." She reached out and took Rolk's arm and led him to a door. They entered the inner temple, in the center of which stood a bright red jaguar throne encrusted with jade disks for the spots and eyes.

"Incredible!" Rolk said, dazzled by the beauty of it.

"It's only part," Kate said, taking his arm again and leading him to an adjoining anteroom, which held a reclining Chac Mool monolith.

Pointing to the reclining statue of the god, Kate explained it was a vital prop in all rituals. "Those to be sacrificed were brought here and disemboweled," she said. "Then their still-steaming, beating hearts, freshly torn from live bodies, were thrown into the lap of the Chac Mool by the priests, as an offering to Quetzalcoatl."

"Jesus," Rolk said, looking around the room, the hair on the back of his neck rising slightly, almost as though he could feel the agony that had filled the room. "I thought beheading was the big thing," he said.

"It was," Kate said. "But human hearts were of next importance."

"Thank God, our killer hasn't taken that part up." He paused. "At least not yet."

"He would have to have a Chac Mool," Kate said. "And, to my knowledge, there aren't any privately available."

They exited the temple, and Kate touched his arm to stop him. Rolk noticed the serious, almost urgent look on her fact.

"I don't want you to get the wrong impression," she began. "Though the Mayans—especially the Toltecs—were in many ways a brutal people, they were also brilliant and very advanced for their time." She turned and pointed to the staircase behind them. "During the spring and fall equinoxes—on March 22 and September 22—a solar phenomenon creates a sunlit serpent on the steps of the northwest side of the pyramid. A design they planned. Quetzalcoatl, the plumed serpent. Their god." She paused, as if forcing herself on. "And the sacrifices were part of their religion too.

They were done out of love of their god, and love of their fellowman, especially the one so sacrificed."

"Some people might find that hard to accept," Rolk said.

"That's only if they thought in terms of what's happened in New York now. What happened here then is no different from what happened in every part of the world at some time in history."

Rolk shook his head. "You're right. I'll try to think of it that way." He smiled at her. "Is there more?"

"Yes," she said. "Next we'll go to the Ball Court."

"Where they played a game with human heads? Then sacrificed the losing team?"

"I'm afraid so. But I want you to see the reliefs on the walls. They're all in the shape of human skulls. Hundreds and hundreds of them."

Rolk let out a long breath. "Lady, you keep this up and I'm not going to sleep very well tonight."

She smiled at him, and her eyes became warm and friendly and understanding. "Yes, you will. You'll have to. We have a long trip into the jungle tomorrow. And the best way is on horseback."

When they left the Ball Court, they went on to the Court of a Thousand Columns, the Temple of the Warriors, El Mercado, and finally into old Chichén, where the Nunnery and Caracol stood.

Kate stopped before the huge building, with its single stairway leading to a large platform that held a domed round tower. "This is my favorite of all the ruins," she explained. "It's the Caracol, the observatory. It was built somewhere between A.D. 900 and 1200, and it has fixed observation points for astronomical sitings."

"No sacrifices here?" Rolk asked.

She shook her head. "Not one, not ever. They came here to observe the moon and the sun, and, without instruments, were able to predict eclipses." She turned back to him. "They developed a calendar that was only two-thousandths of a day off. Their calendar, in fact, lost only two hours every 481 years. Ours, the

Gregorian calendar, loses twenty-four hours every four years." Her eyes became urgent again. "It's what I was trying to explain. They were brilliant and creative people in many ways, even more so than we are, and you have to view everything they did in that light."

Rolk placed a hand on her shoulder, feeling the warmth of the sun on her skin. "I know," he said. "But it would be easier without the beheadings, without the need for all the brutality."

Kate'e eyes hardened. "Mankind *is* brutal. And not only in his ancient past. The gas chambers and ovens of Germany, the thousands who were tortured and killed in Argentina, the camps in the Soviet Union. They aren't the acts of ancient civilizations. For the Mayans, at least it was an act of religious belief. An act of love. What is it for *our* murderers?"

The open thatched-roofed dining room at the Mayaland Lodge overlooked the ancient ruins, seen now only as shadows against the winter sky. Kate and Rolk sat at a small candlelit table, cups of *café con leche* before them. They had just feasted on delicacies of the Yucatán, starting with sweet Moro crab and cazón, baby shark, and finishing with *conchinita pibil*, a suckling pig rubbed with fragrant *achiote*, the juice of sour Seville oranges, garlic, and black pepper, then wrapped in banana leaves and slowly baked.

"I feel as though I'll burst through my dress," Kate said. "But that always happens to me in the Yucatán. I can never say no to their food."

"It's different from the Mexican food I've had in New York," Rolk said. "*Carne asada* and *mole poblano* are about as far as I've gone. This is much more exotic."

Kate made a deep humming sound in her throat. "It's more fragrant than spicy," she said. "And there's something terribly sensual about it."

Rolk studied her face, soft and warm in the candlelight, and decided the woman did not require food to be surrounded in an aura of sensuality.

"When is your local police contact joining us?" Kate asked.

Rolk glanced at his watch. "Anytime now. I invited him for dinner, but he had some family gathering he had to attend. He said he'd join us for an after-dinner drink."

"Would you rather I left you alone? I mean, if you're going to discuss things about the murders in New York, there might be things I shouldn't hear."

"It won't be a problem," Rolk said. "I won't be telling him any more about our case than I have to. Essentially, I want to find out what happened here. When the killings started, and how they were done."

"You want to see if there are any similarities?"

"That's right. And that's why I'd like you to hear what our Mexican friend has to say. There might be something about some ritual that I could miss completely. But I don't think you would."

"And what else do you hope to find?" Kate's eyes bored into him, and the tone of her voice seemed filled with accusation.

Rolk hesitated, then decided he had better be honest with the woman, especially if he expected her help. "I also want to find out how close some people in New York might have been to the killings here."

Kate's eyes widened. "You mean Dr. Mallory and Malcolm, don't you?"

"And Father LoPato. They were all here when this blood ritual started up, and they were all in New York, and they were very close to the scenes of those crimes."

Kate sat back, staring at him. "And that's why you want to go to Chetulak, isn't it? You want to see if you can connect them to anything."

"That's part of it, yes."

Her eyes widened. "And I'll be helping you. My God, Rolk. These people, at least Grace and Malcolm, are my coworkers."

"We could also find something that could clear them.

Or at least two of them. You could think of it that way."

Kate began toying nervously with her cup. "I don't know if I can. You should have told me! When you said we might find something that could hurt someone, I thought you meant professionally. I never dreamed you wanted to prove they were killers."

He leaned forward, his face intense. "We're trying to *find* a killer, Kate. And it's not just some guy who stuck up a grocery store and got nervous. This is someone who's picking out women at random and sacrificing them. And we don't think it's going to stop until *we* stop it."

Kate stared out at the ruins. "It wouldn't be at random," she said.

"What are you talking about?"

She turned back to Rolk. "The women. They wouldn't be random choices. Not if a Toltec ritual was involved." She lowered her eyes to her coffee. "The Toltecs sacrificed only people from their noble class. Only the aristocrats of their society. And that involved both men and women."

"But we don't have a noble class."

"No, we don't, but these women weren't your average office worker either. There has to have been some other connection that made them important enough to be sacrificed."

Rolk looked out to the ruins, frowning. "And only the killer knows what that is."

Kate began to reply, but the words were interrupted by the appearance of a short stocky man with a balding head and an exaggerated drooping mustache.

"Lieutenant Rolk?" the man said, extending his hand as Rolk stood. "I am Captain Rimerez. I'm sorry to be late, but . . ." He shrugged. "This is Mexico."

"That's perfectly all right, Captain. I'm grateful you could spare me any time at all." Rolk turned toward Kate. "This is Dr. Kate Silverman, an anthropologist who's agreed to help me."

Kate glanced quickly, uncertainly at Rolk, then extended her hand to Rimerez.

"I am enchanted, Doctor," the captain said.

"I too," Kate answered.

"I'm afraid I speak Spanish only slightly," Rolk said, extending one hand toward a vacant chair.

"That is good. I would prefer to practice my English," Rimerez said. "It is not bad, no?"

"It's excellent," Rolk said. "I'm afraid I've only been in your country once before. Years ago, in Mexico City."

"Ahh, I was born there." Rimerez wagged his head from side to side. "I also worked there for many years. But . . ." He shrugged. "I offended the wrong person, and I was sent here to his infernal jungle. They said it was because I was part Indian, and that we are the only ones the natives will deal with at all."

"Is that true?" Rolk asked.

"Sometimes, but not always. You do not have these things in your department?" Rimerez asked.

"Oh, yes," Rolk said. "We have them. Would you care for a drink?"

Rimerez nodded, and Rolk signaled the waiter to order a round of Don Pedro, his favorite Mexican brandy. They chatted idly about their trip until the drinks arrived.

When Rimerez had tasted his drink, the required informality satisfied, Rolk raised the question of the blood rituals.

Rimerez sat back in his chair, his protruding paunch forcing its way through his suit coat. "It began, as it always does, without warning," he said. "Women began to disappear. Some very young, some much older. But all of them from the families of village chieftains, or what pass today as chieftains. It's more of an honorary title than anything else."

Rolk glanced at Kate, then turned his attention back to Rimerez. "You said 'as it always does,' " Rolk said. "Is it something that happens regularly?"

"Not often, but from time to time. Perhaps every

twenty years or so. It's hard to say." He smiled regretfully. "Our records here in Quintana Roo are not what they should be. There are no computers, I fear. And things have a tendancy to get misplaced."

"What brings on these things, when they do happen?" Kate asked.

The captain smiled at her. "Who knows with the Indians? Some priest practicing the ancient rites stirs things up, perhaps. Or perhaps the chicle crop has been poor and the natives believe the gods must be appeased. It is hard to say." He raised a cautioning finger. "But do not misunderstand. It is only a small number who still hold to the old ways—who still believe in the Mayan gods. Most are Catholics now, except in some very remote villages."

"Like Chetulak?" Rolk asked.

Rimerez nodded. "A very backward place, I am afraid. The people are very poor and ignorant of the outside world."

"There was a Catholic priest there, I believe. A Father LoPato. Didn't he have any luck converting the natives?"

Rimerez shook his head sadly. "I met this priest. I am afraid he was not successful. It was said he had an eye for the young women, but of course that could just be the gossip of old crones. It is something that is often said about priests unless they are very old."

"In his case, do you think it was true?" Rolk asked.

"It's hard to say. He was very intense about his anthropological work, which seemed to occupy most of his time." Rimerez cocked his head to one side. "Very strange for a priest, no? To be more interested in his studies than his religion?" He sipped his drink. "But then he became sick with malaria. He had—how do you say?—visions when the fevers took him. And the natives, they began to pray for him in the old religion. And it is said he too prayed with them while he was sick with fever. But I do not know this for sure."

"And that's when the blood ritual began?" Kate asked.

Rimerez nodded. "Yes, when the women began to disappear. We never found the bodies, of course. The jungle swallows them up very quickly. But we found blood. The traces of the ritual. And, of course, we found their clothing."

"Did you ever question the priest?" Rolk asked.

"I would have liked to, but unfortunately some other priests from his order came when they learned of his illness. They were very angry when they saw what the villagers were doing, and warned them of the evil of their ways." Rimerez shrugged again. "But the natives only laughed at them. In fact, I've heard that the priest laughed at them too. And it was then that they took him away."

"And did the rituals stop then?" Rolk asked.

Rimerez shook his head. "They continued for maybe a month more. It was then that they stopped."

Rolk sat back, thinking. He glanced at Kate, trying to decide how to continue. Finally he leaned forward. "There were two anthropologists working near Chetulak at that time. Did you ever meet them?"

"Yes. A young man and an older woman."

"Dr. Grace Mallory and Dr. Malcolm Sousi," Rolk prodded.

"I believe those were the names," Rimerez said. "But I would have to check. I do remember that one of the sacrifices took place near to where they were digging. It is how I came to meet them."

"So you talked to them about it?"

"Yes. But they said they knew nothing."

"Do you know if they had any contact with the villagers at Chetulak?" Rolk asked.

"Yes, I believe that some of the villagers worked the dig. It is one of the ways people earn money here. That, and the black market." When Rolk questioned the term, Rimerez looked at Kate and smiled. "I am sure the beautiful doctor could tell you. We have very strict laws in Mexico about allowing our artifacts to be removed. But the natives sometimes sell them to dealers and museums. They are smuggled out of the country, of course."

His eyes remained on Kate, and she lowered her own to her glass. "I'm afraid that's true," she said. "Museums are some of the best customers of black markets worldwide."

Rimerez laughed and raised a hand. "I want no confessions. At least not while we are enjoying a drink together." He turned back to Rolk. "This priest, some say, also took much out of the country. Again, strange for a priest, is it not?"

"Yes, it is," Rolk agreed. "But then, Father LoPato seems to be an unusual priest."

"You think perhaps he is also a killer?" Rimerez kept his eyes on Rolk.

"If he is, I hope to find out tomorrow. We'll be going to Chetulak."

Rimerez wrinkled his nose. "A terrible journey. Do you have a jeep?"

Rolk nodded toward Kate. "The doctor has suggested horseback."

Rimerez looked surprised. "The jungle is full of snakes." He turned to Kate. "You have been here before?"

Kate hesitated a moment. "Yes. The last time was a year ago. I visited the dig Drs. Mallory and Sousi were working on. I was there only a few days. Just to deliver some things Dr. Mallory needed."

Rolk stared cross the table at her. "You didn't tell me you were here then. Did you hear about these killings?"

Kate shook her head. "I never did. And I'm sure Dr. Mallory and Malcolm didn't know either. They would have said something to me."

"Oh, but they did know," Rimerez said. "I told them myself."

Rolk walked Kate back to their adjacent bungalows, but did not ask why she hadn't told him about her trip to the dig. He would just let her worry about when it would come, and see if she would bring it up first. He felt wary and puzzled.

"You're very quiet," she said.

"Just thinking over everything Rimerez told us."

"Did he tell you anything you didn't already know?"

"A few things."

Kate lowered her eyes. "And so did I." She looked up at him. "It just never dawned on me that it might be significant. I was here for only three days, and I had no idea what was happening."

"But Mallory and Sousi did."

"You can't be sure of that," Kate insisted. "They could have found out after I left."

"In New York they told me they didn't know. They said they only heard rumors from the natives that they dismissed out of hand."

Kate turned away. "I don't understand it. Not at all."

"Neither do I. But I'm going to try to find out tomorrow." He released her arm and they moved to the door of her bungalow.

"I'll see you in the morning," she said as she slowly opened her door and disappeared inside.

Rolk stared at the door for several seconds, realizing that he wished she had invited him inside. "Tomorrow," he said to himself, then walked to his own bungalow.

Twenty-two

WHEN KATE MET Rolk in front of the lodge the next morning, she found him seated behind the wheel of a battered blue jeep.

She was dressed in tight jeans over western riding boots, and a tan bush jacket over a red T-shirt emblazoned with the logo of the Museum of Natural History. Her hair was tied back in a ponytail, and as she stood there, hands on hips, legs spread slightly apart, she looked far younger than her twenty-eight years.

"I thought we were going by horseback," she said.

"That was your idea, not mine. And after Rimerez told me about all the snakes out there, I decided to borrow a jeep from him." Rolk studied her, pleased with everything he saw except the slight disappointment in her eyes. "Get in," he said. "We'll both be more comfortable this way."

Kate slid into the passenger seat and glanced back at the wicker basket on the rear seat. "Even more comforts of home?" she asked.

"Food and a thermos of coffee," Rolk said. "I asked the lodge to put it up. What have you got against comfort?"

"What have *you* got against snakes?"

He tilted his head to the side and grinned. "They scare the hell out of me. What's with you and horses?"

"They *don't* scare the hell out of me."

"A regular cowgirl. Straight from the Upper East Side."

"From Tuba City, Arizona, actually." Kate watched his brow wrinkle, questioning the name. "It's where I was raised. And for that matter, it's where I became interested in anthropology. Tuba City's just east of the Grand Canyon, right on the edge of the Navajo Indian Reservation."

Rolk looked at her and shrugged. "I didn't know." He grinned at her again. "But even if I did, I still would have asked Rimerez for a jeep. I've only been on a horse once, and I don't like the idea of making myself look like one's back end."

Kate faced forward and forced back a smile. "Drive on, city boy," she said. "I'll point the way."

They drove through the small village surrounding Chichén Itzá, and were soon on a dirt road headed into the dense tropical rain forest that dominated Quintana Roo. On each side of the narrow, heat-hardened road, lush, tangled foliage rose like a wall, often leaning into the road itself and slapping against the windshield of the jeep.

Rolk looked up at the overhanging vegetation. "I hope those damned snakes don't live in trees," he said.

Kate threw back her head and laughed. "Only the truly bad ones," she said.

They drove on, occasionally passing small thatch-roofed huts. Rolk had seen similar huts from the air as they had flown into the ancient city. From that vantage point they had looked quaint and curious, and Kate had explained that hundreds dotted the jungle, some alone, some in small village clusters, all housing the Indians who worked on the chicle plantations or who fought out an existence from the forest itself.

At close range, the quaintness disappeared, and the huts seemed small and squalid; the people crouching beside them, sad and poor.

"These are the Indians you told me about?" Rolk asked as they passed another of the huts.

"Yes," Kate said. "And this is what's left of the Mayan civilization."

He glanced across at her and noticed the sad, almost weary look in her eyes.

"Makes you wonder how it could happen," he said.

"No it doesn't," Kate said, her eyes fixed on the road ahead. "I know how it happened."

"That's right. I guess you would."

Kate looked across at him, wondering if he really understood; sure that he did not.

Before Rolk could respond, the jeep rounded a curve and came upon a cluster of small huts dominated by a large one with a wooden cross affixed to its roof.

"Chetulak," Kate said, pointing. "And there's the church Father LoPato once ran."

Rolk pulled the jeep to a halt in front of the church. He stared up at the thatched roof, then allowed his eyes to roam the tied-cane walls that looked as though a strong wind would send them crashing to the ground. "Not exactly St. Patrick's."

"Even less like the Temple of Kukulcan," Kate added.

As he climbed from the jeep, Rolk noticed a small group of Indians who had suddenly appeared on the opposite side of the dusty village square. They were small and slender and their facial features reminded him of reliefs he had seen on the walls of temples at Chichén Itzá, with their narrow foreheads, long curved noses, and almond-shaped eyes. They also carried the look of extreme poverty.

He thought back to his interrogation of Juan Domingo, thought of him living here with these same people, this same obvious poverty. A momentary sense of guilt hit him, but he dismissed it as quickly as it came. Domingo was only a pawn in the game, a game that would end only when Rolk found the killer. If Domingo proved to be the wrong pawn, then perhaps Rolk would apologize. But not until then.

"Let's tell them we're here to see the priest," Kate said. "It will make them less suspicious and that may help later."

Rolk nodded and started around the jeep toward her. "I don't think I've ever seen people who look this poor before," he said. "Not even in the city's worst neighborhoods."

Kate smiled wryly, then looked around the battered, dusty square. "This is a fairly prosperous village," she said. "The farther in you go, the more impoverished it becomes." She paused, looking about the square again. "And this is what's left of a culture that built cities that would have rivaled those of ancient Egypt and Rome."

Before Rolk could answer, a small, slender man dressed in black trousers and a wrinkled white shirt came hurrying through the door of the church. He had a day's growth of beard, circles under his eyes, and his thinning hair was badly combed; all of which gave him the look of a man who had had a long, bad night.

The man stopped before them, glancing at first one, then the other, trying to decide what language to speak. "You're American?" he asked.

"My name's Rolk and this is Dr. Kate Silverman. We were looking for the pastor of the church."

The man shifted nervously, looked down at his feet, then back at Rolk. "I'm Father Cordino. Father William Cordino," he said. His hands attacked each other, and he smiled tentatively. A distinct odor of liquor flowed from him. "You'll have to forgive my appearance. I haven't been well the past few days."

The priest stood twisting his hands, awaiting some words of acceptance. Rolk could see now that he was only in his early thirties, a beaten, battered early thirties, and he was reminded of the priest in New York and the sense of pain that had seemed to infuse his very being.

"Is there somewhere we can go and talk, Father?" Rolk asked.

The priest seemed to come back to himself, his eyes blinking momentarily. "Of course. I'm sorry." He turned, gesturing toward the church. "I have a small apartment at the rear of the church. Please, come with me."

They followed him into the church, and Rolk was

immediately aware of the pervading sense of rot and decay. Plain wooden benches had been arranged in rows along the hardened dirt floor. A small golden crucifix hung askew behind a simple wooden altar, covered with dust. The few statues of saints were chipped, their paint faded. A small table to the right of the altar held votive candles, none of which were lit. Rolk breathed deeply, the damp odor of decay filling his nostrils. It was as though something had died there, he thought, and that something was the church itself.

The priest pushed through a curtained archway and led them into a small squalid room that contained an open hearth, a narrow bed, and a table with three chairs.

Father Cordino seated them at the table and offered them food and drink. Glancing toward the dirt-encrusted room, which the priest seemed not to notice, Rolk declined, and so did Kate. He looked across the table at the nervous young priest.

"Things don't seem to be going too well for you, Father."

The priest threw back his head and laughed, almost without control. "They're not going at all, Mr. Rolk. And they never have. Not since the day I arrived."

Rolk leaned forward, his forearms tilting the fragile table. "Are you the one who took Father LoPato's place here?" He watched pain, then surprise appear in the priest's eyes.

"You know Father LoPato?" the young priest asked.

Rolk glanced at Kate, then began a long, slow explanation of his and Kate's presence in Chetulak. With each sentence, more pain seemed to gather in the priest's face, until finally he sat there, mouth open, his eyes staring into Rolk's.

"So it's happening in New York too," he said, then fell silent.

Kate straightened in her chair. "What do you mean, Father? Are you telling us human sacrifices are taking place here?"

The priest seemed not to hear. He stared past them at the small crucifix on the grimy wall behind their heads. "I tried so hard," he began, his voice little more than a whisper. "I did everything I was taught, everything I was supposed to do." His eyes focused on Kate and Rolk again. "And I loved them. All of them." His eyes grew distant again. "But the young women, they just kept disappearing during the first month I was here. And no matter what I did, I couldn't stop it. I couldn't convince them it was wrong. They wouldn't listen to me. And then it stopped suddenly, but not because of anything I did. I knew it would start again. And now I think it has."

"Are you telling me the same type of sacrifices that are happening in New York are happening here? Now?" Rolk asked.

Cordino nodded dumbly, almost as though unable to speak about it. He looked up suddenly. "Yes, I think so. No bodies have been found yet, but yesterday there was blood . . ." He shook his head and his eyes became glazed again. "It's started again, I know it has."

"Did anyone tell you why?" Kate asked.

The priest's eyes blinked as if he had been struck. "It's because Quetzalcoatl has returned. The natives say they've seen him. Talked to him."

"And he urged them to begin the rituals again?" Kate asked.

The priest nodded; then his eyes became suddenly horrified. "They say he told them the religion had been reborn." His lips trembled. "And not only here. Then they said he left them again to carry the message to other people, to other worlds."

Rolk and Kate exchanged glances. "Did they say what he looked like?" Rolk asked.

The priest shook his head. "They only said he wore the mask."

"The mask?" Kate said. "Whoever it was wore the mask of Quetzalcoatl." She looked at Rolk. "And became Quetzalcoatl."

Rolk leaned forward again, pressing himself toward the young priest. "And this first began when Father LoPato was here, and continued for a month after he left? And now it's begun again, right?"

The priest nodded; then his face grew pale. "Oh, my God, man. What are you saying?" His hands began to tremble. "Father LoPato is in New York now. You're saying *he* has something to do with this barbarity *there*? And here?" The priest's head began to shake violently from side to side. "It's impossible. The man was sick, yes. He had a severe nervous breakdown. But it was this place, that's all." He stared at Rolk. "Believe me, I know. It *was* this place."

"He worked with the natives," Rolk said. "He worked as an anthropologist as well as a priest. He studied their past beliefs, became involved in them."

"But not *that* way. Oh, God, no. Not that way."

Rolk sat back in his chair, trying to ease the tension. "There were two anthropologists here from New York, from the Museum of Natural History. Did you meet them?"

"No, they were gone by the time I arrived. I heard about them from the villagers. They were quite revered. But then, they paid the villagers well for the work they did at their dig. The money is important to them. Sometimes it can mean their survival."

Rolk sat forward. "Do you know which people from this village worked on the dig?"

"On, yes," the priest said. "And other villages as well."

"Would it be possible to speak to the ones who are here?"

The priest nodded absently. "Of course." He smiled, almost sadly, Rolk thought. "Whether they'll answer you is another matter."

"I was at the dig," Kate said. "If they recognize me, they just might if I'm with you."

"It's worth a try," Rolk said. "You can translate for me."

Outside, in the dusty village square, Rolk leaned

against the jeep and stared across at a handful of villagers who had gathered around the priest less than a hundred yards away. "Do you recognize any of them?" he asked Kate.

She shook her head. "No. But then, I didn't have much to do with them when I was here last year. It was for such a short time, and I really wasn't involved in the work."

"Well, let's hope they remember you."

The three men who came across the square with the priest were short and stocky, each bearing the broad, flat features and long patrician nose of their Mayan ancestors. They were dressed in tattered work clothes and worn straw hats that looked as though something had been eating at them, and they all seemed suspicious, making Rolk wonder if the priest had warned them not to say anything damaging about his predecessor.

Rolk spoke softly and slowly in English, as Kate translated, trying to keep her face and mannerisms as friendly and nonthreatening as possible. Yet, throughout, the men offered little more than monosyllabic answers, their demeanors docile but their eyes wary.

Yes, they remembered LoPato. No, they knew nothing about this involvement in any old religious ceremonies. They knew nothing about these ceremonies, in fact, only rumors. And the missing women, they were sure, had only run away.

When Rolk asked them about the previous year's dig, the men were only slightly more forthcoming, and when he asked about rituals that might have taken place at that time, they again pleaded ignorance. They had been there, they said, only for the money, and the work had been hard, leaving little time for talk about rumors.

Frustrated, Rolk thanked the men, then took the priest by the arm and led him back inside the church. Once out of the heat of the village square, the priest took a moment to wipe the perspiration from his face and neck.

"I'm afraid they weren't very cooperative," Father

Cordino said. "But you have to understand that they're a simple people, and they're intimidated by any form of authority."

"Did you tell them I was a police officer?"

"No, I didn't. But you're wearing new clothes that are clean. And you're driving a car. To them that's authority enough."

"I don't want you to think I'm down here trying to cause harm to Father LoPato," Rolk said.

The priest stared down at his dust-covered shoes. "It wouldn't matter even if you were," he said. "And even though I'm sure Father LoPato had nothing to do with those killings in New York, there would be nothing I could do to help him, even if I wanted to." The priest looked up, holding Rolk with his sad eyes. "Don't you see, if I did that, and he was the killer, then my sin would be as great as his."

"Tell me, Father, these killings that you think have started again, have you reported them to the police?"

"No, I haven't."

"Why not?"

The priest stared at his shoes again. "As I told you, I've been ill. I haven't had a chance to travel to Chichén Itzá."

Rolk knew where the man's illness had come from, and he thought he understood. He wondered what he might do if he found himself trapped for a year in this dismal, dusty hole set in the middle of a heat-drenched jungle, and he decided that he, too, might find himself going to bed every night with a bottle in his hand. And maybe that had been Father LoPato's only sin as well.

"I'll report it to the police when I get back," Rolk said.

"I would appreciate that, Mr. Rolk, but I'm afraid it won't help. The villagers won't talk to their own police either." He smiled weakly. "Or to their priest," he added.

As Rolk left the church, the three men were still gathered around Kate, but as he drew closer, their eyes darted toward him and they turned away and began moving back across the tiny village square.

"I seem to be making a big impression today," he said as he stopped next to Kate.

She turned to him, her eyes blinking rapidly, almost as though she had been suddenly awakened; then she looked back at the retreating men. "It's not you," she said. "I tried speaking to them in Mayan—and they even remembered me from the dig—but they still responded in the same way." She turned back to him, shielding her eyes against the sun. "Maybe they just don't know anything. Maybe it *is* all rumor."

"It's not rumor in New York," he said. "And I don't think it is here either."

They stopped for lunch on the way back, parking the jeep in a narrow clearing, then making their way inland, following the distant sound of rushing water. The trail they followed was aimless and constricted, little more than an animal path leading to the water they could hear ahead. All about them, steam rose from the vegetation, as shafts of sunlight, directly overhead, pierced the high canopy of trees and heated the dew that had collected on the ground. They paused to look at the colors that surrounded them, orange and scarlet blossoms that seemed to burst from the dark green vegetation, multicolored toucans that flew suddenly from hidden perches, frightened and squawking, their wings stirring the otherwise still leaves, setting off the chattering of monkeys no larger than a man's fist, their small black bodies leaping hysterically from branch to branch, tree to tree.

They entered a clearing with a narrow stream at its center, the water sounds they had heard caused by a three-foot cascade into a small rock-laden pool.

"Not much of a stream," Rolk said. "Especially since it sounded so awesome from the road."

"It's the canopy cover," Kate said. "It creates a tunnel effect that amplifies everything."

Rolk smirked. "Jane of the Jungle," he said, laying the wicker basket on a moss-covered rock.

"Much less threatening than *your* jungle," Kate said.

Rolk looked at the surrounding vegetation, the thick clumps of grass and tangled vines that could hide anything. On the path coming in, he had kept his eyes glued to the ground, expecting something to leap up at him, or worse, slither across his foot. "I'm not so sure," he said. "All our animals have two legs, and you can usually see them coming."

"With evil intent," Kate added. "Here everything is just trying to survive. Leave them alone and unmolested and they'll return the favor."

Rolk eyed the ground again, trying to decide where to sit, or if he even wanted to. "Promise?" he said.

Kate smiled at him impishly. "Unless I'm wrong."

They sat close together, the wicker basket between them, and ate the hotel-prepared lunch of *pollo pibil,* a cold chicken spread with sour orange and *achiote* paste, washing it down with a thermos of still-warm coffee.

Throughout the meal Rolk was distant, his mind fixed on the priest and the villagers of Chetulak.

"You're not happy with what you found in the village, are you?" Kate asked, breaking the spell.

"What's to be happy about?"

"Well, you've eliminated the connection. Between Chetulak and New York, I mean."

"Why do you say that?"

"Because the priest said the killings may have started here again, and just recently. The killer couldn't be here and in New York at the same time."

Rolk stared at Kate, his eyes harder than she had seen them before. "But what if our killer came here weeks ago, before everything started in New York? What if he started everything up here again, and then decided to continue it himself when he got home? What if he has an accomplice here that he reaches by phone or letter?" Rolk shook his head and stared at the ground. "I came down here trying to get some answers, and all I'm coming away with are more questions. Even Father LoPato's breakdown doesn't seem as—relevant anymore."

"Why do you say that?" Kate asked.

"The priest we met today. He looks like he's only a few days away from a rubber room himself. And who the hell wouldn't be, given how he has to live and what he has to live with? Christ, spreading the gospel to people who still believe in human sacrifice. I bet they never warned him about that in the seminary."

Kate reached out and laid her hand on top of his, sorry for his frustration, wishing she could offer some comfort. "What will you do?"

"Tell Rimerez about the new killings, then go back out there with him and see what we can dig up. Then I'll get the airlines to check names against their manifests for the past six months, just in case our killer might have been dumb enough to use his own name. Then the same thing with Immigration, here and in New York and Miami. Then I'll check every damned hotel and every damned taxi driver in Chichén Itzá. How's that sound for starters?"

Kate offered him a weak smile. "Not very hopeful. Do you have any idea how many thousands of tourists visit the Yucatán in six months?"

Rolk nodded. "They'd fill Yankee Stadium a few times over."

"Not quite, but close." She watched Rolk offer a hapless shrug. Her hand was still on top of his and she left it there. "Would you like me to go back out there with you?"

Rolk looked into the soft eyes, felt the hand on his, and thought that he'd like her to stay here a week with him just to see what happened.

"If you don't mind," he said. "But I'm not sure I won't be wasting your time."

"Why don't we see what Captain Rimerez says, and then you can decide," she said, realizing she wouldn't be at all unhappy if Rimerez thought she should go along.

*   *   *

Rimerez arrived just as they finished dinner in the hotel dining room, and Kate excused herself, explaining that she wanted to stroll among the ruins. She had not returned by the time Rolk and Rimerez finished their conversation, and as Rolk made his way along the outside walkway that led to their adjoining rooms, he found himself pausing outside her door and suppressing his disappointment that no light shone from within.

Rolk entered his room and switched on the light. The room was stuffy and hot and oppressive from being closed all day, but the temperature outside had dropped dramatically and he decided against the noisy, rattling air conditioner, choosing instead to open the screenless louvered windows. He dropped his jacket on one of the rattan chairs opposite the double bed, then slumped into the other and began to review his conversation with Rimerez.

He had liked the man immediately, had respected his tough-mindedness. Rimerez asked all the right questions and avoided the obvious. When they had first met, Rolk observed, with approval, the man's easy manner and hard eyes. The contrast was one had found common to most good cops he had met over the years—a mixture of confidence and wariness, friendliness and suspicion.

They had quickly agreed on the tactics they would use the following day in Chetulak—tactics not unlike those Rolk had used to break down Juan Domingo. They would question Domingo's and Roberto Caliento's relatives about past rituals and the recent reappearance of Quetzalcoatl, while implying throughout that serious harm might befall the men in New York if answers were not given quickly and freely.

"It is sad," Rimerez said. "But intimidation, for the police, is still a better weapon than a gun."

Rimerez also offered help—on the Mexican end—in tracing airline and hotel reservations and in circulating photographs, which Rolk would provide, among the handful of taxi drivers who worked in Chichén Itzá.

When they had concluded their business, Rolk walked Rimerez to his car, and they stood briefly in the parking lot discussing the problems the investigation posed.

"If you are right, and someone has come from New York, then he has taken a terrible and foolish risk," Rimerez said.

"Unless he sent someone else," Rolk replied. "Someone I may not even know about yet."

Sitting in his room now, Rolk continued to ponder that possibility, his eyes growing heavier as he sat slumped in his chair. It was something he had not considered, and he knew now that he should have. He would have to call Devlin, have him recheck all the surveillance reports, then run traces on all the people each of the suspects had contacted over the past few days. It would add immeasurably to the work, but there was no escaping it. It would simply have to be done.

Kate wandered among the ruins, the clear skies allowing shafts of moonlight to play across the massive stone facades and staircases, giving each an ethereal, yet living quality, almost as though at night, this city, which had died centuries ago, had come to life again.

Kate imagined living there among the ancients. People who had developed their own astronomy, their own mathematics; who were great artists and craftsmen, working in gold and jade; people who had built great cities that had housed tens of thousands of people, ruled by an established aristocracy. Yes, she thought. If she could will it, she would choose to live in that time.

She stopped before the Ball Court, her mind still overwhelmed by her thoughts, by the place in which she found herself. To be an aristocrat in this city, she thought. To be one of the chosen. She wondered if she could do what would be expected of her: be a living sacrifice to her own people. Could she, as the ancient nobles had, bleed and mutilate herself for the gods? Could she capture and sacrifice the royalty of other cities, while risking the same fate herself?

But it was all moot. And, yet, it wasn't. Someone *had* chosen her, *had* decided she would be sacrificed. Standing there now among the beauty and the majesty of the ruins, she found herself exhilarated and terrified, and she wondered, just for that moment, which she felt more strongly.

The sound of movement filtered in from the outside walkway, bringing Rolk back from the light sleep he had fallen into. He sat quietly, listening as a door was opened and closed. It was Kate going into her room. He sat forward, momentarily thinking he could knock on her door and tell her of his plans for tomorrow; then he smiled at the shallowness of the pretext and sat back in the chair.

The scream brought him out of the chair and sent him rushing through his own door. Kate's door was locked when he reached it, and without hesitation he put his shoulder to it and sent it crashing inward.

Kate stood with her back against the far wall, her face drained of color, her eyes wide as she stared at the center of her bed.

The covers of the bed had been pulled back, and there, exposed against the whiteness of the sheet, lay a large coiled snake, its tail vibrating with anger, its head encircled by a necklace of brightly colored feathers.

Rolk felt frozen in place, then forced himself to move slowly, cautiously, watching the snake's head pivot in his direction, feeling his own pulse rate quicken with each step he took. He carefully eased a small wooden chair from beneath a writing table. It felt light and insubstantial. He thought how much he wished he had the service revolver he had been forced to leave at home, though it wouldn't have done him any good because he was shaking so badly he'd be lucky if he could even hit the bed—provided he had remembered to load it.

He moved closer, the chair extended above his head. He recalled reading somewhere, years ago, that a snake could only strike out at a distance half the length of its body, and he stared at the reptile, trying to gauge the length of its coiled body. Five or six feet, he told himself. It was five or six feet long. Christ.

He brought the chair down with all the force he could muster, so much so that the impact and the natural resilience of the mattress almost tore the chair from his grasp.

He jumped back after the first blow, raising the chair again as he watched the snake uncoil and writhe with pain and anger, its head twisting back to the place it had been struck. The snake seemed enormous, its head almost as large as his fist, its body as thick at its center as his forearm.

He brought the chair down again, and then quickly a third time.

The snake jumped forward, its body twisting wildly, leaving the sheet streaked with blood that seemed surprisingly dark and thick and human. It fell to the floor with a heavy thudding sound, and Rolk brought the chair down again and again and again until it finally shattered with the force of the blows. He dropped it and stared down at what remained. The snake lay still and dead and bloody.

Rolk drew a deep, ragged breath as a violent shudder passed through his body. He turned to Kate. She was sagging against the wall, almost as if she were about to slump to the floor. He went to her and enfolded her in his arms.

"Are you okay?"

He felt her head nod rapidly against his chest.

"I thought you were afraid of snakes," she whispered.

"I am," he said, fighting the impulse to shudder again. "Christ, am I ever."

He pushed her away and stared down into her face. "I thought you *weren't* afraid of them," he said.

Kate smiled weakly, the color only now returning to her face. "So did I. But when I pulled the covers back and saw it lying there with those plumes around its head, it just paralyzed me." She stared up at Rolk. "Someone put it there, Rolk. A plumed serpent. Quetzalcoatl."

"Yeah, I know. Someone who didn't like the questions we were asking." He felt her body tremble beneath his hands.

"What are we going to do?" she asked.

He hesitated, still fighting to keep himself under control. "First, we're going to leave that damned thing right where it is so Rimerez can see it in the morning. Then you're going to get your things and move them into my room." He stroked her cheek. "I want you on the first plane out of here in the morning, and until then I'm not letting you out of my sight."

Kate stared at him for several minutes, then slipped her arms around his neck. "I don't want to be out of your sight," she whispered. "Not for a minute."

Rolk watched her face draw close to his, felt her mouth press against his own with a willing, hungry passion. And he returned it.

Twenty-three

THE REDUCED NIGHT lighting spread a faint glow along the corridor as Devlin stepped out of the anthropology lab and quietly closed the door behind him. It was nine o'clock and he had already spent an hour inside the museum searching for anything that would provide a direct link to the murders.

The search by Devlin and Detectives Charlie Moriarty and Bernie Peters had been approved during a meeting that afternoon with the museum director, who had agreed with Devlin's contention that an unofficial search at night would be less disruptive and upsetting to the museum staff, and would also avoid the need for a search warrant that might be discovered by the press. The only restriction the director had placed on the search was that the detectives be accompanied by the museum's head of security, who turned out to be Ezra Waters, a retired city detective Devlin had known for years.

Waters waited patiently now, leaning against a wall as he watched Devlin move down the corridor toward him. He was a tall, heavyset black man with closely cropped gray hair and a protruding paunch, neither of which had existed before he retired. Devlin also noticed that Waters was far better dressed than he had been as a cop, and he wondered if retirement would also find him wearing a well-tailored three-piece suit.

"Find anything, Paul?" Waters asked as Devlin reached him.

Devlin shook his head. "It's like trying to find an honest vice cop."

Waters, who had spent ten years in Vice, let out a low, rumbling laugh, then fell in beside Devlin. "Yeah, well, it's like I told you, Paul. If I wanted to hide somethin', this is the place I'd do it. Fuckers got so much shit in here, nobody knows what it is, where it is, or how long it's been here."

Devlin grunted agreement. It was one reason he had chosen to search only the laboratory and storage areas dealing with the anthropology and ethnology collections, along with the Bug Room and autopsy lab. A small team of men could never search the entire museum in a reasonable period of time, nor could any massive search, with adequate manpower, be accomplished quietly. And such a full-fledged police invasion would have been vetoed by the brass as politically unwise.

But Devlin had not consulted the brass, or anyone else for that matter, not even Rolk. It was an act of pure initiative, something highly recommended in police-academy training, something that usually put a cop's head on the block whenever it was attempted. Yet he had decided to go ahead, and only some high degree of success could save him now. The excuse that Rolk had left him in charge, and that a search had been called for, would never wash if complaints began to roll in. Rolk might get away with it, but he never would.

"So what now?" Waters said.

Devlin pointed a finger down the hall where Bernie Peters and Charlie Moriarty stood talking. "I'm going to introduce those two overachievers to the wonderful world of bugs."

Waters let out a grunt. "This whole place is a spook house, but that place is even too spooky for me. Man, you just gotta hear the sound those fuckers make when they start gnawin' on somethin'." Waters shook his head as though trying to force the memory away. "If you don't mind, I'll wait in the hall while your boys are playin' with those little bastards."

Peters and Moriarty seemed equally squeamish when

Devlin explained what he wanted. Standing before one of two large containers, the two detectives stared down at the animal body parts wrapped in burlap, then glanced quickly at Devlin as if hoping he would tell them it was all a bad joke.

Ignoring him, Devlin jabbed a finger at the container. "I want you to notice that each one of these things has a number stenciled on the burlap. Don't mix them up, and keep them in order. I want you to unwrap each piece, look at it, rewrap it like you found it, then stack each one on this table so you can put them back in in the exact order you found them."

Peters stared at him. "What difference does it make?" He shrugged. "I mean, if we find what we're looking for, all hell's gonna break loose anyway."

"No it's not. Whether we find anything or not, nobody's going to know we were here."

"You mean we're going to stake the place out if we find something," Moriarty offered.

Devlin smiled sourly at him. "Now I know why they made you a detective," he said.

"Shit," Peters said. "I hope we don't find anything, then. I sure as hell don't want to sit in this place every night waiting for some lunatic to come looking for his trophies." He hesitated, stared into the container, then looked back at Devlin. "You gonna help us with this?"

Devlin offered a second smile, then shook his head. "The boss put me in charge so I wouldn't have to do things like this."

Moriarty groaned. "You fuck. I'll get you for this."

The two detectives worked slowly, their faces grim, their eyes showing their discomfort. They were provided rubber aprons and gloves, and they took turns removing the carefully wrapped body parts, uncovering them, then rewrapping them and placing them on a long stainless-steel table. The overhead fluorescent lighting added to the unpleasantness, flooding the windowless room with a harsh artificial light that made each new offering seem more disquieting than the last. Behind them, in the long metal container that held the

bugs, the faint sound of clicking jaws sent out a dull
hum as the carpet beetles enjoyed their latest feeding
frenzy.

Abruptly, his shoulders hunched as though fighting
off a shiver, Bernie Peters moved to the opposite side
of the container so he was facing Charlie Moriarty.

"What's the matter?" Moriarty asked. "You look
like you're gonna puke."

"I just can't stand having my back to those little
bastards. I keep hearing that noise and it's like some
fucking horror movie. I keep expecting the lid to fly
open and all those little bastards to come swarming all
over me."

Moriarty stared at Peters, his face filled with disgust. "Thanks, Bernie. I gotta work in this prehistoric
butcher shop with a couple of million cannibalistic
fucking bugs behind me, and you gotta start talkin'
about them climbing out and gnawing on my ass.
You're fucking beautiful, you know that?"

A crooked smile spread across Peters' narrow,
hachetlike face. "That's why I want you between me
and them. Those little fuckers get out, the first thing
they're gonna see is your big fat ass. And by the time
they chomp their way through that, I figure I can be
out that door and be home hiding under my bed."

Moriarty glared at him, then shook away his own
shiver. "Christ, this is the worst fucking job I ever
had. This is even worse than the time we were out at
the dump on Staten Island sifting through all that
garbage and shit. How come cops on television never
do any of this crap. They're always driving around in
sports cars and speedboats and wearing fucking designer clothes. And you and me, we're up to our asses
in tiger heads and elephant balls."

He reached down into the container and withdrew a
long, narrow parcel, then carefully unwrapped the burlap, allowing the preservative solution to drip back
inside.

"Jesus Christ, what the hell is this?" he asked aloud
as he glared in disgust at the lower leg of a large

animal, the hair wet and matted, the severed joint trailing strings of tendon and flesh.

Peters stared at the dripping leg. "Musta been a horse or an antelope or somethin'. Maybe a fucking cow."

"Christ," Moriarty groaned. "By the time this job is over, I'm gonna be a goddamn vegetarian."

Malcolm Sousi's office was neat and uncluttered, papers carefully stacked on his desk, books all arranged in an even line on the shelves of a bookcase. The objects he was studying had been set in precise rows on a separate table.

This is a very orderly man, Devlin thought as he applied a lock pick to a desk drawer. His mind went back to the victims, their bodies so carefully arranged, their clothing folded and stacked neatly beside them. But it probably meant nothing, he told himself. Just your own dislike and distrust of orderly people, because you've never been able to manage it yourself.

The desk drawer slid open, and Waters, who was hovering behind Devlin, grunted approval. "Where'd you learn how to do that?" he asked.

"Rolk," Devlin said. "The man can open anything. He can even bypass alarms. Says he learned it during his first years as a detective, on the safe-and-loft squad."

"Yeah, I remember now. Then he went to the major-case squad, then the homicide task force. Too bad he missed Vice and Narcotics. Woulda put a little spark in his life. Yours too."

Devlin knew what Waters meant. His own assignments had all been in the world of plodding investigation —careful attention to small detail, not the world of shoot-'em-up raids and legal entrapments employed by those in Narcotics and Vice. He glanced up at the large, looming man. "I was always too lazy and slow to chase people across rooftops," he said. "Besides, I wanted to be chief of department."

Waters' low, rumbling laugh filled the small office. "Sure you did. That's why you stayed with Rolk all these years, while he went and told those pissy-assed motherfuckers at headquarters to shove it every time they messed with one of his cases. Man, *he* could be a deputy chief now if he had ever learned to play their game. But he ain't goin' noplace, and you, baby, you tarred with the same brush. Look at his boss, Dunne. That pasty-faced little hairbag never was no kinda cop. Even when he was on the street he couldn't find a Harlem streetwalker in the middle of a Boy Scout jamboree. But he's so close to his bosses, and all them limp-dick politicians, they ever stopped short, he'd be halfway up their asses before he knew what happened. And that's what you gotta be in his department if you wanna make it."

Devlin stared into the open drawer and repressed a smile. "Inspector Dunne is an honorable man, and a great leader of men," he said.

"Yeah," Waters added. "And the boys down at City Hall say he gives fantastic head."

Devlin pulled a sheaf of papers from the drawer and began thumbing through them. Each held a detailed description, evaluation, and provenance of a particular piece of pre-Columbian art. He replaced them, then opened the deep bottom drawer.

Again, more scholarly matter dealing with Sousi's work—papers and journals withdrawn from the museum library, along with the beginnings of a manuscript he was apparently writing. Bent over the drawer, Devlin rummaged through the material, then reached down and extracted three pornographic magazines, which he dropped on the desk.

Ezra Waters stepped forward and picked one up and began leafing through it. "Damn," he said. "Looks like our little ole Doc Seuss"—he glanced down at Devlin—"that's what the boys call him around here, 'cause he walks around grinnin' like one of those Wiggly-Piggly characters in those kiddie books—well, it sure looks like he got more on his mind than just diggin' up old pots." Waters shook his head. "Man, where do these magazines find all these dudes with dicks like telephone poles to pose for these here pictures." He glanced back at Devlin. "White dudes, I mean."

Devlin retrieved the magazine and began looking through it. The pages carried explicit photographs of various sexual acts, and as in most magazines of that ilk, they depicted women in poses of abject subjugation, dominated by large, powerful men.

As Devlin gathered the magazines together and replaced them in the drawer, he recalled Moriarty's report on Sousi's verbal altercation with a woman in a West Side bar, along with his own observations of the man's veiled resentment of the women with whom he worked. It all fit neatly with the pornographic magazines. But did it mean anything more?

He closed the drawer and looked up at Waters. "Like the Supreme Court says, we all have the right to buy and read the works of creative minds," he offered.

"What is going on here?"

Devlin and Waters turned to the sound of the slightly strident voice. Grace Mallory stood in the doorway, her face pale, her eyes wide with a mixture of surprise and anger.

Devlin glanced at his watch, then back at the woman. "A bit late for you, isn't it, Doctor?"

The words, or perhaps the calm in Devlin's voice, seemed to stun the woman; she blinked her eyes several times before she regained control, looking from Devlin to Waters, then settling on the security director. "I want to know the meaning of this," she finally demanded.

Devlin raised a hand, silencing Waters, then stepped around the desk and approached the woman. "We're conducting a search as part of our investigation," he said softly. "I met with the director this afternoon and got his permission. The idea was to disrupt the staff as little as possible, and, more important, to avoid any publicity that might hurt either the museum or your exhibit."

Grace Mallory's eyes widened; the muscles along her jaw hardened into a knot. "The director approved this?" When Devlin nodded, her eyes darted to Waters for confirmation.

"Yes, he did," Waters said. "I was there in his office. He told me to be here tonight so nothing was removed without a receipt."

Grace Mallory's head snapped back to Devlin. "Do you have a warrant? You need one, don't you?"

"No, not with the director's permission." The woman began to object, but Devlin held up both hands, cutting her off. "If we get a warrant—and that may still be necessary in the future—there's no way we can guarantee the press isn't going to get wind of it. All that would have to happen is for one clerk who handles the papers to start flapping his jaws about it, and the streets would be full of TV crews and reporters while we were in here conducting our search. And that wouldn't help anyone. Certainly not us, and certainly not the museum, or you, or your staff. Because after that, they'd be camped on your doorstep every day and every night."

Grace's eyes had begun to blink again, and her mouth moved almost imperceptibly before the words began to form. "But people have personal things in these offices. Surely you need some kind of court order to go through those."

Devlin kept his features soft and forced himself to smile. He understood the woman's concern. He had searched her office earlier, and he had found the journal she kept in her desk, which dealt with her personal life and the attraction she felt for other women. He had read it quickly, and he wished now that he could tell her that it didn't matter, that he would treat the information as a priest would. But that, of course, would not be true. Everything mattered. Everything would be remembered and cataloged and considered. There was simply no other way to do the job.

"We won't be removing anything of a personal nature, Dr. Mallory. In fact, we won't be removing anything at all, unless it relates to the murders."

Devlin could see her mind sifting through his words,

trying to find some comfort in what he had said, and finding none. He offered her a weak smile. "I'd also appreciate it if you kept our search as quiet as possible," he added, knowing she would not. "If someone connected with the museum is involved in this, the less that person knows about what we're doing, the better."

Grace stared past Devlin's left shoulder, her eyes suddenly fixed and glassy. It was as though her mind had abruptly divested itself of her body, and he could not be sure if she had heard him, if his final words had made it through the blank wall that had dropped between them.

"I hope you'll cooperate with us," he began, then simply stared in surprise as the woman turned and walked out of the room without a word.

"For Chrissake, will you please shut up?" Moriarty groaned. "When we finish in here, we still got an autopsy room to do, and I can't take your bitching and moaning for another fuckin' hour."

"Look, it makes me feel better," Peters said. He pointed a finger at the table where the animal parts had been carefully stacked. "This is like a fuckin' explosion in a fuckin' butcher shop, and between the stink of all those cold cuts"—he jabbed his finger toward the overflowing table again—"and the stink of this chemical shit they store them in, it makes me wanna puke. And the only way I can keep from barfing all over this shit is to talk about it."

"I'd rather have you puke," Moriarty said. He was working in the lower level of the vat now and was forced to bend over and reach down almost to floor level. He grunted with exertion as he began to retrieve his latest prize, then continued his harangue of Peters.

"At least if you puked I wouldn't have to listen to you describe every goddamned . . . Oh, shit. Oh, shit." Moriarty's eyes bulged in his round, fleshy face as he stared at the long strand of blond hair protruding between the folds of burlap he held in his hands. Carefully, with trembling fingers, he began to unwrap the burlap parcel. He heard himself grunt, and he heard Peters gag, then retch, as they each stared into the contorted, bloodless face of Cynthia Gault.

"Oh, shit," Moriarty said again, almost as though it had become some religious chant. He looked up into the equally bloodless face of Bernie Peters. "You better get Devlin and you better tell him to get the ME down here as fast as he can. He looked back at the head cradled in his hands. "Oh, shit."

The animal parts had been returned to the vat, and Peters and Moriarty had been sent off to calm their nerves with coffee or whatever else Ezra Waters might offer. The once-overflowing steel table was empty now except for the heads of Cynthia Gault and Alexsandra Ross.

Devlin stood off to one side and watched as Jerry Feldman carefully probed the severed neck of Alexsandra Ross. Devlin stared at the white, lifeless face, crowned by its tangled mass of wet black hair. Alexsandra Ross had been an attractive woman when he had last seen her. Unpleasant and self-centered, he reminded himself, but certainly attractive. Now she was far from that. Death had come horribly. Her mouth was twisted and deformed, teeth bared and slightly apart, as if she were trying to scream out against the final horror. But it was the eyes that finally forced Devlin to look away. The eyes on both heads were open, and were now nothing more than milky white orbs staring out of pale contorted faces.

"What can you tell me?" Devlin finally asked.

Feldman straightened up and stretched. "Not a helluva lot more than we already knew." He shook his head slowly. "Damn fine cutting, though. Even better than I thought at first." He reached down and began to unroll a long layer of skin that began at the base of Alexsandra Ross's neck, then gradually widened until it reached a point that would have been her lower back.

When he had finished, Feldman looked back up at

Devlin. "When I first saw the bodies, I thought the head and the skin along the back might have been taken separately. You know, two separate cuts. But it wasn't. It's all in one piece. And that's some fancy cutting."

"I'm glad you admire the work," Devlin said.

Feldman grinned at him, but without humor. "No, it's more than that. A lot more." Carefully he lifted the head, allowing the widening swath of skin to trail out behind it.

Devlin watched with obvious distaste as remnants of the solution in which the heads had been immersed began to flow from the mouth and ears and nostrils.

"What does this remind you of?" Feldman asked as he held the head away from his body, so the dripping, trailing skin hung almost to his waist.

"A bad dream," Devlin snapped.

"Yeah, it's that, all right. But it's something else too." He proffered the head again, extending it toward Devlin, who instinctively took a step back. "Does this remind you of anything? Like a headdress, maybe?"

Devlin stared at the head, at the trailing, capelike strip of skin. He was still repulsed by what he saw, but that emotion was gradually being replaced by the instincts he had gained over the years. "You're talking ritual again."

Feldman nodded, then carefully returned the head to the table. "I know it's not part of my job, but I've been doing a little reading about the Toltecs. Let's just say I've developed an unusual fascination for this case."

"And?" Devlin's eyes were intense now, his body leaning slightly forward as though preparing to jump on some new piece of information.

Feldman let out a long breath. "Seems there was this Toltec city called Tulum. It was unusual in a couple of ways. First, it was built on the coast, right on the Caribbean, the only city they ever built right next to the ocean. Second, this city had a very high religious significance. It was a city devoted to human sacrifice."

"More so than the others?"

Feldman shrugged. "Maybe not more. Some anthropologists describe it as a purer form, a higher form of ritual. Something like high Anglican, low Anglican, I guess."

"So how does it relate to this?"

Feldman slid onto the table, seating himself only a foot from the nearest head. Devlin winced at the proximity, but found himself, as he had before, envying the man's ability to remain aloof from the horror of his work.

Feldman clasped his hands together and began gesturing with them like a professor teaching a dull student. "They had a pyramid at Tulum that was used exclusively for sacrifices. There was a flat platform at the top, and on it was a triangular stone, almost like a fulcrum. Basically, when someone was sacrificed, he was led up the steps of the pyramid in a very elaborate ceremony with the high priests all decked out in plumes and capes and gold and God knows what else. Then the victim would be killed by having his back broken on the triangular stone. The body was then completely skinned, with the head, the arms, and the legs still attached, and the denuded torso was thrown down the steps of the pyramid." Feldman held his clasped hands in front of him. "The important thing is the way the body was skinned—with the head and limbs attached—and the fact that one of the priests would wear that skin like a cloak, as part of the ceremony." He jabbed a finger at Devlin. "You see what I'm getting at? This whole thing is like a modified version of that ritual. I didn't realize it until I saw the way the cutting was done. But dammit, I think there's a definite link."

"So our killer has to be someone who has an intimate knowledge of these rituals."

Feldman grinned at him. "You read me, Paul. This is obscure scholarly information, not something someone with just a general knowledge of the Mayans would know about. Hell, I'm a big fan of pre-Columbian art, and I didn't know it until I started digging into it."

The assistant medical examiner watched Devlin intently, then asked, "So what's your next move, my friend?"

Devlin turned, walked to the door, and turned back again. "I want to keep the lid on this for forty-eight hours. I want to stake out this place, just on the off chance our killer visits his . . ." He waved his hand in the air, searching for the right word, then left it unsaid.

"That's why you asked me not to bring the meat wagon?" He watched Devlin nod. "I'll do the best I can, but both our asses will be in a sling if the families find out we're hiding the heads from them."

"I know," Devlin said. "But I think we're just going to have to take the chance they'll understand." He glanced up at Feldman. "You have any suggestions on what else I should be doing?"

"Yeah, I do. Get that shrink in to take a long look at the people who've been working on this exhibit. It's got to be one of them, Paul. Or somebody else who's so damned close they might as well be working on it."

Devlin nodded again. "The shrink's meeting with us tomorrow."

"And one other thing, Paul. You tell your boys to watch their asses. This killer finds out you've been screwing around with his ritual, God knows what he might do."

Twenty-four

FATHER JOSEPH LoPATO sent a weak smile across the desk. His face was bleak and pale, and his hands, held in his lap, twisted against each other with a life of their own.

"I'm sure you're making too much of this, Grace. The police are only doing what must be done, and probably any intrusion into your personal papers was inadvertent."

Grace Mallory stared back across her desk, her face haggard and angry. "Why don't you stop talking like a priest and act like the scholar you are? They have no right to violate our privacy," she snapped. "I'm not a criminal, and I've done nothing to be treated like one."

"Do you think they searched the entire museum, or just certain areas?" The priest's hands attacked each other again, and a slight twitch had begun at the corner of his mouth.

"I have no idea where they looked, or where they didn't. When I came across them they were in Malcolm's office, going through his desk. I got the impression there were others elsewhere, but I have no idea where."

"Well, perhaps they didn't go through *your* things," LoPato offered.

"Oh, they were *in* here, damn them. Of that I'm sure."

The priest raised a trembling hand, trying to calm the woman. "I understand that you're upset, and that you have every right to be. But I really don't see what can be done about it."

Grace leaned forward, her face red with anger. "Everyone, Father, *everyone,* has things about their lives they prefer to keep private. And if they choose, that is their right!"

The vehemence of Grace's words caused the priest to stiffen in his chair. She seemed to be telling him she knew his secrets as well as her own. Just the thought that she might, left him with a sense of inner rage.

"I understand what you're getting at, Grace. I understand completely. "But you're dealing with a fait accompli, and all you can do is protect yourself from any further intrusions."

Grace sneered at him. "You think they won't be coming to your rectory next? Well, if I were you, I wouldn't count on them letting your church stand in their way."

"Is that why you're telling me? So I can protect myself?"

A long sigh escaped Grace's mouth and she slumped back in her chair. "I intend to tell everyone," she said, her voice softer now, almost defeated. "I think we all have a right to protect our privacy." She leaned forward suddenly, her face angry again. "And I intend to do whatever has to be done to protect my exhibit. I am *not* going to allow it to be turned into the sideshow of some investigation."

The priest stared at her. Was it possible the woman simply didn't understand that the exhibition and the rituals now being carried out *were* connected? There was no way for them not to be. He had thought about it for days now, and had come to believe that the earlier sacrifices in the Yucatán had been connected with the excavations conducted there. The rituals had not simply followed *him* to New York, they had followed the *exhibit.* Surely she could see that as well. He clasped his hands together to quiet them. But he also understood that she was right about the need to protect the exhibit. The work was too important to be lost or denigrated, the advancement in scholarship about the ancient civilization too valuable to be set aside. Even the police would have to be made to realize that.

"How will you do it, Grace?" he asked. "How do you think the exhibit can be protected?"

Grace's face became stern and rigid; her eyes were sharp pinpoints that cut the air between them. "I'm not sure," she said. "But I intend to take all necessary steps to stop this madness. And I intend to urge everyone connected with the exhibit to do the same. I'll make that clear to Malcolm this morning, and to Kate when she returns from Mexico this afternoon. I will not see our work destroyed because of the insensitivity of the police."

Father LoPato stared at her for several moments without speaking. "I think I understand, Grace," he said, then repeated to himself: Yes, I do understand what you really mean.

The dossiers were spread out on the battered, stained table in Rolk's office as Dr. Nathan Greenspan hunched over them, jotting notes in a steno pad.

Devlin sat behind the desk, drumming his fingers on it, his eyes boring into the back of the psychiatrist's head as if he were hoping to divine some information there.

After almost half an hour Greenspan swiveled in his chair, his plump face offering Devlin a look of weary frustration. He ran his hands along the lone tufts of hair that protruded above his ears, then carefully lit his pipe.

"You have an amazing collection of brilliant people here," he began. "And, as you'd find in any such group, you have a collection of emotional problems that coincides with that brilliance. But I don't see anything that makes one a stronger suspect than any of the others."

"What about the priest?" Devlin asked. "Rolk's

leaning hard in that direction. So am I, now that one of his Mayans has disappeared."

"Why? Because he had a breakdown?" Greenspan shook his head. "From what Rolk told you on the telephone, the priest who replaced him isn't far from one himself. Breakdowns come from an inability to deal with problems that overwhelm the psyche. They do not turn someone into a homicidal killer. Those problems would have to have been present before. And from the information you have here, I just don't see any indication of it."

Devlin thought about his telephone conversation with Rolk the previous night. They had exchanged information —Rolk about the events in the Yucatán, Devlin about the discovery of the heads and the sudden disappearance of Roberto Caliento. Rolk had been unusually noncommittal about both, stating only that he did not want Father LoPato approached until he returned. His main concern, in fact, had seemed to be nothing more than increased protection for Kate Silverman.

"What about what happened to Dr. Silverman down there?"

"You mean because it happened after she visited the other priest?" Greenspan waited as Devlin nodded. "My friend, you're grasping at straws. You're suggesting LoPato can somehow communicate with these backward villagers, or has left some instruction that they attack anyone who investigates the ritual. So, let's say that *has* happened. It could just as easily have been done by any of the others. We now know they were each there a year ago. And the incident with the snake could just as easily have been initiated by Dr. Silverman herself." Greenspan drew a long breath. "Right now, based on the background information you've developed on each, I don't find any overwhelming linkage that would allow me to say this one or that one is your killer."

"How would you rank them, based on what you have?" Devlin asked.

"I really don't feel comfortable doing that. The information is so limited that—"

Devlin slammed his fist against the desk, cutting Greenspan off. "Dammit, I'm not asking you to testify in court. I'm just asking you for an educated opinion I can work from."

Greenspan took on a slightly wounded expression, then seemed to shake it off as quickly as it had appeared. He drew deeply on his pipe, exhaling the smoke with a sigh. "If I *had* to list them as probabilities"—he tapped one of the dossiers—"based on *this* information, I'd say: Sousi, Mallory, Silverman, and LoPato. But that's—"

"The priest last?" Devlin asked, cutting him off again.

"Yes. Last."

"Why?"

"First, even though he *is* a priest, and the murderer is imitating a religious ritual, the actions of the killer are diametrically opposed to the long and rather severe religious training LoPato's had. Second, because he's had the least access to the museum, and especially the area where the heads were discovered." Devlin began to interrupt again, but Greenspan stopped him with a raised hand. "I place Dr. Silverman ahead of him because of that greater access, even though she appears to have the most stable background in this group, and also because of the outside possibility that the attacks against her could—and I say *could*—have been engineered by the woman herself, knowingly or unknowingly." Greenspan puffed on his pipe again, sending up a thick cloud of blue smoke. "Now we come to Dr. Mallory. Here we have a brilliant woman who has been forced to struggle for recognition all her life, because of her sex and the generation into which she was born. She has a great—perhaps even fanatic—devotion to her subject matter. This exhibition is her one great opportunity for recognition, and if she is a severely disturbed psychotic, that fact might cause her to do something terrible to gain public attention for it." Greenspan shook his head, openly displeased with his own words. "This is all conjecture, of course, but as curator she does have the greatest access to all areas of the museum. Also, given what you discovered about her probable sexual preference, we have an additional factor. The victims were both women, and they were severely mutilated. Whether that has any significance in this instance, I simply don't know."

"So now we get to Sousi," Devlin interjected. "Why does he make the top of your list?"

"A combination of things. First, his background—and I must compliment your men on the checking they did. Even though it's too limited for hard analysis, they did an excellent job of sketching out the personal, academic, and professional histories of each of these people." Greenspan sent up another massive cloud of smoke. "Sousi, first of all, has a troubled academic history. Now, this isn't unheard-of for a brilliant student, annoyed by teaching he finds inadequate. But in Sousi's case it appears to be combined with a tremendous ego, a sense of self-importance that seems to go beyond what one would expect from your everyday brilliant scholar." Greenspan raised one finger. "The man also apparently resents and dislikes women to an unusually high degree. Now, if he was indeed a psychotic, he might well want to cause professional harm to the women he resents working with, and/or he might want to do terrible things to the women he encounters, and simply chooses methods suggested by his scholarly knowledge. It does fit the ego pattern of a psychotic, but again—"

"I know," Devlin said. "It's only speculation."

"Exactly," Greenspan said, smiling again.

"So where do we go from here? From your standpoint?"

Greenspan rubbed his chin, then laid his pipe in an ashtray. "I'd like to be with you and Rolk the next time you put each of them through some tough questioning. And I'd even like to suggest some of the questions myself. It's the only way I'm going to get a better grasp of the situation."

Devlin leaned back in his chair and mulled over the idea. He sat forward again, taking several more moments to study Greenspan's face. "I'll check it out with Rolk as soon as possible," he said at length. "And I think he'll agree, because what you're giving us now isn't helping one damned bit."

Rolk returned from Mexico late the following day, looking haggard and worn from his jaunts into the jungles of Quintana Roo. His first question to Devlin was about Kate Silverman and the level of protection she was receiving.

Devlin assured him that Bernie Peters had taken on that task, and then informed him of the latest developments in the case.

"So we've got the Bug Room staked out," Rolk said. "Who've we got on that?"

"Peters and Moriarty are splitting it, twelve hours each," Devlin said. "They know the area and all the suspects, and the museum director won't allow more than one man on it. Seems there was a little uproar over our search, so we have to use museum security as backup. During the day it's one of their uniforms set up in a room across the hall with our guy. At night, which is the time we're most concerned about, the backup is the museum's security director, a former vice cop named Ezra Waters, who's as good as anybody I could put there."

Rolk's eyes widened slightly, and at first Devlin thought he would object to the inadequacy of the backup.

"How is Peters watching Kate if he's on this stakeout?" he asked in a a tight voice.

Devlin eyed Rolk closely. He didn't like his degree of concern, or the overly nervous tone of his voice. He waited a moment before answering.

"Bernie picks her up in the morning, then does his stint at the stakeout. Mallory and her staff are working long shifts, getting this exhibit ready, usually from eight to eight. Then Bernie takes Kate home, checks out her apartment, and goes off duty, while Moriarty picks up the stakeout. It's basically what you were doing."

The concern had not left Rolk's face. "What about at night, at her apartment?"

Devlin leaned forward. "What do you mean? There's a patrol car outside. If she has a problem, she calls her doorman, and there are two uniforms outside her door in thirty seconds. You expected somebody inside her apartment?"

"You're damned right I did."

"We don't have that kind of manpower," Devlin said. "And I thought those uniforms outside her apartment were there not only to protect her but also because she's a suspect in this case. Did something else happen in Mexico that I don't know about?" he finally asked.

Rolk's jaw tightened and his face reddened with either anger or guilt, Devlin couldn't be certain which.

"What happened down there was that somebody put a rattlesnake the size of a Buick in her bed—a rattlesnake with a necklace of plumes around its fucking head, so it damned well wasn't something that wandered in on its own. I thought that kind of attack might make you realize a little extra protection was warranted, especially with this clown Caliento missing."

Devlin sat back in his chair and continued to study Rolk. He was more than a little confused by his attitude, unless . . .

"You think Caliento might have gone down to Mexico ahead of you? Maybe was sent there by the priest?"

"It's a damned strong possibility, isn't it?" Rolk snapped. "That day I spent in Washington with Immigration was all he needed to beat me there, and we still don't know where the hell he did go."

"We'll find out," Devlin said. "We'll lean on the priest until he tells us. In the meantime, if you feel Dr.

Silverman needs more protection, I'll take care of it right away."

"Never mind," Rolk said. "I'll take care of it. You just pull that priest in here and find out what he knows."

Devlin rose to leave, then stopped. "Look, it's none of my business, but we've been friends a long time." He hesitated, then continued. "You always told me it was a bad idea to get too involved with a suspect or a victim."

Rolk's eyes glared anger. "You're right," he snapped. "It's none of your business."

Devlin offered a curt nod and left the office.

Rolk continued to stare at the door for a long moment after it closed, then sat at his desk, shuffling reports and telephone messages absently, struggling to control the anger he felt building within him. He knew Devlin was right about his personal involvement with Kate. It was unprofessional and it was dangerous, but he also knew there was nothing he could do to change it, and he had no intention of abandoning Kate to the inadequate protection of Bernie Peters. He also knew Devlin was wrong about the level of protection needed. He had been with her in Mexico and he had seen what they were dealing with, something far more sinister than Devlin seemed capable of understanding. Kate was a target, the ultimate target. He conjured up an image of the two heads, as he imagined Peters and Moriarty had discovered them. It sent a shudder through his body, and he knew he had little choice in what he had to do.

Shoving the papers into one corner of his desk, Rolk glanced at his watch, then reached for the telephone. It took several minutes before Kate came on the line, but the relief Rolk felt would have made any wait worthwhile.

"I'm back," he said. "Are you okay?"

Kate's breath rushed ahead of her words. "Oh, God, it's good to hear your voice. I'm fine. I've been thinking about you much too much."

"I want to see you. Tonight," Rolk said.

"I want that very much too. Will you be taking me home?"

"No. Let Peters do it."

"I'll be leaving at eight."

"I'll wait until I see Peters leave, then I'll be up."

"Oh, Stan, I can't wait to see you."

"I can't stay long, but I have to see you."

"I understand," Kate said.

Twenty-five

"**I** CAN'T TELL you where he went." Father LoPato stood behind a chair in the rectory sitting room, his eyes firm, determined.

"Can't, or won't?" Devlin asked. "He and Domingo were here with you the day before we lost track of him. Was that just a coincidence?"

"You're following him?"

"That's right, Father."

"That's ridiculous."

Devlin stood facing him, Charlie Moriarty standing slightly behind him. Both men still wore their top-coats, offering the implication that they might be leaving soon and might be taking the priest with them.

"I'll tell you what, Father," Moriarty said. "We won't tell you how to say Mass. You don't tell us how to run a murder investigation."

"I'm just telling you about the man," the priest said. "He's not a killer, and you're wasting your time trying to prove that he is."

Devlin stuffed his hands in his pockets and began rocking back and forth on the balls of his feet as if he might launch himself at the priest at any moment.

"It doesn't look too good for Caliento, taking off like that," Moriarty said in a flat, toneless voice.

"Certainly the man has a right to take a trip if he wants to."

"He doesn't have a right to do anything," Devlin said. "He doesn't have the right to scratch his ass in Times Square. The only reason he's still walking around is that *we* decided not to turn him over to Immigration. But all bets are off now. And that goes for Domingo and anyone else we can locate."

The priest's face radiated anger, his breath came more quickly, and his jaw was clenched. "If you want to make an issue out of it, I assure you there are other people willing to stand behind these men."

"Then you better start calling them," Devlin said. "And just to be fair—before they make damned fools of themselves—you better tell them that we're putting out a warrant for his arrest in a murder investigation. A rather nasty murder investigation. And tell them we're doing that because you won't tell us where to find him."

A twitch came to the corner of the priest's eye, and his hands began to move aimlessly along the back of the chair. "And you'll leave him alone if I tell you?"

"Not a chance," Devlin said. "We're going to interrogate him four ways from Sunday, and if we don't like his answers, we're going to lock him up until we do."

"I . . . I meant about Immigration," the priest stammered.

Devlin shook his head. "We don't like the way you play ball, Father. All the rules seem to be on your side. So why don't you just start by telling us why you sent him away."

The priest stared down at his hands, which were now gripping the back of the chair so hard his knuckles had turned white. "I sent him to warn the others who are staying in other cities."

"Warn them about *what?*" Devlin asked.

"That there was trouble with the police. That it might cause them problems too."

"You never heard of the telephone?" Moriarty asked.

"Most don't have them, and in some cases, the people caring for them don't even speak Spanish. I just wanted to make sure there was no confusion, and I didn't want to panic them either." He looked at each of the detectives in turn. "They're a simple people in a strange country, and the idea that the authorities don't want them here frightens them."

"Why didn't *you* go?" Devlin asked.

The priest gripped the chair even harder. "I thought it would be better if they heard the news from one of their own people. I thought it might be less threatening if they saw that he was able to come to them."

"Where's Caliento now?" Moriarty asked.

The priest hesitated. "Philadelphia," he said at length.

"You gave him money to travel?" Devlin asked.

"Yes."

"How much?"

"Just a few hundred dollars."

"And he probably had money of his own," Moriarty added. "He has been working, hasn't he?"

"What are you trying to say?" the priest asked.

"We're just wondering if he had enough money to get to Mexico," Devlin said.

"Why would he go there?"

"Dr. Silverman was attacked there a few days ago," Devlin said. "In Chichén Itzá."

"Oh, my God. Was she hurt?"

Devlin shook his head. "Whoever did it wasn't up to his usual standards."

"But it couldn't have been Roberto. I'm telling you, he went to Philadelphia."

"Then you can get hold of him, can't you?" Moriarty suggested.

"Yes, of course."

"Do that," Devlin said. "And while you're at it, tell him to get himself back here so we can talk to him. Tell him that if he doesn't, every cop on the East Coast is going to be looking for his butt."

"And that anybody who's with him, or who's hiding him out, is going to be in the same kind of trouble," Moriarty added.

The priest stared through the two men and nodded. "I'll call now."

Kate's head was buried in the hollow of Rolk's

shoulder; his arms encircled her, and she felt safe and warm and contented. A thin sheet covered their bodies, still warm from their lovemaking and Kate could hear Rolk's heart drumming against her ear.

"It's almost worth it," she said, her voice still slightly breathless.

"What is?"

"Having a madman chase me around."

Rolk pulled his head back and stared down at her. "Whatever turns you on, lady."

She smiled and pressed her head back into his shoulder. "That's not what I meant. It's just that I never would have met you otherwise."

"Don't forget, I went to your lecture."

"But you only spoke to me for a few minutes, then you left."

Rolk remained silent for several moments. "Yes," he finally said. "Only a few minutes."

She pulled back and stared up at him, still smiling. "Didn't you find me irresistible then?"

"I was just shy."

She threw back her head and laughed. "You? Shy? The infamous scholar of murder?"

"Can't scholars be shy?"

"Never."

"Then I guess I didn't find you irresistible."

Kate jabbed a finger into his ribs, causing him to jump. "That's not the right answer," she said.

"What am I supposed to say?"

"That you were so awestruck by my beauty, you simply found me unapproachable."

"That must have been it."

She jabbed his ribs again.

"Hey, that's assaulting a police officer. You can get locked up for that."

"And you could get locked up for tampering with a witness." She smiled at him again, her eyes glowing with mischief. "Maybe we could get locked up together."

"Not allowed," Rolk said. "They don't allow conjugal visits."

"Then I won't go."

"That would be resisting arrest."

Kate stretched, then slid her arms around his neck. "Never, officer. I'll never resist. Not even a little."

He pulled her to him and kissed her, feeling her tongue slip immediately into his mouth, her body press eagerly against him. He could feel himself beginning to grow, and he marveled at how exciting she was, how easily she aroused him.

Kate pulled back, then reached down and took him in her hand. She smiled at him; the pleasure brimming in her eyes. "So," she said. "What have we here?"

"Just a little something I dreamed up for you."

Her smile widened, and she began stroking him gently. "I like the way you dream, Lieutenant," she said. "I very much like the way you dream."

He drew a deep breath and closed his eyes, concentrating on the steady rhythm of her hand.

"Do you think I'm irresistible now?" she whispered.

"I think you're wonderful," he said.

Twenty-six

CHARLIE MORIARTY YAWNED, stretched, shifted his weight on the hard wooden chair, then resettled his bulk as well as he could. It was almost midnight and he had spent the last four hours seated in the small office across from the Bug Room with Ezra Waters beside him.

"This sucks," Moriarty said, then grunted as he shifted his weight again. "I hate this part of the job. Waiting for somebody who ain't never gonna come."

"How you know that?" Waters asked.

"I can just feel it. You know how it is. I can just tell I ain't never gonna see this loony walk down that hall and into my hands."

"Shit," Waters said. "Devlin never told me about working with no fuckin' clairvoyant. But I tell you right now, you come to work with a crystal ball some night, and I'm gonna throw your ass right outta here."

Moriarty laughed softly, his fat, cherubic face turning pink. "Maybe that's what we need," he said. "A crystal ball. Either that or somebody else getting their head lopped off, so our loony has some reason to come here. Christ, I just don't see him coming by every so often just to check out his goodies."

"It's the search, my man," Waters said. "That's what Devlin's thinkin' about. Our boy, he hears about the search an' he comes by to check out his stash."

Moriarty grunted again. "Even this crazy can't be that crazy."

Waters stood and rubbed his buttocks with both hands. "Man, we gotta get some soft chairs in here."

He windmilled his arms, loosening his shoulder muscles, then lit a cigarette. "I could use some coffee. How about you?"

"Yeah, why not? And I also gotta take a piss, so I'll get it. If the other guards have guzzled it all, I'll make a fresh pot. Shit, maybe I'll make a fresh pot anyway. We gotta get some perks outta this fuckin' job."

Moriarty struggled out of the chair and started for the door.

"Watch your ass," Waters warned. "You run into the bogeyman in the hall, we're liable to be fishin' *your* melon outta one of them tanks."

"Almost beat the shit outta sittin' here, though, wouldn't it?" Moriarty said as he moved his bulk out the door. "Give me a yap on the radio if you see any heads rollin' down the hall," he added as he eased the door shut behind him.

The figure stood in the shadows of a storage case along one wall of the corridor, eyes fixed on the bulky body that lumbered down the hall.

Already the plastic raincoat was in place, the rubber gloves fitted over clenched fists. The only objects that marred the smooth, slick exterior were the stone mask that hung from a leather thong fitted about the neck, and the handle of the long obsidian knife that protruded from the raincoat pocket.

Slowly a hand went to the handle of the knife as the policeman drew closer, then released it and closed again into a fist as he turned, moved through the stairwell door, and disappeared.

Patience, patience, an inner voice cautioned. *They're here, just as you knew they would be.* A harsh smile spread across full lips. *And it was so easy,* the voice said. *So many doors in, and so few guards to watch them. Now you must simply find them*—the smile intensified—*or allow one of them to find you.* The decision came quickly. *Surely a divine intervention. And what better place to punish them? What better place for retribution could there be?*

Ezra Waters sat in the darkness, far enough back

from the glass door so he could see without being seen in return. Moriarty was right. It was boring and it was a pain in the ass, and he wished now he had given this shit duty to one of his subordinates. He grinned at the idea. Just couldn't resist playing cop again, he thought. Even though five years ago you couldn't wait to put your papers in and get away from it all. But that was for the extra bread, not because you didn't know you'd miss it.

And the old lady wanted it too. Not just for the extra bread either, but the idea that your ass was gonna get home safe every night. And, shit, that was part of what you missed, wasn't it? The not knowing. Try to explain that to somebody who wasn't a cop.

Waters was digging a cigarette from an almost empty pack when the figure moved quickly to the Bug Room door, fussed momentarily with the handle, and slipped inside. At first Waters caught only a flash of movement, and when he looked up, he saw only part of someone's back gliding into the room.

"What the fuck?" he muttered to himself, immediately picking up the hand-held radio to send out a call for Moriarty. He depressed the transmit button and spoke quietly into the microphone. Nothing. Quickly he adjusted the "squelch" dial. Again, nothing. Angrily he stared at the red light that glowed from the handset, indicating the battery was down.

"Shit," he growled, realizing he had forgotten to charge the handset the previous night. He withdrew his pistol and eased out into the hall, then glanced down the length of the corridor, hoping to see Moriarty returning. No one.

Set yourself and wait out here, he told himself. He gritted his teeth, knowing such a move would accomplish nothing. You need to catch the dude searching the vats. Just being in there don't mean shit. His mind raced with the reactions he would face if he failed to handle the situation properly, failed to act as he would have when he was still a cop. They'll all know you lost it, baby, he told himself. How you just couldn't hack the job anymore. "Fuck they will," he whispered to himself as he moved across the hall and flattened against the opposite wall.

Using his free hand, he touched the handle of the door. Again he checked the corridor. Still no Moriarty.

Slowly Waters pushed the door open, his body lowered to a crouch, his revolver extended before him as he moved quickly into the room. Ahead of him the figure stood at the long metal table, back to the door.

"You just hold it right there," Waters snapped.

Slowly the head turned, the eyes steady as they took in the hunched man, revolver in hand.

Waters exhaled heavily, then stood, allowing the revolver to drop to his side. "What the hell you doing?" he asked, perspiration beading his forehead.

The figure turned slightly; a hand holding a sheaf of papers extended toward Waters.

Waters reached for the papers holstering his revolver. "Is it raining out?" he asked, taking in the plastic raincoat.

"Yes," the voice said through a growing smile.

As Waters took hold of the papers, the figure turned full forward and Waters saw, for the first time, the stone mask hanging from the neck. His body froze momentarily, and a sudden surge of fear filled his chest; his hand automatically moved back to his holster as the figure's free hand lashed out with surprising speed.

The green blade of the knife sliced into the right side of Waters' throat, severing the major veins and arteries carrying blood to and from the brain. A bright red spray spurted from the wound, and almost immediately Waters' vision began to blur, then darken. The revolver fell from his hand, and the blank sheets of paper he had been handed, fluttered to the floor. His body remained erect for several seconds, the muscles contorting in great spasms, until they finally gave out and sent him crashing to the floor.

The figure stood above him, watching as Waters' arms and legs continued to jerk uncontrollably, the spurts of blood gradually diminishing, until only small bubbles appeared, bursting as they escaped the deep, gaping wound.

From a pocket in the raincoat the killer withdrew a second stone mask and carefully placed it on Waters' motionless chest, then stepped over the body and out into the hall, the blade of the knife hanging down, leaving a trail of blood drops along the floor.

Rolk stood over the body, flanked by Jerry Feldman and Paul Devlin. Waters' cocoa-colored complexion had turned brown-gray in death, and his wide eyes and open mouth made it appear he was crying out some final warning no one could hear.

"He shouldn't even have been here," Rolk said, almost to himself. "And if that damned director hadn't insisted on it, he wouldn't have been."

Feldman placed a hand on Rolk's shoulder and squeezed lightly. "I've never dealt with a murder victim yet who couldn't have been somewhere else," he said softly. "It's the one thing you learn in this job. It happens. And usually there's nothing anybody could have done to stop it."

Rolk stared out of the Bug Room, its spring-operated door tied back to keep it ajar for easier access. Across the hall he could see Charlie Moriarty seated in the small office they had used for surveillance, head lowered into his hands, his heavy shoulders still heaving with remorse. Moriarty had found the body, and after calling for help, had raced through the building, following the trail of blood until it disappeared halfway down the stairs leading to the basement.

I just went to take a piss and to bring us back some coffee. Jesus, oh, sweet Jesus, I was just gone ten fucking minutes.

Rolk snapped away from the memory of Moriarty's words and turned fiercely on Feldman. "I need everything fast, Jerry. Goddamned fast."

"You'll get it, Stan."

Rolk then turned to Devlin. "I want you to get

everyone down to the office no later than nine o'clock. That means Sousi, Mallory, Kate Silverman, and that priest. We'll leave the Mayans for later. Anybody gives you any shit about it, you take some uniforms and drag them in by their ears. Understood?"

Kate rushed into Rolk's mind. She had fallen asleep in his arms only a few hours earlier, and he wished he could spare her this now. He rejected the idea as soon as he thought of it.

"Right," Devlin said. "They'll be there, one way or the other."

"What about you, Stan?" Feldman asked.

"Me?" He snorted. "I've got to see Ezra's wife. Then I'm going to get hold of the museum director and tell him about the new ballgame we've got in town, and what he and his friends at City Hall can do if they don't like it."

Twenty-seven

ROLK PACED HIS office like a caged animal, a cigarette stuck in the corner of his mouth, his eyes glaring at the linoleum floor as though searching for something to crush underfoot. Paul Devlin sat in one corner of the battered leather sofa watching the performance, wondering about the pent-up violence he was now observing in this normally quiet man.

Rolk came to an abrupt halt. "Whoever it was," he snapped, "it was someone Ezra didn't consider a threat, somebody who would naturally cause him to lower his guard." Rolk stared at the floor again, his head tilting to one side. "I checked the department's records this morning, and Ezra was a Catholic, so he probably would feel that way about a priest." Rolk tilted his head the other way. "He'd probably feel the same about the women, so that leaves Sousi." His head began a slow negative shake. "And a guy like Ezra would probably take one look at him, and figure he was a wimp he could have for breakfast. Shit!"

Rolk began pacing again. His sleeves were rolled to the elbow, and the muscles in his heavy forearms did a rippling dance as he opened and closed his fists. His necktie was askew and he had not yet shaved. He reminded Devlin very much of a bear with a toothache.

Rolk turned again and stared down at the other man. "Those blank papers," he said, raising one finger. "They had to be some kind of prop, something to get Ezra to reach for, just that little something to put him off balance, to distract him."

"His gun was out," Devlin reminded him.

"Yeah, but barely," Rolk said, his finger raised again.

"How did you determine that?"

"We both know when a weapon is holstered, the trigger guard is covered, at least with the type of holster Ezra was wearing. That means as it's pulled out, a period of time exits before the finger goes inside the trigger guard. And that's when he was hit."

"How do you figure that?"

"Unless someone is killed instantly—and Jerry Feldman assures me Ezra was not—there's a reflex action. And you know that with a trained cop that reflex always translates into pulling that trigger, even if he's too hurt to point the weapon. I've seen it too many times. And Ezra didn't do it. His finger hadn't even reached the trigger guard, so he was just yanking the gun when he was hit." Rolk paused again, thinking. "And that means he had put it away, because he never would have gone into that room with it holstered."

"All right, I can buy all of that," Devlin said. "But why him? Why did the killer go back there at all. Certainly he had to have heard about the search, and had to at least suspect there was some danger involved."

"Curiosity about the heads, maybe."

"Never. If the heads were that important to him, he would have kept them with him."

"Retribution, then," Rolk said. "Against us."

Devlin nodded slowly, as though considering the thought. "Possible," he said at length. "Or perhaps just to show us that his power was so great no one was safe."

Rolk slumped on the sofa next to the detective. "If that's the case, there's something I don't understand." He paused a beat, rethinking his words. "Last week I leaked a story to one of the newspapers—a derogatory story about the killer."

"Yes, I saw it. I figured you were behind it."

"I thought it might bring the bastard out, force him into the open, maybe even to the point of coming after us. Or me."

"Not a very safe move," Devlin offered.

"No. It wasn't." Devlin nodded, and Rolk continued. "But nothing happened then, and it should have. It's something that's worked in the past, and it should have worked now."

"I agree. But the answer's simple enough. The killer just didn't read that particular newspaper."

Rolk snorted. "That would be a bitch, wouldn't it? If I picked the wrong newspaper to draw him out." He shook his head slowly and rose from the sofa. Then he pointed toward the outer office. "Greenspan should be here soon. Then we can get started."

Before Rolk entered the outer office, he shaved and arranged his rumpled clothing into some semblance of order. The four suspects were scattered about the room, most showing some signs of apprehension—all but Kate Silverman, who was quietly talking to Paul Devlin. Nathan Greenspan walked into Rolk's office to wait.

Initially Rolk had intended to take the men first, then the women. But now he knew he wanted Devlin and Kate separated. She would never understand what he was about to do to her; he wasn't sure he understood it himself. It would hurt her, shock her, and he hoped later he would be able to explain it, make her understand it was something he had to do. Or did he? What if something came out that pointed the finger at her, broke her down? But there was nothing he could do about that. Not now. Not ever.

"Dr. Silverman," he snapped. "Would you come in, please?"

Kate sat calmly, quietly, in an institutional metal visitor's chair in front of Rolk's desk. Dr. Greenspan stood behind Rolk, his pipe sending up plumes of blue-gray smoke. He was introduced simply as Nathan Greenspan, with no indication of his psychiatric background. Just another cop, for all practical purposes, and far less threatening that way, Rolk had decided.

Rolk's forearms rested on his desk; his eyes were

eeply circled and tired. He leaned forward, his jaw
et hard, unrelenting.

"Tell me, Dr. Silverman," he began in a cold, hol-
ow voice, "how would you feel about cutting off
omeone's head?"

Kate stiffened immediately, and her mouth opened
n a circle of horrified surprise. "My God, what are
ou talking about?" she asked. "It's not anything I've
ver thought about." She stared at him, unable to
elieve he was doing this.

"Not even since the murders began?" Rolk pressed.

"Of course not. Why would I?"

"I have. I think it's only natural. You hear about
omething gruesome and you wonder what it must be
ke to do something like that."

"Well, I don't, Lieutenant." She stressed the title,
oping it would shock him, make him realize what he
vas doing was wrong. He couldn't mean this. Not
fter Mexico. Not after last night. He was just staring
t her, and she wanted to return the stare; make it just
s unfeeling as his. "It's your job to think that way,
•ut it isn't mine." She had wanted her voice to sound
ngry, but it hadn't. It had only sounded surprised and
urt.

"You ever kill anything, Doctor? An animal? Any-
hing?"

"No, *Lieutenant.* Unless you want to count spiders
d mosquitoes."

Rolk grunted. "You feel secure in your job, Doc-
or? You like the people you work with?"

Kate was puzzled by the sudden switch in questions.
'Why, yes," she said hesitantly. "Although I guess
've never thought about it much. You see, I concen-
rate on the work. That's the important thing."

"You're dedicated to it, huh?"

"Of course. That's *why* I became a scholar, so I
ould dedicate myself to it."

"Would you be upset if someone threatened it? Or
hreatened your concept of how it should be done?"

"Professional disagreements aren't uncommon. Bu people don't commit murder because of them."

"You're an expert on murder?"

Kate seemed momentarily flustered. "Well, no, c course not. But I'm sure it would take far more than—'

Rolk didn't allow her to finish. "People kill eac other over an unkind word, lady. So please don't te me what it takes to commit a murder." He watche Kate stiffen, her face a mass of confusion. "Tell m about your family," he continued. "Your father o mother ever knock the hell out of you? Ever have an teachers who were particularly unkind?"

Kate was staggered again by the sudden change i the line of questions. "I . . . I'm not sure I understan what you mean."

"Don't give me that," Rolk snapped. "Did anyon ever abuse you, mistreat you in any way?"

"Of course not. Why would anyone—"

Rolk stopped her again, his voice still soft, bu intensifying in its degree of threat. "Don't con me.' He jabbed a finger toward her face. "Before I'm fin ished, I'm going to know everything about you. Every thing. So don't think you can play games." He leane further forward in his chair, his face glowering. "We'v got a killer on our hands. A degenerate who's goin around mutilating innocent women. Who killed a for mer cop—a peer of mine. And you know what I'n gonna do? I'm gonna get this piece of garbage. I'n going to hunt him or *her* down and destroy him. An nobody, *nobody*, is going to stop me."

Rolk continued to stare at her, letting his words sin in. Kate's lips began to tremble, and her face ha become pale.

"Where were you last night, around midnight?" Rolk snapped.

"At home. Asleep," Kate said, a slight tremor i her voice.

"Alone?" Rolk snapped.

"Yes. I live alone." A picture of Rolk in her bec

flashed into Kate's mind, but he had been gone long before midnight, she told herself. What kind of game was he playing?

"I didn't ask you if you lived alone. I asked you if you *were* alone at midnight last night."

A flash of anger came into Kate's eyes. "Yes," she said, her voice cold. "At midnight I was alone, in bed, asleep."

Rolk paused, his eyes boring into her. "That's too bad," he said at length, pausing again to allow the implications of his words to play out. He saw her face begin to redden slightly, then added, "It would have been nice if you had an alibi." He paused again, still staring. "Thank you for coming in," he snapped, dismissing her.

Malcolm Sousi threw back his head and laughed. "How do I feel about cutting off somebody's head?" he asked, repeating the question. "Well, I'll tell you, Lieutenant. On that point I think it is far better to give than to receive."

Rolk stared at him without humor. "Ever done it, Sousi?"

A grin spread over the anthropologist's mouth, exposing perfect teeth. "Not recently, Lieutenant," he said.

"Don't be cute with me," Rolk snapped.

"Then don't ask me stupid questions," Sousi snapped in return.

Rolk leaned back in his chair, a false smile forming on his own lips. "Ever think about killing someone?" he asked.

"Sure," Sousi said. "About once a week, given the idiots I have to deal with. But so far I've been able to repress the urge."

"You're a pretty smart guy," Rolk began again. "Oh, yes," he said, nodding. "I've looked over your academic record. Pretty smart. Except a lot of your teachers thought you were one big egotistical pain in the ass. Did you know that?"

"Doesn't surprise me," Sousi said. "Not given the quality of instruction we have today."

Rolk smiled again. "You know, I thought you might say that. But tell me. How about your job? Do they think you're a pain in the ass? Dr. Mallory for instance."

Sousi's eyes hardened. "You'll have to ask her, Lieutenant. But I haven't had many complaints about my work, if that's what you want to know. Nor should I have."

"Pretty good at what you do, huh?"

"Very good, Lieutenant."

"What about your parents? They think you were very good? Or did they maybe kick your ass around a little bit?"

Sousi threw back his head and laughed again. He leaned forward in his chair, his eyes hard now. "No, Lieutenant. No child abuse. My parents were intellectuals. They didn't believe in that spare-the-rod, spoil-the-child crap."

"You're lucky you weren't my kid," Rolk said, staring into Sousi's sullen eyes.

"Yes," Sousi said. "Especially when it came time for IQ tests."

Rolk ignored him, a fact that seemed to annoy Sousi even more. "Ever kill anything? An animal, whatever?"

"Wings off flies, Lieutenant? Sure. I was your everyday well-rounded, rotten little kid. But they call it 'intellectually curious' when you come from a good family. Or wouldn't you know about that?"

Again Rolk ignored him, and again it seemed to anger and frustrate the man. "Where were you last night around midnight?" Rolk asked, his voice soft.

"In bed." Sousi hesitated, but more for effect than reluctance. "With a lady."

"What was her name?"

Sousi grinned at him. "We never got around to names," he said.

Rolk nodded to himself. "Too bad," he said. "It would have made things easier for you." He scribbled a note on a pad set before him, then looked up. "Thanks for coming in," he said.

Sousi started for the door, only to be stopped by Rolk's voice. "Tell me something, Doctor Sousi. Did the lady enjoy herself?"

Sousi's jaw tightened and he glared down at Rolk. Rolk nodded again and allowed a small smile to play on his lips. "No. I didn't think so."

Grace Mallory sat stiffly before Rolk, her face a carved piece of granite, her eyes flat and devoid of expression. Rolk understood her rigidity, a holdover from the search that had trodden into her private life. Something, he thought, the woman viewed as beyond forgiveness. But enough to kill for? He wondered.

The woman's eyes flooded with derision with Rolk's first question and her voice took on a note of contempt. "How I would feel about beheading would depend upon the culture I belonged to. To some it is a matter of religious necessity. To others, a grave, unwanted punishment, one that could even deny the victim eternal life."

Rolk leaned forward. "I'm not talking about you as part of any other culture. I'm asking how you feel about it as part of your culture."

Mallory shrugged. "I suppose it's a merciful way to end a life. At least modern science seems to think so. But we really can't know for certain, can we?"

The coldness of the answer seemed to radiate out, leaving Rolk with a sense of being internally chilled.

"You ever kill anything, Doctor?" Rolk allowed his eyes to match the woman's, one chilling gaze passing into another.

"Animals," Mallory answered.

"Tell me about it."

The woman's lips tightened, forming a narrow line. "On occasion, on digs, we would come across a badly injured animal. On those occasions one of us—sometimes I—would put it out of its misery. Does that answer your question?"

"No reluctance to do that?" Rolk asked.

"At times, of course." She stared harshly at Rolk. "It wasn't something that occurred daily. But when it did, we did the sensible thing. I was never one who found some point, or religious significance, to meaningless suffering."

Rolk steepled his fingers before his eyes, then spoke through them. "I imagine you've experienced some discrimination in your work. How do you feel about that?"

"How do you *think* I feel about it, Lieutenant?" Grace's tone was cutting, the acid flowing unrestrained. "I despise it. But like most women, I work my way through it, or around it. There isn't much choice, is there? Short of revolution. And you men have all the guns."

Rolk dropped his hands and tilted forward, feigning a more conspiratorial manner. "You prefer dealing with women?" he asked.

The reaction was what Rolk had expected. Pain flashed across the woman's eyes, and her body stiffened in the chair. For a moment he thought he saw tears begin to well up in her eyes, but if they had, they were quickly forced back. A sense of regret and shame passed through Rolk, but he too forced it away, determined to finish what he had begun.

Grace smiled at him, her chin raised in a gesture of defiant pride. "Yes, Lieutenant, I do. I find women far more dedicated to their work—for the sake of the work alone—and much less concerned about the personal benefits to be derived from it. There's also much less of an ego problem to deal with when one is in a position of giving direction."

Rolk began to speak, but she cut him off. "And yes, Lieutenant, I also prefer the company of women in my personal life. I like people who are warm, and I find little warmth in men."

The shame Rolk had felt returned again, and this time he found it more difficult to reject. He studied his hands for a moment, then continued in an even softer voice.

"The victims—at least those whose deaths seemed to follow this Toltec ritual—have been women. Do you see any significance to that?"

The woman closed her eyes momentarily, then offered Rolk another blank stare. "I see little significance in death, Lieutenant. It's something that occurs. Sometimes for a reason, at other times, pointlessly. Given your work, I would have thought you would have surmised that by now."

"Do you see any point in *these* murders?" Rolk asked.

"Yes, I do, Lieutenant." Grace Mallory stared into Rolk's eyes. "Madness," she said at length. "Pure and simple madness."

Father LoPato looked as though he hadn't slept in days. His face had become cadaverous, his eyes sunken, peering out from holes in his skull, his cheeks more hollow and gaunt than Rolk had ever seen them before. The man was on the edge, Rolk thought. The very edge.

The priest's hands fumbled against each other and his shoulders hunched forward, giving him the appearance of a man who had been severely beaten and was now forced to face his attacker.

"It's coming to an end, isn't it?" LoPato asked. "It's all building up to some final, terrible ending."

"Why do you say that?" Rolk asked, thrown off balance by the man's opening words.

"I can feel it." He smiled weakly. "Just as I did once before. It's like that strange quiet before a truly bad storm breaks. I imagine it was like that in the ancient Mayan cities before one of the major ceremonies, the people knowing that a terrible carnage was going to take place, yet believing it was necessary even though it assaulted their senses, the more gentle side of their natures. I suspect they were very quiet and subdued at those times."

"And do you think it's necessary—this final carnage we're waiting for now?"

A pained horror filled the priest's face. "Oh, God, no. If I could stop it, I would. If I could help anyone else stop it, I would."

"You tried once before, didn't you? In the Yucatán."

"Did I?" the priest asked, more of himself than of Rolk, it seemed. "I tried to show them a different way, a different religious path. But it didn't work. Perhaps because I was inept."

"Did you know who was behind it then?" Rolk asked.

"I had suspicions, but never more than that."

"And now? Do you have suspicions now?"

The priest stared into Rolk's face, almost as if hoping to find understanding there, something, anything, he could grasp. "It has to be someone close to the exhibit," he said, his voice filled with pain. "At first I tried to convince myself that it couldn't be. But there's no other explanation. And all of us, all of us who are involved in this exhibit, were in the Yucatán when it happened there." His eyes darted around the room, then settled on Rolk again. "Don't you see? That has to be the connection."

"Who do you suspect, Father?" Rolk's eyes bored into the priest, but the man was looking away now, his gaze fixed on nothing in particular. His head shook back and forth slowly, as if that, in itself, were the only answer he could give.

"Is it you, Father?" Rolk asked.

Slowly the priest's eyes rose to meet Rolk's. "No," he whispered. "It's not me."

"How do you feel about beheading?" Rolk asked, his own voice remaining low, nonthreatening.

A faint, self-deprecating smile played across the priest's lips. "It's death. And death is something I cannot deal with." LoPato's eyes seemed to grow heavy with a deep-felt sadness. "I know that's a strange thing for a priest to say," he continued. "We're supposed to view life as only prelude for a greater and more glorious life to come—and death as a passing into that life we have been waiting for." The sad eyes filled and tears spilled down his cheeks. "But I can't do that. Not anymore. I no longer believe in death as a joyful event." He paused, wiping the tears away with the back of his hand. He tried to smile, but failed. "A priest is not supposed to admit his own failings of faith," he continued. "Others can have their doubts—be troubled by them, but they're supposed to be able then to turn to their priest or minister and find an unwavering faith to give them strength and uphold them. But, you see, Lieutenant, I've lost my faith, and the great sadness is that I don't know where I lost it."

Rolk waited. He was breathing rapidly, feeling close now, so close. "Sometimes, Father," he began in a gentle voice, "when people lose one belief, they adopt another. And sometimes that new belief is more severe than the one they gave up. Do you have a new belief now, Father? A new faith?"

The priest stared at the floor, wondering if, in fact, he did have a new faith, a new belief, even if it was a belief in nothing at all. He reached into his coat pocket and withdrew a worn rosary and slowly began squeezing it in his hand. "There is only one faith, Lieutenant. You see, I still do believe that. I just simply don't know how to find it anymore."

"You're very good," Greenspan said as he took the chair the others had previously occupied. "You hit all the tender areas, and forced all of them to expose themselves as much as they could, or were willing to."

Rolk still felt sickened by his own performance, by the need to probe into open wounds without regard to the pain it caused. Especially Kate. "Yeah, I was great," he said. "But did we learn anything from it?"

"Did we find the killer?" Greenspan asked rhetorically. "No, we didn't find the killer. But I know a great deal more about the suspects we're dealing with."

Rolk's expression remained noncommittal. "So what

do we know now? Or rather, what do *you* know? Let's go backward, starting with the priest."

Greenspan sat back in his chair, lips pursed, the tufts of hair above his ears sticking out like the wings of a fat, ugly bird. "A very disturbed man," he began. "A man who could do something drastic if he isn't helped. Maybe a man who already *has* done something drastic."

"He said he couldn't accept death, and I got the feeling he might even be frightened by it," Rolk said.

"Yes, that's exactly the point. This inability to accept death seems to be at the very heart of his loss of faith—a very, very major event for this man. And sometimes, when confronted with a thing that threatens us so deeply, the unconscious mind forces us to immerse ourselves in the very thing that frightens us. It's how men perform extraordinary feats of bravery in war, and how some women who are terrified of sex become outrageously promiscuous."

"So you think this fear of death could be driving him to—"

"I didn't say that," Greenspan interjected. "But it is a possibility. But even then, there would have to be something else in his background that would trigger that kind of response, something that affected his psyche so deeply that this new failure was more than he could bear."

"And Grace Mallory?"

Greenspan shook his head. "That is a hard one." He raised a lecturing finger, shaking it as he spoke. "But just listening to her, even briefly, I got the distinct feeling that the woman has taken a major step in coming to terms with herself and perhaps even with what she considers her problem. No, based on what I know about her and what I've seen today, I don't think Grace Mallory is your killer. Unless the killings suddenly stop. Then I would have to put her back on the list."

Rolk let out an exasperated breath, shook his head, and went on to ask about Sousi.

"Now, there you have a disturbed personality," Greenspan said. "Delusions of grandeur, the belief that he's surrounded by inferiors. And somewhere inside, I think, a real, abiding hatred of himself."

"And last, but not least . . ." Rolk said.

"Dr. Silverman." Greenspan shook his head. "I just don't know." He closed his fist and shook it for emphasis. "There's something there, something she's not talking about. Something deep inside that's upsetting that woman. But I'll be damned if I can guess what it is. And it may be nothing that has anything to do with this case. It may just be something personal that's troubling her, or simply the result of the fear she's been living with."

Rolk nodded. He knew what that reluctance was, that need to hold something back. But it wasn't a problem for Greenspan. It was his problem and Kate's. And it was something that would have to be dealt with soon.

"So we're back to the problem of getting more information about our suspects," Rolk said.

"I'm afraid so." Greenspan clutched his hands before him. "We're close. Believe me, we are. And somewhere there's something in the background of one of these people that will tell us what we need to know." He pursed his lips again, his body straining against the chair. "Put one man on it. One man who has nothing else to do but dig into the pasts of these people. And tell him to dig deep. What we need is there. It has to be. And if it's as traumatic as I think it is, he'll find it. Sooner or later, he'll find it."

Charlie Moriarty was still tense and agitated when he entered Rolk's office, but the overwhelming regret that had engulfed him earlier now seemed to have been replaced by a quiet anger that simmered behind his eyes.

"I've got a job for you," Rolk said. "And I need you on it right away."

"This case, right?" Moriarty said.

Rolk nodded. The man was afraid he was about to be yanked, afraid he wouldn't get a chance to make up for Waters' death, which he obviously considered a failure on his part. Rolk picked up the files on the suspects and dropped them on the far end of his desk, directly in front of the detective.

"I know we've checked these people," he began. "But somehow, somewhere, we've missed something. Maybe it's some connection with those two Mayans. Maybe it's something else. So I want it done again. And this time I want it done by one person. You."

"Is this make-work, Lieutenant?" Moriarty snapped. "Something to keep my mind off the fact that I fucked up?"

Rolk stared into the angry face, the eyes brimming with personal pain. "No, Charlie, it's not." He leaned back in his chair. "I don't think you fucked up. I think Ezra Waters fucked up by going in there without waiting for you. And then getting careless." Moriarty seemed about to defend Waters, but Rolk shook his head, indicating he didn't want to hear any defense.

"Any good cop would have tried what he tried, given the circumstances. But a good cop—a cop on top of his form—wouldn't have let his guard down the way Ezra must have." Rolk shrugged. "Maybe the poor bastard was just away from the job too long. I don't know. But I do know it didn't have a damned thing to do with you." He reached across the desk and jabbed one finger against the files. "And this is not make-work. This may damned well be the most important thing we've done on this case. And I want you to put everything you've got into it. And that means don't limit yourself to the goddamned telephone. If you think there's more to get, then you get your ass on a plane, or whatever, and go get it. Don't even wait for any okay from me. Just do it. You understand me, Charlie?"

Moriarty blinked several times, his mind reeling with the idea of spending department money without getting specific prior approval. It was something that just wasn't done, yet Rolk was doing it.

"The brass'll have your ass, they find out about this, Lieutenant," he finally said.

Rolk nodded. "Fuck 'em if they can't take a joke."

Twenty-eight

"**H**OW COULD YOU do that to me? How could you make love to me one night, and then treat me like some . . . some . . . I don't know what, the next?" Kate stood in the middle of her living room, her face an angry mask, her emotions so intense her breath came in shallow gasps.

Rolk accepted the onslaught without any sign of concern. His voice remained soft and even, his eyes flat, steady. "It was just part of the job, nothing more. It had nothing to do with you, or us."

"The hell with your job," Kate shouted. Her voice was strident now, losing what little control it had had. "In case it's slipped past that great investigative mind of yours, I'm the one who's been singled out by some lunatic. I'm the one who's been receiving invitations to my own beheading. But when I was in your office yesterday, I was just another low-life criminal you had plucked off the streets."

Rolk's jaw tightened and his eyes became hard. "Everyone had to be treated the same way. It was just part of the game. Now get your coat and let me take you to work."

Kate stared at him, incredulous. "I'm not going anywhere with you. Not now, not tonight, not ever. So unless you have some more insensitive, brutish questions to ask, you just stay the hell away from me." She turned her back on him, her hands now folded across her breasts. The sudden silence seemed overwhelming.

"I'll send someone else to get you tonight," Rolk

finally said. "And the patrol car downstairs can take you to the museum, if you like."

The room was filled with silence again. Her eyes were closed against the pain she felt, and tears ran along her cheeks. More than a minute passed before she heard the door open and close, and when she turned around, Rolk was gone.

Devlin sat nursing his third cup of coffee. His sister was at the sink clearing up the breakfast dishes, and his daughter had already rooted herself before the living-room TV set, fully entranced with a children's program.

"Why don't you invite him out to dinner?" Beth asked. "Philippa loves it when he comes here, and if you're really worried about him, it might be just the thing he needs. Living alone the way he does must be god-awful."

"There won't be time for that until this case is cleared," Devlin said. "Besides, if Rolk even *thought* I was patronizing him, he'd have my guts for garters."

"So what can you do?"

Devlin shook his head. "Too many things are going wrong for him now, and he seems obsessed with each of them."

"Is the case going that badly?" Beth asked. "I've tried not to ask, because I know you don't like to talk about those things at home."

"It's not that," Devlin said. "In fact, I think it's finally started to wind down." He sipped his coffee, then stared into the warm black liquid. "He's just obsessed with this one case and the threat to this Silverman woman. It's reached the point where he's even ignoring other cases we've got pending, and that's not like him." He shook his head. "And he's started the search for his daughter again, and he's doing it with an intensity I haven't seen before." He looked up at his sister, who had stopped her work to share his concern. "He's just beating himself over the head with that one. I know it, everybody knows it. I think even Rolk knows it, but he just can't help himself."

"Maybe the case has just gotten to him. Maybe he's just trying to divert himself from it. It would make sense, wouldn't it?"

"I think he's also gotten himself involved with Kate Silverman," Devlin said, blurting it out before he could stop himself.

His sister looked surprised; then her face broke into a smile. "But that's good, Paul. That's probably the best thing that could happen to him. I've never even heard him talk about a woman, let alone seen him with one. And I bet you haven't either."

"It's not good," Devlin said. "And the brass would put his tail through a meat grinder if they ever got wind of it. It's stupid, and it's dangerous, and he knows better than that."

"Oh, Paul. That's the dumbest thing I've ever heard. If they're attracted to each other, what's the harm? Besides, the case has thrown them together. Anybody in their right mind would understand that."

Devlin offered his sister a wry smile. "I'm afraid you've got that one wrong, babe. Nobody in the department would understand. I don't understand. You don't get personally involved with a victim, and certainly not a suspect."

"Suspect?" Beth stared at him. "How could she be a suspect when somebody's been terrorizing her?"

Devlin raised his coffee cup with both hands. "What if she's doing it to herself? And what if she doesn't even know she's doing it?"

The telephone interrupted them. Beth answered it, then handed it to Devlin. "It's Charlie Moriarty," she said.

"Yeah, Charlie," Devlin said. He waited, listening.

"Shit!" His jaw tightened, the muscles jumping along the bone. "Okay, Charlie. You know what to do. I'll leave right away."

"What is it?" Beth asked as he replaced the receiver.

"The priest just called Charlie. Roberto Caliento
ever made it back to New York. Looks like he took a
owder."

Kate entered St. Helena's Church, which was lo-
ated only a few blocks from the museum. It was eight
'clock and the morning Mass had just begun. She had
ot been to Mass or even to church in years. She
adn't felt either the need or the desire to go. Looking
round at the handful of elderly women who com-
rised the congregation, she wondered if she had made
mistake and overreacted by falling back on the com-
ort she had known as a child.

No, it was right to be here. She felt battered and
bused. She had trusted Stan, had even begun to fall
love with him, and he had turned on her without
eason, had attacked her without any sense of re-
orse. She had been certain she had meant more to
im than just a quick toss in the hay. She had experi-
nced those in her life, and was certain she knew the
ifference. She had felt his intensity, the feeling that
ad poured from him. He had been timid at first, had
old her he had not been with a woman for a long
me. And he had been so gentle, holding and touch-
g her almost as though he had been afraid she would
reak. He had made her feel more loved than she had
ver felt. She had felt special and wanted and adored.
nd she had reveled in it, had wanted it to be true.
nd then . . .

She watched the young priest move about the altar,
echanically repeating the litany, and she wondered
ow anyone could perform the same ceremony day
fter day, week after week, without going mad with
he sheer repetitive boredom of it all.

Kate lowered her face to her hands. It wasn't work-
ng. The comfort she had hoped to find simply wasn't
here. The priest turned, offered his final blessing, and
old everyone present that the Mass had ended. Kate
at there, unwilling to move. She glanced about her.
Banks of votive candles flickered on the side altars,

and she thought about lighting one, of offering up
prayer to her own foolishness. *Votives.* The word no
had a chilling connotation. She rose to leave, turnin
into the aisle. There was a confessional box a few row
behind her, and she noticed the red light above th
center compartment was illuminated, indicating a prie
sat behind the curtain waiting to hear confessions.

Kate stopped and stared at the light. She had though
earlier about visiting Father LoPato or some othe
priest for counsel. But she could do that just as well i
the confessional, and with a degree of privacy sh
desperately needed.

Kate slipped into one of the side compartments an
knelt. Almost a minute passed before the small doo
on the black-curtained window slid back and she coul
make out the faint image of the person who sat behin
it.

"Bless me, Father, for I have sinned," she began
"It has been many years since my last confession
and—"

"Soon, Kate. Soon you will be with the gods. No
because you are evil, but because you are wonderful."

The voice came in a low, whispered hiss, and sh
jumped up in terror, her legs buckling. Only her back
pressed against the wall of the confessional, kept he
from falling back to her knees. She remained froze
there, listening as the words were repeated again an
again. Then anger began to build, and despite he
trembling arms and legs, she shouted at the curtaine
window, "No, damn you! No!"

Kate pushed her way through the confessional cur
tain, stepped directly in front of the priest's partition
and pulled back the curtain with such force that half o
it tore away. The voice droned on as she stared int
the empty compartment. It was coming from a sma
tape recorder that lay on the wooden seat.

Kate turned to the sound of the church's front doo
closing with a bang. She reached inside the confes
sional and grabbed the recorder, then began runnin

up the aisle toward the front door. No, she shouted to herself. You're not going to get away. I'm going to see who you are. I'm going to find out why you're doing this to me, no matter what.

Inspector James Dunne and Deputy Commissioner Martin O'Rourke sailed into Rolk's office at nine o'clock like a hurricane-force gale.

Even from behind his desk, Rolk could smell the previous night's booze wafting off O'Rourke's sweating body, and the feral look in Dunne's eyes told him that City Hall had begun beating the war drums.

"What the hell did you think you were doing telling the director of the Museum of Natural History that he was responsible for Ezra Waters' death?" O'Rourke demanded, his normally florid face taking on a near-purple hue.

"I didn't tell him exactly that," Rolk said, his voice calm and soft and tranquil.

"What did you tell him?" Dunne snapped.

Rolk offered a particularly false smile, even for him. "I told that little prick, quote, that his demand that we have only one cop on that stakeout had gotten his security directors' throat cut, and that if I didn't have his full cooperation from now on, I was going to tell every fucking newspaper in town exactly that, unquote."

"You will like hell," O'Rourke shouted.

"Try me," Rolk said, his voice little more than a whisper.

Dunne jabbed a finger toward Rolk's face. "You can find your ass dumped off this case pretty damned fast, you try anything like that."

"Fine. That'll make what I have to say even better, won't it?"

"And you can kiss your pension good-bye as well," O'Rourke shouted.

"Stick my pension up your ass," Rolk said, his voice still quiet.

The two men stared at him, too stunned to speak.

Rolk stood behind his desk and raised one hand, holding his thumb and index finger an inch apart. "I'm this close to getting this bastard. I know it. But it's not going to happen if the brass downtown throw a roadblock in my way every time some prominent weakkneed sonofabitch decides he doesn't like the way a police investigation has to run. So you go back to whoever's screaming in City Hall, and you tell them that. And you explain to them that they're dealing with a homicide cop who just happens to have a lot of credibility with the press. And you explain that they're either going to back off and let him do his fucking job, or he's going to lay so much shit on their doorstep that they'll spend the rest of the winter shoveling themselves out."

O'Rourke's entire body had begun to shake with rage. "You're finished, Rolk. Believe me, when this is over, *you are finished,* no matter how it turns out."

"And maybe even before," Dunne added. He smiled viciously at Rolk. "You're right. Our asses are hanging out right now. But it won't take us long to cover them. And don't you forget it, mister. Because as soon as this case takes one more turn for the worse, you are fucking history."

"Then I'll be history," Rolk said. "But on my way, I'm going to take this bastard with me. You try to stop me and I'll make sure there's enough shit left over to cover both your shoes."

"But you'll stay away from the newspapers, right?" O'Rourke demanded.

"No, I won't." He watched O'Rourke's face take on the blackened look of a man who has just been strangled. "But I won't make any complaints about you two or City Hall." He glanced at his watch. "In one hour—a little less, actually—this office is going to be full of reporters. And I'm going to tell them some things about our killer that are going to send that sonofabitch into orbit. And when he gets there, I'm going to grab his ass."

Dunne nodded slowly. "And if it backfires, Stan?"

Rolk returned Dunne's stare. "If that happens, Jim, I guess you get the chance to do something you've been wanting to do for years."

"That's right, Stan," Dunne said. "That's exactly right."

Twenty-nine

GRACE MALLORY FELT at peace with herself for the first time in more years than she cared to count. A small smile played across her normally rigid mouth as she realized how hackneyed that idea truly was. Yet, it was how she felt—imbued with an unusual sense of well-being that had come to her shortly after her interrogation in Rolk's office. I am what I am, she told herself now. People recognize it and it doesn't change one thing. Not one damned thing.

The smile faded. So many years of self-doubt, self-rejection, she thought. All those years of hating yourself. It had come, she knew, from her New England upbringing, from the beliefs instilled in her that people who felt as she did were pariahs, outcasts whom God-fearing people would have nothing to do with. Even her years in New York, where almost every attitude and disposition was tolerated, had not removed that sense of guilt, that belief that there was something evil inside her that had to be repressed and beaten down. But never again, she told herself. Self-hatred was something that would no longer be a part of her life.

Grace stared down at her desk, cluttered now with the final documentation needed for the exhibit. And the work would go on as well, she thought. Even the seemingly endless police investigation would not taint the scholarly achievement of the work she had compiled. And that too would bring her the recognition she had long awaited. Her eyes rested on a small stone mask that sat in one corner of her desk, and her mind went immediately to Ezra Waters. She closed her eyes tightly. But that death had not followed the ritual, so it could not be connected to the exhibit. She opened her eyes and stared at the mask again. But that wasn't true at all, she she knew it.

"Grace?"

The voice startled her, and she looked up to find Kate approaching her desk. "What's the matter, Kate? You look so grim."

Kate closed her eyes momentarily. "There was another incident this morning. It just has me a little shaken."

"Another votive? What?"

Kate shook her head. "I don't know what to call it. It was a message. On a tape recorder. Someone left it for me. In a church, no less."

"A church?" Grace asked, incredulous. "But how would anyone know you would be going to a church?"

"That's just it, no one would. It was something I did impulsively. And that means I was followed. By this . . . this . . . "

"Have you notified the police?"

Kate nodded; then her eyes flashed anger. "And one of them had the nerve to criticize me for touching the damned thing." Her jaw tightened; then she drew a deep breath, forcing herself to relax. "I don't know what they expected," she added in a softer voice. "I guess I was supposed to wait there in an empty church until this madman came back."

"Did you see the person?" Grace asked, her body becoming tense, expectant.

Kate shook her head again. "That's the worst part. I just missed seeing him."

Grace eased back in her chair, thinking that Kate was probably fortunate that she had. "You have to try to put it out of your mind, dear. It's the only thing you can do now. Believe me."

Grace smiled up at her. Kate was dressed in a simple white blouse, open at the throat, and a wool skirt that reached the tops of high leather boots. She looked particularly lovely, Grace thought. And even younger than she was, almost like a schoolgirl.

"What is it?" Kate asked.

Grace stood, then reached out and stroked the younger woman's cheek. "I was just thinking how lovely you look today. A bit tense around the eyes, but that's to be expected."

Kate shrugged. "I just can't get all of this out of my mind. It's even affecting my work."

"Your work is fine, dear," Grace said. "It's just the madness we have all around us. You should try to get out in the evenings. Get your mind off the work *and* all this unpleasantness."

A faint, slightly nervous smile played across Kate's lips, then disappeared.

"Actually," Grace continued, "I was thinking of following that prescription myself. Would you care to have dinner with me tonight? And then, perhaps, we could see if there's a concert we could get tickets to."

Kate began to speak, but couldn't quite find the words.

Grace reached out and stroked her cheek again. "It would be nice to see more of each other," she said. "Away from all this, I mean. It seems work is the only time we ever get to spend together."

"Excuse me!"

Grace's head snapped around toward the sound of the voice, and Kate took an abrupt step back. Malcolm Sousi stood grinning in the doorway, an embarrassed Father LoPato beside him.

"What is it, Malcolm?" Grace demanded, her tone annoyed, almost angry.

"Oh, it's nothing that can't wait," Sousi said. "I wouldn't want to interrupt a tender moment among the staff, so we'll just come back later."

Grace glared at him. "Good," she snapped. "Why don't you just do that. Come back later." She glanced at the priest, whose color had deepened, and watched as his eyes darted away. Fool, she thought.

When Malcolm and the priest had left, Grace turned back to Kate. "The man is such an unbelievable boor," she said. "I swear, if he didn't have such a first-class mind, I would have gotten rid of him long ago." She drew a deep breath, then allowed a smile to return to her face. "What were we talking about? Oh, yes, dinner tonight. Would you like to?"

A hint of red crept into Kate's cheeks. "I'm afraid I can't, Grace. I'd love to, but I'm afraid I already have other plans. Perhaps another time."

Grace's smile faded. "Of course, dear," she said. "Another time." A sudden sense of misery crept into her, but she quickly pushed it away. Then the smile returned.

Kate toyed with her salad, her mind still overwhelmed by the events of the morning. Devlin sat opposite her, trying to fight through the reticence she had displayed ever since they left the museum.

Rolk had asked him to handle this latest incident, and also to take over the task of picking Kate up each morning and returning her home each night. Rolk, in turn, would take on Devlin's responsibilities for the priest, and Devlin wondered if that were because of the turn the investigation had taken in that direction, or if Rolk simply wanted to distance himself from the woman. He hoped it was the latter.

Now, seated at a small table in the glass-enclosed section that covered the front of the Ginger Man Restaurant, Devlin continued to struggle against Kate's silence.

"There were no fingerprints on the tape recorder, other than your own," he began.

"And what's that supposed to mean?" Kate snapped.

"Nothing. It means just what I said."

"Was I supposed to guard it and wait for him to come back?" Her eyes were angry, and there was a noticeable tremor in her voice. "Or was I supposed to leave it there so he could come back and get it? That would have been good. Then we could have had some more innuendos about Kate Silverman doing all this to herself."

"No one has ever said that," Devlin offered, trying to diffuse the woman's anger.

"No? Well, it certainly has been implied."

Devlin stared into his half-eaten hamburger as if it might suggest a way to extract himself from this argument. "We had the tape analyzed, and we're reasonably sure it was a man's voice."

"Why only reasonably sure?" Kate demanded.

"It's this rasping whisper he uses. The strange breathing. It makes it difficult to be sure, but our people are fairly certain that the sentence structure and the type of inflection point to a man." He hesitated, trying to decide if he should go on. He decided it was best if he did. "We're going to try to do some voiceprints of our various suspects, and compare them. But that won't be definitive. Our people think whoever's doing this is using a handkerchief or some other device to mask his voice. And any good defense attorney would shoot down the voiceprints on that basis alone. But it could point us in the right direction."

"Will you make a voiceprint of *my* voice?" Kate asked.

Devlin studied her eyes, saw the anger there, waiting to leap forward.

"We'll take them of everyone—"

"I thought so," Kate snapped, stopping him.

He leaned forward, offering her a weary smile. "We have to do that," he said. "We have to remove any reasonable doubt that it could have been you."

Kate began toying with her salad, at first jabbing at it, then gradually with more gentle movements as her irritation eased. "How accurate are voiceprints?" she finally asked.

"As good as fingerprints," Devlin said. "Provided they're clear and unobstructed."

"But these aren't."

Devlin shook his head. "Afraid not."

"Then why even bother?" The frustration was clear in Kate's voice.

"It's just another step. But we don't skip any steps. And that's why we usually win."

"Usually," she said, the frustration even more apparent.

Devlin watched her as she returned absently to her food. There was an edge of fear in her, and he wondered just how frightened she had been when the message had first filtered through the confessional. But she had chased the man, had tried to see who it was. He had learned that from the other detectives who had gone to the scene. She was one gutsy woman.

"What made you go to church this morning?" he asked.

Her eyes wavered a moment. "Just some personal problems. I thought I might find some comfort there." She let out a short, derisive laugh. "Obviously it didn't work."

"I didn't know you were Catholic," Devlin said, probing. "With a name like Silverman, I just assumed . . ."

"I told your lieutenant about that," Kate said. "My parents were killed, and I was raised by my mother's sister. She was married to a man named Silverman. They adopted me."

Devlin nodded, thinking. "Odd Rolk never mentioned it."

"There are a lot of things that are odd about your lieutenant," Kate said, the edge back in her voice.

So that was it, Devlin thought. A bit of a falling-out. He looked at her closely as the silence returned and she gave her attention back to her food. She was an immensely beautiful woman, Devlin thought. But even more than that, she had a sense of self-possession about her that seemed to illuminate everything else, heighten it, somehow. He could understand Rolk's attraction to her; he had to admit he felt it himself. It would be too easy to get involved, he thought. You'd have to protect this woman from all the threats and inflicted fears that seemed to be coming down all around her. That was the wrong way to protect anyone professionally, but he could see how it could happen.

"What are you thinking about?" Kate asked, pulling him back from his thoughts.

"I was thinking that you're a very beautiful woman," Devlin said, the words coming out before he could stop them.

Thirty

GRACE MALLORY BENT over the long table in the anthropology lab, inspecting the fragment of broken pottery that lay before her. It was a marvelous piece, well worth the time and expense of reconstruction, she told herself. She placed a magnifying glass over the fragment and closely studied the pigmentation of the paint that had been used to decorate the bowl. There was no question in her mind it was authentic, and she again marveled at Father LoPato's tenacity in finding each fragment of a piece that had obviously been shattered more than seven centuries ago.

She put the magnifying glass aside and took in the various fragments scattered about the table. A smile played across her lips as she tried to imagine the priest smuggling this magnificent find out of Mexico. She, of course, had done the same herself on numerous occasions. Every anthropologist she knew had. But still, she wondered how he reconciled it all. How he was able to separate the moral questions presented by his two quite separate roles in life.

But thank God he can, she told herself. Or you wouldn't have this wonderful find before you now.

She picked up the magnifying glass again and leaned even closer. Behind her she heard the door open and close, and she glanced quickly over her shoulder before returning to the fragment.

"I wasn't expecting to see you here tonight," she said. "But as long as you are, come and see this pigment. It's really worth a look."

A gloved hand lowered the briefcase to the floor, opened it, and removed an ornately carved bronze ax. The ax rose high into the air, swaying slightly as it poised over Grace's back. Then the breathing came, a harsh sucking in of air over teeth, the faint hum as it was expelled.

"You sound as though you're catching a cold," Grace said. "You should really—"

The ax struck her back six inches below the neck, severing the spinal column. The force of the blow threw her forward on the table, scattering the pieces of pottery she had been examining. Her body, lacking all motor control, slid back, then rolled from the table and crashed to the floor.

Grace stared at the ceiling, her mind trying to grasp what had happened to her. Then the figure came into her field of vision, the stone mask encircling its neck, held in place by a leather thong. She stared up into the face and tried unsuccessfully to speak. *You. It's you.* The accusation played over and over in her mind, as her eyes roamed the face she knew so well. But no, it wasn't the same face at all.

It was as though she was looking into the face of some mad twin. Slowly a hand raised the mask in front of the face, and all she could see were the blazing eyes peering through the holes cut in the stone. That and the long green blade of the obsidian knife.

Kate sat on the sofa, reading through the papers she had brought home with her, making occasional notes in the margin, listing things she would have to remember to check in the morning. Her eyes began to flutter, but she forced them open, fighting off sleep. She glanced at her watch. Eleven o'clock. She was already dressed for bed, a heavy wool bathrobe wrapped tightly around her nightgown.

Carefully she returned the papers to her briefcase and rose from the sofa. She started toward the bedroom, then stopped, remembering to check the locks on the front door. She shuffled slowly forward, her mind on her bed, on her need for blissful, undisturbed sleep. Her hand reached out for the doorknob, then stopped abruptly as she stared down at the light brown carpeting and the stain that seemed to have formed at its edge, almost as though something had seeped under the door.

She continued to stare at it, bewildered. It hadn't been there when Paul Devlin had brought her home earlier that evening. She was sure she could not have missed it if it had been. And surely the detective would have seen it. She couldn't believe they could both have been oblivious of something so obvious.

Kate continued to stare at the stain, which seemed to have been caused by something thick and dark, almost as though someone had spilled syrup in the hall. Her mind jumped to the expense of having it cleaned. But certainly the building would be responsible if it had been the result of something that had happened in the hall, she told herself.

Kate reached for the locks, determined to see what had caused the stain, then hesitated, deciding to first look through the spy hole in the door, just to be certain there was no one there. Assured of that, she unlocked the door and swung it back. A large clear plastic bag lay at her feet. It held a bulky object that was obscured by the plastic.

Kate bent down and squatted before the bag, trying to make out what was inside. Suddenly her body went rigid, and her eyes bulged with terror. Staring back at her through the bag was the face of Grace Mallory, eyes and mouth open in a warning scream that Kate would never hear.

Kate lurched back, stumbled and fell, then scrambled away, crablike. Her first scream filled the apartment and sent a shuddering wave down the hall. Then the screams came in rapid succession, punctuated only by pauses for breath, as she sat huddled on the floor, her eyes riveted on the plastic bag, on the blurred, horrific image that stared back at her.

*   *   *

Rolk and Peters were already at the apartment with the forensic team and the ever-present Jerry Feldman when Devlin arrived.

Devlin moved directly to Rolk. "Where's Kate?" he asked, his eyes flashing a nervous concern.

Rolk's head snapped up, his eyes meeting Devlin's with a hint of irritation. The use of Kate's first name made him bristle. "She's in the bedroom," Rolk said, his voice cold. "She was still hysterical when we got here, and a doctor who lives down the hall gave her a sedative."

Devlin turned and stared back at the now-unwrapped head, which Jerry Feldman was examining. "She found that thing?" Devlin asked unnecessarily.

Rolk glared at the younger detective. "That thing, up until a few hours ago, was Grace Mallory, in case you're interested. A patrol unit found the rest of her in an anthropology lab at the museum."

Devlin ignored the rebuke, his eyes still fixed on the head. "How the hell did he get up here? Didn't we have a unit outside?"

"We think whoever it was came in through the garage," Bernie Peters said. He was watching Devlin intently, surprised by the tone of his voice. "And the unit was gone for about half an hour. An officer-in-trouble call came in to 911 at eight-forty-five, a phony, as it turned out."

"A phony," Devlin repeated. "They should have thought of that."

"Jesus, Paul," Peters interrupted. "You know damned well that no cop is going to ignore a ten-thirteen call in his sector. You wouldn't do it, and neither would I. The sonofabitch just suckered them."

Rolk took Devlin's arm and led him across the room and into the small kitchen. His eyes were hard, unhappy. "Why all the sudden concern?" he asked. "Only a few days ago you were giving me a lecture about not getting personally involved."

"I'm *not* personally involved. But you gave me the job of protecting her—"

"And *watching* her," Rolk interrupted.

"That's right. And watching her. So I just want to make sure nobody screws up." He remained silent for several moments. "If it's bothering you, assign somebody else," he said at length.

Rolk glared at him, then turned abruptly. "It's not bothering me," he snapped as he headed back to the living room.

The morgue attendants had already placed the head in a black rubber body bag when Rolk and Devlin returned. Feldman was seated on the sofa jotting notes in a steno pad, and Bernie Peters was on the telephone, obviously speaking to the team at the museum.

"The same as the others?" Rolk asked Feldman.

Feldman nodded. "Except for the method of disposal," he added. "And that bothers the hell out of me."

"Yeah, it bothers me too," Rolk said. "I think our friend has finally gone over the edge. So we damned well better get him fast or we're going to have an even bigger bloodbath on our hands."

Feldman continued to stare at Rolk. "One of the boys at the morgue had an early edition of the *Daily News*," he said. "You laid into our boy pretty hard."

A flicker of fear passed across Rolk's eyes. "You think that caused this?" he asked.

"No." Feldman shook his head. "From the condition of the body, she was dead before the killer could have laid his hands on a newspaper. But if he *is* over the edge now—and taking the kind of chances he took tonight—those newspaper stories just might drive him right into a frenzy. A bad one."

Rolk ran a hand across his face. "That's what they were intended to do," he said, his voice carrying a note of uncertainty.

Peters approached them, finished with his telephone call. "Forensic is through with the body at the museum," he said. "But they're still dusting for prints. You want to go over there?"

Rolk nodded, then turned to Devlin. "You wait and talk to Dr. Silverman."

"You can do that now, Lieutenant."

The four men turned and found Kate Silverman, standing, fully dressed, in the doorway of the bedroom.

"Are you all right?" Rolk asked, taking in Kate's ashen face, the heavy circles that underlined her eyes.

"No, but I'm ambulatory," she said. "And I intend to go into the museum this morning."

Devlin began to speak, but Rolk's eyes stopped him. "I'm not sure that's wise," Rolk said. "It will be pretty chaotic there most of the day, and I don't think any of you will be getting much work done."

Kate shook her head. "I have to. If I don't, Malcolm will take charge of that exhibit, and God knows what he'll do with it. Certainly not anything Grace intended. I owe her that. The exhibit had been her whole life these last few years." Tears welled up in Kate's eyes, but she fought them back. "But I can answer your questions first. There or here," she added.

Rolk glanced at his watch. It was six-forty-five. "Paul can do it here," he said. "It's going to take some time, and when he's finished, he can drive you to the museum."

Kate drew a long breath and nodded. "I'll make some coffee," she said, moving off toward the kitchen.

Rolk looked back at Devlin. "That's all right with you?" he asked.

"It's fine," Devlin said. There was an edge to his voice, just as there had been to Rolk's.

Peters started for the door. Rolk, his eyes glancing furtively toward the kitchen, followed. Reluctantly, Devlin thought.

They sat across from each other at a small kitchen table. At first, as she described how she had found the head, Kate's hands had trembled so badly that she had had difficulty holding her cup. Now the trembling had subsided, and she seemed far more in control.

"You said you were worried about Sousi," Devlin

said, turning the conversation in a new direction. "Why do you think he'd try to take control of the exhibit?"

Kate smiled faintly."Pure male ego. Malcolm has always considered himself the most brilliant anthropologist in the museum. And now, with Grace gone, I'm sure he feels he's the logical person to take over."

"But you don't," Devlin said.

Kate's eyes hardened momentarily. "I was Grace's assistant curator. Malcolm was just a member of her staff." She smiled wryly. "But of course, that could change. We do operate under an *old boy's* network at the museum, and he could well be named temporary curator."

"Does that bother you?" Devlin asked, realizing for the first time that Kate had actually been Sousi's superior. He was certain the fact had bothered Sousi.

"No, it doesn't bother me. Not personally, anyway," Kate said. "My ambitions are in the area of scholarship, not administration. But the idea of Malcolm taking over this exhibit—Grace's exhibit—and possibly changing it from what she intended, yes, that concerns me."

"I thought you and Dr. Mallory had your own disagreements about the exhibit," Devlin said.

"Not on content," Kate said. "Never on that. Just on the way to bring attention to it. For Malcolm it's a question of content. And he's very wrong about that."

Devlin steepled his fingers in front of his face. "I think Malcolm is going to be very busy with us today, so you might find his ability to do any plotting very limited."

"You don't know Malcolm," Kate said. "He's always plotting. It's part of his nature, I'm afraid."

And what's part of your nature? Devlin wondered, his mind returning to the problem of Rolk. He studied Kate closely. She was still exceptionally beautiful, even in the haggard state the previous evening had imposed on her. And she was so damned bright. No, even more than that. She was intellectually sophisticated. It was easy to see the attraction Rolk had felt.

"You said your interest was scholarship," Devlin began again. "What does that mean as far as your future ambitions are concerned?"

"Fieldwork, hopefully," Kate answered. "I was hoping, when the exhibit was finished, to get approval for a new dig in the Yucatán. Something of my own this time. Not just as part of someone else's team."

Devlin stared down at the table, then back at her. "That's *very* ambitious," he said. "Doesn't that normally mean several years out of the country?"

"Yes, at least that long," Kate said.

"And how would that affect your relationship with Lieutenant Rolk?" Devlin watched her eyes widen, then a slight smile appear on her lips.

"I didn't know you were aware of that," she said.

Devlin offered his own false smile, but his eyes were calm and nonthreatening. "I'm a detective, Kate. Not that I had to be much of one to uncover that little secret. But you didn't answer my question, did you?"

Kate clasped her hands together, assuming a formal position. He wondered if it was to keep them from trembling.

"There's nothing to affect," Kate began. "It was a mistake and now it's over."

Devlin felt a sudden rush of relief. It surprised him, and made him wonder what was really at the root of it.

"I'm glad to hear it," he said.

"Why?" Kate asked.

"It's something the department frowns on, something that could seriously damage his career. It could even end it."

"I didn't realize that," Kate said.

"And . . ." Devlin hesitated, then continued. "He's had a rough personal life. His wife walked out on him fifteen years ago, and took his three-year-old daughter with her. He's been trying to locate the kid ever since."

"He told me about his wife and daughter," Kate said. "I'm sorry for him, I really am." Her eyes had grown sad. "I felt very strongly about him." She hesitated again. "Maybe I still do. But this job you both do, it makes you turn on people, even people you care about. I can't deal with that."

"It's an occupational hazard," Devlin said. "But right now, I just don't want to see him hurt in any way."

"You love him, don't you?"

"Yeah, I guess I do."

Kate stared at him for several moments. "Is that why you want me to stay away from him?" she finally asked.

Devlin stared back at her and wondered if it was.

Thirty-one

THE NEWSPAPERS WERE spread out on the table, each one blaring out its damnable headline in large black type. The figure stood above them, hands trembling, mouth twisted with rage.

They are mocking you, the unspoken voice said. *They are mocking your religion and your gods.* "Yes," the voice hissed, the eyes still staring at the worst words of all.

. . . A detective involved in the investigation described the killer as a "demented madman, fixated with an even more demented Stone Age religion that ranks with the worst in man's history in its barbarity." He went on to say that the number of suspects has been narrowed down and that an arrest is expected before the killer can complete the insane ritual he has been so brutally following.

Hands reached out and grasped the paper, tearing it to shreds, then continued with the others, ripping until the floor was littered with scraps of mutilated wood pulp.

"But the ritual will be completed," the voice hissed. "And it will be completed soon."

But what about those who have offended you, who have defamed your religion? What of them?

"They too will be punished. They too will feel the sword of Quetzalcoatl, the plumed serpent, the morning and the evening star. And their words will be washed away in the blood of one of their own, and the universe will again be pure."

I will wait and see, the unspoken voice said.

James Dunne entered Rolk's office without knocking, his face a mixture of arrogance and anger.

"Nice newspaper coverage, Rolk," he said as he slipped into the visitor's chair, his trilby hat still in place, a tan polo coat wrapped around his lean frame.

"Glad you liked it, Inspector," Rolk said, irritated as always by the mere sight of the man.

"Oh, I liked it. You bet your ass I liked it." Dunne's eyes hardened, but the hint of personal pleasure still came through. "It's just what we needed to dump you from this case. So just for starters, let's consider that done. You're off, as of right now."

Rolk nodded, then reached across his desk and picked up his telephone.

"What the hell do you think you're doing?" Dunne snapped.

Rolk pulled on his nose, then placed the telephone receiver to his ear. "I thought I'd start with a friend of mine at the *Daily News,*" he said. "Then the *Times* and the *Post.* Then I thought I'd go on to the radio and television stations."

"No you won't, Rolk. Because if you do, we'll bury you with it." Dunne's eyes were like coals now, burning with a private personal joy. "That woman who died last night was killed because of your little talk with the press. You challenged the killer and you enraged him. It was in complete violation of departmental policy and you knew it." Dunne paused, offering a ferretlike grin. "So you go back to the press now, and we're going to say it's just more of the same. Just a case of bad judgment, followed up by a rash of phony charges to try to cover up your own mistakes."

Rolk, the telephone receiver still at his ear, snorted in reply. "Won't fly, Jim. Just won't fly."

"And why not?"

"Because the first edition of the *Daily News*—what they call the 'bulldog edition'—doesn't hit the streets until nine o'clock at night. And last night it was even later. You see, I was worried about it, so I checked. Seems they had a press problem, and the paper was a half-hour late." Rolk kept his eyes on Dunne's face, enjoying the uncertainty that was now appearing. "And according to Jerry Feldman, Dr. Mallory was long dead by that time. The killer couldn't have read the paper and reacted to it. Just couldn't have."

"Feldman will never back you up on that," Dunne snapped. "He'll say what he's damned well told to say."

Rolk shrugged. "Maybe he will, maybe he won't. Me, I think he will. But you'll just have to gamble on that, won't you, Jim?"

Rolk reached across the desk and began punching out a telephone number.

"Your pension's gone," Dunne shouted. "You finish that fucking phone call and it's gone. Right now." Rolk hesitated and stared across the desk at Dunne. The pause seemed to give the man added courage, and he grinned wickedly. "Oh, yeah, I checked it all out," Dunne continued. "Twenty-four grand a year. That's what you would have got. Twenty-four thousand if you walked out tomorrow. And I'll tell you something, tough guy. I don't think you're going to piss that away."

Rolk leaned back in his chair, lowering the receiver into his lap. "You know, Jim," he began, "you're just like all the greedy assholes I've met all my life. You only look at things on the surface. You can only see what people *get* if they do a certain thing, or what they *lose* if they don't. But let me tell you a couple of things about Stanislaus Rolk. Just to clear things up in your mind." Rolk clenched one fist, raising the thumb into the air. "First, he's got this little medical problem. It's not one that one of those quacks you hire as departmental surgeons were ever able to find. But it's there, and sooner or later, it's going to kill him. Oh, if he takes real good care of himself, he might last a little longer. But not long enough to make that pension very important to him."

Rolk paused, the corners of his lips turning up slightly. "Second, he really doesn't have to worry too much about that. You see, about sixteen, seventeen years ago, he bought a brownstone up on the Upper West Side. Got it for pennies, actually, because real estate up there was pretty lousy then. But he put some money into it, fixed it up, even put in a couple of pretty nice rental apartments. And now, speaking very conservatively, he could probably unload it for over half a million. Maybe more." Rolk paused again, raising the receiver back to his ear. "And I'll tell you one thing more about that old Polack. It wouldn't bother him one bit to spend some of that money fighting this thing through the courts if he had to. Shit, he might even hire a publicist, just to make sure all the boys in the press got the full story about all the political horseshit that goes on in this department. And if he does that, I don't think the boys at City Hall are ever going to forget the inspector who started it all. What do you think, you sleazy little asshole?"

Dunne's body had become rigid, his face pale. Only his eyes still burned, spewing hatred across the desk.

Rolk reached out and continued punching the telephone number.

"You've got forty-eight hours," Dunne snapped. "The commissioner is going to announce it this afternoon. If the killer isn't in custody in forty-eight hours, a new task force is going to be formed, and you won't have a fucking thing to do with it."

Rolk replaced the receiver, looked at Dunne, and nodded. So that was it, he thought. That was the real message, the bottom line Dunne was *supposed* to deliver. All the rest had been bullshit, a personal gambit to try to force him to quit. And forty-eight hours was all he really deserved, given what had happened. He just hoped it would be long enough.

"Thanks for telling me, Jim," he said. "We'll try to meet the commissioner's deadline."

Kate paced in front of Sousi's desk. They had been

arguing for more than a half-hour now, and her patience with the man had finally run out.

"You just don't seem to want to get the message, Malcolm. You are not changing the exhibit. You do not have the authority to change the exhibit. It has been in preparation for two years now, and its concept of scholarship is sound. It will continue as Grace envisioned it."

"That is your opinion," Sousi snapped.

Kate rounded on him. "And it is the *only* opinion that counts at this moment," she snapped back.

"At this moment," Sousi persisted.

Kate shook her head, her mouth twisting with the distaste she felt for the man. "I know what you want, Malcolm. I know exactly what you want. You think that with Grace dead, you can just step in and steal her work. It's probably the only way you could ever get that kind of recognition, because you lack both the talent and the patience to put together something this good." Kate stared down at him, her eyes burning. "Even your ideas for changes are tawdry. You'd take the creative brilliance of this ancient civilization and turn it into a sideshow. You'd emphasize religious rituals as though they were pagan rites, playing up the brutality rather than the mysticism of the religion, which is at the core of what every true scholar is attempting to understand. But you *will not* do it here!"

Sousi's entire face began to tremble. "You . . . you . . ." His breath came rapidly now, and he had difficulty forming the words. "You dare speak to me like that?" he finally managed. "You silly little bitch. You're a second-rate mind from a second-rate university, and you know nothing about the essence of a civilization about which you claim to be an authority." He snatched a letter opener from the top of his desk and pointed it in Kate's direction. "I watched you when we were on the dig at Chetulak. You had no idea of what we had discovered there. You went off on petty little tangents, collecting obscure, meaningless information."

Kate leaned forward across the desk, almost as if

challenging the blade of the letter opener. Sousi immediately lowered it to the desk. "And that is your problem, Malcolm," she began. "Information you regard as obscure, you also regard as meaningless. Your mind is set in what you believe the truth to be, and you reject even the search for new meaning, new understanding. You're an intellectual zealot, Malcolm, and it is exactly that type of tunnel scholarship that has no place in a growing, evolving science. And I will not allow you to impose it on this exhibition."

"We shall see," Sousi snapped.

"Yes, we shall," Kate snapped in reply. "But until then you will do as you are told."

Kate turned abruptly to leave Sousi's office, but found herself nearly colliding with Father LoPato.

"Father, I'm sorry," she said, bracing herself with her hand against his arm.

The priest, obviously having overheard the argument, seemed momentarily flustered, and his first words came out in a stammer. "I . . . I . . . I'm sorry for interrupting. But I was looking for you, Kate."

"You're not interrupting, Father. Not in the least." She offered the priest a resigned smile. "You just stumbled into a professional disagreement. What can I do for you?"

The priest clasped his hands and began twisting them nervously. "I was just thinking about the pottery that Grace was planning to reconstruct just before her . . ." He found it impossible to complete the sentence, and simply forged ahead. "Well, as you know, I'm familiar with the piece. It came from my collection. And I thought I might offer to do the reconstruction myself, if you think it might save time and be of any help." He paused, uncertain again. "I mean, if you still plan to use it in the exhibit."

Kate nodded. "That's exactly what I plan," she said pointedly, directing her words more to Sousi, who still sat at his desk behind her, than to the priest. "And I'd greatly appreciate your help."

"I don't think the piece is needed," Sousi said to Kate's back.

"And I don't care what you think, Malcolm." Kate returned, staring over her shoulder at Sousi. "If you do not stop trying to impose your will on this exhibit, I will put a very abrupt end to your interference."

The priest stood spellbound as he watched Kate stalk out of the office. He glanced at Sousi, then again at Kate's retreating back. It was happening he thought. Just as he had feared it would. The exhibit was in jeopardy. All the years of work, bringing it all together, and now so close to presenting it in all its beauty, with all its startling revelations about the ancients and their ways, their beliefs. No, he could not allow that to happen. He simply couldn't. He turned back to Sousi and started to speak. Then he thought better of it.

Kate turned into her own office and stopped abruptly. Rolk stood before her desk, and as she entered, immediately started toward her.

Kate took a step back, the anger she had felt for Sousi returning briefly, directed now at Rolk. "I thought I made myself clear," she said.

He reached behind her, closed her office door, then drew her to him. "I love you. That's the bottom line. None of the rest of this matters." Kate began to object but Rolk kissed her, cutting off her words. "This will all be over soon. Probably within the next forty-eight hours."

Kate stared up at him. "You know who it is?"

"I've always known," Rolk said. "The important thing now is us."

Kate raised a hand, stopping him. "You shouldn't be here," she said. "Paul Devlin made that very clear to me this morning."

Rolk's face colored with anger. "What did he say?" he demanded.

"Just that our personal relationship could hurt you

professionally. And he's right, isn't he? Our relationship could affect your job."

Rolk gritted his teeth. "That doesn't stop me from making sure you're all right. That *is* part of my job."

Kate's eyes softened, and she leaned against him. "Yes, it is," she said softly."And I'm glad it is." She closed her eyes for a moment. "I'm sorry. I'm a bit tense. I just had a wicked fight with Malcolm."

Rolk placed his hands on her arms. "I want you to stay away from him as much as possible."

Kate let out a soft laugh. "There's nothing I'd like more. Believe me. But right now it's just not possible."

"Then make sure there's someone else with you when you see him," Rolk said. "And not just him. Do it with everyone involved in this thing."

"But—"

"I just want you to be careful," Rolk insisted, stopping her objection. "This thing is coming to a head, and I've got a lousy feeling it's going to be a damned bloody solution."

Kate stared at him, her eyes wide.

"Devlin isn't going to pick you up tonight," he continued. "I am." He glanced at his watch. "It's three-thirty now. When will you be ready?"

Kate shook her head as if trying to grasp everything he was telling her. "I can be ready by seven-thirty," she said. "There are several things I have to finish, but I should be ready by then."

"Good," Rolk said. "I'll be back then, and we'll get you the hell out of this place. Wait for me."

Thirty-two

ROLK WENT THROUGH the messages on his desk, then cursed under his breath. He checked his watch. It had been three hours since he had left word for Rimerez. He picked up the phone and punched out the number in Mexico he had been given. Rimerez answered on the third ring.

"I was just about to call you," Rimerez said. "I was waiting for one piece of confirmation, and now I have it."

Rolk felt the tension building in his stomach; his hand tightened on the telephone receiver. "What is it?"

"Several things," Rimerez said. "But the most important is Roberto Caliento. He was definitely involved in the ritual in Chetulak. It was years ago, according to his relatives, but there's no question he was part of it. To what degree, I'm not certain, but I will find out. What's more interesting is that he is the one who explained it all to the priest."

"So the priest knew he'd been involved," Rolk said, a small smile forming on his lips.

"There can be no question," Rimerez said.

"What about Domingo?"

"You are thinking Domingo helped him? Gave him access to the museum?"

"The thought had crossed my mind."

"It is possible," Rimerez said. "It seems they are cousins, and Domingo, from what I can learn, is easily intimidated. But what about the priest? I can find nothing that ties him directly to the ritual, other than a scholarly interest."

"He knew," Rolk said. "He knew and he covered it up. That's enough for me to go after him, even charge him as an accessory if I have to."

"I don't envy you, arresting a priest. In my country it would be very difficult."

"In mine too," Rolk said. "But I think I may have an edge."

"There is one other matter," Rimerez said. "Our check with the airlines turned up only your name and Dr. Silverman's. It proves nothing, of course. People do not always travel under their own names, especially when their intentions are not legal. And I have to confess our immigration service is not the best. But there is one thing about it that confuses me."

Rolk listened as Rimerez prattled on, getting to the thrust of the information in his own time. He laughed softly when Rimerez had finished. "Yeah, I knew about that, and I'll explain it to you later," he said. "Your information about Caliento and Domingo is the important thing right now."

"If you need more, please call me," Rimerez said. "And I will send you a written report on what we have found."

"That's all I'll need, my friend. That's all I'll need."

Rolk was halfway out of his chair when Charlie Moriarty entered, a letter dangling from his extended hand. "I found this on my desk," he said. "But it's addressed to you."

Rolk took the letter and sat back in his chair. He glanced at his watch. "Christ, four-thirty. That's a helluva time to be getting your mail. No wonder we can't catch anybody around here."

. Moriarty shrugged. "Sorry, I just got back and found it on my desk. That idiot clerk who delivers the mail musta stuck it there by mistake."

"No problem, Charlie." Rolk tore open the letter and began to read it. When he had finished he turned back to the beginning and read it again.

"Something important?" Moriarty asked.

"Yeah, damned important." Rolk's face had drained of color, and the hand that held the letter had begun to tremble. "But it's got nothing to do with the case. It's something personal."

Moriarty slid his bulk into a chair. "Yeah, well, there's something about the case I think I should talk to you about."

Rolk sat forward. "Go ahead."

"It's about the Silverman woman. The background check I've been running on her and everyone else."

"What about it?"

Moriarty hunched forward and stared into the palms of his hands. There had been talk about Rolk's attachment to the woman, and he wanted to handle it as gently as possible, not just because Rolk was his boss, but also because he truly cared about the man. "We knew she was adopted, right?" he began. "And that her parents were killed in accidents. First the mother, then a few years later, the father."

"That's right." Rolk's face had grown tight and grim.

"Well, it seems her old man was some kind of religious nut. Real devout, and more than a little crazy about it. Seems the cops out in Arizona—they could never prove anything—always thought the car accident that killed him just might not have been an accident. Seems they found a letter at his house, a rambling thing that didn't give any specifics, but the gist of it was that he planned to go to God."

"So what's that got to do with our case?" There was an edge to Rolk's voice.

Moriarty shifted in his chair. "Well, the Silverman woman was in the car with him. The Arizona cops think she was supposed to die too." Moriarty was getting to the difficult part now, and he drew a deep breath. "She was only a kid then, and she was banged up a little, but nothing serious." He hesitated again. "Except emotionally. They had to keep her in the hospital for almost five months. Had to treat her for the emotional trauma. Then her aunt took her in, and as far as I can see, everything's been okay since then."

"So what's the point?" Rolk asked.

Moriarty shifted his bulk again. "Well, it's the type of thing the shrink said we should look out for. Some early trauma, something to do with religion, maybe. I just thought you should know, that's all."

Rolk stared down at his desk, the fingers of one hand rubbing his forehead. "Yeah, it's interesting, and it's something I *should* know about." He looked up quickly, a smile on his face. "But we've got something hotter now, Charlie. And I think it's hot enough to blow this thing wide open." Rolk rose from his desk and picked up his coat. "Where's Paul?" he suddenly asked.

"I don't know. I haven't seen him."

"Then you come with me," Rolk said. "I'll fill you in on the way."

Monsignor John Arpie was seated behind a plain metal desk when Rolk and Moriarty were ushered into his office. Unlike the other rooms they had passed as they were escorted down a long hallway in the archdiocese, this one was Spartan and unadorned, a place strictly for work, the only decorations being a portrait of the Sacred Heart, a crucifix, and a framed photograph of the archbishop.

"You said it was urgent," Arpie began, extending a hand toward two chairs opposite his desk. "I hope it won't also be troublesome."

Rolk sat and stared at the priest with a dispassionate coolness. "About as troublesome as it can get, Monsignor." Rolk quickly explained what had been uncovered about Caliento, Domingo, and Father LoPato's previous knowledge about them; about Caliento's disappearance, and Rolk's own belief that the priest knew where he could be found.

"So what do you want from me?" Arpie asked, his eyes and words suddenly cold.

"I'd like you to help us convince your priest that

he'd better come clean with us, and he'd better do it fast. *Before* anyone else gets hurt."

"I'll have to speak with the archbishop," Arpie began.

"Why?" Rolk demanded.

"Because, Lieutenant, this is a delicate matter. It involves one of our priests—perhaps even to some lesser criminal degree. And it also involves this refugee movement, which is a very delicate question for the Church in itself."

Rolk sat forward abruptly. "I know how the archdiocese feels about the refugee movement. You already explained that to me. I promised you some advance warning if it became necessary, and you're getting that now. But I don't have time for any more delays."

Arpie leaned back in his chair. "What I told you about the position of the archdiocese was offered strictly on an informational basis." He glanced at Moriarty. "Something to ease your mind. But it is something, I assure you, that would never be confirmed, or repeated. So I feel you're just going to have to give me some time, Lieutenant."

Rolk looked like a predator studying wounded prey. "Sure, Monsignor," he said slowly. "I'll give you all of five minutes." He waited, still smiling. "But I want you to know that your little *informational* discussion found its way onto a reel of tape, and if your ass isn't out of that chair and helping me before I walk out that door, that tape is going to be in the hands of a very nasty newspaper reporter I know before you can do anything about it."

Arpie sat upright and glared at Rolk. "You wouldn't dare."

Rolk let out a short, harsh laugh. "You wouldn't say that, if you knew me, Monsignor."

Father LoPato paced the floor of the large sitting room in St. Helena's rectory. His hands were held prayerlike in front of him, more to have something to do with them than anything else, and his voice, when he was able to speak at all, stammered badly. "You

. . . you just don't . . . don't understand," he said. "Yes, Roberto was involved in the ritual years . . . years ago. But . . . but he was only . . . only a child then. He was never . . . never directly involved in . . . in anything brutal."

Rolk, Moriarty, and Arpie sat watching the performance, not an ounce of pity between them. It was clear the priest had gone over the edge.

"Get hold of yourself, man," Arpie demanded, his voice cold and authoritative. "Do you realize you may have brought someone into this city who has slaughtered people?"

LoPato turned to face him, his eyes suddenly glazed, his own voice surprisingly calm. "Yes," he began slowly. "I suppose you may be right." He looked at each man in turn. "But haven't we all killed?" he asked. "Who killed Christ? Wasn't it all of us?" He turned to Arpie, his eyes blinking. "Isn't that what Holy Mother Church teaches?" He smiled. "And wasn't our Lord both the willing and yet unwilling victim?"

Arpie stood abruptly and grasped LoPato by the shoulders. "Dammit, man, we don't need mystical nonsense right now. We need answers to questions. Where is Caliento?" He watched as LoPato slowly shook his head.

"They're part of my flock," LoPato said softly. "I've made a vow to help them, protect them."

Arpie forced his voice to become very soft. "The Church will protect them, I promise you. And if they have sinned, the Church will forgive them." He squeezed LoPato's shoulders gently. "And the Church will care for you too, Father." Arpie turned to look at Rolk. "We have a home upstate," he said. "I'd like to take him there. He can get care, treatment."

"As long as he gives me what I want," Rolk said.

Arpie turned back to LoPato. He took his chin in his hand and raised his head until their eyes met. "You must do this for the Church," Arpie said. "On your vow of obedience, I order you to."

LoPato stared at him. A tic had started in his right

eye, and his lips had begun to move soundlessly. He reached slowly into his pocket and withdrew a slip of paper. Arpie took it, read it, then handed it to Rolk.

"Is this the address?" Rolk asked. "The place we'll find Caliento?"

LoPato nodded, but said nothing.

Arpie turned his back on him, facing Rolk. "We'll take care of him, and we'll take care of him well, I assure you." He paused, forming his next words. "You go get this little animal," he said. "But I'd like you to keep Father LoPato out of it. And I'd like any mention of this refugee movement suppressed." He paused again. "At least until I can find some way to protect the archdiocese from any scandal."

A smile formed on Rolk's lips. "All I want is the killer, Monsignor. It's all I ever wanted."

Rolk and Moriarty stopped on the sidewalk next to their car.

"I want you to put together a team and stake out this address," Rolk said.

"You're not coming?" Moriarty asked.

Rolk glanced at his watch. "I'm supposed to pick up Dr. Silverman at the museum, and I'm already late. You just cover the place and wait until I get there before you move in."

Rolk turned to leave, and Moriarty took his arm, stopping him.

"What is it?" Rolk asked.

"The priest. You think he was involved?" There was concern in Moriarty's eyes.

Rolk shrugged. "I don't think we'll ever know. I don't think anybody's going to see Father LoPato again for a long time."

Thirty-three

KATE LOOKED AT the clock on her desk. There was time, she told herself. Just enough time. She would leave him a note telling him where to find her. She wrote the note quickly in large bold print, then propped it on her desk so it could be seen from the doorway. She gathered up her briefcase and started out, stopping briefly at the door to look back and make sure the note was visible. Yes, she told herself. There's no way he can miss it.

Paul Devlin stood in the open doorway and stared at Kate's empty desk. He hadn't been due to meet her for another half-hour, but he had hoped to find her there and convince her to leave earlier than she had planned, perhaps even to stop off somewhere where they could talk. He spotted the note, walked to it, read it. The old library, he told himself, trying to locate it in his mind, then remembering it was one flight up.

Devlin took the stairs three at a time, pulled open the stairwell door with such force it crashed against the wall, and hurried down the hall to the library.

He called Kate's name as he opened the library door, then stood glancing about the apparently empty room. He crossed it quickly, looking down each row of bookcases, then climbed the spiral staircase that led to the mezzanine and checked each aisle there.

Standing at the edge of the balcony that looked down on the main floor, he slammed his hand against the railing and cursed aloud. He could feel the tension building, the sensation that something was wrong. It was instinct, he knew. But over the years he had learned to rely on it.

He hurried down the staircase, his shoes slipping on the metal steps, only his hand, clutching the twisting banister, keeping him upright. Outside the library he checked along the hall in both directions, then again called out to Kate. Nothing.

To his left, Devlin saw the open door of a storage room, the same room where Kate had once been attacked, and moved toward it, instinctively unbuttoning his suit coat to provide easier access to the revolver on his hip.

The room was dark, and Devlin ran his hand along the wall until he found the light switch. As he turned it on, fluorescent ceiling fixtures flooded the room with light, and Devlin stood mesmerized by the collection of mounted animals that loomed up before him.

It's like a goddamned zoo without bars, he told himself. But it's a zoo for the dead.

Slowly he moved across the room, stepping around a male lion, its glass eyes seeming to follow every step. Far to his left, a leopard was posed in mid-spring, teeth bared, claws unsheathed. A chill ran down Devlin's back as he stared at the gleaming eyes that somehow, even in death, seemed to spew hatred across the room.

He backed away and turned, then stepped around the stuffed remains of a massive crocodile, its mouth open as if preparing to snap out at his leg. Behind the croc, a huge bear rose to the ceiling, its mouth contorted into a twisted snarl.

Devlin stopped in mid-step, his eyes fixing on a flash of color between the animal's legs. He moved quickly around the beast, then knelt. A pool of fresh blood lay before him.

Standing, he continued to stare at the blood, then turned and began searching the room with his eyes, moving from one animal to the next, struggling to find what he hoped he would not see. His eyes stopped on the mounted body of a large ostrich. Next to it, a plumed cape seemed to hang in the air, a high collar protruding above it, the feathers—a brilliant mixture of iridescent reds and blues and greens—cascading in an ever-widening flow until they reached the floor.

There was something about the cape, something that nagged at him. He moved slowly toward it, one hand extended, reaching for it.

Devlin's hand shot back as the cape suddenly spun around, and he found himself staring into a stone mask, two eyes glaring at him through the cut holes.

Devlin's hand moved quickly to his revolver, but as he began to pull it free of its holster, a heavy bronze ax flashed toward him and slammed into his upper arm, cutting deep into the flesh and smashing into the bone.

Screaming in pain, Devlin staggered back, the revolver falling away, the hand of his damaged arm no longer able to hold it. As he stumbled away from the plumed figure, the back of his legs struck the mounted crocodile and he fell across it, his body twisting helplessly as he hit the concrete floor.

Gasping for breath, his left hand holding his wounded arm, Devlin struggled to his knees and stared across the body of the reptile at the unmoving plumed figure.

The figure bent slowly and dropped the bloodied ax into something at its feet, then rose back majestically to its full height, a long green-bladed obsidian knife now in its hand.

Fear and anger mixed in Devlin's mind as he watched the advancing form. He staggered to his feet, his memory assaulting him with visions of severed heads—Cynthia Gault's, Alexsandra Ross's, Grace Mallory's—and now, somewhere, he was certain, Kate Silverman's as well.

But not mine, you sonofabitch, he told himself as his mind screamed at him to turn and run.

The figure reached the crocodile and stopped. Then the hand lashed out with surprising speed, the length of the blade and the extended arm reaching over the

creature, allowing the tip of the knife to slash into
Devlin's cheek, cutting it from cheekbone to jaw.

Devlin screamed again, and he felt the warm flow of
blood running down his face and neck. He turned and
began to run, his knees threatening to buckle with
each staggering stride. He lurched into the hall, his
body momentarily losing control, and he crashed into
the opposite wall, smearing it with a wide swath of his
own blood.

He glanced over his shoulder as the plumed figure
filled the doorway, and his ears were filled with a
loud, rasping hiss, followed by a pulsating hum. Flat-
tening his hand against the wall, he pushed himself
away, then turned and hurtled down the hall, his feet
stumbling beneath him, his body swaying dangerously
from side to side.

Suddenly his feet were gone, and he fell facedown
and sliding, his own blood greasing his path. He struggled to his feet, his head twisting to see behind him,
his good arm raised protectively to ward off any blow.
The plumed figure was moving toward him in long,
majestic strides.

He lurched forward again, his body bouncing off the
wall with each step, leaving a crimson trail of gore in
his wake, as his mind screamed at him to find a place
to hide.

Ahead, a glass-paneled door broke the plane of the
wall, and he hurled himself toward it, his good hand
seizing the doorknob and twisting it. It was locked.
Panic raged in his brain, and with his good hand he
smashed through the glass panel, then reached inside
and twisted the inner knob, the weight of his body
forcing the now-unlocked door open.

He staggered forward, fell to one knee, then righted
himself. The room before him was filled with row
upon row of large glass bottles, and within each, float-
ing in alcohol, were the remains of long-dead animals.
Thousands of them. Devlin staggered against one of
the wooden racks, his hand encircling the base of one
of the bottles, and he twisted around, forcing himself

to face the plumed figure as it stepped through the doorway.

Devlin flattened his palm against the base of the bottle, then, reaching down for every ounce of strength he could summon, he hurled the bottle at the advancing form as his wounded arm matched the scream that rose from his throat.

Helplessly he watched as the bottle crashed at the feet of the plumed figure, and he staggered back, knowing that he lacked the strength to try again, knowing that he was about to die.

Slowly the figure grasped the handle of the knife with both hands, the blade pointed toward the ceiling, dissecting its mask, then rising still higher until it loomed above its head.

Devlin staggered back, inching his way along one of the aisles formed by the racks of bottles. The figure stood there, the huge shimmering cape filling the aisle.

Then, without warning, the arms dropped. The blade remained motionless, then slowly began to move until it pointed at the opposite rack. Devlin's eyes followed it, his feet still inching back. A sudden gasp rose in his throat, and his legs buckled beneath him, sending his body crashing to the floor. But his eyes remained fixed on the bottle singled out by the long green blade, and he stared in horror at its contents. The severed head of Malcolm Sousi stared back at him.

Devlin's head snapped back to the figure that loomed above him, and his mind filled with terror at the sound of his own voice as it echoed through the room.

"Nooo," he screamed. "Nooo."

The blade rose again, but the arms holding it began to tremble as it reached its apex. Then the figure turned and ran.

Devlin remained on the floor between the racks of bottles, Sousi's face staring blindly at him from one directly above.

His breathing was shallow, and he felt weak from the loss of blood that had already begun to pool around him. He struggled to right himself and failed. He undid his belt, fought it free of his trousers, and tried to fit it into a tourniquet above the wound in his arm.

He heard footsteps in the hall and tensed, then searched the area around him for something to defend himself. All he could find was a jagged shard of broken glass from the bottle he had thrown at the killer. But it was ten feet away.

Devlin swung his body around and began pulling himself along the floor with his good arm. His body screamed against the pain, but he ignored it, eyes fixed on the daggerlike piece of glass. He was determined to reach it, to find a way to fight against the madman who had tried to kill him.

He heard the footsteps falter, then start again, more quickly this time, then pause outside the door just as he reached the glass. He grabbed it with such force the glass cut into the palm of his hand, but he felt nothing and quickly struggled to his knees, preparing to fight in whatever way he could.

Kate stepped into view, her eyes wide and frightened. She stared down at him, her mouth forming a circle of disbelief. "Oh, my God," she said, hurrying forward as Devlin, all adrenaline gone now, slumped back to the floor. She cradled him in her arms, ignoring the blood, one hand moving to the makeshift tourniquet to tighten it as best she could.

"The killer," Devlin gasped, still fighting for breath. "He's here. Go get help. Fast."

A shadow filled the doorway, blocking the light from the hall. Kate turned, terrified, as she felt Devlin struggling to gain his feet.

Rolk stepped cautiously into the room, his revolver held before him in a two-handed combat grip, his eyes scanning each corner, each potential hiding place. "Are you all right, Paul?" he asked, his attention still fixed on his search.

"Yes."

"No, he's not," Kate said, her voice broadcasting her fear. "He needs a doctor. Right now."

"Where is he?" Rolk asked, ignoring her.

"He ran out," Devlin said. "A couple of minutes ago."

Rolk lowered the revolver and hurried to his side, quickly checking the wounds, the tourniquet. He looked at Kate, eyes hard. "Did you see him?" His voice was demanding, angry.

She shook her head. "I was in the ladies' room. When I came out, there was blood all over the hall. I followed it and found him. There was no one else."

Rolk stared down at Devlin. "Dammit. I was going to call you and tell you not to come. Then things started happening and I never did." Rolk clenched his teeth, the muscles jumping along his jaw.

"You know who it was, don't you?" Devlin said.

Rolk nodded. "Caliento. And as soon as we get you an ambulance, I'm going to get the little bastard."

Devlin lay back on the floor, his breath coming in gasps now. His eyes blinked and he fought to keep them open. "You said 'little.' " he said, still struggling for breath. "He didn't seem little. Smaller than me, but not little."

"What was he wearing?" Rolk asked.

"The cape. A stone mask."

"That's why," Rolk said. He turned to Kate. "Get to a phone. Call 911 and get an ambulance."

He turned back to Devlin as Kate hurried from the room. He placed a hand gently on his shoulder.

"You sure it's him?" Devlin asked.

Rolk nodded. "Ninety percent. But I'll make sure, damned sure, because of what he did to you."

Thirty-four

SEVEN DETECTIVES PUSHED their way into the room. The door to the tiny Brooklyn apartment had been kicked in without even a knock. It had caught Roberto Caliento sitting on a battered sofa watching an old black-and-white television set.

He sat there now, not quite believing what he saw. Seven men stood before him, six of them pointing revolvers at his head. But the seventh man was even more frightening. He had no gun, but the murderous smile he wore was worse than any weapon.

"Hello, Roberto," Rolk said. "Spending a quiet evening at home, are we?"

Caliento stared back, but said nothing.

"Frisk him," Rolk ordered, then watched as two detectives pulled Caliento to his feet, spread-eagled him against a wall, patted him down, then pushed him roughly back onto the sofa.

"He's clean."

"As driven snow," Rolk said. He turned, walked to the small kitchen, bathroom, and bedroom, looking into each. Then he turned back to his men, jabbed a finger at two of them. "You two watch the front. Keep an eye out for this Domingo." He jabbed again. "You two, out back. Do the same. Moriarty, you watch the front door. Lopez, you question this little prick while I toss this dump."

Rolk started in the kitchen, ripping it apart as he went, listening to Lopez question Caliento in Spanish.

"Says he doesn't know what we're talking about," Lopez shouted in English.

"Hit him," Rolk called back, continuing in the kitchen, nodding with satisfaction as he heard the sound of Lopez's blow.

He moved on to the bathroom. It was dirty and smelled of stale urine; the porcelain fixtures were stained brown with age and ill care. He walked back into the living room. There was blood on Caliento's lips, but Rolk ignored it. He stared across at Moriarty, standing by the door. "Toss this room while I check the bedroom," he said, making a mental note to find out who had rented this pigsty for Caliento to hide away in. If it was the priest, so be it, he told himself. His deal with the archdiocese didn't include somebody trying to kill a cop.

Rolk entered the bedroom and began pulling it apart. From the living room he could still hear Lopez interrogating the Mayan, his voice more threatening with each response. Rolk heard the sound of another blow, then another. Caliento would soon tell them what they wanted to know.

Rolk grabbed the edge of a ragged double mattress, pulled it up and away, then stared down at the sagging box spring.

He returned to the living room, hands behind his back, his body rocking back and forth on the balls of his feet. "What's he telling you?" he asked.

Lopez had been holding Caliento by the front of his shirt, and he turned now to face Rolk, still maintaining his grip. "Says he was involved in the ritual, but only in the Yucatán, never here. Says he was here alone all day. Hiding, because he knew we'd be looking for him. Says the priest warned him and he was scared."

"You believe him?" Rolk asked.

"Not for a fucking minute," Lopez spat.

"Good for you," Rolk said, extending his arms away from his sides.

Lopez stared up at him, at the plastic bags hanging from Rolk's hands, one containing a bronze ax, the other a green-bladed knife.

"Under the mattress," Rolk said. "Not very original, but handy when he needed them."

"Any blood on them?" Lopez asked.

"Yes, indeed," Rolk said. "Paul Devlin's blood would be my guess."

Lopez turned and stared into Caliento's eyes. Then his right fist drew back and smashed into the man's face again.

Thirty-five

TWO DAYS PASSED before Paul Devlin was able to receive visitors. As Rolk entered the private room at Bellevue, Devlin smiled weakly at him, his drug-hazed eyes failing to notice the sharply tailored suit and crisp regimental tie that Rolk now wore.

Rolk sat on the edge of the bed and deposited a box of chocolates on the table beside it. "Keep an eye on these," he said. "Those damned nurses steal." He reached out and gently patted Devlin's undamaged shoulder. "How you feeling today?" he asked.

"As lousy as I look," Devlin said. He gazed off toward the window. "The specialist still doesn't know if I'll have full use of the arm. Good enough for most guys, but he's not sure if it will be good enough to stay on the job." He shook his head. "Hell, so I'll take a disability pension, and I won't have to worry about guys in feathers chasing me with knives." He laughed weakly. "Christ, I thought only cops who worked Greenwich Village had to worry about that."

Rolk grunted, then stared down at his hands, struggling to suppress the regret he felt rising within him. "It'll work out. The department will give you time." He winked at him. "And if it doesn't, I understand they've got a real demand for one-armed paperhangers out in Queens."

Devlin laughed softly, then reached out and squeezed Rolk's hand. "Thanks," he said, his voice slightly choked. He shook the feeling away. "Tell me what happened. They've had me so doped up, I haven't even seen a newspaper."

Rolk shrugged. "Caliento finally confessed. It took a little persuasion, but he coughed it up in the end."

"Anybody in it with him?" Devlin asked.

"Domingo. But only to the extent of getting him in and out of the museum. Apparently Caliento scared the shit out of him, and he did what he was told."

"What about the priest?"

"Caliento won't talk about that. And the archdiocese has him holed away in some sanatorium they run upstate. Nobody's going to get to him for a long, long time." He shrugged again. "That's the DA's problem now, because that's the way the game works. Always has, always will."

"Well, I guess I was wrong," Devlin said. His eyes seemed perplexed and Rolk wondered if it was about the solution or about himself.

"How?" Rolk asked.

Devlin gave a slight shake of his head. "He seemed so small. When Lopez and I interrogated him, he just seemed small. But the other day, the guy struck me as bigger, bulkier."

"It was that plumed robe," Rolk said. "And the high collar and the mask. It just made him *seem* bigger."

Devlin nodded absently. "I suppose," he said. He looked toward the window again, thinking, then back at Rolk. "Did he say why he killed Sousi? I can't quite figure that one either."

"Just in the wrong place at the wrong time," Rolk said. "Same as with you."

Devlin nodded, but his mind was far away. "You know," he said at length, "for a long time I had this gut feeling it was Kate Silverman. Maybe with somebody helping her or covering up for her."

Rolk shook his head. "Never fit," he said.

Devlin nodded. "Yeah, that's the way I started to see it too. Toward the end, anyway."

Rolk grinned down at him. "Maybe you started to fall for her at the end. Ever think of that?"

Devlin nodded. "Yeah, I thought about it. Maybe you're right. How is she? What's she going to do?"

"Stick with the museum, I guess." Rolk smiled with uncharacteristic warmth. "Unless I can talk her into something else."

Devlin returned the smile. "See, that's why I backed off. I hate losing to a better man." He started to laugh. "I'll have to send her a sympathy card if she takes you up on your offer. Poor woman. Having a relationship with a homicide cop who sleeps in his office half the time."

"I won't be sleeping there anymore," Rolk said. He watched the confused look on Devlin's face suddenly turn to comprehension.

"You did it? You finally did it?

"Put in my papers today. I'm officially retired. Put them right into Jim Dunne's hands. Never saw the bastard look so happy."

Devlin laughed. "Christ, I wish I could have seen that sonofabitch's face."

"Watch your mouth," Rolk said. "He'll probably be chief of department someday. Maybe even commissioner. He's got all the qualifications they look for."

"Tell me," Devlin said. "What finally made up your mind? Kate?"

Rolk patted the breast pocket of his coat. "Couple of days back, I got a letter from a private investigator I hired a year ago. He found my daughter. In Seattle, of all places. I'm going to head out there tomorrow."

"Stan, that's great." Devlin shook his head. "I never thought it would happen. I really thought you were pissing in the wind on that one, but I never had the guts to tell you so." He reached out and squeezed Rolk's hand. "When will I get to meet her?"

Rolk gazed off toward the window as if distracted. "When we get back. If we can work things out between us, that is." He smiled, a little fearfully Devlin thought. "But, who knows, maybe I'll like it out there and decide to stay. I'll just have to see what happens."

Devlin took Rolk's hand again. "It'll work," he said. "And if you decide to stay, I'll jump on a plane one of these days."

Rolk smiled down on him. He knew Devlin would never do that. After all, he had a child of his own to take care of. But he was glad he had said it. It mattered to him that he had.

Rose Delacroix was already seated at the kitchen table when Rolk walked in, and the usual uneasiness she felt upon seeing him lately turned to surprise as she took in his new clothes.

"Mother of God," she said. "Don't tell me you finally bought a new suit."

"Three of them," Rolk said as he slid into a chair opposite her. "And a couple of sport jackets and slacks too."

"I don't believe it. What got into you?"

"I retired," Rolk said. "And this is my new image."

"Retired? I don't believe that either."

"It's true. So you don't have to worry about me blowing the whistle on this little bookmaking operation of yours anymore."

"I never worried," she said. "It's just that my husband always taught me to be nervous when a cop was around."

"That's probably what killed him. Nerves."

"You know how he died," she said, a sharpness to her voice now. "You ran the investigation." She looked at him levelly. "But you never caught the bastard who shot him."

"He was a pro," Rolk said. "You don't catch pros. That's why they call them that."

Rose poured herself a drink but didn't offer Rolk one. He wasn't a cop anymore, so she didn't have to. "So what made you decide to retire?" she asked at length.

Rolk reached into his breast pocket and withdrew the letter he had received two days earlier. It was wrinkled and worn now from repeated readings. He handed it to Rose.

She began reading it; then her head snapped up, "So," she said. "You finally found her."

"PI I hired about a year ago to run down some leads I couldn't check myself."

Rose stared at the letter, which was printed in pen and ink. "Some PI," she said. "He doesn't even have a typewriter."

"He got the job done. Who knows, maybe he considers it the personal touch."

Rolk's face broke into a smile, and Rose realized it was the first time she had ever seen him smile. She reached out and poured him a drink. "How's your partner, Devlin? The newspapers made it sound real bad."

"He's in Bellevue right now. But he'll be okay."

Rose looked at the letter again. "Seattle," she said. "You going out there?"

"Tomorrow."

"I'm happy for you, Rolk. You were a cop—and I don't particularly like cops—but you never gave up trying to find your kid. I'll give you that."

Rolk sipped his drink, his eyes lowered to the table.

"You have an address, Rolk?" Rose asked. "I'd like to send the kid something. Maybe make her feel somebody else is pulling for the two of you."

Rolk took the notebook he had carried for years from an inside pocket and carefully wrote the address. He dropped it on top of the letter.

Rose stared at it for several moments, then looked up at him.

Rolk retrieved the letter, then stood to leave. "We'll see you, Rose. And thanks for the thought. About the kid, I mean. Who knows, maybe it will help."

Rose watched him go; when she picked up her drink, her hand was trembling.

Devlin put down the telephone and stared blindly at the far wall. His eyes were still fixed on the empty white plane when Nathan Greenspan entered his room, and Devlin realized he was there only when Greenspan touched his arm.

"Are you all right, Paul?" Greenspan asked. There

was a look of professional concern on his face, and he leaned closer to get a better look at Devlin's eyes. "Were you just medicated?"

Devlin focused on the short, pudgy psychiatrist. He forced himself up, then swung his legs over the side of the bed, momentary pain flashing across his face. "No, I'm fine," he said.

Greenspan placed a hand on his shoulder. "Paul, perhaps you shouldn't get up."

Devlin waved him off, then drew several deep breaths, waiting for the pain to pass. When he turned his attention back to Greenspan, the psychiatrist's concern seemed to have deepened, but Devlin ignored it.

"How do you feel about this case? About Caliento?" There was an urgency to Devlin's voice, and the sound of it seemed to confuse Greenspan.

He hesitated, suddenly uncertain how to answer. "Why do you ask?"

Devlin shook his head. "I don't want to talk about that yet. Just tell me how *you* feel about it."

Greenspan turned, paced a few steps, then turned back. "It's hard to say. I never had an opportunity to interview him. There just wasn't any need. The physical evidence was there, and then there was the confession."

"But how do you *feel* about it?" Devlin's voice was demanding now.

"Well, it doesn't fit the pattern I'd anticipated. Some past trauma—especially something with religious undertones—or some brutalization or great that loss produced a psychopathic reaction was more or less what I had expected." He paused, shaking his head. "But this also fits, Paul. A strange, obscure religion brought here from another culture—"

"Goddammit," Devlin snapped. "Can't you stop the bullshit, the constant hedging, and just tell me how the hell you *feel* about it?"

Greenspan blinked several times, then retreated into his professional shell. "Why don't you tell me how *you* feel about it, Paul? Then perhaps I'd understand what you're getting at."

Devlin shook his head in frustration, then picked up the phone and punched out Charlie Moriarty's number.

"Yeah, I'm fine, Charlie. Looks like I'll be away a month, then they'll check the arm again, and if everything's okay, I'll be back." He waited as Moriarty launched into the latest office gossip, centering around Rolk's retirement and who their new boss might be. Finally Devlin cut him off. "Yeah, listen, Charlie, I need some information. The background checks you did on the Caliento case—did you ever turn up anything?"

Devlin's hand tightened on the telephone receiver. "Did you tell Rolk about that?" He waited. "And what did he say?" Devlin closed his eyes; his jaw tightened. "Listen, thanks, Charlie. No, it's nothing. Just something I was lying here thinking about. Yeah, I'll talk to you soon. Let me know who the new boss is going to be."

Devlin replaced the receiver and sat rocklike, his eyes again glued to the wall.

"What is it?" Greenspan said, his voice slightly agitated.

Devlin waved him off again, opened the drawer of his bedside table, and pulled out his notebook. He flipped through the pages until he found the telephone number Rolk had given him, then picked up the phone and dialed Mexico.

Captain Rimerez answered on the second ring, and Devlin quickly explained who he was.

"I just wanted to double-check something with you, Captain. It's about your investigation, and anything it might have turned up." Devlin listened, his face growing pale, almost frightened. "And you mentioned this to the lieutenant?" He waited again. "No, nothing's wrong. It's just that the lieutenant's just retired, and I wanted to double-check. . . . Yes, thank you. I'll be in touch if there's anything else."

Devlin replaced the receiver and slowly stood.

"What *is* it?" Greenspan demanded. He listened as Devlin explained.

"Oh, my God. And you think they're together now?"

Devlin nodded.

"What are you going to do?"

"First, you're going to help me get dressed," Devlin said. "Then you're going to get me out of this place."

Thirty-six

DEVLIN RANG THE doorbell, waited, rang again, then waited a full minute before removing the set of lock picks from his pocket. Despite images made popular by film and television, opening a decent lock takes several minutes, and Devlin found himself glancing over his shoulder repeatedly, fearful some neighbor might happen along and call the police. And other cops were the last thing he wanted now. By the time the lock finally gave way, he found he was sweating freely.

He entered the apartment quietly, stood in the living room listening for any sound of life, then quickly checked each room before returning to where he had begun.

He stood in the living room now, staring about him. Everything was immaculate, almost as though some professional cleaning service had been called in; the floors were highly polished, the carpets recently shampooed and vacuumed, there was not a mote of dust anywhere, and except for a cluttered desk in one corner, not a magazine or book was out of place. A wave of uncertainty washed through him. He was challenging the conclusion Rolk had reached, challenging the arrest he had made on his last case. It was something he had never done before, not in all the years they had worked together, something that had never before crossed his mind. But he knew he had to do it now. The alternative was too overwhelming.

Devlin moved to the desk and hunched over it, trying to study each item without altering its position.

331

There were several books on Toltec ritual, which seemed perfectly understandable. Carefully, without moving it, he lifted the cover of the first book, hoping to find which passages had been underlined. On the flyleaf the name of the original owner had been crossed out and a new name inserted. Next to it was a date, followed by an inscription: *Study this well for Quetzalcoatl's sake, for now the knowledge is required.* He closed the book's cover, knowing now it had been right for him to come.

The restaurant on Columbus Avenue was small and quaint and littered with hanging ferns, exactly the type of trendy café that Rolk had always despised. But Kate seemed to melt into it, perfectly in her element, choosing from the menu a leek soup and vegetable crepe that made Rolk wince. He settled for a Reuben sandwich and potato salad, much to the chagrin of the effeminate waiter, who rolled his eyes with such distaste it caused Kate to fight back laughter.

"In the old days a Reuben sandwich and a glass of wine would have been considered *haute cuisine* in this neighborhood," Rolk told her, forcing out the laughter she had tried to restrain.

The laughter was infectious and Rolk joined in, then reached across the table and took Kate's hand. "You seem to be in exceptionally good spirits today," he said. "Is it the present company or something else?"

"The present company *and* something else." She smiled at him, a look of relief in her eyes now. "It's just so good to have all of this over with. It's as though the air has suddenly become cleaner, easier to breathe."

"There's still the trial, unless they find Caliento mentally incompetent," Rolk said.

"That doesn't matter. It's over. Don't you feel the same way?"

Rolk toyed with his fork. "I guess I feel a little guilty, leaving my men when there's still a lot of shit work to do."

"Like what?" Kate asked. "I thought it ended with the arrest."

Rolk shook his head. "Over the past five years there were some murders that were never solved. Strange mutilations where the killers were never found. The DA will want to see if they can be tied into these killings. They're not at all similar, but it's the way it works. You always have to try to clear old cases." He shrugged. "So my guys will have to go back, see if Caliento, or Domingo, or anybody connected with them was in New York at those times. They'll probably have to check out LoPato too, but nobody will want to prove that part of it."

The waiter served Kate's soup and she sat studying it for several moments. "It's hard for me to think of poor little Juan Domingo being involved in this," she said through a weak smile. "And I never met Caliento."

"Didn't you?" Rolk asked, an enigmatic smile playing across his lips.

Kate drew a deep breath. "Yes, I guess I did, didn't I?" She shook her head thoughtfully. "And if you weren't right about him, the murders would have continued, wouldn't they?"

"Yes, they would have," Rolk said, looking up as the waiter served his sandwich and Kate's crepe. "But let's forget that," he began again when the waiter had left. "You're right, it's over, and there's something else I want to tell you about."

He reached into his pocket, withdrew the well-worn letter, and handed it to Kate. He watched her read it, hoping it would be important to her, wanting her to understand how important it was to him.

When she looked up, her eyes seemed sad, almost melancholy. "So you've finally done it," she said. "After all these years you've finally found her." She smiled at him, and the smile seemed to have a touch of sadness as well. She reached out and took his hand. "I'm happy for you, and I'm happy for her. It will be wonderful for her to know she has a father who so desperately wanted to be with her." Kate stared out the restaurant window, but Rolk could tell she wasn't looking at anything in particular. "It's hard about parents," Kate continued, still staring off. "You're sort of trapped with what you get." She looked back and tried to smile. "In most cases, of course, they try to give you great love—maybe even ultimate love—but they find they just can't. They simply fail."

"Everyone fails," Rolk said. "It's part of living."

"But it shouldn't be that way, should it?" The smile finally forced its way through. "You won't fail," she said. "I know you won't."

Devlin sat at the desk, unconcerned now about disturbing what was there. He looked through the material quickly. Things that had been hidden away—that must have been hidden away—seemed to have been taken out for some final review. He picked up three sheets of paper. Each held slightly different versions of the second votive message, and he realized for the first time how carefully worded those messages had been, how important it had been to the person who had written them that they be correct in every respect. He picked up several more sheets. They were copies of letters, some long and rambling and confused, others distinct and to the point, as if two different minds had conceived them—one lucid and intelligent, the other irrational and tortured.

He replaced the letters and began going through the desk drawers. In the bottom-right-hand drawer he found what he was looking for. Slowly he closed the drawer and stood. The pain in his arm was getting worse, but there was little he could do about it, not until he had finished.

In the bedroom Devlin methodically went about his work, as he had learned to do over the years. He searched the least obvious places first, so none would be inadvertently overlooked, then went on to drawers and shelves and boxes on top of dressers and tables. Everything seemed to be in order, and like the rest of the apartment, everything had been cleaned and polished and dusted. It reminded him of an elderly woman he had known as a boy, who every week thoroughly cleaned every item in her house, no matter how obscure, or hidden away. He had asked her about it once and she had told him she was afraid she might die unexpectedly and that she didn't want anyone to remember her as a poor housekeeper. Devlin thought about that now and wondered if a similar reasoning had prevailed here. Or was it something else? Was it in preparation of some anticipated event?

He walked to the closet and opened the door. He stood staring at the contents for several moments, then closed it softly. The pain in his arm was worse now, and it seemed to intensify with each breath. There was only one other place to search, and then he would be finished. Then he would decide what to do, and how.

They sat lingering over coffee, the subject of Rolk's daughter exhausted, their conversation drifting in and out of events that had dominated their lives in recent days.

"It seems so inconceivable that Grace and Malcolm are gone," Kate said. "And killed in a ritual they had spent so much of their lives studying and trying to understand." She stared into her cup. "I wonder if they understood what was happening. At the end, I mean."

"I think they may have been the only victims who did," Rolk said.

"Of course." Kate looked up suddenly. "Except Mrs. Gault. She might have understood, if she really did go to my lecture."

Rolk nodded, thinking about that possibility. "I am almost looking forward to the trial," he said at length.

"Why?"

"It will be fascinating to study the defense, especially if insanity is ruled out."

"But it has to be, doesn't it? If Caliento was a

believer, and was simply following a ritual of his religion, then there could be no question of madness."

Rolk smiled at her. "That's what I mean. A defense that claims the killings were not acts of murder, but acts of ultimate love and respect, mandated by religious belief." He sipped his coffee, then returned the cup to the table, his eyes never leaving Kate. "They'll still convict him, of course. No jury will ever understand or accept the argument. But the speculation it will cause . . ." He shook his head slowly and let the thought die.

Kate remained silent, her mind mulling over the scenario Rolk had offered.

"Of course the newspapers have already picked up on the idea," Rolk added. "I think they'll run with it."

"Do you think so?"

"It was too good a story for them to pass up, especially the tabloids." He shrugged. "But who knows, it might catch the imagination of some editor at the *Times,* and then some scholarly piece might even find its way into print." He leaned closer, lowering his voice. "They might even ask *you* to write it."

Kate dismissed the tease. "I don't think I qualify as an objective observer."

Rolk finished his coffee and signaled the waiter for more. "No, I suppose not," he said. "But I hope someone writes about it. I've spent so much of my life studying killing, the motives, the methods, the attempts to hide *what* was done, and how, and where. The idea of a killing as a great act of love, something not hidden away, but celebrated—now, that would make fascinating reading."

Kate drummed her fingers thoughtfully on the table. "But as you said, no one will ever accept it, even intellectually. People are very parochial in their views. Everything that's not part of their lives as they know it and deal with it each day is considered primitive." She paused, then laughed. "New Yorkers even consider square dancing primitive."

"Sometimes I wonder," Rolk said. "Look at the

Shiites in the Middle East, and God knows how many other sects, who believe in suicide as a form of martyrdom—believe that an act of self-destruction is the greatest gift they can bestow upon themselves, because it guarantees them a place in heaven." He smiled at the idea, at himself for mentioning it. "How big a step is it to offering that to someone else?"

Kate nodded but said nothing.

"Do you think it's possible?"

"What?" Kate asked, the question bringing her back from her own thoughts.

"That someone could kill as an act of great love. I don't mean euthanasia, I mean taking a healthy, normal life because it would offer that person some greater good."

"Or save the person from some greater evil," Kate said. "Yes, I believe it's possible someone could think that way, could act that way, could even, in his or her own mind, love someone that much."

Rolk watched her, the distant look in her eye, almost as though she had gone back in time. Far back. He thought about what Moriarty had told him about her father, and he wondered if she were reliving that part of her life now, trying to understand it as she had not been able to before.

"You must have experienced something of that yourself," Rolk said.

Kate's head snapped up. There was a look of concern, almost fear, in her eyes. "Why do you say that?"

Rolk leaned forward, lowering his voice again. "You were the primary object of this ritual, the final sacrifice. And you understood the ritual. You knew that someone wanted to kill you, not because they hated you, but because they loved you. That must have produced some strange feelings."

Kate nodded absently. "Yes, very strange." She shook her head as if driving the worst part of those memories away, then looked at Rolk and smiled weakly. "It terrified me, of course. But it also fascinated me. Intellectually, if in no other way. I kept asking myself why anyone would consider me so special, why anyone —anyone who *really* believed—would consider me worthy. And then that thought started to frighten me as well." Her face became serious, intent. "But I couldn't stop thinking about it." She closed her eyes momentarily. "But then you put an end to it. You stopped the ritual."

"Yes," Rolk said. "Finally."

Unlike the rest of the apartment, the final room in Devlin's search was dusty and cluttered and forgotten, a miniature warehouse with boxes piled in every corner, boxes of books and clothing and old papers intermingled with discarded lamps and chairs and unused household items, many far older than seemed reasonable. Maybe an inheritance, Devlin thought. Things that weren't needed but still could not be thrown away.

Devlin began moving boxes so he could reach others, his wound screaming stabs of pain each time the muscles were called upon to work. Sweat glistened on his forehead, more from the pain than the exertion, and his breathing grew more labored.

He moved a final set of boxes in one corner, then stopped. He stared down at the long narrow metal box that had been hidden under the clutter. He had seen boxes like it at the museum, hermetically sealed containers that kept all air out to protect old and rare and fragile artifacts. He knelt before the box and carefully worked the complicated locks until there was a rush of air as the seal was broken, the old, putrid air rushing out.

Slowly he raised the lid, then stared in horror at what lay within. He began to gag, and fell back against the pile of boxes he had moved earlier, sending the contents scattering across the floor. Then he turned his head to one side and was violently ill.

They stepped out into Columbus Avenue, the winter air biting at their faces after the warmth of the restaurant. Kate slipped her arm into Rolk's and offered him a smile.

"Now that you're retired, I guess we can be seen together," she said. "They can't suspect you or punish you for flirting with a witness after you're retired, can they?"

"They can't do a thing to me," he said. "As long as you're over sixteen."

She laughed at the idea. "Twelve years over. That should be a reasonable margin for error."

They walked slowly along the sidewalk, oblivious of the people who hurried past, as though they had never had anything more pressing on their minds than the casual pleasure of each other's company. Even the biting cold seemed unimportant.

Kate squeezed Rolk's arm against her side. "Didn't you tell me you lived near here?" she asked.

"About two blocks," Rolk said.

"I'd love to see your place," she said. "You've never even talked about it, and this may be my last chance."

"Why do you say that?" he asked.

"Well, if you don't come back from Seattle . . ."

He looked at her curiously. "Of course I'll come back. All my things are here. I can't just walk away from them." His features suddenly changed, replaced by a smile. "But come, I was going to suggest it myself. You just beat me to it."

"Then I wish I had waited."

"Why?"

"It would have been more proper, waiting for you to invite me."

His smile widened. "You're proper enough for me. In fact, you're perfect."

Devlin sat on the floor, trying to fight off both the nausea and the intensified pain in his arm. He had managed to close the box, but now he had to move, to act on what he had found. He would go to the museum and see if Kate was there. He had to get to her, and he had to do it before she got to Rolk.

Kate turned in a full circle, taking in the large living room and dining area. "This is lovely," she said, turning back to him, her face both curious and surprised. "I'm ashamed to admit I expected something more primitive, more the bachelor-cop image."

"Here come those cliché attitudes we were talking about at lunch." Rolk smiled.

She smiled back at him, raising her eyebrows in surrender. She looked very lovely, very delicate, and Rolk watched her as she placed her briefcase on a large round coffee table, then moved to a wall of bookcases and began scanning the titles.

Kate turned back, her look one of pleasure. "And I didn't expect this either," she said. "I thought most of your books would deal with murder. But you seem to have very eclectic tastes."

Rolk walked behind a high-backed chair and rested his forearms on top of it. "Some of them belonged to my wife," he said. "But I have read them." He stared at the floor for a moment, then back at Kate. "You see, she was a very well-educated woman. Had a doctorate in art history. In fact she worked at your museum until she left me."

Kate seemed jolted by the news. "But . . . I'm surprised no one connected the name. Especially Grace or—"

"She didn't use my name. She worked under her maiden name. Thought it sounded better professionally." He stared at the floor again, unable—or unwilling—to look at her. "I think she was a little ashamed. About my lack of formal education, I mean. Especially when we were with people she worked with." He looked up and smiled wryly. "We never went to functions there, at least not together. Then the Star of India case came along. That was a famous jewel theft at the museum."

"Yes, I've heard about it," Kate said. She wished

the chair wasn't between them, so she could go easily to him.

"Well, I was with the safe-and-loft squad then, and the case was assigned to me. So I was there every day until we broke it." He shrugged. "It was right after that she decided to leave."

"I'm sorry," Kate said. "I've known people like that. Unfortunately, academia is rampant with them." She stepped toward him. The chair was still between them. "But now you've found your daughter, and things will be different." She looked around her again, seeking something that would change the subject, put them both back at ease. She wanted him at ease; wanted him happy, relaxed. "I'd love to see the rest of the apartment," she offered. "Or do you occupy the whole house?"

Rolk shook his head. "No, I own it, but I just keep the duplex apartment. There are two more apartments on the third and fourth floors that I rent out." He glanced around casually. "But there really isn't much to see." He gestured to a doorway behind him. "That leads to the kitchen. Pretty basic, but adequate." He turned toward the hall. "That door in the hallway leads to the basement, and the stairs go up to two bedrooms. One is mine, one is my daughter's."

Devlin hurried out of the Museum of Natural History, his face pale and drawn, both from the renewed pain in his arm and the increasing fear he felt building in his gut. Kate had left for the day, and she had left with Rolk.

He stood on the sidewalk and realized his hands were trembling. He had to find her before it was too late, and that meant he could no longer do this by himself. He needed help. He hurried to a sidewalk telephone and quickly dialed Charlie Moriarty's number. The knot in his stomach tightened.

Kate stared into his eyes. Rolk had been speaking about his daughter, about the years he had spent in search of her, and there was a deep sadness etched into his face now, perhaps even pain. She stepped closer to him and smiled. She knew she had to dispel the pain. She wanted him calm and happy. She wanted to help him forget the past and think only of the great joy that lay ahead, the joy that she could give him.

Kate reached out and stroked his cheek. "You're such a wonderful man," she said. "I don't think you realize how wonderful, and that makes it all the more perfect." He returned the smile, his eyes brightening. Now the sadness was gone, she thought, and she turned and walked to the coffee table where she had left her briefcase. "I brought you a present," she said, her voice bright and cheerful. "Here. Let me show you."

Kate reached into her briefcase and withdrew a small mask of Quetzalcoatl. "It's only a replica, but I thought you'd like . . ."

"No."

His voice stopped her, and she turned to face him, puzzled.

"First I have something for you," he said.

Kate watched as he went to a small desk in one corner, and, with his back to her, bent and opened a bottom drawer. When he turned, the stone mask of Quetzalcoatl hung around his neck, and his hands held an intricately carved bronze ax and a long obsidian blade.

"It's the final sacrifice, Kate. The one we've both been waiting for. The one that was *always* meant to be."

Kate's body swayed, her feet rooted to the floor. Rolk's eyes bored into her, glazed and wild, yet somehow oddly rational, as if madness had brought him some serene inner knowledge.

Kate came back to herself, her eyes moving quickly, searching for some route of escape. He had come to the center of the room now, and there was no way past him, no way past the reach of the weapons he held.

Rolk seemed to sense her thoughts; his face darkened. "You mustn't try to run. You mustn't do anything to destroy the beauty of the ritual." A small smile came to his lips. "You are the one who's wonderful. Who's perfect. And you understand it all so well. I could never have found anyone else like you. Even your name is perfect. Katherine." His smile grew larger, madder. "My wife's name was Katherine, you know. And she had blond hair, soft and beautiful just like yours."

Kate began to tremble uncontrollably, and she could feel the perspiration beneath her clothing. She fought for breath, for words. She was terrified and she wanted to run. But she wanted to know what had brought him to this, what had brought him to the ritual, and to her. It couldn't have been only her name. There had to be more.

Kate struggled for words, wanting to know, yet wanting to stop him as well. But only one thought came to mind. "The cape," she said, her voice hoarse, almost strangled. "You don't have the cape. And you must."

Rolk's eyes clouded momentarily; then the confidence, the assurance returned. "It was too large. I couldn't get it out of the museum," he said. "But I took some feathers. They're in my pocket. I think they'll do." He gestured toward the large round coffee table. "Just as that table will do for the sacrificial stone." He waved his arms, taking in the apartment. "And I've had everything cleansed, purified. The cleaners have been here for two days making everything ready." He stared at her, his eyes loving, tender now. "And it is. It's ready."

Kate took two steps back, unable to control herself, realizing she might provoke him, but afraid he might lunge at her. "But you can't believe in the ritual. You're not Mayan. You can't even have known of it until . . . until . . ."

"Oh, I knew. It was all in my wife's books. Books that I read years ago." He shook his head almost as if dismissing his own inadequacy. "I didn't understand then. Not the way I do now. But I knew about it. Yes,

I knew about it all." He took a step toward her and stopped. His head tilted slightly to one side. "It was your lecture. It made me remember. And it made me understand."

"What? What did it make you understand?" Kate's voice was shrill, overcome by her own terror now.

Rolk hesitated, the weapons dropping to his sides. His eyes squeezed shut as pain racked his head. When he opened them they seemed distant, clouded. "Years ago, something terrible happened. At least I thought it was terrible. I lived with it for a long time. But I never understood." The small smile returned. "But it wasn't terrible. It was wonderful. And your lecture made me understand that." His arms spread apart again, the weapons rigid in his hands. "What I did wasn't evil. It was an act of great love, the greatest act of love anyone could offer." He took another step toward her, then stopped again. "And you gave that to me, and I loved you for it. And I knew then I had to give you my love in return. And it had to be perfect. Perfect in every way."

Rolk lowered the ax to the coffee table, then raised the knife high into the air. Kate's eyes followed its ascent, mesmerized, unable to move. It was over, and there was nothing she could do. In her mind she could almost hear the chanting, the hundreds of voices, not unlike the beating of a human heart. But it was only Rolk's breathing, she realized, the breathing she had heard before, breath drawn sharply but faintly, then expelled through the mouth in a barely distinguishable hum.

"I loved you," she said, her voice barely more than a whisper. "And I know you loved me."

"And I still do," Rolk said, his lips curving into a small smile not unlike the one on the mask that now hung about his neck. "And that's why I'm offering you this gift, offering you to the gods. And then I'll come to you. I promise. Soon I'll come to you. And we'll be together forever. Just you and me and my daughter. It's the way it was meant to be, Kathy. Always, always."

Devlin moved down the hall and into the living room. He stood quietly, his revolver held loosely in his hand, resting against his thigh. He had listened to their conversation, hearing what he had hoped he would never hear, trying, even now, to understand it all.

Rolk and Kate stood before him, poised in some strange dance of death, unaware of his presence, engulfed by a belief that had lived for hundreds of years and that now had to die quickly and finally.

"It's over, Rolk. The ritual's over."

Rolk froze in place, eyes blinking, the sound of the familiar voice destroying his equilibrium. His body swayed momentarily; then he turned, the knife dropping to his side.

"Paul. You shouldn't be here, Paul." His voice was soft, soothing, his eyes distant and confused.

"I had to be. There was no other way. I had to clear the case."

"But the case is cleared. I cleared it myself."

Devlin shook his head. "No, not yet."

Rolk let out a long, ragged breath. "You're a good detective, Paul. But then, I taught you, didn't I?"

"Yes." Devlin's voice was little more than a croak, and he stopped with the one word, knowing he would not be able to say more.

"How did you find out? Tell me. It's time for the pupil to teach the teacher." Rolk's eyes were wild, full of madness now.

Devlin breathed deeply. The pain in his arm was gone, but not the pain that still grew inside. "Caliento always bothered me," he began. "His size, lots of things. The fact that the killer ran away, that he didn't kill me when he had the chance." He stared into Rolk's eyes. "Why did you want to kill me? And why did you change your mind?"

Rolk's eyes blinked uncontrollably, and his mouth worked for several moments before the words came. "You were trying to take Kathy away from me, just like someone else tried to years ago. I knew you didn't mean it, but you were trying." The eyes continued to blink. "But then I couldn't kill you. Even now I don't know why. I just couldn't."

Devlin nodded, understanding for the first time. He pushed it away. He had to keep talking. "Then today, Rose called me. You showed her the letter about your daughter, and then you gave her an address so she could send your daughter a present. But the writing was the same, and she thought you might realize that later, and it scared the hell out of her."

Devlin took another step into the living room and stopped. Rolk remained motionless, but his wild eyes seemed filled with an odd approval, much like the look of a mad father listening to the unbelievable exploits of a son, Devlin thought.

"So I called Charlie," Devlin continued. "He told me what he had found out about Kate, about her father and what it had done to her. And he told me how you had dismissed it out of hand. Then I knew. It was all so simple. You understood the information meant nothing, because you already knew who the killer was. You had known all along. And you knew that the rituals in Mexico had nothing to do with what was happening here. It was just a coincidence you used to throw us off." Devlin watched Rolk nod, and saw that his eyes were glowing with approval.

"I didn't want to believe it," Devlin said. "But I had to know, so I called Rimerez, and he told me about their check with the airlines, and how he had already told you about it." Devlin paused, fighting to get his emotions under control. "There was only one person who had shown up early, and that one person was you. You didn't go to Washington to check with Immigration, you went straight to the Yucatán to get everything ready, to convince those villagers you were one of them, so they'd help you. What I don't understand is why you didn't kill Kate there. Why did you wait? If you had killed her then, no one ever would have known."

"It wasn't time," Rolk said, his voice distant again.

"When I saw those ruins, the majesty, the perfection of it all, I knew I wasn't ready. I knew how perfect it really had to be." He glanced back at Kate, smiling. "Kate taught me that there. Oh, she didn't realize she was doing it. But she did." He looked back at Devlin. "So then you came here and searched."

"Yeah, I came here and searched." Devlin stared at the floor, unwilling to look into Rolk's face. "And I found the books about Toltec ritual. Books that had been your wife's, that you had made your own." He shook his head, still staring at the floor. "Then I found the copies of the messages you sent with the votives, the ones you practiced until you got them just the way you wanted. And the first drafts of the letter you sent yourself about your daughter. And the mask and the weapons."

Devlin looked up now, unable to avoid the final confrontation any longer. "And I found your wife and daughter. In the basement. In the box where you've kept them all these years."

A rapid tic appeared in the corner of Rolk's eye, and it twisted the corner of his mouth, turning it into a grimace of unbearable pain. His hands began to tremble, the weapons shaking violently at his sides.

"But my wife's here," he said, turning and smiling at Kate. He turned back to Devlin. "And my daughter's in Seattle. I have the letter."

Devlin shook his head; his lips trembled. "No, they're not. They're in the basement. It's where they've been all along."

Devlin watched Rolk struggle with the fact. At first his eyes clouded, then suddenly he seemed to understand, or perhaps remember, and the wild, glazed look returned. "Of course," he said. "I just forgot for a minute."

Devlin took another step toward him.

"Where are the others, or did you decide to do this alone?" Rolk asked.

"I sent Charlie to Kate's apartment, in case you went there. I decided to come back here alone."

"So it's over now," Rolk said.

"No! Dammit! It's not over." Devlin was shouting at him, his voice filled with anger and despair. "Now it just begins. You know what they're going to do to you. The trial, the press, and then, if you're lucky, years and years in a mental institution."

Rolk took a step back, shocked by Devlin's sudden rage. "No, it won't be like that." His voice was soothing, as though trying to comfort a child. "They'll understand. They will. I know they will. They'll even write articles about it. Scholarly articles." Confusion suddenly spread across his face, and the tic and the grimace returned briefly. "But maybe they won't. Maybe they'll never understand."

Rolk took a step forward and raised the knife menacingly above his head. "Clear the case, Paul," he whispered. "Just clear the case."

"Oh, God, no!" Kate screamed.

Devlin raised his revolver, held it in both hands, and sighted the barrel on the center of Rolk's forehead. His eyes filled with tears.

Rolk smiled at him.

Epilogue

FATHER LoPATO STOOD before the flower-draped casket and prayed fervently for the soul of Stanislaus Rolk. There were few people at the graveside. The members of the squad had come, but none of the brass, and Devlin thought that Rolk would have preferred it that way.

It had not been the traditional "Inspector's Funeral," and the press had been kept away. Off-duty cops, in uniform, had seen to that. It was quite illegal, but they had done it anyway, and Devlin thought that Rolk would have liked that as well.

Kate stood next to him, her arm in his, her body pressed against him for comfort. There was no one else there, but then, Rolk had had no one else for many years. The sky was bright and sunny, the day, a cold clear winter day, a good day to end things.

Father LoPato's voice carried across the grave, speaking of eternal life and forgiveness and the end of earthly pain. Then it was over, and Devlin and Kate turned and headed back to his car.

"I'm glad Father LoPato could officiate at the funeral," Kate said absently. "It seemed to please him, but I was surprised the archdiocese released him so easily."

Devlin looked off in the distance, past the rows of endless gravestones. "Seems he got his hands on a tape recording," Devlin said. "It made the archdiocese see things a little differently."

"He seems to have recovered again. He told me he's going back to the Yucatán," Kate said. "But just as an anthropologist this time, not as a priest. Did the tape accomplish that too?"

Devlin shrugged. "You never know. God moves in mysterious ways, or so they tell me." He looked at her and tried to smile. "It will be good for him. Maybe it'll help him sort everything out."

Kate squeezed his arm against her. "What's going to help you sort everything out?" she asked.

They walked on, Devlin silent for several moments. "Maybe you will," he said at length. "Maybe we'll help each other that way."

They reached Devlin's car and stood quietly facing each other.

"Maybe we shouldn't forget," Kate said. "Maybe it's better to remember."

"There are some things I'd rather forget," Devlin said. "Especially how it all ended."

Kate lowered her eyes. There were tears in them and she didn't want Devlin to see. "I loved him too," she said softly. "But I think the way it ended was best for him."

Devlin stared off again, back toward the grave this time. The few mourners had gone, replaced now by two men with shovels, waiting to complete the task they had been given.

"That's what the Toltecs believed, isn't it? That killing someone under the right circumstances was the ultimate act of love."

Kate nodded, her eyes still avoiding his. Devlin reached out and pulled her to him. "Maybe they were right," he said. "Maybe just this once they were right."

ABOUT THE AUTHOR

WILLIAM HEFFERNAN, a former New York City news reporter, is the author of *The Corsican* and *Acts of Contrition*.